The

Path of a

Titan

The Proving

John Bennett

Book One in The Path of a Titan series

http://www.facebook.com/AuthorJohnBennett/

Cover Design: Mark Reid

Editors: Maria Bennett and Gina Nagy

Printed in the United States of America

First Printing, 2021

ISBN 9798720092320

Prologue

"**S**aintdamn it!" I scream in frustration. "Three thousand credits for this overpriced piece of garbage and it crashes again."

I roll back in my desk chair and let out a groan as I wait for my computer to restart for the third time today. The two moons gleam through my office window, the stars soothe me like a warm blanket after coming in from a snowy day. I flick my wrist to open my palmphone and read through the half a dozen missed messages from my wife. She went into labor an hour ago and is asking me if I left work. I promised her I'd meet her at the hospital but this saintdamn computer keeps crashing and stopping me from finishing my work. I'm about to just log off and say hex it but I'm conflicted on the time I could be losing on my project.

While my computer slowly awakens once again, I slide myself back into my work. I skim over the endless notes and calculations in my notebook for my Subdermal Parasite Inducing Nanorobotic Enhancers project, also known as Project SPINE. If I can perfect the nanites and develop them properly, my project alone could put Harmony back in the United Territories. My home territory of Harmony has been looked at as a plague by the other territories of the world for nearly two hundred years. Trade routes were demolished from Dalton, imports from Alannah were seized, and we were left in the dark to rot and prey on each other to survive. SPINE will be exactly what this territory needs to show the Sovereign that we are civilized, and Harmony can receive the resources to modernize.

Project SPINE is a spinal implant that is surgically implanted onto the brain stem. Once induced, millions of microscopic nanites will deploy into the body and through the cerebral cortex of the patient's brain. Their job is to split neurotransmitters and increase the reproduction of red blood cells, then divide and morph into grey matter to create a faster, more ingenious subject over time. The only thing that is stopping me and causing the countless delays is that all my test subjects have been murdered by it. My nanites are freakishly adaptive but also extremely picky when it comes to feeding. They feed on stem cells, the lifeforce of the human body. Without stem cells, humans can't heal, and eventually the nanites will literally eat the host from the inside out. Knowing that, there's no way I can show this to the Sovereign until I can find some kind of way to develop a stem cell multiplier. To do that, I'd need outside help...

Ah! Finally, my computer is back on. A cute picture of my wife, Isabella, appears in a small circle above my log-in. Her smile is infectious, and always brings a smile to my face like a hypnotic spell. As the prototype loads and codes start flooding through my screen, work is finally back underway. Just as I'm back in the groove, my palmphone rings. I ignore it guessing it's Isabella. If my wife needs me, she will call the secretary. I can't get work done if she keeps distracting me. My phone goes off again. I look to see who it is and it's a unknown outside number.

"Saintdamn it, are you serious? This better be good." I flick my hand to open my phone and answer the call. "Christian Paul, who is this?" I ask in my headset.

"Hello, old friend. Late night, as usual?" The man's hoarse voice is remarkably familiar. The voice of AlphaTitan Robert Fox, commander of one of Tyke's military legions, and Viceroy of our two moons. He is also my unforgivable emancipated half-brother who forged his way into the military at the illegal age of sixteen.

"What do you want, Robby?" I scorn. He hates being called that.

"You know exactly what I want, Christian. Let's be frank, you know why I am calling." My brother knows about SPINE and has been trying to buy it off of me for about five years now. Except what he wants to do is change my invention to create super soldiers for a worldwide planetary defense system. He talks about making the world safer, but I know him, he wants to rule, he wants to be Sovereign. As much as I agree with his opinion of our absolute ruler, I cannot, in good faith, sell my patent to a sociopathic narcissist who will use it for treason.

2

"Can't say I know any Franks, Robby, but if you don't mind, I am extremely busy. My wife just went into labor an hour ago and I don't have time for one of your monologues. Good day."

"Do you honestly believe you can do this by yourself? Aren't you tired? What does Isabella think of your late nights? It must be a real strain on your marriage."

"My marriage is perfectly fine."

"Right!" he chuckles. *"You don't need SPINE to see that your marriage is a car crash on the Skyline. It's just a matter of time before it all comes crashing down in a ball of fire. Oh, and that baby of yours is just a—"*

"Did you call to insult me or to pitch a partnership?" I interrupt starting to feel impatient. "Because I really don't have time for this," I say trying desperately to stay calm and keep his words above my skin.

"Of course not," he rasps and clears his throat. *"Project SPINE. Name your price. Any price, Christian. It is yours. You can move out of that wretched house of yours in that saint forgotten territory. Come work with me on the moon and start a new life with your wife. Hell, you can even drop Isabella or maybe live the polygamy life if you fancy options, you know I do,"* he chuckles in his burner ridden voice. Saints, I hate it. *"You'll have the money for it, that's for sure."*

I exhale a ball of frustration and roll my eyes. "Let me make this perfectly clear—"

"No, let me be perfectly clear with you, Christian, I will not interfere at all. I'll give you a team of engineers just as ambitious as you. I have all the resources and credits to finance any experiments or hypothesis you have. Finish the project here, we'll throw it into a few jimbo's and see if it works. If not, then there's no problem. Lunens are reproducing like saintdamn ovats up here. Life ain't all bad either, we got some of the brightest minds you could ask for to teach your children. C'mon, I'll even name a school after you.

"This project is *mine*, Robert. I didn't make this to wage intergalactic war. I—"

"Who said anything about war?" he interrupts me again, always has, always will. He just loves hearing himself talk. *"I hear you, Christian, truly I do. But do you understand that you cannot do this alone anymore? Think of a sole military corps filled with men and women with superhuman abilities. Battlesuits won't have to be equipped with rune, the military would be unstoppable. I could finally stop trade with those land loving Daltonese, and we can rebuild*

Harmony and all that jibber jabber, but you're wasting the potential of this. Forget about Harmony, this could prepare us from aliens."

My brother was always obsessed with the idea of intergalactic species. That's why he left for the military at such a young age. He wanted to be the first to find aliens. Humans travelled two lightyears to escape Earth in search for new life in other galaxies. They landed on Tyke and had done nothing to explore the rest of the galaxy until my brother finally made contact last week.

"You and I both know I can and will do anything to get that tech, Christian. Stop being selfish. Jingoty can shine a new light on this project of yours and you are squandering this chance for us! You think Silva will give you another chance after what you showed him last time? His office still smells of the disgrace you left in there from your last failed attempt. Keep that in mind when Isabella leaves you and Carson resents you because you didn't see a good opportunity when it lands on your lap."

I'm about to unleash a whirlwind of curses, but that name catches me off guard. "What does dad have to do with this?" I ask.

"Oh… You didn't see him yet? He's all over her Novapage." he laughs. *"Congratulations, brother. Family is such a precious thing. It's a lot of responsibility. A whole lot to gain, a whole lot to lose, too. Too bad dad didn't see it that way."* The call ends.

Anger and rage fill my body and explode through my hand as I rip my headset off and throw it across the room. I curse and scream at it as it hits the wall.

"Dr. Paul? Is everything ok?" A lady's voice catches me off guard. I look sharply at the sound of my door opening. My assistant, Janet, is at the door. I was unaware anyone was still here.

"Yes, yes. Everything is fine." I walk over to the door and pick up my communicator. "Please, if you don't mind, Janet, I have work to finish. My wife went into labor an hour ago and I need to—"

"Dr. Paul," she interrupts me crookedly. "That was four hours ago. But um, your wife just called and left a message. Shall I send it to your communicator?"

"Yes, please." I rush to put my headset back on and Janet sends me the message with a click from her headset to mine. I can't help but break into tears as I hear my wife's panting voice.

"Hi. I guess you're busy, but if you care to know, it's a boy. A beautiful, perfect, and healthy baby boy. He's even got your nose. I told the nurse we are naming him Carson, after your father. Call me when you can… I love you."

1

My name is Carson Paul

Present Day, year 1010 A.E. (After Earth)

After a long day of my sophomore year in high school, I find my sister on the student transport and take my usual seat next to her. As the massive machine of metal and magnets lifts off the ground and takes off, my head hits the seat cushion and my ears pop. Soaring through the air on the Skyline Expressway, I watch the tops of trees sway from the light breeze outside. My sister, Kylie, is quieter than usual. Normally, she's eccentric and talkative but today, I can sense there is something wrong, probably something about a boy. I stare at the back of her head attempting to telepathically get her attention away from the window, but she is in her own world and I don't own such power. Before long, the transporter merges off the Skyline and into our small neighborhood of Redding.

My mother sits on her rocking chair on the porch waiting for us to get home. As always, she's sipping on her afternoon coffee. Her affectionate smile makes me forget about the unsettling territory we live in. If there is one good thing about living in the slums of Harmony, it's coming home to see my mother's comforting smile. My mood changes when I see her, something about her just gives me a sense of bliss. She is all that I have, besides my father who's never given me the time of day. He works long hours and constantly complains about making enough money to finance his project. He's very vague when I ask him about it. He says I simply just won't understand it, but when it comes to my sister, he talks her ear off with his big words and technological terms.

Kylie is the spitting image of our mother, but she is all daddy's girl. Born a little over a year after me but shares the same academic prowess of our father. As miraculous as it sounds to be categorized with a 140 I.Q. at such an early age, she's extremely clumsy. She's always walking into things and stumbling, like her brain is working too fast for her body to react, yet she'll go on and on about the origin of a bananapear.

Our house isn't glamorous. It's just a small bungalow held up by bug infested support beams and a lot of dad's charm, as he calls it. It started out as two bedrooms, but with the surprise birth of Kylie, my dad had to split my room in half.

"Do you need help with any of your homework?" Kylie finally says after twenty minutes of silence.

"Wow, she speaks," I humor her by grabbing her hand with both of mine and shaking it. "Hi, I'm Carson, your brother, record holder for most marshmallows he can fit in his mouth. Who are you again?"

She tries to hide her smile and playfully yanks her hand away from me. "You're a dope."

"How'd you do on that test?" I quickly change topics to a more suitable one that will get her talking.

"Test?" she asks confused. "Oh, yeah, I did fine. I knew all the answers."

"What? What are you, some kind of genius?" I question, knowing she enjoys hearing me say it.

Her cheerfulness finally emerges with a flip of her hair. "Well, I don't mean to toot my own horn but I—" A flying object hits Kylie in the back of her head. I turn to see a black-haired boy laughing and pointing at her. He sticks his tongue out and pushes his nose up out the window of the bus. "Don't forget!" he yells as the bus ignites its thrusters and lifts off.

"Who was that?" I snap at her.

"Nobody," she snaps back quickly and walks away with a growl.

I click my tongue. "Right. It's always nobody." Kylie gets bullied a lot. Her petite stature doesn't help her much. She was born two months early and by a complete miracle she is alive and well. Mom tries to fatten her up, but Kylie rarely finishes her food. All mom's been doing is fattening up my dad. Lucky for me, I have a fast metabolism. My dad however…

"Who was that?" Mom calls out.

"Not now, mom," Kylie says and walks past her with her head down.

6

I try to walk in, but I get stopped by the ferocious grip my mother has.

"Who was that?" she whispers intensely. Her crazy protective eyes sneer at me, a slight smell of coffee on her breath. She's oddly dressed today, like she's going out somewhere fancy and wants to impress someone.

"I don't know, but I'll handle it," I dismiss her.

"Good." She releases her grip on me. "Hey, Car, can you run to the corner store for me? We're out of milk."

I roll my eyes, but I know I have to say yes. I must do my part to help. "Sure, ma."

"Thanks, kiddo. Credits are on the table."

I walk down the hall and peek into my parent's room. My dad sits in the corner of his room on the computer. Boxes of papers everywhere, scattered all over his desk and on the floor. My dad has been a robotics engineer for as long as I can remember. He rarely ever takes a day off, so seeing him is a gift. Supposedly, this project of his is this bug looking thing that will change how humans act or live, or something like that. I'm not into that kind of stuff. I would rather play starball or quite honestly anything else. I'd try out for the school team, but at this point of my high school career I rather just focus on getting into college. Where, and for what is the problem. What I dream is to attend the Titan Academy at Atlantis University in Alannah and get recruited into the military.

My dad stares at his computer, typing as fast as lightning. "Hey, dad, want to play catch?" I ask. "It's a nice day out and—"

"Not today, kiddo," he replies. Not even skipping a beat in his typing and refusing to give me his attention. "I'm only home because your mother and I are going out to dinner for our anniversary. You don't mind staying with your sister tonight, do you?"

"Sure," I grumble. "You really can't take an hour to throw the star around?"

He finally gives me his attention. His beard consuming half of his face like a mask. The bags under his eyes are getting wider as well. He keeps his hair slicked back, covering the weird scar he has on his neck. "No. Like I said, kiddo, I'm only home because—"

"Whatever, dad." I throw my hands up and walk away. Jealousy and hatred fill my heart as I close my door to my room, feeling shunned from the love and approval I've always strived to get from him. He refuses to give me even a sliver of hope, a tiny morsel that he cares. When I have kids, I'll be different. I won't be like him. I'll give my kids all the attention they could possibly ask for. Work won't consume me like it does him.

I gaze at my holoposters on my wall. Tyke's four alphaTitans rotate around in an epic pose. Robert Fox of the moons, Collin 'The Cannon' Caldwell from Dalton, Tori Castaway from Alannah, and the greatest of all, Malcolm Suez welding his legendary Hammerscyth in his one of a kind battlesuit. Lightning sizzles from his hammer as he roars a mighty war cry before pummeling his foe into the ground. I would do anything to meet them one day. I dream to be a titan, but all my dreams come crashing down to reality when the realization of it all is clear. The only legitimate Titan Program is at Atlantis Academy in the territory of Alannah. The territory that will never accept a Harmonian. We are a disease to Alannicans. It is a felony to even step foot on territory grounds without written permission from the Viceroy of the territory. It disgusts me to know I am not accepted anywhere else than this saint forsaken place.

I walk into the kitchen and spot the credits on the table. Kylie is frantically finishing up her homework and stuffing it in her tattered book bag. I don't take a second look, but I would have sworn I saw someone else's name on that paper.

"Hey, I'm going to Mickey's for milk. Wanna come?" I ask.

She agrees with a shrug, and I meet her in the garage where I unplug our hoverbikes from the back of the garage and lug them into the road.

The sky is an unsettling hue of purple with plenty of dark clouds throughout the sky. The grass is finally coming back to its healthy baby blue from the warm spring weather, and rain we've had recently.

We take off and race to the corner store about half a mile away from home. A soft thunder mumbles in the distance. It's going to rain soon.

We park our bikes along the side of Mickey's Corner Store and lock them to the bike rack. Large windows cover the front of the building, with bright luminescent lights advertising mint flavored burners. We walk in the store and I observe the cashier on his palmphone. He swipes his finger along the projection in his hand. He doesn't greet us, or even acknowledge we are here. I assume he's waiting for a girl to answer him. Hah, not with that haircut, buddy. Looks like his grandma with Parkinson's did it for him.

I send Kylie to get the milk and I walk into the candy aisle. I take one last look at the oblivious cashier and carefully swipe a few candy bars into my bag. I zip up my bag and meet Kylie at the register.

After paying with the credits mom gave me, I stuff the milk in my bag and swing it over my shoulders. I thank the man casually pretending like I don't have twenty credits worth of candy in my bag and confidently walk out the door with Kylie behind me.

Here in Redding, I've learned to fend for myself and in doing so, my hands are quick, sneaky, and sticky. It's a bad habit for sure, and if Kylie finds out, she'd be furious. She constantly complains of the level of character this town has and how inconceivable the townspeople are.

A commotion comes from the back of the store. Laughter and chatter get louder as we get closer to our bikes. I find a boy tugging on my bike lock with bolt cutters in his hands. Three more of them watching behind him.

"Ey! What do you think you're doing?!" I yell.

The whole group snaps their heads to me. I recognize one of them immediately. That kid from the transporter makes a face at Kylie and smirks but covers it when he sees me. I notice an unsettling gulp in his throat. Fear sets in, but he composes himself. "Well, well, well, look what we have here, boys. Seems like someone already did our shopping for us."

"What do you want, kid?" I blab, not caring if I make a scene.

"Nothing from you, *nerd*." He looks over at Kylie and nods with a smooth looking smile. "Sup, girl, you finish my paper yet?"

"Hey, Kenny. I… um," she stutters, and fidgets with her hair.

"Yah musta got my homework done if you're out here, right?" he says in a distinctive southern Harmony accent. "It bettah get done or else I'ma tell everyone your uh, little secret, yah heard?"

"No! Don't. It's done. I have it in my book bag at home. I can give it to you tomorrow." She looks at me ashamed.

What secret is he talking about?

I walk up to him and get uncomfortably close to him. I'm taller than him, and noticeably stronger than him or either of his friends individually. "You like picking on girls, don't you, Kenny? Makes you feel big and bad, huh? How about you try and bully me?" My mother's crazy eyes come out of me as the fire in my heart ignites and spreads throughout my body. Adrenaline floods as I embrace the calm before the storm. My heart revs, my excitement grows. "C'mon, twerp, swing. I dare you."

He shoves me and I use the momentum like a slingshot. I take one strong step forward and shove Kenny back into the boys crowded behind him. His friends yell back at me and start to surround me. Two with clenched fists, one with the bolt cutters and another one has his hand behind his back. They're not afraid to take me on as a group. Separately though, I'd have no problem.

"Yo, back up, joker!" Kenny makes his way back to the front and pushes me again. I'm barely moved. "I'm just tryna get my homework. Mind yah business before I do something I might regret, yah heard?"

I clench my fists ready to fight, confident I can take them, but then reconsider my odds. Five on one isn't the best odds for me. One may even have a gun on him. Is this something I might regret? I eye the bolt cutters and envision a scary and uncomfortable use for them. Got to be smart and think fast. "How about some candy, you want a candy bar, kid?" I swing my bag around and toss him one of my candy bars. As it glides out of my hands, I realize it was my favorite one. Crap. "Will that get you off our backs? We got to get home before it rains. You don't want to be fighting in the rain now do you?"

He catches it and examines the candy. "It's a start," he says. He unravels the wrapper and takes a bite. Now that I got his hands full, I could swing right now, and he wouldn't be able to do a thing about it. All I need to do is worry if his friends have anything on them. Any knives or anything else could leave me in an exceedingly tricky situation I may not be capable of getting out of. If I swing, his friends could jump me, or worse, Kylie. He looks back at his friends. "What about my boys? I know you didn't go in there for just one measly candy bar."

I huff and unload my collection of candy bars. Leaving only one more that I wanted to give Kylie. "Kylie, get your bike, we're going home."

"Nah, I want the bike too," Kenny says.

"Excuse me?" I question.

"Yah heard me, as collateral." He snaps his finger and points to her hoverbike. One of his friends walks up to Kylie and yanks it out of her hands. Kylie does nothing but watch as her favorite thing in the world is stripped from her. "Bring me my paper tomorrow, and you can come by my place after school for yah bike back." He blows Kylie a kiss. "I'll see yah tomorrow, baby girl." The group turns and walks away.

Kylie's shell-shocked face turns from shock to despair. She never would have lost her bike if I didn't ask her to come with me. I think quickly. "Hey, Kenny! Take mine instead!" Kenny turns around with a mouth full of chocolate. The giant smile on his face quickly turns upside down as my hoverbike launches into his sternum, running him over like a wild animal. With all his friends distracted, I lunge forward and break the nose of the kid with the bolt cutters. Bones shatter on impact. I slip to the side and dodge a knife swiping across my neck. I grab his wrist and bend it backwards, breaking his grip and drive my knee into his chest. A fist finds my jaw from behind me but I'm able to slip under his next swing and land a quick combo of punches to another kid, finishing him with a swift uppercut. Mom trained me in her backyard martial arts for years. It pains her that Kylie never wanted to learn, but I took full advantage of my grandpa's teachings from her.

I grab the bike and slide it backwards to Kylie. "Kylie, let's go!" I scream.

Kenny is barely able to push the hoverbike off him, I jump on it from the back and ride over him again as we make our escape. "You'll regret this!" I hear behind me as we speed around the corner onto the main road.

After getting a few blocks away from the store I can't help but ask. "Who is that guy, Ky?"

"Nobody. Just a friend."

"A friend?"

"Yeah, I'm uh, doing his homework for him."

"What secret was he talking about?"

"Nothing. It's all lies. He said I kissed this boy in my class, and I didn't. I *really* didn't."

"That's it?" I say realizing a fourteen year old's definition of a secret is astronomically less serious than someone my age would define as a secret.

"Carson, it's the smelly kid I was talking to you about. I don't want to be associated with the likes of him," she says. "So, where did you get the candy from? Mom gave you five credits. How'd you buy twenty three credits worth of candy and a three credit gallon of milk with only five credits?

"I always carry candy, Ky. What kind of big brother doesn't?" As lame of an excuse as it is, Kylie doesn't need to know about that part of my life. I love her, and I'd do anything for her, even if that means giving up my favorite chocolate bar.

2

Promise

As we ride home, and the cool afternoon air whips my face, I can't help but think of my sister's wellbeing. She is so much more than what she portrays. She's strong and fierce like our mother when it comes to standing up to me, but she refuses to stand up for herself when someone else messes with her.

"You want to know something, Ky? I ask rhetorically. "One day, you're going to be in a situation where you're going to have to stand up for yourself. What if next time, he touches you? What will you do?"

"I'm fine, Carson," she insists. "The probability of—"

"No! This isn't a math problem, Kylie. I'm serious, you need to stand up for yourself. This world isn't rainbows and summerflies. There are worse people out there, who won't stop at just homework. This world will eat you up and spit you back out without even flinching, and you will have to deal with the consequences. What if I wasn't there? What would you do?"

She doesn't answer. She just stares at the ground with a disgruntled face, like she does every time we have this conversation.

"Kylie?!"

"I don't know! Just leave it alone."

The rain starts coming down and thunder begins to rumble, as we pull into our driveway. I tell Kylie to go inside and I'll put the bikes away.

She nods and looks down looking ashamed, maybe even embarrassed "Hey, Car."

I slide the bike back in its place and plug it in. "Yeah?" still a little annoyed but curious.

She walks in the garage, outside of the rain, a few rain droplets have claimed her shoulders. "I know I need to stand up for myself. I'm just... scared. You know? I can't fathom how it feels to be physically assaulted."

"We all get scared, Kylie," I say. "But you got to do something. Anything. Say no, scream fire, or something to grab anyone's attention."

She chuckles with a huff. "I can't just scream fire every time. I'd be screaming that every day."

I laugh but it makes my heart break knowing Kylie gets picked on so often. If only we were twins and I could be in her classes. "It's better than getting your bike stolen. Then he said to go to his house for it? Who knows what he'd make you do there?"

"I know. I wouldn't go, obviously."

"So, you're saying you'd do this kid's homework, let him take your bike, and be fine with it? Kylie, have some backbone."

"No!" she scrunched her face and clicks her tongue. "Maybe I'll mess up his homework. That will show him, right? I'll change the answers, make them all wrong. When he gets an F, he'll think I'm inadequate and leave me alone. Would that suffice?"

"It's a start but what happens when you get an A? He'll know you did it on purpose. It'll only make him angrier. You got to do something immediate, something that will catch him off guard, not build him up. You got to scare him. Make him look bad, embarrass him. A punch in the mouth will—"

"Carson, no, I will not jeopardize my perfect attendance to be suspended for a meaningless fight. Not everything has to be about violence. What if I casually explain to him that what he is doing is wrong, maybe then he'll comprehend his delinquent behaviors and realize that he's been wrong to bludgeon me."

I look down at my hands and feel the violence radiate off it. A patch of blood has hardened on my bruised knuckle. It's not the first time this has happened. It definitely won't be the last. "Ky, he's bullying you to do his homework. How about you rip up his paper and throw it in his face tomorrow on the bus? Do it in front of everyone. That will embarrass him."

"What if he hits me?"

"Has he hit you before?"

"No, but what if he does?"

She's not wrong to think that. Plenty of women have been reportedly beaten for less. "Don't get hit. Duck, bob, and weave." I mimic some boxing moves. "Get out of the way." Kick him in the shin, the shin *hurts*! Or worse." I point to my groin. It makes her laugh. "You're fast, Kylie. Look at mom, she could kick dad's butt. Don't you want to be strong like her?" I reach over and wrap my hand around her bicep. "Give me a squeeze." She flexes her arm muscles for me. I feel a small bump, but nothing impressive. "Wow, look at you," I joke. "Some bad ass chick from the slums of Harmony is here to take on Tyke's fiercest foes."

"Stop it, Carson, I'm not strong like you." She yanks her arm way from me.

"I'm not that strong, Kylie," I lie. "But kids don't mess with me because I fight back. I always tell them this. If you want to fight, fine. I don't care if I lose, but know this," I step to her and put a finger in her face to show her my intensity. "I will get you at least once, and trust me, you will remember it." I step back seeing Kylies face turn feeling the intimidation of my words. "It really gets in their head." I point to my temple. "Makes them second guess themselves. It creates doubt."

"You're not scared?" she asks.

"Sure. Just back there, seeing that goon squad he had behind him, I was intimidated," I admit. "Just be smart about it. Remember what I did? I filled their hands with candy, got them off guard. They never saw it coming. They thought I was scared but they all fell into my trap."

"Yeah, and about that. I know you stole that candy, Carson. Don't think I don't know."

"I don't know what you're talking about."

"Yes, you do! Why does one carry around four bars of chocolate in the spring months?"

I swing my bag around and pull out the last candy bar I have. It was Kylie's favorite. I hand it to her. "Five, actually," I say with a smile.

"Carson…" She looks at me stunned with disappointment but snatches the candy bar out of my hand. I laugh it off, but she doesn't. Although I believe my point is made, she must do something next time she sees him. The rain starts coming down harder and the thunder gets louder. I finish putting the bikes away and climb over the countless boxes and containers we have in here. The garage is dark and clammy, packed with boxes and cobwebs my parents have neglected over the years. Some would call them hoarders but in a strange kind of way. If anyone wants anything valuable in here, they will have to go through *a lot* of junk to get in here, I call it brilliant. I hop and lunge over all the boxes, and other things in here. I end up tripping over a box and stumble around it. I curse and look back at it, my name is on it. Curiosity consumes me as I swipe a pile of dust off and I open it. What I find is unlike anything I've ever seen before. A curved looking contraption, it feels wooden as I pick it up in my hands, but it's brown and feels different compared to the blue trees we have here. I feel an otherworldly energy radiating from it, dormant inside. It's wrapped in cloth where it looks like handles, with some kind of insignia or language I don't understand. I grip it in my hands and stare at it for a moment, examining this wild toy my parents have kept from me. What is this? I feel it crack and a glowing yellow light flashes me from the middle. It frightens me and I slam it shut and drop it back in the box cursing at myself for thinking I just broke it. I fold the box back up and slide it in a corner where it's hidden.

I open the front door and I'm greeted by both of my parents in their jackets on like they are about to walk out.

"Where are you going?" I ask confused.

"Brooklyn's, kiddo. Didn't dad tell you?" my mom questions.

"Um, yeah, I—"

"Can we come?" Kylie asks.

My dad butts in the conversation grabbing his jacket and putting it on my mother. "Not this time, kiddos," dad insists. "This is something your mother and I want to do together."

"Ok? What are we supposed to eat? Do we even have anything?" I ask.

"I made a casserole," mom says. "It's in the oven. Set the timer for twenty minutes and take it out." They edge by me. "We got to go, Carson. Love you," mom says cheerfully walking out the door being held open by my dad.

"Hey, kiddo," my dad says before closing the front door. I pick up my head and look at him eagerly. Kiddo has always been our nick names. I always find it comforting when my parents say it. I feel more connected that way. Reminds me of when times were better, at least for me. "Please don't burn the house down, ok? We'll play starball tomorrow, just me and you. I promise."

"Whatever you say, dad," I say. Dad smirks as I close the door and lock it. Kylie jumps on the couch and watches them leave out the window.

"Want to watch cartoons and help me with my homework?" I ask her.

She smiles and nods.

As night follows and Kylie goes off to bed, I stayed on the couch in the living room watching TV, waiting for my parents to come home. I usually stick to sports or cartoons, but being that it is so late, there wasn't much to see. I end up watching the storm and listen to the sounds of the rain crash down on the house along with the sudden sounds of thunder and lightning dancing through the clouds. After watching a few meaningless videos on my palmphone, I realize time has flown by, its midnight. Mom and dad still aren't home. My eyes are heavy. I tuck myself under a blanket and before I know it I'm woken up in a brightly lit room.

"Car, where is mom and dad?" I hear.

My eyes open and the blinding bright lights of the morning fill the room. "What?" I say half awake. "What time is it?"

"It's time for school. Did mom and dad ever come home?" Kylie asks. "They're not in their bedroom."

"I don't know," I mutter rubbing my eyes. My brain still isn't computing what's going on. I roll up off the couch and look outside, no sign of the car but I have no time to think about it. I rush into my room to put on some clean clothes. I don't even worry about what I find. I hurry and call my mom's phone as I get outside but she doesn't pick up. Maybe they are asleep in a hotel. I call my dad, hoping he answers, but his phone actually goes straight to voicemail. Kylie is already at the bus stop waiting for the student transport, so I make haste to get down the block.

Akron Avenue and First Street is where our transporter stop is, about four houses down the road. A group of kids are playing kick hockey with a crushed soda can. I see Kylie by the stop sign. Pessimistic thoughts circle around me, an unnerving feeling follows but I try to stay optimistic for Kylie.

"They must have had a few too many drinks last night and stayed in a hotel. Probably the smarter thing to do, Ky. Dad is always cautious like that. Last thing he needs is getting put in jail or losing the car for driving drunk, on their anniversary, nonetheless. I'm sure they'll be home when we get back from school," I insist.

As optimistic as I try to be, I have an eerie feeling that they may be in trouble. My dad never over drinks, I know him better than that. Mom, on the other hand, is usually the drinker in the family. I've found mom several times sprawled out on the couch holding an empty wine bottle and a half filled glass on the floor.

"Did you call them?" Kylie asks once I make my way to our stop.

16

"Yeah, no one picked up. It's early, Ky. They'll be home when we get back from school."
She lets out an anxious huff and shakes her head looking down at the ground. I put my hand on her shoulder but before I am able to say something, the student transport blares its engines and initiates its landing sequence. A bushel of air smacks my face as it descends to the ground. Once it hits the street, the doors open for us. The old man who drives us smiles as we get on and take our normal seats. The thrusters ignite and the floor shakes underneath our seats. We feel ourselves being lifted, my stomach lurches every time and my back is thrusted against the seat cushion. For the first time ever, we leave our home without mom waving us goodbye.

Once the transport is in the air and settles at a consistent speed, I am able to lift my head off the seat.

"Dad isn't normally a drinker, is he?" Kylie asks.

She knows dad just as well as I do. Even though she's two years younger, she is no idiot to our family's behaviors. I try to conjure up a lie, but it'll only make matters worse "It was their anniversary, Ky. The man works twelve to sixteen hours a day. He can have a few drinks if he wants to. He deserves it," I argue.

"Kylie, baby! You got my paper?" a more than familiar voice shouts from behind us.

I turn around and find that punk kid, Kenny, from yesterday. He's out of his seat, standing right over us with a cut on his lip. I completely forgot about him, I hope Kylie didn't. I glare at him with all intent to reach out and wail his ugly pimpled face in like I did his friends who are nowhere to be seen. I look and see Kylie reaching into her bag.

"C'mon, what did we talk about yesterday," I whisper to her. I look back up at the kid. "No, she doesn't have your saintdamn—"

"Shut up, Carson," she whispers back to me. "Yeah, I have it. It's uh—" She hesitates and takes a deep breath. "It's right here." She takes her hand out of her bag, but with no paper. Just a big middle finger pointing straight in his face.

My jaw drops in disbelief. "Oh snap!" I shout. A few ease droppers from around us make their own comments.

Kenny growls angrily. "Are you serious?! What did you do with my homework?!"

"Oh yeah, now I remember." She reaches back in her bag and pulls out shredded pieces of paper. "It got caught in the shredder. Clumsy me," she giggles and tosses the shreds of paper in the air. They flutter to the ground like winter's snow.

He's flabbergasted, just as I hoped. "You think this a joke? I need that homework or I'm gonna fail. You said you'd do it!" he growls. His power and control over Kylie is dwindling by the second. Groups of eyes linger to us, eavesdropping on the most interesting and loudest thing on the bus. Kenny notices it, his face flushes. Embarrassed, and caught off guard, his intimidation to Kylie is gone. She is finally standing up to this punk.

"Yeah, that was before you tried to steal my hoverbike and forced me to kiss you," she yells for everyone to hear. "Newsflash, Kenny, they came up with this wonderful new product. It's called toothpaste. You might want to get some!" The transport bursts in laughter. Everyone, including the old man driving, is cracking up from Kylie's outburst.

Kenny's face gets beat red and is face twists into a raging scared little boy. He grabs Kylie's hair and brings her face to his face. "Hex you! If you think I'd—"

"Get off her!" I yell and throw a wild punch, connecting square in his mouth, knocking him back into some poor girl listening to her music. He bounces off her and he falls in the center aisle. "Touch her again, Kenny, touch her one more time and I swear to the saints it'll be the last hexing thing you ever do." Blood rushes out the boy's mouth. He peers up at me with a missing tooth and fear in his eyes. He gets up and quivers like he's about to cry. The bus erupts in a frenzy of laughs and mockery towards the young and defeated boy as he scurries back to his seat. I sit back in my seat and wrap my arm around Kylie. "I'm proud of you, baby sister."

3
Where are they?

School was long, and tiresome, I couldn't focus at all. All I could think about was what was in that container in the garage, and where in saint's name are my mom and dad? I tried calling both of them in between classes but still no answer from either of them. Countless scenarios twirled around my mind. Some good, some bad, and some were hard to get out of my head. After the final bell rings, I am rid of this place for the weekend. I hop on the transporter and look for Kenny. I don't see him. Good, I was lucky to get away with that. I know I preach defending yourself, but I can't keep explaining to my parents why I keep getting detention for fighting off Kylie's bullies. I find Kylie and take my seat next to her. She's starring out the window, doesn't even realize I sat down. I'm sure she's been thinking the same thing as I have been.

I tap her shoulder. "Hey."

She jumps and turns in shock but is relieved when it was me. "Holy saints you scared me," she pants and composes herself. "You think mom and dad are home?" she asks gently.

"Of course, they have to be. It'd be weird if they weren't home by now," I say staying optimistic. "Has Kenny bothered you today?"

She smiles. "Nope. He didn't even show up to class. Probably called his mommy and went home early."

I smile back at her. "Nice! Hopefully, he learned his lesson."

"Yeah, it was so invigorating to stand up for myself. For once, I felt as if I could breathe again, like I've been holding my breath for so long, and finally I can exhale and relieve myself of the madness I put myself through. Carson, I feel like I can be myself again."

"Wow, that's... that's fantastic," I say.

"Thank you, Carson."

"You know I always got your back, no matter what, you heard?"

We share a genuine laugh and relax as the transporter takes us home. The ride home went faster than usual. Kylie was in high spirits and hopeful for our parents return. We enter our neighborhood anxiously hoping that there's the dark blue beat up car sitting in the driveway with our mother waiting for us with a hot beverage in her hand. We arrive at our stop and see a Gesicki Backlash in the driveway, a lightning fast hovercar used mostly for law enforcement, made to reach speeds nearing three hundred miles per hour. A sleek and aerodynamic design, windows are all tinted, and some even have a cloaking device inside to hide in plain sight to catch speeders. A thousand questions rush through my head, but one thing is for sure, someone is in our house. We rush off the transporter and run full sprint towards the door.

I barge open the door. "Mom?! Dad?!"

We find two officers staring at us. Black, sleek sunglasses cover their eyes with a bulletproof vest and a full duty belt with a pistol holstered to their hip. They're mountains compared to my sister and I.

"Are you Carson and Kylie Paul?" one demands in his intimidatingly deep voice. His name plate reads, Ldt. O'Neill. LowDelta, the lowest ranking officers of Tyke's military law enforcement, an entry level ranking at best.

"Yeah. Who are you?" I ask. "Where are my parents? Do you know where they are? Are you here to help us look for them?"

"Yeah, are you some kind of detective?" Kylie adds.

The man ignores our questions and kneels down to get eye level with us. "Listen to me very carefully, kids. You both need to gather your things, a few sets of clothes, and if you want to bring a toy or two you can, but you are leaving with us. Do you understand?"

"Wait, what?!" I say baffled. "Who the hell are you? Get the hex out of my house!" I violently snap back at him. Fist clenched with a hand pointing out the front door.

He exhales and drops his head. "Hexing Harmonians." He looks back up to us. "Listen to me, youngling," O'Neill says kindly putting his hands up. "Everything will be explained in the car, we need to get you out of here. You are in danger. I'm sorry but this is no longer your home anymore. Your parents committed treason and are no longer owners of this house. I'm sorry it has to be like this but please, go pack your stuff."

I am dumbfounded. To think my parents actually made it home in a new car. Now to hear they are criminals, and this man is taking us away.

"Treason? What could they have possibly done?" Kylie shouts. "My mom barely ever leaves the house, and my dad never stops working. What could they possibly have done?"

"That is none of your concern," the other one says. "Now c'mon, go get—"

"I'm calling the cops," I say unlocking my phone on my wrist and attempt to walk back outside. I'm then grabbed by my wrist and my phone crushes in the man's grip. A shooting pain scorches down my arm. I shriek in pain, but he won't let go. I watch as a family picture on my palm disappears as the sheer force of this man's grip turns my palmphone into a stress ball.

"I *am* the cops, boy." His breath smells like coffee and burners. His dangerous eyes peer out of his sunglasses. Om. Robbins is his name, an omega, a rank higher than delta. He's much grungier looking than his partner. "Your parents are dead, your father shot your mother and then killed himself."

My world stops. The realization of the most horrible image in my head has come real. My parents are dead? They were criminals? Treason? These thoughts going through my head like a haunted merry go round.

My consciousness returns and I'm still in this man's face. "Do you understand?"

"What?" I say shaking my head out of the trance.

"Holy saints!" the delta yells flailing his arms looking at his partner. "Just go pack your stuff. Suitcases are on your beds."

Kylie is sobbing, still in shock by the man's orders. I'm sure everything going through my head is spinning even faster in hers, the poor girl. I take her by her hand and lead her to her room. She yanks out of my grip.

"Please tell me this is some cruel joke," she begs them. "Who are you guys?"

"No more questions," Robbins shouts. "You," he points at me. "go pack your things. And you," he points at Kylie. "grab some clothes and some lady toiletries and pack your things. There

21

is a suitcase in both of your rooms. Fill it with what you can fit in them." He looks down at his watch. "I want both of you done in the next ten minutes. We are late and we have to go. Now!" he orders.

I scan the omega, looking for any sign of what legion he's in. Cannon Legion normally patrols Harmony, not always, but definitely wouldn't be breaking into houses to take kids away. I realize he has no patch on his shoulder, it looks taken off. "Why are you missing your legion insignia? Who are—"

Robbins pulls his pistol out and strikes it an inch from my face. Kylie shrieks, I step back and pull Kylie behind me. The barrel of a pistol staring directly in my eyes. My stomach drops and fear shivers down my spine.

"Mind your business and do as I say. Now," Robbins orders.

With no other choice, I pull Kylie down the hall and into her room. A foreign suitcase is laid on my bed. I stuff as many sets of clothes as I can fit in the suitcase. The realization of it all finally hits me like a hydrogen train. Tears crawl out of my eyes, my vision blurs with sorrow and pain as I punch my bed and throw my blankets across the room. I feel hopeless, my life is over. I feel powerless for the first time in my life. My parents are dead, and I don't know what to do. I can't think of any way to escape this horrible fate. I'll never get to see my mother's smile ever again, smell one of her home cooked dinners after coming inside from playing, or feel the warmth of her hugs and kisses goodbye when I go to school.

I don't understand. How could my dad shoot my mom, it's not like he has his gun…?

My mind races, did he have his gun? I burst to the threshold of my door and sneak a peek. The soldiers are talking to each other in the living room. I take my chance and tip toe over to my parent's room down the hall. Kylie's crying in her room, there's no time to coddle her. Quietly, I open the door and jump inside the room. Dad usually hides his gun in his end table. I open it up and there it is. Placed plainly in all its glory, a 96 plasma pistol.

"Hurry up!" I hear outside the room, one of the soldiers are walking down the hall. I quickly conceal the pistol in my waistband and dash over to the door. I'm met by the delta who towers over me.

"What are you doing in here?" he demands.

"None of your business." I snap and wedge myself around him.

"Well, hurry up."

"Or what?!" I snap back.

"Or we'll arrest you for trespassing. This isn't your house anyone, boy!" the omega yells from the living room.

I grumble walking back to my room. Outmatched again. I shove the gun into my suitcase in between a pair of socks and a pair of boxers. With no more room to fit anything, I zipper up my suitcase and take one last look at my room. I gaze at my holoposters, hating myself for not being as strong as them to fight off these brutes. Wherever I am going, I will be back. My parents aren't dead, they can't be. How could my dad shoot himself if I have his gun? I walk out into the living room where the soldiers are. I stand there quietly.

"You ready, kid?" the delta asks.

I don't answer. He doesn't deserve my response.

"Ok then, just waiting on Kara."

A nerve strikes me in the back of my head like an arrow unleashed on its target. "It's Kylie!" I snap aggressively. "You ransack my house, point a gun at me, and tell me my parents are dead! *The least,* you can do is get her name right!"

"Mind your tongue before I cut it out," he threatens completely unfazed by my angry rant.

With a sneer, I settle in my silence. As I told Kylie, pick and choose your battles. Kylie drags her feet into the living room shortly after. Sobbing, tears run down her face, she looks awful. "Ok kids, let's go," the delta says getting up off the couch and puts his hand out pointing at the front door."

"We are not going anywhere until you tell us where on Tyke are we going." I demand.

Omega Robbins looks me dead in my eyes with a small grin on his ugly and battled ridden face. "Your new home."

4

Future of Harmony

We're loaded into the hovercar and I gaze out the window in silence. Kylie still sobs beside me as we lift off the ground and drive out of the neighborhood and onto the Skyline Expressway. The delta explains to us that my father was arrested for withholding government property with the intent to sell it. That lead to him shooting my mother and then proceeded to shoot himself after resisting arrest.

Kylie is distraught by the man's words and also refuses to believe any of his story. "You're a liar!" she screams. "You killed them, didn't you?! You wanted dad's project and he wouldn't give it to you, so you killed them. My father would never kill my mother! It was you! You repulsive, malodourous—"

The omega swivels around in his seat and backslaps Kylie. She shrieks and grabs her face.

The line has been crossed and I finally find the courage to lash out. "What the hex is your problem?! You like hitting little girls? Can't handle the truth, big guy? I bet you're some worthless, puny shell of a man outside all that equipment. Look how pathetic you look, had to suit up to handle two children? Are you really that big of a pathetic—"

"Shut up!" yells Robbins. "Stop the car!"

The delta slams on the breaks so hard, the seatbelt locks to catch me. He flicks a button on his side console and turns around again. Thinking he's going to hit us again I jerk my arms towards Kylie to catch his next strike. But he moves towards the door and opens it. The powerful breeze floods the car, and a shockwave enters my body. We're hovering about two hundred feet from the ground. He wouldn't...

He upholsters his gun and points it at Kylie. "I don't care about you." Then to me. "I don't care about you." He flicks the gun towards the open door. "If you want to be on your own, jump. See if I care. See if I come and save you. You think I want to be transporting orphaned children? No! I'd rather be swimming in a pool with a whiskey in my hand, and actually enjoying my day. But no, I couldn't care less about either of you Harmonian scum!" His partner remains silent, refusing to intervene. I'm sure he feels the same way. "Go! Jump!" he yells. We sit still in our seats. Closing our lips and choosing to obey the ballsy omega. After a few more moments he reaches over and closes the door. "I don't want to hear another peep out of either of you. Do you understand?!"

I nod, I don't know if Kylie does. She grabs my hand and I see a cut slightly bleeding down her face. I pull her face into my shoulder and press my shirt against it to stop the bleeding. As blood changes my white shirt red, tears follow. For the first time in my life, I feel helpless. I feel like I can't protect her. "I'm sorry, Kylie," I whisper to her head and tighten my grip on her.

The car ride time went by like it does on a treadmill. Minutes feel like hours. I watch tears roll from Kylie's face. She refused to look at me, it's painful to see her like this. Painful to see such a bright young girl being stripped from everything she knew and loved. This whole situation is baffling. How did my dad get ahold of another gun? Why would he shoot mom? He's told me countless times this project was his life's work. There's no way he stole this, and if he did, how did it take so long for the government to find out? There is obviously something shady going on here. I need to get to the bottom of this, but how? I don't even know where I am going to be sleeping tonight.

As I watch the sun set on the worst day of my life, we land near this dirty, broken down house, bigger than anything I have seen in Redding, but the siding is dirty with a hint of blue mold over it. The roof looks in bad shape, some of the shutters are falling off on the second story.

Several farm animals come into view. It smells of manure and shame. Animal odor consumes my nose, and I hear some voices of children. I see some playing tag in the far back of the house.

"What is this place?" I ask.

"Welcome to your new home, kid," Robbins says. "*The Future of Harmony.*"

We walk up to the front door with our suitcases and an older woman opens the door before we can get up to it.

"Hello, children," she says looking down at us from the top of the steps. Grey hair stretches down the roots of her hair and fades into a bright yellow. Wrinkles create a maze on her face.

She greets the omega, and he whispers something in her ear. She nods and turns to us. "Why don't you two get settled in. Go inside and unpack your things. You are..."

"Carson, ma'am. And this is my sister, Kylie. Is there any chance we can share a room? I don't want her to be alone."

"Unfortunately, Carson, we cannot take requests like that here. Everyone must deal with what we can offer," she says cheerfully. "Your room is upstairs the second door on your left. Kylie, your room is down this hallway and to the right. I hope you two don't mind having some roommates."

"Ma'am, please, there has to be something we can figure out."

"I'm afraid not, Carson. We split the boys and girls up here. The boys are upstairs, and the girls are down here."

"I promise, ma'am, I won't be any harm. I—"

"It's fine, Carson!" Kylie interrupts. "It's fine," she says softer and disappointed. She's just as finished with this day as I am.

I take a deep unsettling breath, and watch Kylie get escorted to her room. I turn around and see Omega Robbins typing something on his data pad on his wrist. His delta beside him. "Robbins," I call out. He peeks his head up. "When I'm your titan, you'll be scrubbing toilets for the rest of your career."

The delta step forward, but Robbins stops them. He unhooks the lever on his holster and grabs his gun again. "I'm sorry. What did you say to me? Something about being a worthless piece of Harmony trash?" he says.

I feel safe in this doorway. There's no way he would pull his gun on me. "That's no way to talk to talk to your future commanding titan, Robbins. You look like such a fairy waving your gun at children, smacking little girls, and calling us names. To wonder what your wife would think of you if she were here. I'll tell her when she makes me dinner." I slam the door as hard as I can and hope he doesn't charge the door to fight me. He doesn't. Thank the saints, I'd probably soil myself if he did. I take a deep relieving breath and try to collect myself. Second door on the left she said, right?

I head up the stairs. The carpet looks like it hasn't been cleaned in years, it's an old looking dirty grey. As I get up the stairs and look down the poorly lit hallway, I wonder what kind of roommates I'm going to have. I get past the bathroom that is littered with dirty clothes, and head into my new room. It's small and compact, possibly the size of my room but with a lot more stuff and two bunk beds all unmade but no sign of my so-called roommates. The smell of body odor and farts linger in the air so they must be around. The walls are painted white with several fist sized holes and scuff marks on them. No desk or nice chair to sit in, just three unmade beds with different colored sheets on them, and one bare mattress with stains of who knows what all over it.

I'm taking a wild guess that the top bunk with no sheets is my new bed. I look around and find some drawers with a small TV on top and candy wrappers lining the whole surface of it. I open the drawers and find it is stuffed with someone's belongings and a muscle relaxer stim hidden away in the back. I've never seen stims before, besides in movies. I hold it in my hand and pop open the top. A small needle with directions to stick it in your neck are displayed on the side, next to a visible screen showing the liquid inside. Mom didn't want them in the house. She always told me they rot your brain out. I drop the medicine back where I found it and look elsewhere, finding no empty storage spaces for my stuff. Figures.

I take another deep unsettling breathe to calm my nerves, and exhale. The rotting stench of body odor makes me nauseous. I feel like a bird with no wings, or an ovat without long floppy ears. Something crucial and worthwhile to me has been stripped from me and I just don't know how I'm going to live with myself. I'm exhausted. I throw my suitcase on the bed and I walk out of my room and find a closet. I open it up and find some crumpled up sheets. I make my bed and feel it out. Stiff. The bed is as stiff as a saintdamn board. Ugh. This is definitely something I'm not going to get used to. I climb in and accidently bash my head on the ceiling. I groan in frustration, barely able to sit up, I give up on today and lay down. I miss my home. I miss my parents. Tears finally escape and roll down my face, I finally crack and cry myself to sleep.

5

The Boys

A loud voice rudely interrupts my nap. I jump out of my sleep and find two boys walking in the room. Sweat stains drench their shirts and dirt covers their pants and shoes. We make eye contact.

"Who are you?!" the kid demands. His short blonde hair doesn't fit his caramel complexion. He looks a little younger than me but seems to hold himself quite confidently.

"I'm Carson," I say wearily rubbing my eyes. "I'm new, I just got here." I flick my wrist to unlock my phone but realize it's been broken.

The boy takes one hop and clears my bed and lands his dirty behind on my bunk. He examines me for a long second. "I'm Kevin, and this here," he points to his companion in the doorway. "is Anderson."

Anderson seems quieter, maybe even shy. He has a much darker complexion like most Daltonese people. His black hair poofs up in an afro. "Sup."

"You from Dalton?" I ask Anderson boldly.

"What's it to you?"

A man of few words. "Nothing, I guess. Is there anywhere I can put my clothes? I looked around and—"

"What did you find?!" Anderson snaps violently. He looks outside the room and abruptly slams the door.

"Uh, nothing?" I reply confused, then realize that stim is probably his. He rushes to the drawer it's in. "I was just trying to find a place to put my clothes."

"Liar!" he snaps in a malicious tone, rummaging through the contents of the drawer.

Kevin looks at me like he's about to jump me and beat out whatever they think I took. I must act fast. I roll out of the bed, swinging my legs around Kevin and landing swiftly on my feet in a ready stance. If they think they are going to bully me, they have another thing coming. I've fought off more than one person at a time before. They don't know me, but then again, I don't know them. I'll stay defensive and try to deescalate, no sense in getting into a fight on my first day. "Let's be civil here, what could I possibly have taken that is so precious to you? I swear on my life I just got in here, took some sheets from the closet and fell asleep." Anderson reluctantly pulls out the stim and immediately injects himself in the neck. He falls on his bed and lets out a sigh like he just plopped in a hot bath.

Kevin laughs. "We're just messing with you," he says. "I'm from Harmony, born and abandoned, just like everyone here besides Andy, he's from Dalton."

"Wow, Kev, way to blow my cover."

"Pshhh, what does it matter? Stop being such a shade ball man." Kevin says and hops off my bunk and starts taking his shirt off. He rolls onto his bed and takes out a towel from behind his bunk against the wall. "I'm jumping in the shower. Carson, since you're new and haven't done any work at all today, you don't shower."

"I can't shower?" I ask.

He rolls his eyes and lets out a huff like he has explained this a dozen times. "Carson, buddy, there are twenty-two kids in this house. We wake up at five in the morning and we go to work. We share that bathroom down the hall with twelve other boys. Good luck getting in there in the morning to brush your teeth before roll call."

"Roll call? What about school?"

"*What about school?*" he mocks and laughs with Anderson. "There is no school, Carson. We live in an orphanage. You want to go to school, and be a smarty pants, then you better get adopted."

"So, this *is* an orphanage?" The realization finally hits me.

Kevin snaps me out of my thoughts. "You start work tomorrow morning, Carson buddy. I get it, it's hard to come to terms with your parents giving you up or whatever happened. Sad really, what are you, sixteen?"

"Yeah, just turned actually."

Kevin nods. "Same. Been here about four years now. I'm no high school graduate, but I know how to work with my hands and handle myself in the real world. I'm doing whatever I can to live the best life I can."

"I can respect that. Did the military show up to take you here?"

"Military?" Kevin's head turns lopsided. "Uh, no, not that I remember. I was taken from the hospital after my ma killed my pop in a car accident. Supposedly they were both doing drugs and when we got to the hospital, there was a nice lady there with candy who told me I needed to go with her. My ma didn't even fight it, she just... waved... Anyways," He walks over to what is assumed as his stuff. "these are my drawers." He opens one up and takes out the context of them and stuffs them into the one above it. "You can have this one for ten credits a week. We get an allowance at the end of every week. If you want new clothes, or whatever, we can take a bus to Levi after we get off work. Curfew is at nine. If you're caught outside after nine, you'll be locked out. I've slept in that barn about a dozen times now." He back slaps Anderson's leg. "Remember that time we snuck out to meet up with those two freckled girls? Ah, that was a great night."

Anderson smiles and nods, still enjoying his little daydream he's having.

"How much do we make a week?" I interrupt.

Kevin ponders. "Hmm, bout thirty to forty sometimes. You want it or not?"

"How about five?" He huffs but agrees to my terms. Hopefully I won't have it for long. "Did you see a little girl around here? My sister came with me, the old lady said her room was downstairs."

"Hah, that's Sally. As a matter of fact, the girls downstairs were talking about a new girl. Hasn't stopped crying ever since she got here."

"Can I go down there?" I ask. "That's my little sister, I told her I'd check on her."

"Sure. Go for it. Dinner will be ready in a bit. Don't get caught down there after curfew through, we're supposed to stay on our floor. Ron will cut all our wages if he finds one of us snooping around afterwards. And believe me, friend, you do not want to get on some of the bad side of the boys."

30

I nod. "What kind of work do we do?" I ask Kevin.

"You see them animals on your way in? We all take care of them. Have you ever hunted before?"

"No. Have you?" I ask.

"Once. I went out with Mr. Ron hunting ovats. That was fun. Those floppy eared thangs are quick. I didn't capture anything, but Ron caught like six. Sally made an ovat and veggie stew that night for dinner, and let me tell you, it was so much better than the food packages they get from the government."

"Ok, how often do people come and try to adopt?" I ask.

"Hmmm... maybe two or three in the last two months? Little Dillon was the only one who got adopted recently. These people love the young ones. Dillon was about six, I believe, right Andy?" Anderson nods, still smiling and humming a song in his bed.

"So, not a lot. Great, I'm going to be here forever." I say as my optimism slowly keeps depleting. "Is he ok?"

"Who, Andy? Yeah, Andy's got a bit of a stim stick." Anderson then shouts some foreign curse at him, and then proclaims that Kevin has a stim problem.

"Anyways, once you turn eighteen, you'll be told to leave. So, no, we won't be here forever."

"What?"

"Yeah, legal age is eighteen. Y'all grown up. Adults can't be adopted, Carson. This place will kick you out in the rain in a heartbeat and you'll be replaced with another youngster soon after. If you act up and disobey Ron or Sally, you won't be fed. They don't care much about your health." He pauses. "Well, they do to a point, can't say they're heartless, but honestly, if you died, they'll probably just bury you in the woods," he chuckles.

This place just gets better and better. I search around the room feeling a bit more comfortable. "So where is the other guy? There's three made beds."

Kevin looks at me strange. "Oh, Rocky? Yeah, he comes home late every day. He's turning eighteen soon, so he's pretty much given up staying around to be adopted. He works hard, but after work you'll find him off trying to catch some tail, or whatever he does. He's got some crazy stories."

31

I wonder if I will have the same faith, living here every day with a timer on your back. At least I have a few years until that happens. Kevin leaves to shower and that leaves me and Anderson alone. It's quite sickening to watch, but I'm oddly curious how it feels.

"You want a hit?" he asks pulling the needle out of his neck after injecting himself again.

"Um, no thanks. I'm going to go check on my sister."

6

The Girls

It's been about an hour since I have gotten here, and I feel like my eyes are all dried up. I can't stop myself from crying no matter how hard I try. All my emotions are digging their way into my heart and exploding into a frenzy of sorrow and remorse. I feel so helpless. I have found what I believe is to be my room. It smells like cheap perfume, and manure. The walls are painted some off-white color with young pop singer posters all over the wall. Two bunk beds sit along the sides of the room with a fluffy pink carpet in the middle, covering a dirty wood floor. I place my suitcase on the empty bed on the bottom bunk of one of the bunk beds and I curl up in a ball and wonder what I've done to deserve this.

A blonde girl barges into the room, gives me a vile look and says, "Um, who are you?"

I sniff up my sorrows and attempt to compose myself. "Hi, I'm Kylie. I'm—"

"Don't care," the girl chimes before I can explain myself. She walks in and grabs her towels from behind the door and walks out without another word.

I shiver in fright; I can't do this. I lay back down on the bare mattress and replay the same scenarios I've thought of about my parents. I knew they were dead from the first morning they didn't come home, but I prayed to the saints it wasn't true. Why would dad kill mom? He loved her. I don't understand. I want to go home, back to my family, back to Carson. There must be something I can do to see him. I get up and look outside in the hallway and see a group of kids stampeding down the hall. I get pushed by a boy back into my room and I nearly fall. I look at my shirt and see a mud stain the size of a hand placed right in the middle. I try to wipe it off, but I only smear it more.

I'm about to pull my hair out of my head in frustration but a voice catches my attention. "You the new girl?" the voice asks. I look up and find a tall girl, with a tanner complexion and long caramel legs. Her black hair's like a ball of yarn.

"Yeah. I'm Kylie. I just got here."

She huffs and shakes her head. Her bangs sway as she lets out an innocent laugh and tells me about the handprint on my shirt. Her light brown eyes peek through her hair, they say, welcome.

She gives me a baby wipe from her drawer. "I'm Nala."

Her accommodating demeanor calms my nerves. She sits on my bed with me and gives me a general run down of our days here. This thing called role call is at six in the morning, and she tells me the jobs the girls normally get stuck with. I begin to feel comfortable talking with Nala, her voice is soothing and warm. Nothing like the girl from before. She makes me laugh about one of the girls next door and tells me she will help me get through this place. Nala was orphaned at the age of ten, after her parents couldn't afford to take care of her anymore. She thinks they had a drug problem, but at the time, she had no idea why they abandoned her. She cried for days after coming here and now she plans to open up a hair salon when or if she gets adopted.

The girl from before comes in the room with her towel around her body and another one on her head. "You tell her what's what, Nala?" her blue eyes snare at me like I stole something from her.

"Yeah, she knows. Don't you… Kylie?" Nala says. I nod. "That's Courtney. Don't let her scare you, she's all talk."

"Shut up you fat cow" Courtney snaps at Nala. She looks at me. "You should be very, very afraid of me." She jerks her head close at me and I can't help but flinch back.

"At least I don't smell like one. Didn't you just shower?" Nala snaps back.

Courtney rolls her eyes and laughs at the comeback. She walks to the corner of the room by a dresser and unravels her towel, exposing her perfectly proportioned body. I quickly look away, suddenly feeling embarrassed to even look. I peek over at Nala and see her eyeing Courtney with a smirk on her face. Interesting.

A knock comes from the door. "Hello? Kylie?" A familiar boy's voice comes from the door. I look over and find Carson. He peaks inside the room and sees me. He smiles then I see his

34

eyes wander to the corner of the room. His face turns beat red as he makes eye contact with Courtney's naked body. He swivels back outside the room in a flash. "Holy saints, I'm sorry! I didn't know!"

"Uh, who was that?" Courtney says still unashamed.

I chase him out of the room and hug him. "Carson!"

He awkwardly hugs me back. "I'm sorry. I swear I didn't see anything."

"Shut up, it's fine. How are you? Are you ok?"

"Yeah. I'm…" He hits himself in the forehead. "Holy saints, I'm so sorry, I didn't mean to barge in like that, I—"

"Who's this?" Nala asks behind me.

Carson looks up at Nala with wide eyes and an open mouth. "I'm Carson, hi. I'm sorry the door was open and I, um… I'm Kylie's sister, *brother*," He quickly corrects.

Nala laughs and looks him up and down like she did me. She smirks and bites her lip. "I'm Nala," she says pushing her hair out of her face and sticks her hand out.

"Hey," Carson says embarrassed rubbing the back of his head. He shakes her hand. "Look, I wasn't trying to snoop on you or anything, I just wanted to see how Kylie was doing."

"Well, you see her, now don't you? She's fine, I got her. I'll keep her safe. Don't you worry yourself so much, she's in good hands." Nala wraps her arm around my shoulder. I smile and give Carson a thumbs up.

"I," he laughs nervously. "Thank you, and please, I hope I didn't—"

"Who the hex was that Nala? Another one of your dirty boyfriends?" Courtney says from inside the room.

Carson stutters and his face turns red again. "I'm uh, um—"

"Hex you, he's just the new girl's brother," Nala shouts back.

He touches my shoulder to get my attention. "Hey, Ky, listen, mom and dad can't be dead. Dad never took his gun, I have it."

"You what?"

"Yeah, it's in my suitcase. Which means Robbin's story is completely untrue, it has to be."

"Hey, you," Courtney interrupts, and pokes her head out the door, still indecent in her bra and underwear. She gives him a slanted look. "You see anything?"

"No!" Carson says defensively. "Honest, I—"

"Because it would be ok if you did." She winks at him and slips back in the room.

"Holy saints." Carson wipes his hand across his face. He's as red as last summer when he forgot sunscreen on the hottest day of the year. "I'm going back upstairs. It was nice to meet you, Nala, and um... I'll see you at dinner, Kylie?"

I smile and squeeze my brother one more time. For such a dreadful day, watching my brother stutter over his words and make a fool of himself made me laugh and reminded me I still have him. I'm not all alone. "Yeah. I'll save you a seat."

I watch him leave and I walk back into the room and see Courtney finally all clothed. She sure took her time, and obviously has no shame in herself. Her confidence is radiating, makes her quite intimidating to look at.

"He's a cute one. Hope you don't mind if I take a turn at him," Courtney says.

"Take a what?"

7
First day on the farm

I wake up to someone yelling in my face. I open my eyes to a boy with pimples all over his face. His amber eyes feel as though he is looking through me into my soul. "Yo, new kid, get up! You're going to be late," my last and least tolerable roommate, Rocky bellows in my ear.

He climbed in through the second story window in the middle of the night and scared the living hell out of me, then didn't stop badgering on about some broad he was seeing to Kevin for two hours. He's taller than I imagined with a light red beard and a tight man bun wrapped up by a rubber band. He looks over to me again. "Are you deaf? Get up. Let's go," he snaps.

The room is still dark, the sun hasn't even risen yet. I slowly climb out of bed and slip on my shoes. Lucky for me I kept the same clothes on from the day before, a plain, white t-shirt and blue jeans. Both Anderson and Kevin are already gone and out of the bedroom walking down the stairs. I follow the crowd down the stairs and into the kitchen leading towards the back door where I bump into a younger girl coming out of the bathroom.

"Oh, sorry. I—" It was that Courtney girl from last night. I instantly forget how to speak.

"Watch where you're going!" she snaps. We make eye contact and her demeanor instantly changes. "Oh, hey, it's you." Her long light blonde hair sways from her radiant blue eyes. They make me nervous.

"You're gonna be late, boy," a deeper rougher voice says over what Courtney was trying to say. A balding man with snow white hair marches down the hallway. He's in overalls with a dirty red flannel on and worn out brown boots walking past me and out the back door. That must be Mr. Ron.

"I'll see you—" I look back and realize she is gone.

I snap back into my wits and get shoved forward. I follow the crowd and rush out the backdoor through the kitchen. Just as my foot hits the first step outside, my body is launched forward by a forceful push. I fall down the small flight of stairs and land directly on my face at the bottom. I look up and Rocky is laughing at me with a group of kids around him. Courtney was one of them.

"Gotta be faster, new kid," Rocky says as he bellows along with the group. He intentionally tries to walk over me, barely missing my face with his dirty boots in the process.

I could feel the dirt brushing against my face from his boot hitting the ground. I try to close my mouth in time, but it is too late. I cough and spit up the dirt that flies into my mouth. As I watch more kids walk down the stairs and run through the field for role call, I catch the eyes of Nala looking at me, she turns away with a smug and disappointed look on her face.

Completely embarrassed, I get up and brush myself off. I get the taste of blood in my mouth and feel a cut where I bit through my lip. The sun is barely over the tree line. A bead of sweat already escapes my body, my arm pits already moist from the humidity. I'm going to smell worse than these farm animals. Ugh, it's going to be a long day.

I find my new companions from my room in the middle of the line. I try to wedge my way in there, but I get shoved back.

"Get to the end of the line," I'm told by another kid.

I look around for Kylie but can't find her. I end up walking to the end of the line next to a boy with short brown hair and a few pimples on his chin. He has a plain white t-shirt on and overalls, full of dirt stains. Mr. Ron walks in front of the group and waits a few more moments for the stragglers. He then walks down the line pointing a finger at each of us as he goes by, counting us. I hear him mumble something about missing one.

"Where's the new boy?" Mr. Ron announces. My heart drops, is he talking about me? No, he can't be… He scans the line and sees me. He walks right up to me. Oh crap…

"What's your name, boy?"

"I'm uh, Carson, sir."

"Great! Thanks for volunteering," he says in an upbeat voice. "You will be on manure duty. Go to the barn over there where all the horses are and clean up the barn. After that, come find me, I'll be working on the fence around the perimeter. If that's too hard for you, you'll have manure duty all week. You hear me, boy? I wanna see you in an hour, tops. Dismissed."

"Yes sir," I say nervously. I feel frozen to the ground.

"Everyone else, same as yesterday unless I tell you otherwise. Damion, you are excused from manure duty. Go pull the weeds in section one with Kevin and Anderson. I want it clear by breakfast. Dismissed!"

Everyone goes their own way, except for me. My legs still won't move. Mr. Ron looks back at me with a crooked face and sees that I'm still standing exactly where I was.

"MOVE BOY!" he yells. It jumpstarts my legs and I take off running unbeknownst where the barn is. "Wrong way, boy! Saintdamn it!"

I turn to Ron with a confused look. "Where's the barn, sir?"

He turns and points at a big red house in the corner of the property. "You see that giant building over there?"

I take off before getting yelled at again. I get into the barn and get a full whiff of the putrid aroma. Ugh, saints almighty, I just swallowed that. I can't do this. I take a step outside to clean out my nose of that disgusting smell. I gag and try not to puke. Ugh… I have to do it. If I don't then I'll just cause more trouble. I take a deep breath of fresh air, scope out the shovel, and make my move. There is so much of it, piles and piles of dung everywhere. I scoop up the droppings as fast as I can and dump them in a wheelbarrow. I charge out the barn doors with my shirt over my nose and a wheelbarrow full of manure. I leave the wheelbarrow outside. Figure Ron just wanted it picked up. He never said anything about dropping it off anywhere in particular.

I search for Mr. Ron outside and find a shed door wide open. Maybe he is in there getting his tools. I peak my head in and find him picking tools out and placing them in a bucket. "Mr. Ron, I'm done with the manure." I tell him.

He looks at his watch, smirks and hums a pleasant sound. "Good. Where did you put all of it? he asks.

"I just left it outside, I didn't know what to do with it, sir."

He inhales and lets out a long and disappointed exhale. Then spits something black and foul into a plastic cup. "That's fine, boy. What was your name again?"

"Carson, Carson Paul."

"Well, Carson Carson Paul, have you ever built a fence before?"

I had to think about it but after some thought, I don't even think my dad knew how to build a fence. "No, I don't believe I have."

"Well, I'm going to show you how to build an electric one."

I started off by hammering stakes in the ground and watched Mr. Ron hook up the wires. He showed me how to properly hook up the wiring through the fence and connect it to the panel. We ended up talking for quite a while. He asked a few questions about me and I answered accordingly. He told me a story of his childhood, how he was abandoned and left in the woods. He said he was picked up by two drunken hitch hikers who just took him for their own, gave him a second chance at life. That's why he does this. To give a second chance for kids.

After that, I asked him about Rocky. I didn't snitch on him for pushing me down, or coming home late, but I wanted to know more about him. Ron tells me his name is Rocco McKenzie. Apparently, he has been an orphan since he was a newborn. He's been moved from orphanage to orphanage his whole life.

A loud ringing noise sounds off. It rattles my ears and frazzled me. "What is that noise? What's happening?" I ask Ron.

"Breakfast time, Carson Carson. Let's grab some grub and finish afterwards," Mr. Ron says. "Got to say, you got a knack for this kind of thing. Keep up the good work and I'll just have to keep you around."

I chuckle at the awkwardness, not knowing if he is just messing around. "It's just Carson, sir."

"I know what your name is, boy. C'mon. Best not keep Sally waiting."

After a breakfast of cold eggs and half cooked bacon, I get a chance to look around and still I see no sign of Kylie. As I step inside to hand in my plate to the dishwasher, I realize it's Kylie.

"There you are," I say to her.

She turns around. "Oh, hey Car. How is everything going?"

"I'm fine, Ron and I are fixing the fence. Where were you at role call?"

"Nala didn't wake me up until she was walking out the door. It's no fair, how was I supposed to wake up at the crack of dawn with no alarm?"

"Don't worry, Ky, when we get paid, we can go buy you an alarm clock or something. How's that sound?"

Kylie looks at me confused. "Why are you so... calm? I know you like being optimistic about everything, but our parents are *dead*. We're at an orphanage, living with seventeen strangers who, not for nothing, smell unfathomably putrid."

I chuckle and fold my arms. "I... I know. I'm just... I don't know, making the best of it?"

"Making the best of it? You can make out a good thing about any of this?"

It's hard to think about, knowing my parents are never coming back, but something in me says they will. Like they took a cruise to some far away land but will eventually come back home and find us. "Well—"

"Did you know we're not going back to school? You're not going to graduate? I'm not going to go to college, I'm not going to be a robot engineer like daddy. I'm going to be a—" she stops midsentence and looks around suspiciously.

"A what?" I ask.

"Like these people," she whispers. "I don't want this, Carson. I want to go home."

"This is our home now, Ky. At least for the time being."

"So, you're saying you're ok with this? Living with all these strangers? Sharing a bathroom? Living on this... this labor camp?" she says sounding panicked. "Where we may, or may not get adopted together to other strangers, who may or may not treat us the way we are accustomed to? I can't, Carson. I can't do this."

I put my hand on her shoulder. "Relax. They won't separate us, they can't and I won't let them. We just have to make the best out of it. Plus, every week we get paid. After work we can go and do whatever we want," I say.

"You think we can save up enough money to buy our own place together?" she asks.

"That's always a possibility," I reassure her. "I don't know how much money we can make in two years."

"Two years?" Kylie looks at me crooked.

"Yeah, once I turn eighteen, that's it. Apparently, Ron and Sally will kick me out. Technically, I'd be considered an adult.

"What? That's not enough time!" she shouts in a whisper. Kylie's eyes stare off like she's hard at work doing some kind of numbers problem in her head. A plate then comes flying into the

41

sink and splashes her. Water hits her chest and face. I turn and see a little brown haired boy licking his fingers.

I sneer at him. "What?" he asks sarcastically and walks away.

I look at Kylie, expecting her to lash out at the boy but she doesn't do anything. She just kept her head down and continues to wash. I grab her a paper towel and wipe up the water that splashed her. "I'll make you a plate."

8
The Watch
One week later

As I watch Kevin barrel into our room in front of me, he shouts that he calls first in the shower. His baggy shirt waves back and forth as he weaves in and out of the incoming children with his shirt halfway off him. I hear the bathroom door slam shut. I slip off my dirty shoes underneath my bunk and watch as Anderson doesn't even hesitate to pull out his stim dispenser from his drawer and dig it into his neck. The euphoric sensation he describes consumes him. His eyes flutter and he plops down on his bed with his legs hanging over the edge with a gazing look in his eyes.

"You really need to lay off that stuff. It's gonna rot your head."

"I swear to the saints, my friend, it's the best feeling in the world. Just you wait, you'll have the time of your *life* once I get you on this stuff."

I gaze at my troubled friend nodding off in his little galactic adventures he has while being induced under the erotic feelings those things give him. While he was born a Daltonese boy, his family was killed by racist cultists. He was rescued by a young family from a small part in Harmony who got him hooked on stims and then later overdosed.

My first week at the orphanage is over. One whole week of nonstop work and picking up disgusting, stomach turning manure. I can see how this kind of life can affect my young fourteen-year-old Daltonese friend. It gives him some kind of alternate reality of the world like how a pair of sunglasses would enhance your vision.

Today was a good day. The work was tedious but I will always take tedious over strenuous any day. With the electric fence all done, I think I deserve this paycheck more than most. I hardly saw Rocco lift a finger or do anything at all for that matter. He's more of a finger pointer than a worker. Since he's one of the older kids, he feels more inclined to tell other people what to do like he's a young Ron.

After budgeting the five credits I need to give Kevin, I'm hoping my first paycheck is enough for a watch. Something with an alarm to help me wake-up earlier to get myself prepared for the day. At least four days this week I was woken up with nearly five minutes to get outside. With no clock in the room, I feel so uncoordinated. Kevin said there's a store in Levi called *Al's Warehouse* that sells watch. It's supposed to have a little bit of everything from jewelry, to clothes, to palmphones. After Robbins destroyed mine, I've felt lost without one, naked even. It was always something I checked on or had on to be updated on the world. I still find myself flicking my wrist to open it. Maybe one day I can save up enough money for a new one.

Kevin yells my name from down the hall. It freaks me out at first, so I jump up out of bed and peak my head out into the hallway looking for some kind of emergency. I see him in his towel, still newly out of the shower waving me in. As quick as I can, I rush inside the steaming bathroom. "Thanks, buddy," I say as I slide past him.

"No problem, waters still hot so use as much as you want," he says with a goofy smile. I ignore his selfish ideas and philosophies of first come first serve, or something about a bird waking up early to get food first. I want to get into Levi as soon as possible so I shower quickly and save some hot water for the next boy in line. When I'm finished, I open the door and find a line of shirtless boys waiting for the shower. Some ask if there is still hot water and I just nod and keep it short. I slide back in my room and see Kevin already dressed for our night on the town. Anderson, however, is still in his dirty work clothes enjoying his magical land of splendor or whatever he feels.

"Hey, Andy, you coming with us to Levi? Carson wants to get himself one of those fancy wrist watches," Kevin asks.

He looks over at Kevin grungy and out of it. "Nah, I'ma gonna stay here tonight and chill," he says drunkenly.

I click my tongue in an annoyed disgust. "Yo, get up, stop being such a bum."

44

"Hex you! Can't you see I'm—" he looks at his dispenser and realizes he just used the last of what he had. He shakes it and tries to look for something inside, but it looks like it's been stripped clean. "Alright. I'm coming."

I groan. "You coming to hangout or are you going to get more of that crap you're on."

"No, no. I'll come hang with you to get your fancy watch," he says mockingly.

Before I come back with more negative comments, Kevin jumps back with his enthusiasm. "Great. Get ready, Carson. Civvyshuttles come around once an hour. We don't want to miss it. We can't come back in if we get home late. Remember that, nine o'clock."

"I gotcha, I gotcha. Hey, do you mind if I invite Kylie?"

"Ahh, c'mon man. Guys night! No offense to your little sis broham, but she's…"

"She's… what? You don't want her to come?"

"It's not that, she's just… you know, guys night?"

I can respect where he's coming from. Kylie has been different ever since we got here. Can't blame her much, but we all need to move on eventually. Some grieve differently than others. I miss my parents. I do, I truly do, but as of now, they aren't going to magically appear and take me home. This is my home and I have to make the best of it, and work towards a better future for myself. I can't be a Titan if I cry all day about… ugh. I drive the thoughts of my past in the back of my head. I hold back a sudden rush of emotions and pull back into reality. "Fine. Then let's go before it gets too late. You gonna shower, Andy?"

"Nah. I'm good like this."

All Ron gave us is thirty this week. He said that food was expensive this month. But he lies through a straight face as all Harmonians can. He has his own addictions like Anderson, except his is through a glass bottle, not a dispenser. The civvyshuttle ride to Levi costs two credits. Kevin told me he'd waive the rent for the drawer if I pay his way, and Anderson pulls the guilt trip on me and says he forgot his credits just as we walk onto the shuttle so spot him as well. I don't see how a little dinky watch can be any more than eight to ten credits. So, if I'm right, it'll leave me with just enough credits to save at least five and get us home.

As the shuttle lands in the middle of Levi, my heart races with excitement. I have a love for exploring unfamiliar places and seeing new things. Levi is one of the nicer established towns in Harmony. Buildings are built sturdier than most places. Huge apartment complexes and stores are down the strip next to a massive park in Town Square, where concerts and other festivals are thrown.

Walking into Al's Warehouse parking lot looks like a scene out a movie. Dozens of hovercars land into parking spots and others ascend and zip away from the stores in all directions. In Redding, most people don't own hovercars, they're simply too expensive. Most have to use the roads with battery powered quadromobiles that don't hover, like back in the Old Earth days. It was a bit of a culture shock to see so many unique style hovercars all at once. Anderson is curiously looking around on the ground and around us like he's about to do something crazy. He nods to Kevin and they pull away from me and walk through the rows of cars. They start deviously and discreetly pulling on the car doors. After the first few rows I grow confused and annoyed at their actions. "What are you guys doing?" I ask.

"Keep your saintdamn voice down. Can't you see we're trying to find a jellybean?" Anderson snaps.

"A what?" I ask confused.

"An unlocked car. If you find one, say jellybean," Kevin explains.

"I didn't come here to rob people. I'm—"

"Then hex off," Anderson snaps in a whisper. "I don't know about you, but I like free credits when I can get it." Anderson's wrist beeps and he stops instantly and answers the burner palmphone his "guy" gave him. He flicks his wrist, and a conversation of text messages lights up his wrist. He looks in the distance at a group of guys on the side of the store in a small alleyway. "That's the call. I'll... I'll be right back," he says to us.

"What? No, Anderson, where are you going?" I try and pull him back but he's too quick. He sprints through the parking lot towards the side of the building.

"Let him go, broham," Kevin says. "He can make his own decisions."

"What is he doing? What's going on?"

"Didn't you see he ran out of his stim?" I nod and realize what is happening. "You know damn well he scammed you before, right? He has money. He's got plenty for stims. Don't expect to be paid back."

"How does that not bother you? Didn't your parents die from stims?"

"Nah, I don't think it was stims. Had to be something stronger like luna salts."

"What's luna salts"

"Pshhh, I don't know. Never seen it before. I'm just guessing, but apparently it makes people overdose." Kevin stares at the ground with his hands in his pockets.

I worry for my new friend. Such a young and hopeful child can be stripped of everything in a blink of an eye because of that crap. I hope there can be something I can do for him. Kevin on the other hand seems like a good kid, just dealt a bad hand in life. I stroll up to the front entrance and wait for Anderson. He comes wobbling up to us with his eyes dilated and a big smile on his face. "You good?"

"Oh yeah. Let's get some food, my dudes."

"What? No. I'm getting my watch."

He looks at me dumbfounded. "I thought we were getting some food?"

"No? I'm—"

"Man! I'm starving. Whatever! I'ma chill out here. You ain't gonna ruin my high again."

"Cool. Cool." Kevin pushes him away from me before I get angry. Anderson is really starting to aggravate me. "See if you can find a jellybean," Kevin shoos him off.

"Ight! You got that." Anderson turns around and moseys on into the parking lot.

"Is he going to be ok?" I ask.

"Yeah," Kevin says shortly. "Let's go find your watch and get home before we're locked out."

In Al's Warehouse, Kevin didn't disappoint, this massive store has everything. Rows upon rows of anything you can think of. I eye up several shirts and shoes and things I find appealing and find myself making a mental shopping list to go back to when I save up my money. But I keep my head on straight and follow the path I need to find the small section of watches. I find sparkling crystal watches all ranging from a hundred to over a thousand credits. I try and look for a person to help me get pointed in the right direction to the clearance rack. This is ridiculous. I end up finding the cheapest watch with an alarm was twenty credits. It's got a velcro strap that wraps around my wrist but it's as basic as it comes.

9

Courtney

Four credits left. Anderson better have credits for the bus home because I am not paying for that bum again. I thought he wanted to hangout, but he just wanted to find a fix. It's disgusting to live like that. Small time thieving is one thing but he's breaking into people's cars, not taking a two credit candy bar from a multimillion dollar franchise. I wonder if he'll get arrested for doing that one day. Will anyone break him out, or will he rot in a prison cell because no one ever taught him how to live sober?

As we exit the store, in the distance, I hear a car alarm going off. Its loud sirens can be heard from a mile away. Anderson finds us quickly and yanks us away from the noise, insisting that we leave. I find out he made his own jellybean. He saw a compartment with a small amount of credits, so he broke into the car and swiped it up. The sharp glass left a mighty gash going down his forearm. "Yeah, man. I got like twenty credits. It was awesome. You should have been there."

"Oh good, so you got money for the civvyshuttle, right?" I question. "Better yet, you can pay me back, right? Pay my way home and we're square."

"Um, yeah, I um, I don't got it anymore," he ends his sentence softer. Guilt in his voice.

"What happened to it, Andy?" Kevin adds.

"Well, my guy had more stims so I—" The truth comes out.

"You're hopeless!" I snap. I can't care about his emotions. If he wants to be mad at me, I can care less "So how are you getting home?" I ask sarcastically.

"Oh, you can't spot me, Car? I thought you had credits."

"Yeah, had. This watch was twenty credits."

"Wow, that's a rip off. Could have gotten another week's worth of stim for that."

"I don't want your disgusting stims, Anderson. You know one day you're gonna—"

"Mind my own business?" Anderson snaps back. "Yeah. I just might." Awkward silence collapses on my little group as we walk back to the bus stop. It's getting late. We have a little less than an hour to get home. We have to get on the next bus.

As we make our way back to the bus stop, we pass a smaller group of thuggish looking men with a group of girls who have oddly familiar voices. With a mound of makeup over their faces and clothes I've never seen them wear before, I recognize the girls from the orphanage. Heather, Naomi, and Kylie's roommate, Courtney.

Without a second to think about who they are with, I stretch my arm out and wave at them. "Hey, girls. What's up?"

I get smacked from my side, I turn and see a worried face on Kevin. "What are you doing? You know those are Bone Breakers, right?"

"Who?"

The group of four men stand up with grueling grotesque looks at their faces. They all wear the same sleeveless jacket but the smallest one with a spikey mohawk, he has a pudgier face and a white undershirt on. A lengthy man with a thin face and a pointy nose leads the group with two wider brute looking guys behind and the smallest one to his right. "Who the hex are you?" The lengthy one asks. He's got a short mohawk, dyed jet black with matching ripped jeans and boots. A white cracked skull is stitched on his jacket along with everyone else in his group.

An uncomfortable intimidation wraps my throat and words can't come out. I look back at my friends and they have already found extra distance from me. "I'm uh, Carson. Are you—"

"Your worst nightmare is who I am, kid. These girls are property of the Bone Breakers. If I ever see you again, I'll pummel you into the ground and bury you with your puny friends."

"Listen," I back up out of the guys face and hold my hands out defensively. "There seems to be a misunderstanding here. I live with those girls. We're friends. I was just saying hi."

A vein pops out of the man's head. "What did I just say?!" He looks towards his friends "This guy must be stupid." Then looks back at me. "Are you one of those dimwit kids in special classes?"

"Excuse me?"

49

He looks at the girls. "Do you know this guy?" Both Heather and Naomi shrug me off, but Courtney walks up to him and puts her hand on the man's shoulder and starts massaging it.

"He's my roommate's brother, Bonez. He's harmless. Isn't that right, Carson?" She looks at me with wide blue eyes and a hint filled face to go with the flow.

"Yeah? Yeah, man. I'm, uh, I'm harmless."

"Great. So, since you've insisted on wasting my time, give me that watch, your shoes and all the money in your pockets. We can call this *harmless* discussion over." I see the two brutes behind him laugh and rotate their shoulders, stretching them out for a fight. Along with the smaller one pounding his fists into his other palm.

"Woah, woah, woah. I just got this. I need this for—"

"Back talk, huh?" Bonez questions. "You two," he points at Kevin and Anderson. "Empty yah pockets, yah heard? And you, Dalton boy, you look high as a kite. You must be holding. Fork it over! Your dumb harmless friend just screwed you guys too."

"No!" Anderson freaks out. "I don't have anything. I swear."

I get shoved out of the way and the gang of men stomp over to Anderson and Kevin.

"I would run if I were you," Courtney whispers in my ear. Her blue eyes are surprisingly dazzling with the amount of eye makeup she has on.

"Empty yah pockets yah Daltonese runt!" Bonez orders.

Anderson covers his pockets. "No! Please, I just—"

The smaller one steps forward and punches Anderson in the gut. He drops to his knees as Kevin gets blindsided from one of the brutes and crumbles to the pavement. The group of men encircle them and all I can see is hands flying and feet swinging.

"Stop! What are you doing? They're kids!" I yell as I watch the horror of my friends yelping as a punishment that was supposed to be mine becomes theirs.

Images of Kylie being bullied engulf me, the countless scenarios I've been involved in. This is no different. I tighten my fist and prepare to give it my all. I'm out numbered, out muscled, and outmatched but no one gets to hurt my friends without me having to say something about it. I choose wisely and aim for Bonez first, hoping if I take out the loudmouth first the rest will follow along. Without Bonez even seeing it coming, I leap onto his back and pull him away from my friends. I hop off and immediately duck from a sloppy swing. He's taller than me and has a much longer reach. I lean forward and dig into him. Closing the distance quickly, I clutch his head and pull it down into my knee before he can swing again. I feel his nose crunch and crack over the solid technique my mother taught me. I grab his waist and fling him over my shoulder, body slamming him into the ground. I look onward. The smaller one turns to me and sees what I did.

Shock drives through him in an unexpected panic. "What the?" he says in his whiny voice. Before he says anything else, I drive my foot into his collarbone. He's much shorter than me so pushing him off Anderson was easier than expected. I follow up with another fully loaded kick to his jaw as he tries to get back up, leaving him in the middle of the street with two missing teeth. I snap around towards my friends and see I have gained the attention of the two brutes.

"Back up!" I yell. They stop their onslaught and back away. I run over to my friends and see the carnage they've endured. They each have sweltering black eyes and bruises all over their faces. "C'mon, let's get out of here." I try to pull them up, but Kevin is unconscious.

Anderson is slow to get up holding his stomach. "I told you not to ruin my high," he mumbles with a small gash around a swollen lip. I try to get Kevin up over my shoulder, but I come face to face with a switchblade pointed directly in my face.

"You're not going anywhere," Bonez says with blood dripping out of his nose. "You think you can come around these parts, *my parts*, and make a fool of me? Blaze! Twig! Hex him up."

Courtney gets in the middle of us again. "Bonez, stop. You don't have to do this. He's—"

"You do not have a say in any of this, you hear me?" Bonez slaps Courtney with his blood-filled hand.

"Hey!" is all I can yell before I'm distracted by a punch in the chest. The wind shoots out of my lungs, and I'm decked again by another fist coming from both the brutes spinning me and tumble into the road. As I try desperately to give myself ground, realizing I can't fight them off, the only solid hit I get is a kick to the shin to one before I am pummeled. I get picked up off the ground by my neck and I feel the tightening of a bulky arm wrapped around my throat. I'm strangled by one of the brutes and I feel my feet leave the ground. Vascular muscles tense up around my neck and I feel the squeeze pulsing towards my head. Blood rushes, my vision blurs, I feel unconsciousness start to set in as I try my best to squirm free, but I can't seem to get loose.

"Stop! Stop! Put him down now!" I hear in Courtney's pleading voice, but it doesn't stop. I open my eyes to see Bonez with an evil, conniving look with his switchblade pointed right at my eye. I panic, thoughts of what could happen terrify me. I lurch forward and swing my legs up like you would on a swing set and drive them into Bonez's chest. With the same backwards momentum,

I pull back and heel my captor in knees. He yelps and his grip loosens but I hold on to his arm and heave him over my shoulder. With the brute's wrist, I twist and pull on it till I hear a pop. His shoulder dislocates and I curb stomp his head into the grass. In a ready stance, I face Bonez and the second brute. He's bald with a lazy eye, about a head taller than me. I lock on to Bonez, he holds his blade up at me. Intensity thickens. Adrenaline fills my body and flows through me like a herd of illans prancing through an open meadow.

Courtney screams for this to stop again and pulls the blade away from Bonez. He struggles with her for a sheer moment in time, I have an unexpected opening. With his face completely exposed, I lunge forward and detonate the man's left side of his face. Bonez is blasted backwards and falls with a thud. The brute looks on at me with Courtney in front of me. I pull her behind me and she rips my arm away from her.

"Stop! Just stop! I can't take this anymore! Blaze, enough!" the brute puts his hands out and submits. She looks at Bonez slowly inching himself back up. "You're a coward, Jack. Keep your hexing necklace. I'm going home." She rips off some kind of necklace and throws it at him. She races to me and helps my friends up. I pull Kevin over my shoulder and look over at Courtney. "Are you taking the bus home?" she asks me.

"Yeah. Why?"

"Good, I'm coming."

Courtney follows us to the bus stop. Kevin wakes up with a pounding headache and is mostly quiet for the walk to the bus stop. Anderson is furious with me for getting him jumped. His three dispensers broke in the thrashing. The bus arrives as we approach the bus stop and I help Kevin on to his seat behind Courtney. I pull out my remaining four credits, and I realize that I can't afford for all four of us. Courtney already paid her way and I try to come up with some sob story about how we got jumped and four credits was all I could hide. The driver doesn't falter even with my bruised chest and puffy face. He tells me to get off the bus. As I drop my remaining four credits in the money tank for my friends, I decide to let my friends stay and I will walk home. With defeat growing on me, and with the realization that I have lost this argument, I step off alone. As I watch my friends in the windows, the bus door surprisingly opens again. I let out a sigh of relief thinking the driver let me slide, but Courtney walks off the bus.

"What are you doing?" I ask.

She looks slightly embarrassed. "You um, you looked lonely, and that was really sweet how you helped your friends, so I thought I'd walk you home."

Still a little frustrated with her, I find myself feeling more defensive than flattered. "I don't need anyone to walk me home, I know the way."

The shuttle pushes off the ground and strolls ahead down the road. Leaving Courtney and I to ourselves.

"Well, looks like your stuck with me. Oh well," she giggles. "Plus, you're new, how do you know your way home? It's a seven-mile walk."

With a click of my tongue, I embrace her wishes and start the long seven-mile walk back towards the orphanage. I've come to realize I did not know my way and thanked Courtney for leaving the bus to walk with me. The first few miles dragged, but it became slightly tolerable when we started talking. Courtney starts asking about me and Kylie, such as what our story was, how we ended up in the orphanage, and where I learned to fight. I don't shy from details as she requested. I tell her about Omega Robbins, and how I almost punched him. She laughed and called me crazy for thinking I'd get away with that. Also, how big of a lunatic I sound when I say that Robert Fox was behind all of it. She admits that she admired how I stood up for my friends and fought back. She's never seen anyone stand up to them before nor fight so cunningly. I asked about her friends, she says they are part of a gang called the Bone Breakers. They're mainly in Levi but have small sets in other parts of Harmony. They were trying to recruit her, but Courtney doesn't see how she can fit in. With her orphanage clock winding down to a measly ten months left, she's trying to figure out a place to live once she has to leave. The Bone Breakers are a mosh pit of misfits who run most of the town of Levi. They make a living by issuing a rent to stores for protection and run a few recharging stations and body shops that runs through most of Levi and into parts of Southern Harmony.

Courtney explains the wall she has when she's uncomfortable, and that whole gang made her wall into concrete. When she feels that way, she shelters herself as she has her entire life. When her mom overdosed and died, her father left her at a gas station shortly after. She's lived most of her life thinking it was her fault her mom died, and why she was abandoned.

As we finally make it back home, I'm a sweaty embarrassing mess and all I want is my bed. As I expected, the doors are locked. It's midnight and I have had just about enough for one night. Courtney walks to the gate and an electric jolt shocks her when she touches the handle. She yaps when it bites her hand. I can't help but snort uncontrollably.

"Saintdamn it. Why didn't you tell me it was on?" she snaps.

I laugh. "I don't know. I thought it'd be funny."

"You jerk!" she shouts shaking her hand. "Oh my saints, my hand is numb."

I hush her. "Shh, you don't want to wake anyone up. C'mon, I have an idea."

I walk her to the other side of the fence where there's a small power box near the edge of the house. It's where Ron came up with a backup code to turn it off if he, for some reason, had it on when he was locked out. "I looked over his shoulder when he installed it. Figured if I ever got stuck with some annoying girl late at night, I'd be able to get back in."

"Ew, shut up. Did you forget that I saved your life back there? Bonez would have killed you."

"Please," I say confidently. "He had nothing on me." I hear her hum a soothing spurt of approval as I punch in the numbers 0828. The fence makes a muting sound and I pull the gate open.

"Look at you," she says impressed.

Thanking the saints, it actually worked, I attempt to act pompous. "Yeah. I'm pretty awesome if I do say so myself."

"Oh my saints. Cocky much?"

"What, me? No, never," I say sarcastically. "I'm just a humble gentleman escorting a fine young lady home."

Courtney rolls her eyes. "Pshhh, you're stupid."

We share a laugh. "What did Bonez call me, a dimwit? What is he, eighty?"

"Twenty-three, actually."

"Ew, shouldn't he be talking to girls his own age?"

"I don't think girls his age like talking to him."

We share another light laugh as we walk the distance of the farm towards the barn. I open the barn door for her, and we shuffle our way inside. It smells as it should, like farm animals but not as bad as it did the first day. "Hope you don't mind the smell," I say.

"Oh, this is fine. I'm so used to it, I barely even smell it nowadays."

I rake up two big balls of hay for us to lay in. I plop myself down and feel it out. Surprisingly, its more comfortable than my bed. We end up telling jokes about everyone in the house. She educates me more on the Bone Breakers and how I may be a wanted man for what I did. She says she'll talk to Heather and Naomi, but from what she assumes, Bonez will never admit he got beat up by some kid. As I finish telling her a story about how I stopped Kenny from picking on Kylie, she snuggles up to me. "You're really something, Carson. A knight in shining armor."

I feel nervous from the embrace but I'm too tired to fight. Although, why should I? Her hair smells like fresh fruit as she lays her head on my chest. Her long blonde hair melts into my hands as I find myself weaving my fingers through it. "That is so relaxing," she mumbles and lets out a satisfying moan. She kisses my cheeks and looks up at me. Waiting for a move.

Our eyes lock for the first time, bliss and desire swish around between us. She wants a man who will do what he wants when he wants. I want to be that man, but I realize the embarrassing truth. As shameful as it sounds, I have no idea what to do. "Good." is all I can say. I smile at her smile. Her lips are glossy, her face is blush, her eyes sparkle. She slides her hands down my chest and around my thighs.

"Do you want to?"

I blush. "I, uh, what do you mean?"

"You know," she giggles as her eyes dazzle and point downwards biting her lower lip.

Feeling powerless to her charm, but ashamed, I start to stutter. "I, um, I never…"

"Oh saints." She covers her mouth. "You're a—"

My face blushes a deep red as I wasn't expecting anything like this to happen. Not in a million years would I expect my night to end like this. "I… um. Well…"

She straddles me, her hands slide from my chest to my face. She leans forward, cradles my head, and pulls mine into hers. Our lips lock in the most intense and electrifying moment of my entire life. My hands gravitate to her sides and my animal instinct kicks in as I pull her into my embrace. In that moment, my worries wash away, my past is forgotten, and the pains in my body and mind clears in one pure moment of desire and ecstasy. The world around me closes and becomes just me and her. For the rest of the night, I was hers and she was mine.

10

Kylie's breaking point

It's been three months since we lost our parents. Ninety-two days, sixteen hours, and fifteen seconds to be exact, but who's counting? No one has been adopted, no families have even come to try. My brother doesn't seem to mind it very much. He has made friends with his roommates and even mine, but me, I haven't gotten close to Nala like I thought I would, and Courtney isn't much of a shoulder to cry on either.

I can't fathom the fact that my father killed himself and my mother for no reason. Everything just doesn't add up. Those officers said my father killed my mother with a gun but Carson has his gun. There's no reason my father could ever do that, no reason whatsoever. I can't find any information on Fox Legion or if there's been anymore disappearances in the span of time that connects with Fox. My palmphone has also been disconnected and I feel as though I'm living in the dark.

I've been living out of my suitcase for the time being. None of the girls will give up any of their closet space or drawers so I can unpack, even Nala won't budge. Then, on top of all that, I'm forced to go and clean these filthy animals and get verbally abused by those two old geezers, Ron and Sally. I hate this place and I want out.

Today is the first time I have the bathroom to myself. It's not every day I can sneak in here and have the stench of feces and mildew with a garbage can filled to the brim with hair and used tampons all to myself. Some of these girls are disgusting. No wonder their parents abandoned them. As I finish brushing my teeth, the doorknob flickers back and forth. Someone tried to get in and failed.

A loud knock comes from the door. "Hello! I need to pee! Hurry up in there, please," a girl's voice announces.

"One minute," I respond.

I want to take my time, nothing like rushing out the bathroom just so someone else can take their time in here. I was able to buy a cheap watch like Carson's with Nala at the corner store in Levi last week. I planned out my mornings by the minute. Wake up ten minutes to five, shower for ten minutes, then dry off and change is close to fifteen minutes. By then its rolling around 5:30, I can make my way outside for roll call and if I am one of the first ones out there, Mr. Ron could be generous and give me an easy job like help Mrs. Sally with breakfast, I like cooking with her, or maybe even milk Ol' Dotty. She's an earth born cow cloned twelve times and one of the most docile animals here. Especially considering the demon horses here. Nasty suckers they are. A kid got bucked yesterday and got sent to the hospital with a concussion. Poor kid is only twelve and possibly now has brain damage. Didn't even know who Ron was when he came to.

I walk out of the bathroom to see a little girl named Caroline waiting with her legs twisted like she was about to burst.

"Oh, sorry, Caroline. If I knew it was you, I would have opened the door. You sounded like Heather or Jacklyn." Caroline is an innocent little girl of ten years who lives in the next room from me. Her dad left her mother and she then became a raging alcoholic. She left her in a cart in a grocery store parking lot. Heather and her sister Jacklyn on the other hand are the worst, always playing pranks on the other girls for their amusement. One time they threw gum in a girl's hair and Mr. Ron had to cut it out and it completely ruined her hair. She had to get it cut embarrassingly short and she cried for days. I wish I could have given her my hair. I don't need it, it's not like I'm trying to impress any of these inbred boys. Although, there is this one boy who is kind of nice to me, his name is Rocky. I've seen him pick on Carson a few times, but he seems to do that with all the boys. He doesn't pick on me or the girls though, so maybe he just likes to horseplay. His eyes are different too, a passion red color that flows with his pale freckled face and his fading ginger hair. Carson thinks it's scary looking, but I think it's intriguing.

I make my way out to the back yard and find Carson right behind me. "Hey, Kylie. You doing ok?" he asks me in his caring and heartwarming tone. His tone is always different when he talks to me. It's quite comical whenever I catch him talking to a girl, he makes sure to stand up straighter and talk in a deeper voice.

"Yeah, today seems like it is going to be a good day," I reply. Carson is all I have here. He promised me that we would stick together, and although he couldn't get us in the same room for obvious reasons, he is making a huge effort to keep an eye on me and make sure I don't feel alone. He's told me about nights where he has snuck out with his roommates and went around playing pranks in town, leaving brown bags of cow feces at people's doors, and dingdong ditching.

We get in roll call together. Mr. Ron comes out in his usual overalls, flannel shirt with his sleeves tucked into his overalls, and his dirty, old boots. He rolls off a few names and tells them their jobs. He tells Carson and Kevin to go clean the gutters and then looks at me.

"Kylie and Rocco!" he calls out. "I want you two to milk the cows, clean the pen, and gather the eggs for breakfast. Make it quick so Mrs. Sally can get everything started." He flicks his hand, insinuating us to go. "Away with you two."

Rocky taps my shoulders and challenges me to race him. I accept his challenge and take off running. He gets a good head start but I have much better endurance. I catch up to him and gain an extra step on him before we make it to the barn.

"Hey," he says out of breath. "Wow, you're faster than you look."

"Thanks." I smile and strikes a pose.

He catches his breath. "Why don't you milk Dotty and I'll start cleaning up the barn. After you're done, I'll run the milk to Mrs. Sally, and you go on and collect the eggs from the coup," he says in a gentle voice.

"Hah, so I do all the arduous work and you get to sweep and have a nice relaxing stroll back to the house?" I say sarcastically.

He huffs. "Do you want to carry the milk back? No offence but—"

"I'm joking," I stop him before he says something insulting. "I don't mind." I smile at him and go about my assignment. Dotty is a bit of a handful today. Maybe she had a rough night. I learned that when she gets in these fits to grab a brush and stroke her mane. It helps soothe her, and calm her down. Maybe no one has done that for her in a while so she's acting out on purpose. I grab the hard bristle brush and approach her. She moos at me seeing the brush and moves in a position to be persuaded. I brush her for a good five minutes, she loves it, I can tell. "Ok, Dotty, enough of that. Let's get down to business." She moos in a disappointing tone. Funny how it seems that she can actually understand us. With some practice in milking cows, I've gotten in a good habit of how to handle myself around her. With two full buckets of milk, I carry them outside and try to find Rocky.

"Rocky?" I call out.

"Right behind you, sweetheart," he calls from behind me.

"Sweetheart?" I ask in a higher pitched voice than I wanted to. He's never called me anything like that before. Maybe this is a good sign. He ignores the question and puts the remainder of the shovels and rakes back in their hooks inside the barn.

"I want to show you something before breakfast. It's in the woods behind the pen it'll be perf... I mean, it looks perfect," he insists.

"What's behind the pen? Isn't the electric fence on? We can't get back there," I say.

"It is, but I broke a section off so I can slip through. If you don't want to go, I could bring Heather or someone else who likes being more..." He pauses because he knows he has me intrigued.

"Oh, shut your trap, Rocky. What is it?" I ask feeling intrigued.

"Just come with me. I promise you'll love it," he says as he grabs the milk. "Meet me over there, I'll be right back."

He puts the buckets of milk on his shoulders and charges the house in a sprint. I watch him go for a few paces and he doesn't seem to slow down much. I wake up out of my trance and make my way over to the coup. Ideas bounce around my head. I am thoroughly intrigued. What could be back there? A dead animal? What is something I would love to see back there? I get to the chicken coup and start collecting the eggs and putting them in egg crates, another skill I have acquired over the months. The coup smells foul, the humidity is horrendous, and when the taste of ammonia hits my tongue, I gag. I have to hold my breath and try to collect as many eggs as I can, making sure none of them are broken because last time I brought back three cracked eggs that slimed the rest. Mrs. Sally was *pissed.* The chickens are all out marching around pecking at the chicken feed I laid out outside, so it makes collecting the eggs so much smoother. As I am collecting the last of the eggs, I see Rocky making his way over.

"Follow me," he says with a smile waving his arm over his head.

I drop the two crates of eggs by the door and follow him behind the coup. He motions me to a broken part of the fence. It looks like he smashed it down with a plank and a few bricks.

"Did you do this?" I ask. My imagination runs wild, what could possibly be back there?

"Let's not ask too many questions, sweetheart. Just don't touch the fence, you'll get shocked if you touch it. It'll be easier to jump over," he points out. "Watch me," he says backing up a few steps. He angles himself in a runner's stance and takes off. He leaps over the fence and glides through the air, clearing the fence, and sticks the landing.

"Wow! Look at you," I say giving him a little clap.

"You like that?" he says as he turns around. "The guys say I should be an Olympic long jumper.

"Oh yeah?" I say, feeling a bit warm inside. I mimic what he did, starting where he stood, and line myself up for the jump. I'm nervous, I've never did anything like this before. I close my eyes and wipe a bead of sweat from my forehead and think of a bigger, braver, and more powerful me, someone who can stand up to anyone, someone who can fight back, who can take anything life throws at them. As a fire ignites in my heart, I take off and jump the fence. I stretch my legs out and fall short, landing awkwardly on the fence and feel the bite of the electricity. It shoots up my leg and numbs my foot. I shriek and crumble to the ground.

"Woah, woah, not so loud, you don't want them to hear us. We would get in so much trouble," Rocky says as he reaches out for my hand.

I laugh it off. "Sorry." I try to act strong and shake it out. No need to panic and cause attention. Everything will be ok.

He helps me up. "Are you ok?"

No! My foot is numb! "Yeah, I'm strong. See?" I show him my arm muscles to hide my lie.

He smirks and doesn't entertain it like Carson does. We start walking through the woods, listening to the treehoppers chime their tunes, communicating with other insects. The grass is a healthy shade of blue back here, perfect summertime weather. We cover a fairly good distance following a stream and scaling a few small rock formations. Anxiety races, I don't want to get in trouble, and we are far beyond that walking in the woods. What would happen if Ron found out? Would I get blamed for it? Would I have to pay for the repairs? A pack of ovats dash across our path and catches me off guard. Two babies follow the pack.

"Did those little things scare you?" Rocky asks.

"No… What are we doing out here, Rocky? Let's head back, I don't want to get it trouble."

"We'll be fine. Ron knows I like going off and doing my own thing from time to time. The work is done, he'll leave us alone for an hour or two if the work is done."

His optimism helps. He's so sure of himself. "Did you know you can tell an ovat's age by the size of their curved horns on their head," I ask.

"No. No, I did not."

"Did you know that a female can have up to thirty babies in one litter?"

"Nope," he says less enthusiastic, like he's getting annoyed. We approach a vast field of white pedaled flowers. I recognize them instantly and grab on to his shirt.

"Rocky wait!"

He pulls back before stepping and looks at me funny. "What? You don't want to hurt the delicate little flowers?" He laughs at his own joke but stops when my face doesn't change. "Want me to pick you some?"

"No. Those are venenum sporae, they're poisonous. If their spores touch your skin, you'll swell up like a balloon. Then Ron and Sally will definitely know we were here."

He looks down and back at me. He kneels and looks at them more carefully. "How do you know?"

I kneel with him and nudge myself close to him. "You see how the bulb of the flower is shaped like an araneae?"

"A what?"

I click my tongue. "You know those creepy crawler things?"

He squints trying to see what I'm saying. "Uh, ok." Obviously not the brightest crayon in the box.

I huff and roll my eyes, ignoring his lack of an education. The ambition to constantly educate one's self isn't for everyone, especially when your idea of life doesn't go past the farm. "You see those string like tentacles around it? They're sticky, it's used to catch bugs and other things. Even small animals in some rare cases. Once the flower catches something, it emits this toxic pollen to kill its prey."

"So that flower could possibly kill me?"

"Nah. Well, maybe. Not sure. I suppose if you sit there and let it wrap you up, eventually your body will decompose from its poison."

"Woah, wanna see if it catches anything?"

"Is this why you brought me out here?"

"No, no, no. Sorry, that flower just looks really cool. You're pretty smart, Kylie." He gets up and walks around the flower bed. "Any other crazy killer plants I should know about?"

"Oh, there's plenty, and I'm sure there's so many more to be discovered. Did you know scientists have explored only twenty percent of Tyke? There's an entire world left to discover."

"Hah, really? Well, if I ever become a titan and get a chance to explore it, I'll be sure to send pictures."

"You want to be a titan, too? That's Carson's dream."

"Carson? Really? That little joker ain't gonna be nothing."

What? Stand up for him, don't let him talk about Carson like that. "Hey, that's my brother you're talking about. Did you know he beat up four Bone Breakers a few months ago?"

"Pshhh, yeah, I heard about that. Don't believe everything you hear. That guy's been crazy over your one roommate ever since you got here. It's kind of pathetic how desperate he is."

"Hah, right? I don't know what he sees in her."

"Um, she's uh," he stops himself from saying something. Probably some inappropriate comment. "Yeah, I don't know. I like a more intelligent woman, you know? Like, how can you even talk to her? She's like those blonde girls you see in movies, no brains all—"

"Yeah. I get it," I stop him.

He picks up a long branch to let me walk under. I smile at him as he lets me through. We follow down the man-made path for a few more minutes. The view of the forest intrigues me. Life lives here. For well over a million years before humans arrived, animals ruled the world, or maybe some other kind of intellectual life. Tyke was one giant forest before humans arrived and started creating cities and pollution like they did on Old Earth. So many people died during The Crisis. Billions of lives were sacrificed so the few who survived could flourish on another planet, two lightyears away.

The trees are massive in these woods. Dark blue trunks with great big, swaying leaves layered over each other. In the summer season, the leaves are blue. Once it starts getting colder out and summer turns to fall, a beautiful sequence happens. The leaves change colors to purple, then red, then by winter they're orange. Once you see that, you know they're going to break apart and blanket the ground. These leaves are very thick, yet light and soft to the touch. Perfect for smaller herbivores to devour and make little houses to shelter them from the elements.

"How far are we going? I don't want to get lost," I say getting nervous.

"I know where we are, it's actually right up this hill," he says.

After a test of endurance, we climbed this huge, oddly steep hill. My arms and legs burn from the trip but it's all worth it. My eyes sprout open and my jaw drops at the spectacle on top the hill. Tree tops in the distance, big flowing leaves look like slides, the fresh aroma of hilltop trees are in the air as we reach the summit. The roaring sounds of water loudens. I race over to the other side to find jaw dropping sight of a beautiful waterfall. It's so close that I could reach out and feel its waters. It spews out from inside of a cave above me down into a clear magenta pond below. I have never seen anything like it before. "Rocky, this is beautiful."

"Yeah. Isn't it?" he turns to me and smiles.

I walk over to the ledge and stare at the beauty of nature. I reach out and cup my hands to catch a handful of water. It's clean to the taste, spring water. "Where does the water comes from? We could gather the water for the farm. The animals could get clean water. We won't have to use the well anymore and poison those poor animals anymore."

"I'm not sure. I'm guessing there must be an underground village or something in there. Wouldn't that be cool?" he says walking up to me and wrapping his arm around my shoulder.

A thousand ideas flow through my head. "We need to find out. This could be huge for the farm." I start looking around for any signs of where the water is coming from and Rocky stops me.

He pulls me into him. "You are so saintdamn beautiful right now," he says. I smile and we lock eyes. I feel passion radiating from his gaze. A twinkle comes from his red eyes. He leans in and kisses me gently. My first kiss.

I untangle myself from him before he tries to claim another one and I look over the ledge watching the water crash into the stream we followed, trying to imagine how to transfer all the water. Maybe we can make buckets or maybe some kind of—

"Don't fall." Rocky leans his hand into my back and scares me. My stomach drops as he whips me around and pulls me into his chest and picks me up off my feet. His vehement lips drive into mine and a moist tongue is forced into my mouth.

I push off him, and squirm to get him to release me. "Woah, Rocky. A bit aggressive don't you think?" I try to laugh it off, wiping the saliva off my mouth.

"Oh, *c'mon*, Kylie." He rolls his eyes.

"C'mon what? Slow your role, bub," I demand, and spit out the foreign saliva out of my mouth. "I wasn't ready for that."

Rocky rolls his eyes. "Well," he walks up close. "You ready now?" He leans in but I sweep around him and distance myself. "C'mon, Ky, you look so stressed. I think you deserve a little, relief is all."

"Relief?" I question. "No, no thank you, Rocky. This is perfect, thank you for this, really. Can we just enjoy the view?"

"I'm enjoying the view right now," Rocky says as he looks me up and down. I start to feel uncomfortable. What is he thinking? "C'mon, Kylie, let me show you what a real man can do," he says in a deep masculine voice that isn't his real voice. He approaches me as I take a few steps backwards. It scares me, this whole thing starts to scare me.

"Right, how many girls have you said that too? In fact, I bet you brought all the girls back here. Don't lie. Tell me the truth," I trying to deflect my fear.

"Only you, sweetheart. I wanted to impress you. I told you I'm into smart girls," he says. I look behind me and see a steep drop. "Watch your step, sweetheart. You don't want to fall." I turn back and watch Rocky approach me slowly with a worried look on his face. "C'mon, get away from the ledge, I won't hurt you," he says innocently. "Look, I took a risk for you, I picked you out of everyone else, and brought you out here to impress you. This isn't impressive? I *deserve* something in return," he says arrogantly.

"What exactly do you think you deserve?" I say disgusted. "This is nice, sure, but you will not take advantage of me just because of a pretty waterfall."

"Take advantage? No, of course not. I want this to be a mutual understanding." He steps closer.

"Well, it is not, I'm not ready for this kind of thing. I've never done—"

"And why not?" he says waving his arms. "You don't like me?"

"Rocky, I... I've never done anything like that before" I start to feel embarrassed and ashamed. Thousands of scenarios go through my head. I'm scared, I can't think straight. I've always pictured my first time being intimate with someone would be like this, in a beautiful setting with a boy I've come to admire and trust, but Rocky is being way too aggressive. I take another small step backwards and look behind me. I'm at the edge and I have nowhere to go. What do I do? Before I can think of my next move, he tries and reaches for my hand. I pull back out of his grasp, and the momentum of me jerking backwards makes me slip. I feel my body start to fall. I shriek again.

Rocky grabs hold of my hand and he pulls me off the ledge and into his chest. I feel his arms wrap around me and I feel my butt being squeezed. "See. I saved you. I'm your hero." He forces his lips into mine.

I entertain him and grab his face. I kiss him hard and give him what I hope he is after. "There. Happy now?" He pulls me back in and tucks his other hand around my butt. He tries to kiss me again. "Rocky, stop, please." The fear becomes real. I move my face and cup his mouth with my hand. He pulls my hand off and pins it in my lower back. He continues to pursue me and bites my neck. "Ow! Rocky, stop!" I growl at him as I slap his face.

Rocky huffs and grabs my face and pulls it into his. "Fine, then if you won't give me what I want, then I'll just bring Heather back here. Or maybe I'll give Courtney another chance. Make sure you tell Carson that too. Tell him I gave her the time of her life," he sneers, staring devilishly at me. His red eyes feel as if they're piercing through me. "She'll give me what I want. Not like you, who is as *useless* as everyone says you are."

"Screw you, Rocky!"

He steps back and swings his arms out. "Let's do it then, baby. I'll be quick, I promise. I just like you so much." He tries one last time and I kick him between his legs. He jolts back holding his groin. He grunts and I see the rage building in his eyes.

"No!" I shout at the top of my lungs. "Help! Help! Carson! CARSON!" I scream, hoping he or anyone hears me. "Carso—" My world jolts, I get pushed hard enough for my head to jerk forward and bite my tongue. I can't catch myself. My feet fly up over my head and I feel nothing but air as my body plunges off the cliff. I scream for my life, feeling my soul being stripped from my body. Feeling death about to catch my fall and bring me to the afterlife to reunite me with my parents, I close my eyes and embrace for impact. My back slaps the water and I wail in agony. Little air bubbles race up to the surface as I descend deeper and deeper into the depths of the pond. The soothing sound of the waterfall crashing into the pond is all I hear. My eyes flutter, and darkness consumes me.

11

What's the plan?

With a large gasp for air, my eyes jolt open and my lungs find oxygen. I cough and gag up water and phlegm and hurl into the sand. I find myself ashore in the sand next to the stream. I'm alive. A brutal agony stings my back like sunburn after laying in the hot sun, but I am alive. My clothes are soaked with mud, and my throat hurts when I try to pull in air.

How am I even alive? How could I fall for something so stupid? I look up at the ledge where I was pushed from and ponder the fact that I am still able to stand and breath. I fell about a hundred feet into the pond with nothing to slow my fall. As much as I am relieved to be alive, I feel worthless. I feel stupid for believing anyone would truly have feelings for me and not aspire to use my body as a plaything. To think a decent human being lived in Harmony, I feel like a fool. Who am I kidding? I'm a loser. No family, no friends, I have nothing to show for, no hope for any real future, no way to get into college. Even Carson has been giving me the cold shoulder. All he does is hang out with his friends after work, he barely makes time for me anymore, like I am some chore to him like taking care of the animals.

Why even bother anymore? Carson is going to turn eighteen and he'll be kicked out and sent to live on his own. I'll be all alone once he is gone. I'll have no one to protect me, no one to love, or care for. I'll have nothing. What if Rocky or any of the boys ever try to take advantage of me again? What if two of them try together, or…

I pick myself up and brush the dirt off my pants. I get nothing off. All I do is dirty my hands and smear the dirt over my pants. I can't even do that right. With no future, no education, no career, my life feels empty. I feel worthless as Rocky said. *"Fine, then if you won't give me what I want, then I'll just bring Heather back here. She'll give me what I want. Not like you who is as useless as everyone says you are."* Did he really mean those words? Did he really mean to push me? Did he really try to kill me?

My mind wonders for what seems like hours. I sit in the sand and watch the water pass by, thinking of... ways.

It's getting dark. My stomach grumbles my body shivers from the wet clothes. Carson will be better off without me. The world will be better off without me. Mom, dad, I've decided I'm coming to see you. Wherever you are, please come find me. Please hold my hand and bring me to the paradise I hope you've found together, the peace you must feel in the house you built in the afterlife together. I stand up and walk back up the hill where Rocky pushed me, expelling the rest of my energy to climb the awkward terrain. After reaching the top for the second time, I find the waterfall and realize I am unable to take my eyes off it. The most beautiful thing I have ever seen in my life, is attached to the most horrifying event I have ever experienced.

All of it could finally come to an end. The pain, the suffering I have endured all these years. Being premature at birth, being so fragile, so delicate. I hate myself. I don't deserve to live, I never should have existed. I look over the ledge and aim myself to fall. Just tilt over the ledge and plummet in the pond headfirst, and never come back up for air again. It'll be easy and painless. Once my body hits the water, my head will hit the ground, shattering my neck and paralyzing me. Being unable to move, my body will go into shock from oxygen deprivation, my lungs will fill with water and I will drown. It'll be easier than waiting here to be eaten by some predator or go back to that farm soaked and embarrassed to have ever thought a boy like Rocky was ever a decent human being. Carson will be better off without me. He will figure out a way to live without having to worry about the likes of me. I look into the stream and I close my eyes for the last time. "Goodbye, Carson. I'll say hi to mom and dad for you. I lov—"

"Kylie!" a voice echoes.

My eyes flare open to the sound of a familiar voice. I look down at the choice I was about to make and stumble backwards and fall in a panic. Oh saints, what was I about to do? I look out into the foggy woods, frightened, numb to reality. Was that for real? "Carson!" I scream and start to cough uncontrollably.

It sounded like Carson's voice. I turn around and look for my brother, but I don't see him. The late afternoon fog blinds me from beyond the trees. I huddle up in a ball and stop myself from calling back. It wasn't him. My mind is just playing games with me. No one is coming for me. A cold breeze hits my damp back and I start to shiver again. Flashing back how Rocky looked at me, those red eyes *are* evil, Carson was right.

"Kylie!" the voice echoes once more.

It was real. That is my brother. "Carson!" I scream back but my throat is throbbing. I could barely get the words out before my body stops me. I cough again.

"Kylie! Where are you?!" he calls.

"Over here," I mutter out with what was left of my energy. I hear movement, it sounds like footsteps. Could it really be him? I look over the lip of the hill and see his face emerges with his brown hair and big brown eyes. The face of my brother peaks over the hilltop, and he makes eye contact with me. Holy saints in the afterlife, it was really him.

"Kylie!" My brother found me. Oh my saints, he actually found me. He runs up to me and grabs me in a warm embrace. He's a sweaty mess. His wet shirt smacks mine and his body odor hits my nostrils, but I don't care. My brother, the only friend and family I have left saved me from ending my life. I squeeze him tightly and silently thank him with all of my heart for finding me.

He looks at me. "Holy saints, you're soaked. What were you doing here? What happened?"

I'm speechless, tired, sore, and I don't have it in me to tell him. I don't think I'll ever be able to tell him. I just grab him once more and hug him. "I got lost," I tell him.

"Lost? Are you kidding me? And what happened to your clothes?" He takes his shirt off and wraps it around me.

Unfortunately, I accept it. "Carson, I..."

"Is this where you've been all day?"

"Yes. I hate that farm, Carson. I... I had to get away from that horrible place. Let's find somewhere else to live. Just you and me. No one to tell us what we can and can't do. No filthy animals to care for, no—" I hesitate. Images of what I've been through haunt me. Tears begin to roll down my face.

"Woah, woah, woah, Kylie, look at me," Carson says trying to get my attention.

I try and hold back my emotions. Snot spills out of my nose and on to his sleeve. I sniffle up as much as I can and look at him. Pain and agony in my eyes. He looks down at me with all the love and care I could possibly have asked for.

"You should have told me first. If you really thought you were going to run away, by yourself, *and without me?*" he says starting to sound offended. "I feel betrayed. How could you leave me behind? How *dare* you leave me behind."

"I know. I just figured you were happy here with all your new friends and I know you and Courtney kind of have a thing going. You wouldn't notice if I left."

"You're saintdamn insane if you think for a second, that I'd be fine without you, Ky. You're everything to me... And no! Me and Courtney don't have a thing... did she tell you that?"

"I'm not stupid, Carson! I know you've been seeing her. I see the googly eyes you give each other. The silly faces, heck, Kevin even told me you would sneak out most nights. Is it me or just by some coincidence, Courtney would sneak out the window on the same nights you do? She's my roommate for saint's sake, Carson. Girls talk, she's crazy about you. She even told Nala to back off because you're *hers.*"

"That's Courtney for you." He laughs nervously with his hand behind his head. "I thought Nala was, um, into girls?"

I shrug my shoulders.

"How is Courtney by the way? We haven't... She hasn't really talked to me lately."

Now that he says something, she has been weird. "She's... well, Courtney, I guess. I don't know what you mean by weird, I hardly ever see her besides when we sleep. I think she's been sick. She was throwing up in the morning. Besides that, she's been more to herself recently."

"Throwing up? When did that start?"

"About a month ago, maybe? I don't know." I can't think straight. Just thinking about it makes my stomach turn. "She has been eating strangely too, maybe that's why. Like some nights she brings carrots and ice cream in the room."

"What? That's super weird." He laughs nervously again. "But um, you ready to go back? Rocky's worried about you. He said you were right behind him when he came back with the eggs."

That filthy liar. How dare he just leave me back here to fend for myself. I really thought he liked me, I really thought he cared for me. I realize Carson is still talking. "—found that hole you

69

made in the fence. Thanks for that, I'm going to have to explain that somehow when we get back home."

The most embarrassing moment of my life spirals through me, and what will happen if I show my face at that farm again? Thoughts of walking back into that house to be laughed at and ridiculed for not showing up to breakfast. Then being blamed for breaking the fence, that could come out of my pocket, not Rocky's. Going back could ruin my life. I'd be laughed at, I'd be shunned, I'd be looked at as an idiot, as a nuisance. I'd... I can't. Rocco nearly took my life for not giving him what he wants, that rejection will drive him to do, who knows what else. He'll probably start a rumor and tell everyone some provocative story about how I did everything he wanted. I will not stand for that; I will not be made a fool for other people's enjoyment. "No."

"No? What do you mean, no?"

My mind is made up. "I can't go back."

"Wait, what? Why in the saint's name not? We have everything we need right here," he replies pleading his case.

"Carson—" I hesitate. "*You* have everything, I'm... I'm just a nuisance here."

"What are you even saying, Kylie? You just want to leave? Don't you want to get adopted?" he says plainly.

"No. Not in the slightest. Face it, Carson, our lives are hopeless here. It's only a matter of time before you're kicked out and I am left here alone. Please, Carson." I look directly in his eyes. "I want to leave, right now. I'm going to live in Levi, find somewhere to stay or something. I don't know. I'll figure something out. All I know is I can't stay here. You are either going to follow me, or I am going by myself."

He looks at me with his big, brown, caring eyes. I know he sees me for who I am, what I have endured these last few months. "What are you hiding from me?" he finally asks. "Did Rocky hurt you?" he quickly examines me and stares at my neck. "What happen to your neck?" He must have found the bite marks. "Did he do that?" He points right at them.

I look down in shame and try to hide my neck with his shirt. "I, he... Not now. Please, Carson, not—" I stand up and wobble, flaring my arms, nearly falling off the ledge. Carson grabs my hand and pulls me in, just like Rocky did. He stares at me, looking deep into my eyes with so much concern it reminds me of our mother. How she cared about every little thing in our lives like she had nothing else better to do. She's always cared for us, like a mother canahound to her little

70

pups. She always knew when something was bothering us, the look in her eyes, her motherly instincts kicking me. Carson has those same eyes, the same intensity my mother had. He can sense something happened, and now I look at my mother's son and gaze at those same eyes once again. The fire has lit in his eyes, and it burns brightly with the desire for revenge.

"What did Rocky do to you?" he demands. "Answer me, Kylie!"

I stutter, I can't get it out. All I can do is look down in shame. I can't tell my loving brother about the monster that did this to me. That, again, I couldn't stand up for myself. I couldn't think fast enough. I couldn't be him for a change. It is just so hard to admit that Carson was right. He was right all along. "He, well he…"

I see him examine my wet clothes and looks behind me at the cliff from which I fell. The puzzle pieces come together, and Carson figures me out. My silence answers all his questions. "I'm gonna kill him." He releases me and turns around. He starts walking back to the farm. "Rocky!"

"Carson, wait!" I shout. Wincing from the pain I forgot about. "That's why I can't go back."

"Are you kidding me, Kylie?!" He turns back at me with fire in his eyes. "So, you're telling me he—" He stops himself and puts his hand on the bridge of his nose and turns away from me frustrated. "What did he do, Kylie?!" he snaps back to me and questions me. "Did he push you off that cliff?"

"He, he didn't, mean to." I feel stupid trying to defend him.

"Holy saints. Are you insane?!" Carson shouts dumbfounded. "He tried to kill you, Ky. Why would he do that?" He looks at me in a state of massive confusion. "What did you do?"

"I didn't do anything! I…" I can't get it out. *Why* can't I get it out? I feel so ashamed, so powerless. Now Carson sees me in all my worthless glory. He watches me crumble in my own body.

"What didn't you do? Did he… Did he try to…" I shudder to his words. My emotions take control of my body, I can't hide the guilt anymore, the mask of strength I wear has come off. I peek up at my brother standing firmly with his fist clenched. With a fire brewing in his heart, his eyes fill with vengeful rage, his mouth loosens with wild accusations and profanities to send Rocco on an avalanche of pain. The animal inside him has broken its cage. "Rocco!" he shouts at the top of his lungs. Carson starts to run.

71

I have to stop him. "Stop!" I scream. "Just stop, Carson!" I plead chasing him down. I'm much faster than him and catch up to him. I jump on his back and hold him, hoping my body will slow him down. He trips and we tumble into the ground. I land on top of him. "Please, stop. You're going to get yourself hurt."

He violently shoves me off him. "You do *not* get to tell me how to handle this, Kylie Josephine!"

I start sobbing as I look at the fresh scrape on my elbow. "Carson! I don't want to go back, *ever*! I just want to run away and never see him, or anyone ever again. Please! Just stop…" I plead. Feeling the rush of tears fall down my cheeks. "We can… We can figure something out in Levi, together. We can make something of ourselves. I promise I will figure this out. I will get you into Atlantis University, and—" My breath is cut short from the lies, my energy is depleted, and false promises keep spilling out of my mouth. I feel like my father.

He looks at me intensely. The animal inside of him walks back in its cage and locks itself away, but for how long can I distract him? I can't let him do something stupid that will put him in jail. He paces back and forth, an internal argument is brewing in that head of his, waiting for me to say something that could contradict myself, but I stay firm. "I can't live in the farm another day. This isn't the first time I've thought about this, but today…" I take a deep breath and own my thoughts. *Stay strong.* "Today was my breaking point," I say as firmly as I can. "Please, run away with me, Carson. Forget about this farm and we can start a new life together."

He looks at me baffled with his own worries and concerns. How could I expect him to want what I want when our lives are so different here? "What about Courtney?" he asks.

"I'm not going back there to wait for you. I'm leaving, right now," I say sternly.

"C'mon, Ky, don't be like that. I can't just leave her, she has abandonment issues as it is, I can't just ghost her."

"Then so be it. Go back to your *girlfriend* and leave your sister to herself. I guess this is goodbye," I bluff.

"C'mon," he exaggerates. "You're not being fair, Kylie."

"Not being fair? Look at me, Carson." I lift my arms up and show him the damage this day has given me, my soaked clothes, the bruises creeping through my body, and my neck. "I will not embarrass myself walking back there to get laughed at. Then what? I can't tell on Rocky, he'll… I'll be labeled as a snitch. No one will ever want to talk to me." I start thinking of worse scenarios.

Thoughts of him invading me in my sleep. The rumors he'll start of me, my dignity will be forever tarnished. No one will ever look at me the same. "Please, leave with me, Carson. I have a plan. Please don't let me go by myself."

He takes in another breath and shakes his head. A slanted look on his face makes me believe he doubts me. He clucks his tongue knowing he doesn't have a choice. He knows the right one to choose. He hugs me tight around my head and kisses the top of my head as I lay mine into his chest. "I'll never leave you, Kylie." He sighs and shakes his head. "Courtney's going to be so pissed."

12

Levi

Being a big brother is a lot of hard work. Not only that, but it requires you to sacrifice a part of yourself to ensure your baby sister is safe. Kylie wanted to leave and, as her big brother, I cannot allow my sister to run off by herself and get killed, even if that means sacrificing everything I had at the farm to do it.

Luckily for us, we held on to the money we've accumulated during our stay at the farm. It wasn't much but we learned quickly that if we leave anything worth something, it goes "missing". I couldn't prove it but I know Anderson snooped around my stuff and took small increments of credits from me for his stim addiction. It was sad actually; he never was able to save credits for fresh clothes or snacks and I knew when he ran out. He begged us to go with him to Levi and was shady when he wanted to go to this certain store. He never went inside, he always wanted to go behind it, and we weren't allowed to go with him.

For the rest of the day, we hiked. The ground is still muddy from yesterday's storm, my feet are swimming inside my shoes. Wild animal noises scare Kylie, she's so tense from what ever happened with her and Rocky. I can feel it in her grip as I pull her along the path. It tightens at every sudden noise.

Once the sun went down, it was hard to see in front of us. Kylie, being optimistic in our new journey through the woods, figured out a way to makeshift a tent using fallen leaves from the trees held up by some branches. It wasn't much and wouldn't survive longer than we needed it to.

As the late night hours passed, Kylie snuggled up next to me to keep warm and that was my only priority, to keep her safe. Through our sleepless night, Kylie finally opens up and tells me what happened. She thanks me over and over again for staying with her through this, but I can't understand why she wouldn't let me go back and confront Rocky. I wanted to go back and beat his face in for what he did, but as she stated, I can't be doing something stupid to get myself locked up in jail.

The night hours crawled, the moons are the only source of light we have, and even that barely helped. The nerve wracking sounds of nature at work kept me up. The buzzing of bloodsnatchers flying around trying to grab a sample of blood out of my neck, and the other insects interacting with each other, roaming on the ground, were wondering why this massive man is invading their home. The howling of canahounds, and eerie noises of branches snapping or leaves crunching from small varmints surround us. I can't think straight, at any moment a canahound could sneak into our tent and end our lives if I wasn't up to fend it off. So, I hold on to my dad's pistol tight in my hand and point it at the entrance of the tent, waiting, hoping I don't have to use it. I squeeze Kylie tight in my other arm and stroked her hair through the night. I had to choose between protecting her and getting sleep. The choice was easy.

As the sun rises and shines its rays of sunshine on the world, I wake Kylie up as soon as I'm able to see the path in front of me.

"Did you get any sleep?" she asked rubbing her eyes.

"Yeah, slept like a baby," I lie. She doesn't need to worry about me. I can muscle through this. "Did you?"

"Yeah, for a little bit."

For the first few hours, we hiked. My shoes are soggy, and my socks are still soaked from the day before. I feel miserable, how did Kylie ever persuade me to leave the farm? Right now, I could be doing some meaningless chore to get through the day and filling my belly with freshly made eggs. But instead, I am sleep deprived, my body aches, my clothes are wet, and I just want some coffee.

Eventually, we escaped the clutches of the forest and all that inhabited it. We found ourselves looking at a bridge over the main road that leads us into Levi.

"We made it!" Kylie jumps in the air with her hands up.

As much as I was ecstatic to be out of that jungle full of bugs and who knows what, we're about to enter another one, except this one is full of people and concrete. "Ok, first things first, let's get some food and dry clothes. There was a corner store just before we get into town. I say we go in and stock up before we set out to find us a new place to stay."

"What do you mean, stock up? Do you have credits to stock up?"

"No." I say plainly. "But we'll just have to go *borrow* some."

"Borrow? You mean steal? Carson, we could get in trouble."

"Not if they don't catch us."

"Carson…"

"Look, Ky," I snap getting frustrated. "*You* wanted to do this! *You* wanted to pick up and leave with nothing and—" My sharp words startled Kylie. She stops in her tracks.

"And what, Carson? Would you have wanted to go back if that happened to you?"

I calm myself. "No. Hey, I'm sorry Kylie. I just—"

She puts her hand up to stop me from talking. "It's fine."

"No. No, it's not." I put my hands on my head and compose myself. "I lied. I didn't get a lot of sleep. I'm tired and cranky, and all I really want is a cup of coffee. But I know I can't get that if we need to buy new clothes, plus we don't have money to go to a diner. We need something quick, something to walk around with so we can plan our next move."

Kylie's eyes turn into concern. I think I have her back on my side. "Fine, so how are we going to do this?"

13

Here N' There

We finally get into the town of Levi, and walk into the first convenient store we find, 'Here' N' There'. I quickly scope out the place, look for the cameras, and send Kylie to the corner to make a distraction. Anything she can think of, but I told her to make it sloppy and exaggerated. Maybe spill a gallon of milk or slip and fall. Anything to distract the cashier. I find a rack of novelty shirts with Levi, in big letters with its slogan on it. "Rely on Levi". Normally I try to calculate the blind spots of the cameras, but I'm planning on taking what I want this time. No sneaking around and slipping a few things in my pockets. It's going to be a grab and go operation. I walk up to the counter and ask for a Vita-stims pack behind the counter in a lock box. The cashier looks at me with a crooked face and asks me for my license. He has a south Harmonian accent, like Kenny from the bus that was bullying Kylie. I give him a smart mouth comment and tell him to just give me the stims, making a bit of a scene so Kylie can get herself ready.

"Forty-eight credits," he says with a huff as he puts the four stims on the counter.

What is taking Kylie so long? As I rummage around my empty pockets acting like I have money, expecting Kylie to be making some kind of noise, I hear a loud clumsy banging noise and a loud crash. I turn around to a milk carton flying into the ceiling and crashing down over the gondola, splattering everywhere.

"Awww, shucks," Kylie says.

The cashier curses and rushes over to the mess. I slip the stims in my pocket and follow the man over to where Kylie is. I can't stop myself from snorting as I find Kylie, in a puddle of milk and soda. Chips and pretzels are everywhere.

"I'm so sorry, sir. I'll clean it up," she says holding her side. I hold my hand over my mouth and hold my laugh. She looks like a drunk mess. A perfect distraction. The man is in disbelief, he cannot believe the sight.

"You got to be kidding me. Are you ok?" the cashier says.

"Yeah, I'm—" He tries picking her up, but she shrieks in agony. He drops her back on the floor with a thud. "Oh saints!" she shrieks grabbing her back. "Sir, I think I broke my hip, can you please call an ambulance?"

"Um, yeah." He curses under his breath looking frazzled. "Do you want me to get you an ice pack?"

"Go call an ambulance, dude!" I yell to motivate him. "She's hurt, can't you see that? She needs medical attention!"

"Um, yeah, ok. Stay there. Don't move, I'll call an ambulance." He turns and rushes into the back office.

As soon as he leaves, I see her get up like nothing happened. "Are you ok?" I say convinced Kylie actually hurt herself.

She hops right up on her feet. "Yeah, c'mon, let's get this over with."

Within a minute we barricade the door with a gondola, so the man is trapped in the office. We grab all the shirts and shorts off the clothes rack and fill them to the top with bags of chips, cereal, instant soup cups, breakfast sandwiches, and other snacks and candy. I notice the man left the cash register open. I rush to the cash register and fill my pockets with credits.

"Carson, are you serious? We're going to get in huge trouble," Kylie panics.

"Shut up," I snap. "We need this." I finish stuffing the bigger credit bills in my pants. We finish our raid by swiping a few gallons of water and burst through the front door. I run out the door behind Kylie and race down the block. We run awkwardly trying to hold on to everything but luckily there was no one in sight. I get in front of Kylie and tell her to follow me down an alleyway around a dump. Once out of sight, we unload our shirts and shorts we used as bags and count our loot.

"Two dozen candy bars, eight bags of chips, a dozen breakfast sandwiches, four boxes of cereal, four gallons of water, six shirts, seven pairs of shorts and... one bathing suit," I add up.

"Nice job, Kylie. Why did you grab these swim trunks?"

"I just grabbed what I could."

I hold them up and see it is a size small, I'm a large. "These are way too small."

We share a laugh. I pull out three hundred and three credits, out of my pants. A dozen instant soups, a dozen microwavable breakfast sandwiches, four gallons of water, two boxes of my favorite treenut butter chocolava bars, and four Vita-stims, perfect for if we get sick all stuffed into six shirts and five pairs of shorts.

"What are those?" She points at the Vita-stims. "Are you some drug addict now?"

"No! Of course not. They're vitamins, see?" I show her the label. Most stims are pain killers or mood enhancers, so I see where she got the idea. "Vita-stims are used to help get over a cold or bring down a fever. It injects all thirteen essential vitamins directly in your bloodstream. Most well-off rich people use these as an everyday vitamin."

"That's weird. You're going to inject yourself?"

"Only if we get sick. Yeah, we need to prepare, Ky."

"You're right. I guess you got some smarts in you," she jokes. "Oh yeah, and I almost forgot." She pulls out a to-go cup of coffee out of one of her shirts.

My mouth drops and spreads wide into a smile. She actually got me a cup of coffee. "You're the best," I say taking it from her. "I guess this makes up for ruining my favorite shirt."

"You mean your only shirt?" We share another laugh. For the longest time I haven't heard Kylie genuinely laugh. So, this was a special moment for me. "You know we're homeless, right?" She ruined that moment quick. She gets it in my mind that we can't just do this for the rest of the day. We need to find shelter and we need to establish ourselves with something.

"Well, let's think of something," I say as I open up a breakfast sandwich. "How much money do you have?"

"Um," she pulls out a wad of credits and starts counting. It looks pretty impressive actually, compared to what I have. "two hundred fifty... three. Yeah, two hundred fifty-three."

"How did you get so much money?" I ask while changing into new clothes. "I thought you said you had no money?"

"You never asked. You're not the only one that knows how to *borrow* things," she confesses in a giggle.

"You stole all that? Kylie, you savage. I thought you were against stealing?"

"Hey. Those girls made fun of me every day. *Everyday,* Car. There were only so many places three girls can hide things from each other. So, when they were out shopping or hanging out with those gangster wannabes I borrowed a few credits from each of them here and there and put it aside so we can get our own place one day."

In any other circumstance I'd be disappointed with her. I was supposed to be the delinquent, she was to be the perfect child, but she definitely came in the clutch on this one. I take the first sip of my coffee, and it tastes old and cold. Ugh. Whatever. It was a good try. Old and cold coffee it is. I take a huge gulp and try to down the coffee before I grow disgusted by it. "Ok, so I see it this way," I say starting to feel a spurt of energy. "A hotel is maybe sixty to a hundred credits a night. We can get a room for a few days, have a shower to ourselves, but that'll drain our money very quickly. Maybe we can skim through for another day but then we would be out of money unless we are going to go on a spree of robbing places but that could get messy really quick. We could buy a tent and a blowup mattress and live in the woods. We could possibly meet someone and ask to stay where they are but that seems kind of risky," I contemplate. I find myself talking to myself before I look behind me and see Kylie starring at the sign. I walk back to her.

"Levi Scrapyard." It shows. The sign is on its last leg, hanging by a tip of a chain.

"Kylie, were you even listening?" I ask her.

"Here," she says.

"What?" I ask in disbelief.

"Here." She points up at the sign and, looks at me. "It's secluded, no one will know we are in here, and it's perfect to set something up. If we can somehow get inside here, we can live here. It's obviously abandoned, no one would even think we are living in here. This is perfect, at least for a few days before we can figure out something else."

We figure out a way to get in by breaking a piece of the fence off and pushing the mesh behind it up enough to slip in.

Kylie puts her hands on her hips and takes a good look around everything. "I think this could really work for us. We need tools though. I can make anything given the right things we find."

80

"Since when can you make *anything*?"

"I'll learn. *We* will learn. We will make ourselves a home here, and in the meantime, we'll figure a way to get you into Atlantis University." She looks up at me. "Do you trust me, Carson?"

I stare into my little sister's eyes and see all the hope she has. She may only be fifteen, but she's all I got. "Do you trust me?"

"You're the only person I trust, Carson."

14

The Battlesuit

One year later

I

t's been a hard and struggling time making a new home with Carson. I wonder how different my life would've been if we stayed on that farm. We had fresh food every day, a roof over our heads, our own bed to sleep in, and a shower to bathe in. Living in this scrap yard has had its difficulties, but one thing is for sure, I am content here.

I remember the first day we got here, we found a broken-down school transporter and spent all hours of the day fixing it up to live in. It was horrid inside, there were bugs infested everywhere, seats were torn to shreds, and the roof had bullet holes in it. The entire interior was ruined from the rain leaking in, it smelt like mildew and mold. I scrubbed for days to clean out the dirt and scraped out all the grime on the floor, then bleached the entire transporter to kill the mold the best I could. After that, we painted the inside with old paint we found in a dumpster at the hardware store. None of the colors match, and the inside looks like a toddler did it, but it will stop the mold from growing and made our makeshift scrap yard home a bit more tolerable.

Carson was able to buy us a socket set, some screwdrivers, a soldering set, and a few power drills with the money we had from the corner store heist. Carson used them to take out the seats and repurposed them into two beds for us both to sleep in. The first few months were great until it started to get cold. I rewired the transporter's battery to a generator and gave us a working heater and air conditioning. The worst part of all this was spending the holidays without our parents. We suffered with blankets over us and huddled next to the heater most the night.

I've spent a lot of time at the Levi Library, and snuck into some classes at hardware stores with Carson to learn how to use my tools and what I could do with them. I learned how to wire and program lights and how to construct them into the roof of the transporter using solar panels. It has been one tough year for us, but we are surviving. Carson managed to get a job at Here N' There for the time being. Ironic, too. He asked the owner about the cashier we met in his interview, he said he was let go for making a fake emergency call. Those cameras in the store were fake! There was no footage of us. Carson works there pretty much all day getting paid under the table. Sometimes he takes the leftovers after he closes the store. His boss, Rick, never knows about it, nor do I believe he cares. It goes in the garbage anyway.

One of the biggest problems we faced was the roof that was rusted out with all the bullet holes in it and leaked every time it rained. I soldered the holes the best I can but what I thought of is to divert the water out the sides like a real roof would, so I cut PVC pipes in half and triangularly attached them to the roof. The drain system fills up buckets of rainwater we use to shower, cook, or water the small garden we have. It's been keeping me busy. There are so many more possibilities now. I've been able to experiment on some things too. I can imagine something and simply find some things and put it together.

About a month ago, I went scavenging around a massive pile in one of the corners of the yard. It was off the beaten path, but for some reason I was drawn to it, like a saint was shining it's light on it and was drawing me to this pile. I was hoping to find something useful like car parts or anything tyketanium but what I did find scared me half to death. At first, I thought I found a dead body and I shrieked when a hand fell out when I touched it. At a second glace, I realized it couldn't be human, so I swallowed my fear and pulled it out to discover that it was an exoskeleton. Its similar to the ones the military uses but it was completely stripped of its armor and power core. With the right tender loving care, I can make Carson his very own battlesuit.

The exoskeleton is a complete mess. Dirt piles, rust build up everywhere, and broken connectors, and wires infest it but I have committed myself to getting this in working order. It's going to need a lot of love and elbow grease. Supposedly, real battlesuits weigh as much as a ton when it is fully armored, but I was able to pull it out of the pile and stow it on a cart we walked off with from the hardware store. They have plenty, they won't miss it. My goal now is to get it to power on. Carson has been talking about this fighting tournament he's been itching to go see. Of course, he just wanted to watch it, but when I show him a working battlesuit and tell him he can compete, he'll go nuts.

I work on it day and night when Carson is away. I don't want him to know I have it so I keep it hidden from him, hoping when we search for fresh supplies that he doesn't run into it. He has found me some excellent pieces like road signs, aluminum cans, and cast iron that I can use to make the helmet and a chest plate. They work perfectly since I can mend them and curve them on the exoskeleton. Carson even found a solid tyketanium pipe he's been using as a walking stick. Unfortunately, it's been difficult finding an alternative power source to start the suit up. Rune, the delicate crystals used as power for the suits, isn't sold in its purest form like I need it, so I had to settle with a small car battery. The only way I can imagine it to run is to hook up jumper cables to the battery and jump it to life. Hopefully doing that will activate the exoskeleton and work as if rune was in it.

I plan to surprise him with it tonight. The winner of the tournament gets an invitation to some proving event at Atlantis University. The only thing is the entry fee, a hundred credits, I know I don't have that anymore. I've been spending the few credits I have on tools and food. I hope Carson has enough to get him in.

That night, before Carson came home, I finished constructing an incredibly special present for him to go along with his suit. I made, what I would like to call, Turbo Boots. I have amplified a set of magnets to produce an anti-gravity friction field. Enabling the user to hover when wearing the boots. Using the same technology, we see in hover bikes and hover cars, I was able to condense it into a smaller compressor to be worn inside the sole of the shoe. This won't make him fly like the cars, but it can give him a quick burst in a direction he pushes to. I'm going to let him be the first to try them out.

I get goosebumps from the excitement for when Carson comes home, but my excitement turns to concern as he walks in with his head down. I hope he didn't get fired or anything.

I pop out of the transporter and surprise him. "Hi, big brother," I say with my hands in the air. It didn't even seem to faze him. "What's wrong?"

He looks at me with a small frown. "Rick is cutting my hours. He told me business isn't going well and the Bone Breakers just raised his protection rent. I made up this elaborate story and I think he bought it but I'm only going to have half the hours I usually get." He slicks back his sweaty brown hair. It's been getting long in these past months. He's able to tie it back in a small ponytail. Even his patchy beard is growing in. "I'm going to start looking for another job tomorrow."

"What's more elaborate than escaping an orphanage to end up living in a scrap yard with your sister?" I ask sarcastically.

He rolls his eyes. "Right, which is all completely illegal by the way." He exhales and shakes his head. "I don't know what to do, Ky, we are running out of money and I need to get another job. I really wanted to go see that tournament, too," he complains. "Ugh, this is the first time Atlantis University is sponsoring a Harmonian to enter the Proving. I really wanted to go see if there is anyway I could apply to the school even if I can't compete."

My heart drops and my emotions burst out. I can't hold in the surprise any longer. This has to be the perfect time to tell him. "Carson." He looks at me. "What if I told you, that you could enter the tournament yourself?"

His eyes light up in curiosity. "What did you do? Steal a battle suit?" I laugh but my face doesn't falter as it would if I told a joke. "No... No, Kylie, no. Don't say that, we are in *serious* trouble if you did."

"No, silly. I *made* you one," I say with a huge smile. I couldn't hold back anymore. I am so excited for him, I just wanted to show him. "C'mon, let me show you! I've been hiding it from you over here."

"You've been hiding... Wait, are you serious?" He drops the bags at the front door of our home and chases me down and around the back. Just behind the transporter in the pile of scrap he has never looked through, I pull the suit out of its hiding place "You made a battlesuit?" he asks surprised. His eyes light up and a smile covers his entire face. "Does it work?"

"I found the exoskeleton and welded pieces you found to it. We just have to jump it with the generator and see if it works."

"So that's where these went." He finds all the pieces that he found over the months. The stop sign chest plate, down to the forearms which are quarter panels from cars. "Kylie, this is amazing. Can I try it on?"

"I'd be insulted if you didn't. But, before you do, we need to power it up first. If you jump in unpowered it'll be like walking with four hundred pounds on your back. The exoskeleton won't carry the weight."

"Is there a helmet?"

"No helmet yet," I tell him annoyed. "I'm still working on that. Just, slow down." I take the pair of boots that were behind the suit and leave them at his feet. "Try these on, I call them Turbo Boots. I know this suit isn't like the real ones so when you're fighting in the tournament, you're going to need to be light on your toes. These will help you dash from side to side and jump three times your normal vertical."

"Woah, woah, the tournament? You mean the Tournament of Titans?" he asks surprised. "Kylie, you really think I could win? Who knows what kind of experienced fighters will be competing? Do you understand that I have no real training at all? Mom's backyard martial arts won't match up to years and years of real professionals. How would I even stand a chance?"

"Because… because it's your dream, right? To be a titan? This is your dream, isn't it?" I ask sounding unsure.

"Yeah, yeah it is… I just figured it was hopeless at this point…" He looks at his gloves, little pieces of jagged aluminum cover the knuckles of snow gloves. "You did this all for me? So I could enter the tournament?"

I nod. "Before you decided to leave the farm with me, I promised you I'd get you into Atlantis University. I know you didn't believe me, or see any way of getting in, but you still gave up everything to stick with me. With no diploma or residence in Alannah, it sounded close to impossible, but the winner gets an invitation to the Proving. This is the first time Harmony gets a chance to represent itself. You need to be the representative. I know you'll give us a good name. You can show Alannah and the rest of the world that Harmony isn't what they think we are." I look deep in his eyes and only wish good fortune for my brother and the idea of peace among the territories just like dad always wanted. He means the world to me and I only want to see him happy. This is his chance to do something better, to be someone better. "So, will you do it?"

He knocks on the chest plate and finds the small car battery stuffed in the center console of the suit that will power this mighty beast. "Do we have the money to enter?"

"We will make it happen. I can sell some of my little knickknacks at the pawn shop on 2nd Street. I'm sure they will give us the money we need." His face cringes with doubt. His lack of faith bothers me. "If not, I guess we will just give up," I say hoping to get a reaction.

"Wait, what?" he panics. "No way. We can do it."

"That's right, big brother. Now stop looking at all the negatives." I grab his face and look into his eyes. "This is your dream. I made it possible. You have to make it a reality."

He gives me a sneer look, then smirks. "I won't let you down. Now, let's try this out."

That night started off with tragedy and disappointment. The suit didn't power on, but with a slight change of circuitry, it finally comes to life on the fourth try. To get in, we must unzip the shoulder pads in the back and remove the casing to open the exoskeleton. Once opened, Carson awkwardly slides his legs into the leg slots and squeezes himself inside. I strap him inside and if the suit works, the immense weight of all the scrap metal becomes weightless. Carson's dream of wearing a battlesuit becomes a reality, he laughs and hollers in joy punching and kicking in it, then activates the Turbo Boots and jumps, and the jumper cables detach from the suit. In seconds, the suit seizes and Carson panics as the suit engulfs him in the full weight of the armor. He groans and panics when his body fails him, and he falls face first into the ground feeling the hundreds of pounds of force collapse on him.

"What just happened?!" he shouts. He tries to get up but the suit doesn't budge. "I'm stuck! Kylie, help! I can't move! Kylie, this isn't funny. Get me out." I wish I still had a phone, this would be an awesome photo moment.

I undo the zipper and help him escape the clutches of the suit. "Carson, it's a car battery, you have to let it charge for a bit before you detach the jumper cables." With a huff, he crawls out of the suit and helps me stand it up right. Thankfully for us, the suit isn't a ton like a real suit, but it was difficult to get it back upright. "Let it charge overnight. Tomorrow, we can really try it out," I instructed him.

He groans and folds his arms. "Saintdamn it, Kylie, you sure sound a lot like mom sometimes."

"I'm not mom, you've always been mom. You're strong and fearless like she is… was." Talking about her still hits me like a punch to the gut. It's been over a year since we've been orphaned. Some would call us miracle children to survive this long without the comfort of adult figures in our life. We've done plenty of growing up since our days in Redding.

The next morning, I wake up early to find Carson sitting crisscross next to the suit. He isn't touching it or playing with the armor like I thought he'd be, he's just admiring it. I tell him to gather our credits because we are forty credits short of the entry fee. Carson doesn't have much to give but the shirt off his back, so he helps me bring two of the little decorations I have put together. One was a lamp I made from washers, nuts, and bolts, and the other was a statue of an ovat made from pieces of scrap welded together. I would guesstimate that all of this is worth three hundred credits. Sure, they aren't the most amazing things in the world, but we aren't looking for top dollar.

We make it to the discreet hole in the wall pawn shop named, 'Curly's Pawn Shop.' Thousands of things line the walls and shelves, from phones, toys, anime trading cards, tools, sports paraphernalia, and jewelry. There's so much in here. I'm in awe until a sharp outburst from an elderly man at the counter argues with the clerk trying to pawn off a book. He seems to be giving the man an awfully hard time.

He drops his fist on the table in anger. "What do you mean this is only worth two credits?!"

"Sir, it is all about reselling. To me, this is worthless. I'm trying to give you something but there's no value in it," the shop owner states.

"Impossible! I bought this when I was a child for a hundred and twenty credits. This has to be a collectable of some kind," The old man argues. "It just has to be."

"I'm sorry, sir, it's just not worth anything to me. I don't see anyone coming into my store looking for." He looks down at the book and gives it a smug look. "The Rebound Effect." What is the rebound effect?"

"It's a classic!" the man blurts out as he grabs the book and storms out.

We walk up to the counter, after watching that scary looking man nearly bump into Carson and place our things on it for the store clerk to examine.

"Good morning, sir," Carson says.

"How are you doing, kids?" The man looks at us, then eyes the two items. A nametag says his name is Mosley. "You steal these things?"

I'm appalled. "No! I made them," I say annoyed.

Mosley gives us a crooked look and eyes the lamp. "*You* made this?" he asks in disbelief and clicks his tongue. "I'll tell you what, kids, run home and get your parents to come here and we can make a deal. I'm sorry but I don't buy from kids."

I start to fume up. "We don't have par—" I get stopped by Carson grabbing my shoulder. He puts his finger in front of his mouth and shushes me.

He turns back to the clerk. "Sir, I'm twenty," he lies. "We just need to buy some medicine for our dying grandmother. We really don't have anyone else. Please, it will help us a great deal if you can give us a good deal for this. My sister here worked very hard on these things to make our grandmother proud of her."

"You got any I.D?" He takes a closer look at Kylie's work.

"Afraid not, sir. I do most of my traveling on my hoverbikes. This was kind of a quick decision thing."

He pulls out a magnifying glass and takes a closer look. "What is this? Some kind of school project gone wrong?"

Oh, now I'm boiling. "Excuse me? I—" I get nudged by my brother and we exchange looks again. He gives me the look to breathe and that he has it under control.

"I'll tell you what, you kids don't look like bad kids. How many credits you need for the medicine?" the clerk asks.

"One fifty," Carson comes back.

Mosley laughs. "Listen kid, it's cool that you're trying to help your grandma, but I don't even want these things. Where did you find this stuff, a junk yard? I'm trying to do you a favor," he insists.

"Eighty," Carson tries. "Sir, our grandmother is dying. Medicine isn't cheap," he pleads in a convincing tone. "There must be some sort of bozo that'll come in here and see these things and give you any price tag you want. C'mon, look at it. It's a freaking ovat. Also, look at this lamp. Tell me you've seen this before because I know you haven't."

The store clerk looks up at me. "You really made this, kid?"

I nod my head trying to look sad even though this man just insulted me, and I want to rip his ugly mustache off of his face.

He hesitates. "Thirty is more than fair."

"Eighty is more than fair, how about fifty?" Carson calmly points out.

The clerk gives him one final look, checks out the details on the ovat once more, pulls out a wad of bills and smacks down forty-five credits. "Go get your grandma's medicine, kid. Hope she feels better."

Carson bites his tongue and takes the money. "Have a nice day, sir."

He turns and walks away. I give the man one final look. I see concern in his eyes. Maybe the lie actually did get to him. I turn and follow Carson. Even though we wanted more, we got exactly what we needed.

"Hey, little girl!" The clerk calls for us.

I turn around to see what he wants. "You ever make anything like this again, bring it my way. This is actually incredible work.

A smile uncontrollably wraps around my face. Maybe I was wrong about him. He doesn't seem so bad.

15
Prepare

With the entry fee and a fully functional battle suit, my sister is making my dream come to life. Finally, something good is happening. A year of struggling and loss is finally coming full circle.

"Don't get too excited, hot shot," Kylie says seeing my excitement. "You still have to win."

"I know." I look at my watch and realize I have to get to work soon. "Crap, it's almost one. I got to get to work."

"Work? Carson, you got training to do. I say you take off today and focus on preparing for the tournament. You need to be accustomed to the suit. You are going to be in a ring with another person who wants this opportunity just as badly as you do. You need to know your suit's minutiae," Kylie expresses.

"My suit's what?" I question.

"You need to know every detail of the suit. You need to know your capabilities, your limits, your strengths, weaknesses, everything, Carson, everything. This could be your one and only chance to get into Atlantis University."

"You're right," I agree. As much as that job means to me, my importance there is dwindling. Any day now I could be fired. So, I listen to my sister and focus on what is important. I just feel bad for leaving Rick high and dry. We start walking back to the scrap yard. The pawn shop was a bit of a walk. Maybe about a half mile.

"So, what are we going to do if you win?" Kylie asks.

"What do you mean? If I win, I get to go to Atlantis University," I elaborate.

"Yeah, *you* do," Kylie states. "Don't get me wrong, this is your dream, I don't want to get in front of your dreams, but it just hit me... If you win, where am I going to go?"

"You can come with me?" I figured. "Why wouldn't you?"

"Carson, A.U. is a college, I'm not old enough to go."

My world stops me in my tracks. She's right. If I win, I may just have to leave her. A.U. is in Alannah, about a four-hour trip, by car, for that matter. On top of all that, Alannah isn't fond of Harmonian visiting their territory. They think we are some kind of virus. Harmony may be massive compared to any other place on Tyke, but four hours away from my baby sister is like being on a completely different planet. I can't abandon her, not after all she has done for me.

"I'll make it work, I promise. There has to be some kind of dorm you can stay in, or school you can go to and you can stay with me in the dorm," I insist. "They can't honestly separate us, can they?" Ugh, how could I promise something like that to Kylie? I feel like my father.

"It's Atlantis University. It's the most prestigious school on Tyke. They can do whatever they want," she says. "The school was funded by the Sovereign himself."

Our Sovereign, Donavan Silva, has been in charge for nearly thirty-five years. His family has been ruling Tyke for as long as I can remember. Even when my great grandparents were alive, his family ruled.

"What if I say you're on my team? I need you as my mechanic or something?"

"I'm sure they would expect the recruits to learn how to fix their suits."

My mind goes blank. She is on a completely different level than me. It is honestly hard to keep up with her sometimes. "Let's just focus on the task at hand," I interrupt Kylie. "I may not even win. I may not even get past the first round."

She turns to me in a fit of frustration. Hands curled into fists, ready to punch me. "Shut your mouth." She swings and hits my shoulder. "I didn't just work on that suit for the last two months so you can say you're going to lose!" she shouts. "Carson, don't you think it was weird seeing Fox soldiers in our house? Like, what were they doing in Redding? They don't belong here, they should be on the moon where Fox Legion is stationed. They were astronomically out of their jurisdiction. I know those guys had something to do with our parent's murder, disappearance, whatever. Haven't you been thinking about this? This wasn't all just some weird coincidence."

"Kylie, that is a long shot and you know that."

"No, it's not! That Robbins guy rubbed me the wrong way. Every time I talked, he had something else to say or he stopped me. He slapped me; don't you remember?" I remember that vividly. I remember the rage, and fear I had for such a man, like nothing I have ever felt before. "You need to win this tournament and get into Atlantis University. Find out what happen to our parents. This is our chance."

"Ok, and how would I even begin doing that? If you haven't noticed, I'm not some expert private investigator."

"Figure it out, dummy. You're resourceful, you're smart, talk to people. Get information on Omega Robbins. Find out if they have information on dad. There has to be something going on, I can feel it in my gut."

I mock her. "You sound crazy, Kylie." The thought of staring my parent's killer in the face scares me. If I knew it was him who took my parents life, I would have shot him right then and there in the house. What if I did? The repercussions of it all, I wouldn't be here right now, I'd be in a jail cell rotting in prison for shooting a Fox soldier, living the rest of my life behind bars while Kylie lived at the orphanage wondering what went wrong. "Why would Fox Legion go through so much trouble for some random engineer? Was dad's project really all that important?"

"Dad was not some random engineer! How dare you insult him like that! Maybe if you paid attention to his work, instead of patronizing him because he didn't want to waste his time throwing a starball around, you'd understand he was trying to revolutionize the world. He wanted to give Harmony a second chance. He wanted everyone to have the gift of a genius intellect. Do you know how special that could have been? Doctors, scientists, teachers, students, everyone would be sophisticated and intellectual. We could peacefully work together hand in hand to make the world a better place. Are you just going to let someone get away with murder? Carson, dad did not shoot mom, he couldn't, he wouldn't, he loved her."

I've thought the whole scenario over a thousand times. Every time I do, I end up right back to where I started; reality. It doesn't matter what he might have or could have done. It's what did happen, whether he killed my perfect mother or not, they aren't here, and we are on our own. "It was hard to tell. You've heard them fight. It was always about not having time to spend with each other." She drops her head. "You don't understand, all I ever wanted was a normal dad. Why was it so hard to throw the starball around?" I complain. "I never asked for much, and look, this genius of a father was arrested for treason. For what? For being selfless? How is that fair? How is it fair for us to suffer like this for his consequences? How is it fair that mom only wanted love from him, and when he finally showed some kind of compassion, she was shot." I rant. Feeling the betrayal I've always felt for my father. "Why was it fair for us to be taken from our homes and put in that orphanage to rot. Right? How is it—" I look down at Kylie and realize I brought up a very touchy subject. "Kylie?"

She sniffs back her emotions and straightens up. "Yeah. Whatever."

Without another word to each other we get back to the scrap yard. Even after all these months, that sign still holds the same position it always has, a bit more rust but still standing strong. "Kylie," I call to her. She looks back at me, a lonely tear falling down her face. "Come here for a second." She walks over to me, looking like she's been beating herself up this whole walk back. "You see that sign?" I point to it.

"What about it?" she mutters.

"This sign has looked like that this whole time, probably even longer than we have been here, but it still holds on, that's you."

She tilts her head in confusion. "I'm a broken-down sign, hanging on for dear life?"

"No, c'mon, you're smarter than that," I say rolling my eyes. "Whatever the world threw at you, you hung on. You got knocked down but got right back up, you never gave up." I try to instill confidence in her. I need her now more than ever, I can't have her hating herself, not now, not ever for that matter.

She sniffles and composes herself. "No, no, that's not me at all."

"What do you mean? Of course, it is. You—"

"No, Carson, it's not." She takes a deep breath. "I was going to kill myself back at the orphanage. I truly felt that I was in a situation that I couldn't handle, and… it got the best of me. I looked at that waterfall and I wanted to die. The most beautiful sight I have ever seen is where I felt my lowest. I remember closing my eyes and saying my goodbyes. Goodbye to you, goodbye to the world. I just want mom and dad back so bad, that jumping off that cliff was the easiest way of getting them back, but then I heard your voice, and I opened my eyes and saw what I was about to do, and… you stopped me. You, alone, are my world. You are all I have left. You." She points to the sign. "If I'm that sign, you're the chain holding on to me. You are the reason I have purpose."

I pull her into me and wrap my arms around her. Comforting her in her moment of weakness but also for a moment of absolute strength. "That is exactly why I'll never walk away from you, Kylie. You're all I have, too. Those guys at the farm... I wouldn't consider them friends. We all stole from each other when no one was looking back and forth, it was like a game of who wouldn't notice."

"What about Courtney?"

"What about Courtney?" I repeat her in a confusing tone. "She was just... a girl, I guess."

"You liked her, didn't you?" Kylie asks.

"Yeah, but it's fine. If I ever see her again, I'll have to figure something out, but I think I may have screwed that chance up."

"I'm sorry."

"Don't be. I'll find another Courtney someday. I only have one Kylie."

She squeezes me tightly. "Anyways, I'm happy you saved me. You're right, I am strong. I am better than this." A newfound confidence emerges. "Let's get you in that suit. We have a lot of practice to do."

16

Time to enter

A buzzing noise wakes me up. My eyes flutter open and I peak down at the wristwatch I've had since our times at the orphanage. My muscles are sore from practice and for the first time in a long time, I slept through the night. I roll out of my makeshift transporter seat cushion bed and feel the cool morning breeze through our cracked windows. I wake up Kylie and tell her to get ready. We have two hours to make all our final adjustments before we have to head over to the tournament in Levi Square.

I walk outside and take in the rotting stench of garbage all around us. The cool morning air hits me in the face and sends a shiver down my back as I relieve myself in the wastebasket with an inflatable tube as a toilet seat. I am so sick of this place but, for now, it is the only home I have. It has given me a chance to do what I have always felt was impossible.

Kylie powers up the suit with the generator and the suit comes to life. I wedge myself inside and make sure everything is operable. The exoskeleton molds to my body, squeezes my arms and legs, contracts across my chest and back, and relieves me of the weight of the armor. An outrageous and unworldly feeling it is to be in one of these suits. Although I appear to look like a garbage monster out of a movie, I fully intend to bring my inner beast to life in this tournament. My heart pounds as I wait for Kylie to get ready, anxiety tickles my stomach, and I soon become impatient. I want to jump and run around but I'm scared to burn my energy, I'm going to need every last bit of it to survive today.

Kylie finally walks out of the transporter with a backpack on. "You ready yet, Kylie?" I ask. "Is everything tight? I don't need pieces flying off of me today."

She walks around me and knocks on a few pieces. "I think we are ready."

"You think?" I ask.

"Hey! I'm no expert on this stuff."

"Ok, but you built this?" Kylie gives me a snide look. She isn't a morning person by any means. She takes another quick lap around me looking and pulling at something on my side, mumbling about trying to find something. "What is it? What are you looking for?"

"I'm looking for your testicules, you must have lost them last night."

I huff and roll my eyes. "Very funny. Is everything good though? I just want to make sure everything is working. I don't want this thing crashing out on me today."

"Neither do I, Titan Obvious, but as I just said, I am no expert on this stuff. We're taking a gamble here."

"You're right. It's a gamble we need to take. A gamble I need to take."

Everything seems to be working. Walking is a bit awkward, but I feel walking is more fluent and easier than it was yesterday. She slides herself out of the broken pocket in the fence. I take one look at the hole and realize… I can't get out. Just looking at the opening we made. I realize my body is twice as wide as it was with the bulk of this suit. "Kylie, I can't fit through the gate! The suit is too bulky to get out. How did we not think of this before? I can't get through the gate." I start to panic and look for alternative ways to get out.

She, on the other hand, starts laughing. "You shouldn't have had the last candy bar."

"Shut up! What am I supposed to do?"

"Umm… Jump?"

"Jump?!" I look up at the eight-foot fence. "Do you think I can make it?"

"If you can, then you won't have to break more of the fence. Plus, I made those boots for you to jump higher. C'mon, we're going to be late."

She really has thought of everything. These Turbo boots were an excellent accessory to my strategy. With a little practice, I was able to get the hang of pushing myself side to side, but I never tried to jump as high as I could. Scary at first to move at such a quick pace but being in a four hundred pound metal deathtrap does have its flaws. These Turbo boots exploit this flaw, giving me an edge against slower and heavier opponents. I take a couple of steps back and activate the Turbo Boots. The magnets inside pulse to life.

Here it goes. I take a deep breath and take off. Pumping my arms as forcefully as I can, I launch myself into the air. Never in my life have I jumped this high. I feel like a superhero soaring the massive heights of the fence. My body clears but something catches my foot. Gravity pulls my body back towards the fence and the next thing I know, my face smashes into the other side of the wooden fence and I flip over on my back. My body makes a boisterous crashing noise as I fall to the ground.

Kylie guffaws out a loud uncontrollable laugh. "Nice one, dingus! Nimble as can be!"

The pain is not as bad as I thought. I hop up and shake it off, trying not to feel embarrassed around my sister. She's seen far worse of my character and even more of my stupidity getting the best of me back in Redding. I clear my mind and pretend what just happen doesn't faze my confidence with an honest smile on my face and a chuckle to go along with her spastic laughing. I start walking, checking to make sure nothing came loose. I go over my shoulders, my arms, and my knee pads. Everything seems ok. I look behind me to find Kylie looking at me, seemingly like she's waiting for me to see something I'm not.

"What is it?" I ask.

"Where's your pipe?" she says plainly. Being a smarty pants, as always.

I check my back strap where its holster is. It's not there. Crap, it's still inside.

"Kylie," I say desperately.

A sinister smile forms on her face. "Yes? Oh, what ever could it be?"

"Can you get it?" I plead.

She nods with a cackle as she squeezes through the hole in the fence so easily, like always. She comes back moments later with it and slides it in the holster on my back, still carrying that silly know-it-all smile.

"Thank you," I say plainly. "Ok, anything else I forgot?"

"Probably a snack or two could work."

"Kylie!"

"I'm kidding." She pulls her bookbag around and shows me a couple of Quickmeal bars we usually have for snacks during the day, along with a set of sockets and screwdrivers, and her pocket welder for quick repairs, if needed.

We make our way down the block. I notice people are staring at us, more or less me. You don't see people in battlesuits often walking down the street. They are usually transported in containment cases or in a bed of a truck at least, not walking around in it like it's some kind of costume.

"What is that supposed to be?" I hear. "Where did they get that from?" another voice comes from behind me.

I wave and smile at them like I would normally do trying to ignore any negativity. We pass by my store, and I see my boss Rick cleaning the windows.

"Carson?" he says disgruntled. "Carson, you were supposed to be at work yesterday, where have you been?" he sounds more concerning. His thin slanted eyes glare at me with wonder and curiosity. "And why do you smell like rotten seashellwalkers?"

I stop for the moment and think fast. "Hi, Rick. I'm entering in The Tournament of Titans. Didn't I tell you?" I lie.

"No!" he says with raised eyebrows. "Where were you yesterday? You don't like showing up anymore since I cut your hours? You were supposed to be here working the store not playing dress up in your garbage cans. I missed my family dinner because of you." He points his thin callused finger at me. "What is this anyway?" He wants an excuse or some kind of explanation for not showing up, but I don't have one that he wants. He's never had a care in his life that didn't benefit him so anything I say won't help my chances.

"Well, it's—" I start.

"It's a battlesuit, can't you tell?" Kylie butts in.

"You look like you got that out of the scrap yard," Rick says sarcastically.

"I made it, Mr. Rick," Kylie interrupts again. "Carson is going to fight in the tournament today, so if you don't mind, we have to go," Kylie says as she grabs my hand and pulls me down the sidewalk.

"You're fired, Carson. I hope this is worth it," Rick shouts out to us walking past his store.

I say nothing and put my head down. "Thanks for that," I say sarcastically to Kylie.

"You don't need that job. Now, you have to win. There is no going back now."

"Easier said than done," I huff.

Finally, after many more ugly looks, and whispered insults walking through town, we arrive in Town Square where the tournament is being held.

99

"Is this the place?" Kylie asks.

"Yeah. That's what it says on the flier."

A big sign that looks to be written in marker on a poster board reads "Sign ups here", with an arrow pointing down the alley.

Kylie inches herself closer to me. "There's no reason to be afraid, Ky." I tell her.

"Easier for you to say. I'm not the one in a suit."

We walk down the alleyway and find an interesting looking group of people standing around. All of them have crazy hair styles, oddly placed piercings, and tattoos. I try and make eye contact with one of them, but no one is giving me a second look. I finally grab the gaze of a lady with black makeup around her eyes with a sprayed in picture of a skull in her hair, dressed in all black, with black stockings with spiked boots that go up to her knees, Valkyries, the Bone Breaker's fearless women. "Excuse me, is this where we sign up for the tournament?" I ask her.

She looks up from her phone and checks me up and down not moving any other part of her body besides her eyes, she points with her eyes and nods down the alleyway. We continue down the path and the voices and screams are getting louder. We start seeing other people holding tools and spare parts. A broader man in front of us leaves the table and we walk up to a booth where a man with a spikey mohawk sits with a clipboard on it.

"Is this where I sign up for the Tournament of Titans?" I ask.

The man has a clear picture of a cracked skull on his chest; Oddly familiar as well. He ignores me as he finishes typing a message on his palmphone. He looks up with an obnoxious stare and flips the clipboard over in my direction with a pen attached to the forms. "Fill this out and wait for your number to be called. Do you know the rules?" he asks in a nasally voice like he's congested. His nose is wildly crooked. Is that Bonez? No, I can't ask, I do not want that kind of attention right now.

I grab the clipboard and hand it to my sister. "Rules? No. What is it? No low blows or something?"

He rolls his eyes and sits up in his chair. He closes his hand and the holo- projection of his phone dissolves, then flicks his wrist to lock it.

Saints, do I miss having a phone.

He takes a deep breath like he's annoyed he even asked me. "No, you can absolutely low blow. Low blows are one hundred percent legal. It's single elimination. Knock your opponent out of the ring, yah win, yah kill'em, yah win. Winner of each fight gets a choice between a piece of armor or a weapon from the losing competitor." He looks at my suit with a glare and smirks. "Looks like you have nothing to lose," he snarls. A small group of people walk up with him, all wearing gang paraphernalia. One of them I recognize instantly, Courtney. "Winners move on. Rounds are all chosen randomly. The winner of the tournament gets an invitation to Atlantis University's Proving in one month's time."

I make eye contact with Courtney through my caged helmet. She matches the group wearing black stockings and spiked shoes. Her blonde hair has pink underneath. She sneers at me with a disgusted face. A tag on her jacket reads, "Pinky". "Ok, so what is this Proving?" I ask.

"Are you saintdamn new to the world? Do you know nothing about any of this?" Bonez snaps.

"Not really, to be completely honest. Lived under a rock most of my life."

Courtney snorts, and quickly composes herself.

Bonez wasn't so keen on my comedy and smacks his face and shakes his head. "Oh, saints help me." His group of friends behind me snicker to each other. One of them wraps his arm around Courtney's shoulder.

"The Proving is how you prove yourself to the legions that you deserve to be drafted. Once you get drafted you will be housed at Atlantis University for four years and blah, blah, blah. I'm wasting my breath. Let's be honest, you sorry excuse for a trashcan, you don't have a chance in hell of winning. You look like a trash can, and smell like Blitzkrieg's stomach virus's over here." I look up at who he's pointing to. A clean shaven man with a strong chin and a scar over his eye rolls his eyes to Bonez's comment. "Where did you even make that, the junk yard?" Bonez laughs. "Holy saints, is that a stop sign on your chest?" He turns around to Courtney. "Check out this guy, Pinky."

She nods and laughs, "Yeah, he looks like he got stuck in a garbage press." The group chuckles. Oh Courtney, if only you knew who was under this helmet.

"Put this dweeb up against Mean Machine, Bonez. Let him know what wasting our time means to us," Blitzkrieg says.

Being talked down to is starting to make my blood boil, especially in front of Courtney. "You know what," I slam my hands on the counter in frustration and lean into him. "I've had enough of you clowns thinking you're better than me. I'll take on this Mean Machine, and I'll show all of you neanderthals that I'm not one to mess with." From the corner of my eye, I see Kylie slam the application down and the entry money with it right next to me. "Anything else you wanna say to me? Any sweet tips, or maybe where I could get one of those sick jackets?"

The group behind him eyes me up, looking insulted. Bonez takes the clipboard and flips through the application. "Carson Paul, huh, that's a stupid name." Courtney instantly looks down and back up at me. I smile through my helmet and know she's connecting the dots. "What kind of parents gives their kid two first names? Ugh, you got a stage name, Carson?" he asks.

I look over at Kylie for a name. She shrugs her shoulders.

"How about Trash Can, or Tin Can," one of the Bone Breakers says. The group laughs. "No, no, how about The Dumpster Diver?" another says. They mock me, trying to get me on my heels.

"How about Ghost, that sounds suitable, right, Carson?" Courtney says.

"Ghost?! No, that's stupid, he doesn't look anything like a ghost," Bonez says and shoos her away.

Courtney squints her eyes at me.

I gaze at her as she walks away. Oh, yeah, she remembers me. I snap back into reality. "Yeah, I like your style, Bonez. Call me… Scrap."

"Scrap?" Bonez and Kylie say simultaneously.

I fold my arms. "Yeah, Scrap. I like Scrap."

"Scrap? Is that really the best you can think of?" Courtney questions loudly.

Confidence consumes me. "Yeah, you know me. I like to scrap, kind of like these dimwits!"

Courtney's eyes bulge out of her head like she actually saw a ghost and steps to me but Bonez and the rest of the group springs up and gets in my face.

"Ey! No talking to my girls here, you got me?" Bonez points at me with his pen. "If you see anyone with this skull on their jacket do not talk to them. All these girls are mine and property of the Bone Breakers. If I, or any one of us, see you trying to shoot your shot with any of them, we'll hex you up. You hear me?" Without causing a scene, I nod, ending something that shouldn't have been started, especially around Kylie. I do not want her in a mess like that or anywhere around these guys for that matter. He writes my newly claimed name on the top of the application, and hands me a number, #16. "Nice knowing you, Carson. Our man, Mean Machine, is gonna hex you up good but I'll tell you what, I like your attitude. If you put on a good show for Mean Machine,

I'll consider you trying out for the Bone Breakers. That is, if your cute little sister over here joins too."

A hand comes out of nowhere and smacks Bonez in the back of the head. "She's only sixteen, you weirdo. Get a grip."

Bonez snaps back at her. "How do you know?!"

She stumbles over her words, "I, uh, just... just look at her." She gestures to her.

"She's not interested," I step in. "Say Bonez, are you entering this tournament?"

"Me? No. I mean, uh, I would but I wouldn't want to take any glory away from Mean Machine."

"Right, right, still recovering from that broken nose?"

Courtney snorts and Bonez's face gets red.

I feel Kylie tug at me to leave but I want Courtney to notice me. I take my helmet off and whip my hair back. I look right at her and wink. The group steps up at once, defending and protecting the only female in their group like a herd of wild canahounds.

"You tryna die today, boy? You sure got a big mouth with no back up," the one called Blitzkrieg shouts manically.

I pull out my tyketanium pipe. Squeezing the thread on the grip part and tapping the other end in my hand. "I don't need it." I say, feeling the fire start to light up inside me.

Kylie tugs me harder and I let her force pull me away.

"He didn't mean any of that. Thank you, have a nice day," Kylie says pushing me away.

"Yeah, that's what I thought!" Bonez yells. "Thanks for donating to my stim fund, *Scrap*! Really appreciate it, *Scrap*," he shouts and bellows. "Just you wait, Mean Machine's gonna make an example outta you, kid!"

17

Scrap

W̲e walk past the sign-up booth and down another alleyway into a massive festival where the tournament is being held. Walking under a homemade banner that says. "Levi's 7th annual Tournament of Titans."

"You're going to get us killed one day, you know that? You have to control your temper. You were about to get us kicked out before this tournament even started."

"Pshhh, I had everything under control. I wasn't going to swing. You just can't show them you're scared. That's all those goons are, they feast on fear."

"If you say so… So… Scrap, where'd you pull that one out of?" Kylie ponders out loud.

"I don't know. First thing I could think of. I'm a fighter, so I scrap, and I'm made of scrap metal. Makes sense, right?"

"Sure," Kylie says sarcastically. "So… Courtney's a Bone Breaker, who would have thought?"

"Yeah. She's changed."

"This town seems to do that to people. Please be careful, Carson. She's not the same girl she was at the orphanage."

"I won't, I won't… It's hard, you know? I left her so abruptly."

Without another word on the matter, Kylie and I immerse ourselves into the festival. Concession stands, souvenir booths, and all kinds of food trucks surround the tournament with colorful signs and lights to pull eager customers to their wares. One food stand in particular catches Kylie's nose by surprise.

"What is that smell?" she asks looking around. She searches vigorously, sniffing around and finds this small stand with a heavy path of steam coming from the top being dispensed out of a fan.

"Welcome, youngling, what can I do for you?" the man behind the counter asks.

"Um. I don't know, what is that smell? It smells delicious."

I find my way behind her looking up at their menu. The smell of grease, and some kind of roasting aroma has caught my attention as well.

"It is my famous shishkabob. Try a piece. A gift, if you will." The man welcomes us into his stand and hands us both a small plate with a tiny piece of meat on a toothpick. The meaty substance is a brownish color, looks very tender and well cooked with some kind of sauce on it. Kylie devours it in one gulp but I take a second look at it.

"Oh my saints, this is amazing!" Kylie proclaims.

The man behind the counter smiles and giggles like he has heard that plenty of times before.

"What is this sauce you have on it?" I finally get in to ask.

"Ahhh, family secret I'm afraid. Go ahead. Try it, youngling. Please, I insist. I will be insulted if you don't."

I stare at my plate for another second and consume the so-called tasty morsel. I find the savory flavors mouthwatering. "This is really good. Thank you for the sample, sir," I say.

The man looks a bit disappointed and annoyed, maybe he was thinking he was going to get a paying customer out of us. "But of course, of course. Are you a contestant here, youngling?" he asks. Unbeknownst to him, we only got five credits to our name and can't afford the napkin on my paper plate.

"Yeah. My name is Ca—" I stop myself. "Scrap."

"Ahh, very good, very good. Your suit is uh, unique. Yes, very unique." A small boy peaks his head out the window. He jolts back just as fast as he came in. "Any contestants get a discount of my famous shishkabob. So, if you are hungry after your fight, do not hesitate, my friend."

"Sure, thank you, sir."

"The pleasure is mine."

We find a seat on a nearby picnic table. It's off to the side and secluded from the main crowd that covers the perimeter of the fighting stage.

A man comes over the loudspeakers. *"Welcome all young and old to the 7ᵗʰ Annual Levi Tournament of Titans! My name is Skip, and I will be your devilishly handsome announcer for today. Thank you everyone for coming! Please try any of our delicious and nutritious food trucks and drink stands. My, oh my, they are heavenly! Look at me, I am getting ahead of myself. Let's, get this, Tournament of Titans going and a'flowing!"*

I lean into Kylie. *"Going and a'flowing"* I mock.

She smirks. "Do you need anything? Want me to check over everything again?"

"Yeah, sure. If my name doesn't get called," I say. "Oh, and don't worry, my testicles are in place."

Kylie giggles, "You're such an dope."

"And if you can—"

"No."

"No, what? You didn't give me a chance to—"

"I'm not going to see if Courtney will talk to you. I'm not doing it."

I laugh at the familiar gesture. I used Kylie to properly introduce me to Courtney. It took me about three days to give myself enough courage to walk up to her and properly introduce myself. Something about her was so intimidating. "I'm appalled," I say sarcastically. "No. Screw her. If you can, try and pickpocket some of the drunks by the bar. See if you can get some food money."

"Carson, no. I'm not doing it."

"Do you want the shishkabob or not?"

Kylie grunts at me and snarls. I know I got her. "Fine. After this fight."

"OK!" Skip the announcer says. *"Our first fighters are,"* he pauses. *"Reno, and Vector!"*

The surrounding crowd of fans start to cheer. Several huge projection screens face outwards. Half a dozen aftermarket camera drones hover around the stage. I watch as the fighters make their way on the stage. The stage is massive, it has plenty of room to maneuver around, just like I wanted to.

"Those guys look pretty tough. Look at them, Car." The doubt is slowly rising in Kylie's tone.

I stay quiet, patiently studying each one. Reno is a smaller, stocky man with exposed muscular hairy arms, with two block sized hammers and wears a sleek black set up. His shiny helmet visor shines against the glare of the sun. He may be big, but every man has about four pressure points that can be taken advantage of.

Vector, however, is taller and skinnier. His deep blue armor is covered in polished yellow pinstripes. He has some kind of metal glove that's way bigger than his other hand.

"Kylie, you see that on his hand, what is that?"

"Not sure, but it's huge," she answers.

If I'm going to have any chance at all, I need to focus. I need to know how each one fights and how they like to wear down their opponents. No one is going to bat an eye to me. Maybe that will be my advantage.

A horn blares an obnoxious tune, and the crowd starts to roar throughout the tournament.

"Begin!" the judge shouts.

The two warriors shout and charge in a frenzy and clash into each other. Fists fly, clanking against armor. Reno blocks a kick and grabs hold of Vector's leg. He twirls it around in a circle and heaves him in the air. Vector summersaults in the air and lands gracefully on the far edge of the stage. The crowd roars.

"Try this one on for size!" Reno yells. He throws one hammer at him like a hatchet. The hammer goes scorching through the air. Vector takes a stance and punches through the hammer with that oversized hand. The hammer crumbles with a wave of air that I feel from the side of the stage. As impressive as that was, Reno got himself distracted and pummels Vector square in the forehead, knocking Vector on his back and skids nearly falling off the stage.

"Wow, what a move," Kylie says excitedly.

The crowd cheers and Reno is bathing in the positive reaction from the crowd of misfits. Profanities and territorial slurs blast out into the stage. He gloats at his opponent as Vector gets back up. "Yeah! What now! You got nothing on me!" Reno laughs and waves his hands to the crowd.

Vector has a small dent in his helmet as he gets up and cracks his neck. "Was that a pillow?" he says in his smooth tone of voice.

Reno growls. "That dent in your head doesn't look much like a pillow!"

Vector feels out the dent, and chuckles. "Didn't feel a thing."

Reno growls, and charges him. "Oh yeah? Well, feel this!" Reno manically rushes Vector and swings with a giant roar. He dodges it easily, comes right back at Reno with a kick to the throat. Reno curses and spirals to the ground. He punches the floor. "You think you're tough?! I'll show you tough!"

The two warriors are relentless. Kicks fly, punches connect, and bodies tumble but recover quickly. The crowd roars and cheers for their favorite contestant. Each fighter is giving everything they got, neither side giving any room for error. Vector finally gets a sweet roundhouse kick to connect. Reno flops to his stomach. Vector's oversized glove turns on, changing color, creating an aura around it. He runs up and punches Reno, launching him the distance of the stage and into the crowd, crashing into an unoccupied wooden picnic table in the process. A miraculous and exhilarating feeling envelops me, and I jump out in a shout. One of the coolest things I have ever seen. Vector stands proudly in the center of the stage; the judge runs up to him and throws his hand up. The crowd goes wild, hands flailing in the air, and shouts of his name echo the festival. He walks down the stairs and takes his helmet off. He flicks his hair backwards. "Strange thing, confidence is," Vector says boldly. "The simpletons are always full of it."

Kylie looks on in fear. "That was brutal. I hope he is ok."

"That glove of his is powerful," I point out. She looks at me in curiosity. "I wonder if he didn't have it, would he be so good?"

"Even when he got hit, he barely seemed to care."

"Reno had him, but he stopped to mock him like a pompous meat head. Just like Vector said, he's a simpleton. That glove is going to be a problem. I should find out more about that."

I watch as Vector picks up one of his opponent's hammers and shows the crowd his new prize.

The next few fights went by like the first one. I send Kylie off to scout around and try to pick up some credits so we can eat. I stay back and watch the fights unfold. Several distinctive style fighters make their way to the stage and some are more impressive than the next. A small boy named Needle destroyed an overpowering brute while another massive sized brute dressed up as an Old Earth spartan clobbered his feeble foe and threw him off the stage in a matter of forty five seconds. Skip called them up, the judge began the fight, and a victor was named. I made small notes of each one. Each winner has a weakness, each winner can be beaten. Vector impressed me the most with his glowing sonic wave fist thing.

Kylie eventually returns with a huge smile on her face. "How'd it go?" I ask.

"Super easy. I was able to grab around thirty credits from around the bar and this guy even gave me some."

"Let me get this straight. A guy from Levi, Harmony, handed you money? Like, from his hand? Out of the kindness of his heart?"

"Strange, right? I thought so too. I thought he was going to take it away like a cruel game, but he let go and didn't freak out."

"What does he look like?" I ask. "You got to be careful with being—"

The announcer comes back on the loudspeaker and interrupts our conversation. *"Ok, folks, we have an interesting new competitor coming up on this next fight."* He chuckles. *"Let's see what he is made of. Everyone please welcome to the stage, Scrap!"*

18

Begin!

My heart races with anticipation as my name is called. Bile bubbles up my throat and I have to force it down as I stand up and put my helmet on. Kylie took a rusted old fashion starball helmet and welded a piece of scrap metal to guard my face. It obscures my vision slightly but for the most part, it'll work. I get booed as I make my way through the gang bangers, and civilians looking for cheap entertainment. People start to laugh as gestures and jokes fly through the crowd like rotten tomatoes being thrown at a horrible comedian. I walk three steps up to an enormous platform. Elevated from the floor, a stage where bands usually play during music festivals was repurposed into a fighting ring. The only thing holding the crowd back from storming the stage is a dinky railing and Bone Breaker security guards surrounding the stage. The floor is solid concrete, so falling on this is going to hurt. Got to be light on my feet and stay focused. Camera drones hover around trying to get the perfect angle. Kylie stands on my side off stage, she seems to be the only one rooting for me.

Skip clears his throat. *"And now, for his opponent, the man we have all been waiting for. Get ready, folks! Please welcome to the stage, our protector, our hero of the streets, the man who you've all traveled to see! Let me hear you folks, for the three time Tournament of Titans winner, The Head Skull of the mighty Bone Breakers, the man, the myth, the legend! Brett, The Mean Machine, Breaker!"*

"Mean Machine, Mean Machine, Mean Machine!" the crowd erupts in a chant.

"We love you, Brett!" Courtney screams from his side along with other surrounding Bone Breakers. She shakes her body and swings her sign around as he walks up to the stage waving his hands in the air. He has a white cracked skull helmet with horns protruding out of it. He wears a black protective chest plate with red trim around it, a cracked skull wearing a crown with "Mean Machine" labeled on his chest, black padded legs like a starball player would have, and khaki work boots. A long shafted sledgehammer is holstered on his back. He doesn't have the same gloves Vector had but they are plated like something of the sort. He walks over to his side and faces me with a sinister stare, like a hound looking to pounce on his fresh meal of the day. His thick brown goatee covers his mouth as Mean Machine takes off his helmet. His long brown hair falls to his broad armored shoulders as he smiles cynically at me.

"Before we begin, Jeffery, I have something to say." He turns to the crowd. "Ladies and gentleman, may I have your attention for a moment. I just want to thank everyone for showing up today. Waking up as the Head Skull of Bone Breakers every day is a blessing from the saints themselves, and the fights today have been amazing to watch so far. So much talent is wasted in Harmony when each and every one of these contestants here today should have the same chance to enter the Proving as I do. However, the world doesn't work like that and there is only one invitation. That is why I promise that after I win this tournament, for the fourth time in a row, I will solemnly swear that I will rise the ranks and be the greatest titan ever. The Bone Breakers will reign, and Harmony's honor will be restored!" The crowd cheers in a riot. Hopsguzzer cans, food, drinks, everything goes flying in the crowd. Absolute pandemonium ensues until Mean Machine gestures the crowd to quiet down.

"Now, let's get down to business. As you were, Jeffrey."

The judge nods to Mean Machine and brings us towards the center of the stage. "We appreciate everything to do here, Mean Machine. Thank you for all you do for us."

"The pleasure is mine," he replies. His breath smells like old burners. Ugh.

"Do any of you have any questions before we begin?"

"Yeah, what am I supposed to take from this... whatever you are? I might have misspoken when I said everyone deserves a chance at the Proving." He bellows out a laugh that contagiously travels through the crowd until everybody in the crowd is laughing.

Saints, this is so embarrassing, why did I say yes to this... Snap out of it, Carson. Say something.

"You can take one of my breath mints."

"So you admit defeat already?" He bellows again and the crowd joins in.

My blood starts to boil, he's just trying to get under my skin, and it's working. "I'd be more worried about keeping your promises. You talk a big game, I hope you don't disappoint anyone."

"I've never disappointed anyone in my entire life!" Mean Machine yells.

"Then best of luck." I put out my hand in good faith for a handshake. My mother always told me that even in the worst of times, you must choose to be the better man, no matter what the case is.

Mean Machine back slaps my hand out of the way. "Get that disgusting thing out of my sight, you disgusting pile of dung," he snaps.

The crowd enjoys the comedy show on the stage as they continue to laugh and scream words that I've never heard of before and demanding I get off the stage and for Mean Machine to pound my face into the ground.

The slap hurt. My hand throbs already and the fight hasn't even started. His gauntlets are like cinder blocks. Holy saints, my hand is throbbing!

Harmony definitely missed a meeting in culture when it was founded. The people here are such savages. No one will even bat an eye to this guy if he wins. Alannah is class, proficient, and flawless. As soon as anyone hears this guy's raspy voice, they'll turn tail and humiliate him. He's no man of worth, he's just a guy with a big mouth. I guess whoever yells the loudest is the one who people listen to, especially here.

Unlike most fights I have watched here, I am going to hold my ground in the beginning. No sense in using all my energy in the first seconds of the fight. I'll wear him down, find his reach, and try to get him when he's catching his breath. Hopefully I can tire him out, but he's a three-time winner here. There's a good chance I'll run out of energy before that.

The judge raises his hand. "Ready." His arms drop. "Begin!"

"Get ready, cause here I come!" Mean Machine roars like a wolleybear and rushes me. I put my hands up and try to anticipate what he is going to do. Before I can think out the situation, his fist flies and connects with my face. I'm bulleted off my feet. My head smacks against the floor and skids across the stage. My vision blurs. I look up and see him standing with his hands on his hips laughing. The crowd roars his name.

112

"This isn't the playground anymore, my man. You're in Mean Machine's house now!" he bellows out another confident laugh. "I've won this tournament three years and counting. I am an elite warrior, destined for greatness. I am in a league of which you will never be a part of, a league of my own. I am the *only* one—"

"Yeah, you're a tool, I get it," I say regaining my feet. The battery is still holding strong, nothing tampered. I get into a fighter's stance, legs a little more than shoulder width apart with my hands up, knees a little bent, and eyes on the prize, just like mom taught me.

Mean Machine bellows. "Hah! A tool of destruction is more like it."

"We'll see about that." I run up and take a swing and strike only air. I swing again trying to do something, but he is quick. He smacks my hand out of the way, side steps, grabs the back of my head, and spikes my skull into the ground like a starball player scoring a pylonbreak. My face meets the stone stage and my legs scorpion up. The crowd starts hysterically laughing.

Mean Machine bellows yet again. "Are we done yet, Mr. Official?"

"Wow, what a waste!" I hear from the crowd.

"Who let this guy in?" another voice says.

"I told you he'd hex you up! I told you!" Bonez screams from the side. "Finish him, Mean Machine!"

Mean Machine's name is chanted again. Anger and adrenaline start to mix in my blood. I will not be embarrassed like this, not by him, not by Bonez, not by anyone! I peak over to his side and see Courtney holding her sides laughing hard with her group.

The judge appears in my sight. "Hey, you good? You gave it your best shot. I'm calling the fight."

"NO!" I shout trying to catch my breath as I struggle myself back to my knees. "I am not done!" The bars on my helmet are crushing my forehead, I can't use this anymore. I rip it off and throw it off the stage in aggravation.

"Holy saints, you're just a youngling," Mean Machine says.

"I'm *not* a youngling! I have been through more than you have ever gone through," I say panting. "You think you're some… elite warrior… you're just a…" I can't catch my breath fast enough to talk.

"Please, kid, catch your breath first," he mocks me.

I take a deep breath. "How about you catch this!" I pull out my pipe and swing, he catches it mid swing and pummels my side. I hear the sound of metal giving way, and a bone crack. I desperately step back from another swing for my head. I start to panic and hyperventilate. Every time I breath in the pain gets worse, but I can't give up. I gave up everything to be here. All my money, my job, my self-worth. Not like this. I pick my head up and see him looking right at me with his hands on his hips.

"Gotta say, kid, you got heart, but heart isn't gonna save you now. Quit while you still have some dignity."

"I will never quit! I can't!" Fire ignites in my heart, teeth clenched, face exposed, but he's not hitting me again. I click my heels. Time to go on the offence.

I take a two-step wind up, cock back, fake left, pivot my body and push my opponent with my anti-gravity boots in his stomach. He doesn't see it coming and falters backwards. Here's my chance, I unleash a fury of haymakers, swinging manically, gaining ground on every swing. He bobs and weaves through them and tries to swing back but I dash out of the way and finally clip him with one in the chin. He feels it. I lunge forward and jab my pipe into his side and swing for his head. He dips under it and retreats back to his corner.

The crowd is astonished. Gasps come from a few spots in the stands.

Mean Machine laughs. "You got guts, kid. Not enough though." He reaches behind him and reveals his massive sledgehammer. "I call this bad boy my Skull Splitter. It's made of pure steel. Perfect for crushing runts like you!"

He roars and charges me, swinging his hammer fiercely aiming for my exposed head. He's intentionally trying to kill me. I duck and dodge, fearing for my life, blow after blow I weave through and dip under his swings. I duck under the next swing, spin around and connect with his side. He surprises me with a swing for my leg, I jump. Not realizing the height I can jump in these boots, it exposes me as I defenselessly descend. He smiles, winds back and times his swing perfect for my landing. I land and lean backwards just in time for the hammer to skim the tip of my nose. I dash backwards, land, and shoot upwards to land a flying kick square in his helmet.

"Ooh," the crowd goes.

Mean Machine grunts and has to catch himself.

He growls angrily, "How dare you think you stand a chance against me. I am the Head Skull of the biggest gang in Harmony! No one can trump me, and I will not be beaten by a mere child!" Mean Machine screams like a savage animal and tries an overhead strike. I dodge it easily, dashing around his swings more fluently than before. His swing cracks the stage, fracturing it as I sweep to his side with my Turbo boots and lay wreckage into his kidney with multiple full swings of my pipe, then finish with a swift kick to the back of his knee. He drops to a knee and growls. "Saintdamn it!"

He swings wildly and I have to dash backwards. He rushes forward with rage filled attacks that have slowed down dramatically. Technique is fading as he pants after every swing of his hammer, missing more and more embarrassingly every time. "Get over here!" He swings once more, a lot slower and sloppier than the last. I easily evade him, lunge to his side, and shoot my Turbo Boot in his inner knee. The force alone inverts his knee along with the momentum of his swing. He topples over himself and I swing my pipe into his face as he falls. Connecting beautifully, he spirals backwards and his back hits the stage floor. The crowd is pitch silent. Kylie is screaming her head off as the judge rushes over to Mean Machine's side. Dazed and confused, he pushes the judge out the way and quickly wobbles to his feet.

Just before he gains his footing I run up and grab hold of the horns on his helmet pull down as my knee collides into his face. My knee plate, made of the corner of a car bumper, indents his helmet. His helmet flies off him as he ragdolls backwards and bashes the back of his head against the stage. The sound of the helmet clanking off the stage is the only noise in the entire park. The judge panics and rushes back to Mean Machine's side and calls the fight. Courtney and the small group of Bone Breakers jump on the stage and circle their inglorious leader.

I sheath my pipe and lift my arms in victory. The judge moves over to me and raises my hand declaring me the winner. My celebration is short lived as he lets go and orders the paramedics to the stage. The crowd is unfathomably quiet. I just defeated everyone's favorite, the Head Skull of the Bone Breakers. I hear Kylie cheering and screaming my stage name. That brings a smile to my face, she is the only fan I need.

My newly defeated foe sits up with the help of his companions. Wearily and dazed from battle, his nose gushes blood down his face. A massive bruise covers the lower part of his face and a swelling black eye forms in his right eye.

The judge gets in my ear. "Choose your prize quickly. He needs immediate medical attention and needs to get to the hospital."

"Oh, right! Um…" I liked his helmet but I kind of ruined that. "I choose his chest plate."

Mean Machine hears me and perks up. "What? No! This is my identity! You can't take my chest plate! I'm Head Skull of the Bone Breakers, one of its founding members. You can't take this from me!"

I start to reconsider the helmet and think we can just try to fix it before my next battle. Before I had another moment to think, one of the paramedics pulls out a stim and shoots it in the man's neck. He grunts in agony and falls back on the floor unconscious. Without another word, a group of bulky, sleeveless jacketed men with "MEDIC" stickered on their back escort him off the stage on a self-loading gurney.

"Unfortunately, he is correct. That would be very unwise of you to take that. You can, but I advise you to consider the repercussions of it," the judge says.

"Ok, yeah. You're right. Um," I look at my snow gloves with glued on pieces of metal on it. "give me those gauntlets instead. Those things nearly broke my hand when he slapped my hand away."

"Splendid choice, sir. I don't see any problems with that. Go see the medical team, they'll examine you and clear you for the next round," the judge says as he strips the gauntlets off the unconscious man and tosses them to me. The weight of them both catch me by surprise but once I slide them on and feel the weight of them mold to my hands, I feel exhilarated.

"You did it," Kylie loudly whispers as we walk down the stairs off the stage.

She collides into me with a hug. I embrace the love and feel a huge weight fall off my shoulders. The anxiety, the fear of losing, the amount of pressure that has bestowed upon me has lifted. For now, I can relax. I watch Courtney and her group of spikey haired friends pile into the medical tent where Mean Machine is being escorted into. They argue and yell at the paramedics, throwing threats out at them like a child would throw popkernels at animals in a petting zoo. They advise the group of worried Bone Breakers that they need to examine him before they can clear him to leave. With that, they all turn their attention to me.

"You'll regret this, kid! I swear it, with every bit of my being, you will regret this!" the man named Blitzkrieg threatens me.

I try and keep my calm. Confidence is still flowing, and I'm in a battlesuit. While I'm in this, no one will dare take their shot at me. "What was I supposed to do?"

"Shut up! Don't you dare speak another word. You ruined us!" another says. They scream and yell at me but hold their ground, creating a barrier between Kylie, me, and them. I hold Kylie behind me and hold on to my pipe just in case they come at me.

"Listen, listen." I put my hand out and try to deescalate. "I had to do what I had to do."

"Hex you! Go jump off a cliff and die, you scum!" another one says.

Out of the pile of angry looking men, Courtney spouts out of them and we lock eyes. All distractions leave my mind and I enter a tunnel vison of just me and her. Her perfect wavy blonde hair actually goes well with the pink underneath. Her hair is loose and her tightly worn Mean Machine shirt is ripped in the collar, so her shoulder is exposed. She's as beautiful as she ever was.

"Hi," I say softly to her.

"Hex off! she sneers.

Blitzkrieg rushes me and tries to push me but in my suit he can't even nudge me. "You think you're some tough hex or something? You're not! You got lucky! Just wait till you lose, you're Bone Breaker bait as soon as you walk out those doors. You hear me?! You're done! Finished!"

Courtney and three others have to restrain him and pull him back.

"Ey, yo, Pinky! Get away from that trash can!" Bonez shouts. He walks by from behind me. "You better watch yourself, Scrap! If you think you're getting out of this freely, you're wrong. I told you not to talk to my girls."

"Woah, she came up to me, man."

"Shut up! You do not speak here. Say another word and you will regret it!"

"Shut up, Bonez," Courtney snaps. Bonez looks at her weird. "As long as he is competing in this tournament," She rolls her eyes. "he has immunity. No matter who or what he did. He didn't break any rules, so—"

I laugh, and interrupt Courtney. "Tell me something, Bonez, what did happen to your nose? I heard some little kid did that to you." His face softens and the realization unfolds. He realizes the little kid that broke him nose a year ago has grown up. "I'm talking to Courtney. Mind your hexing business."

"Yo, Bonez, you just gonna take that from this kid?" Blitzkrieg charges back in. "Don't let him disrespect us like that. Hex the rules, let's hex this guy up! He won't be able to take all of us."

I clench my pipe and push Kylie behind me.

"Carson, no," Kylie finally steps in. "Stop causing drama," Kylie says pulling me away from the situation and turns to the group. "Sorry everyone. I'll keep this juvenile under control. We don't have to resort to unprecedented measures. We're all here for the same reasons. Let's just be civilized, that's what Mean Machine wanted, yes?"

Bonez looks at her and looks back at me. Then to his group and back to us. Without a Head Skull, these guys have no idea what to do, no leader to tell them what to do. Courtney scoots in front of Bonez. "She's right. Let's get out of here. Brett would want all of us by his side. Let's go."

Bonez and Blitzkrieg sneer at her but eventually settle. "Lead the way." Bonez says.

All but Blitzkrieg obeys. He stands his ground with clenched fists. His eyes twitch with anticipation. His clenched teeth show in the corner of his mouth. An internal battle of loyalty and chaos argue in his head. He wants action, but deep down inside, he knows he can't take me alone. "You'll regret this, Scrap. I swear to the almighty saints, you, will, regret this." He turns around and storms off after the rest of the Bone Breakers.

19

Jinx

After Mean Machine was finished getting examined and the gang cleared out, I made my way into the tent. The paramedics told me he's being transported to the local clinic with a mild concussion. I gaze at Courtney hoping she would give me the attention I desire but she never looks my way. Maybe she was distracted by her friends or maybe she just wants nothing to do with me. The adrenaline finally wore off and an aggressive pain finds a home in my side. After being examined by the medical team, they tell me I broke a rib. The examiner walks me through some breathing exercises and recommends that I should quit the tournament for health reasons, but we all know I can't quit. They asked if I wanted a stim but I can't get myself to do it. Thinking about Anderson, how he looked on pain stims, worries me. I don't want to end up like him, addicted to that crap.

"I'm good, sir. I don't need it," I say regretfully.

The five o'clock shadowed medic looks at me crooked. He holds an orange dispenser with a small needle pointed out the end. "Uh, you sure? The pains gonna be really bad for the next few weeks, kid."

"A few weeks?" I question coughing from the lack of oxygen. "I hada friend who was dangerously addicted to that crap. I don't want to be like him." I can barely get out a full sentence without an agonizing pain slipping around my body, squeezing my chest feeling like I'm suffocating. "Is there anything else?"

119

"Kid, you're not going to get addicted. I'll tell you what." He puts the pain stim away and reaches into his bag of assorted medical supplies. He opens it and it is filled with several orange tubes, all labeled long medical words, probably all meaning some other kind of treatment. He fingers around the labels and decides on one. "This is a numbing agent. It'll help with the pain, but it won't last long, but it'll get you through your next fight though." I let him pin me in the fist sized bruise growing on my side. The pain dissolves in a matter of a minute. I still find trouble taking in deep breaths, but it becomes more comfortable to deal with and walk around. They wrapped my torso up in a bandage wrap, something with some padding on it to help with contact. He hands the stim to my sister. "There's three doses in here, use them scarcely." They send me on my way.

I focus on relaxing before I have to endure another fight. This scares me now, creating more doubt in my head than I had before. It's difficult to breath correctly. I've never experienced anything like this before, which worries me even more. With my mind spinning in a thousand directions, I relieve myself of my suit and plop ~~myself~~ on the grass where I can soak in the mid-morning sun and try to find some kind of tranquility.

"You like the boots?" Kylie asks.

"Yeah, they're great." I say trying to act happier than I feel. "Did you see how much distance I got?" I pick them up and the heels click. They activate and fly out of my grip and crash into the souvenir stand in front of me, making a loud noise and causing an arousing amount of unneeded attention. My face blushes and I try to laugh it off while I run through the mud in my socks ~~on~~ to retrieve the boots. Luckily, I didn't create any damage, the last thing I need is to be paying for repairs on someone's stall.

"You're lucky you didn't break a window, Carson," an unknown voice comes from behind me.

I huff, thinking I'm in some major trouble. "Yeah. I'm so sorry for that I—"

"I have to say, I was impressed with you, kiddo." I look up at a man who has blue eyes, with short brown hair and a darker, tannish complexion. By no means Daltonese but who knows nowadays, Daltonese citizens have come and left Harmony for generations. Definitely not what Harmonians normally look like, however, most Harmonians have fairer skin. "Mean Machine has never lost in the first round before," he continues in a chuckle with his hands folded. "Quite honestly, he's the reason why I drove all the way out here. You have just made my job a whole lot harder."

Confusion wraps around my head. "Thanks, and uh, don't call me kiddo, sir."

The man stumbles on his words like he was caught off guard. "I, um, ok. I'm…You're Carson Paul, right? And this must be your sister, Kylie?" His voice, his mannerisms, proper speech, he's definitely not from South Harmony.

"What are you some kind of stalker? How do you know me? What are you some pervert? Because listen here, I—"

The man sticks his hands out in a defensive way. "I know your father," the man says.

"You…" I look over at Kylie and we share the same shocked expression. "Yeah, well a lot of people know of him apparently. He was… he was special, you know?"

"He is."

"Was."

"Is."

"My dad is hexing dead, sir. Now if you don't mind, I'd like to relax before my next fight."

"Carson…" Kylie hisses at me softly.

The man nods and smirks like he doesn't believe me. "Right. Well, my name is Jinx. Do you need any help with your, uh… suit?"

"What makes you think I need help from you?"

"You need a helmet, don't you? How about food, you guys hungry? Does your sister need more money? I can always spare a few more credits if you're hungry" I see him reach into his pockets.

"No!" I snap. "I have a spare."

The man laughs. "Right. Well, if it looks anything like that other one, you'll be dead in the next round."

Having absolutely nothing more to say to this Jinx fellow, I try to end this awkward encounter as fast as I can. "Sir, I don't know who you think you are walking up to me to tell me things like that, but you need to back the hell up. Keep your hexing helmet and mind your saintdamn business."

He hums. "No, no, that won't do." He pulls out a wad of big credit bills and swipes through them. "How about this instead, I'll give you *my* spare helmet, and we will call this awkward encounter a productive one. Ok?" He smiles and hands me a few bills. I refuse to take them. He tries to stuff them in my shirt, but I swipe it away from me.

"We don't need your money, sir."

He clicks his tongue and pockets his money. "Wait here, I'll be right back." He walks away, leaving Kylie and me in an extremely questionable situation.

"How much was he trying to give you?"

Regret fills my head. "I don't know, but I saw a hundred in there."

I don't wait for Jinx. He rubbed me the wrong way. It's hard to trust anyone now a days, especially ones coming up to you with your shoes off. I felt so defenseless. if he wanted to hurt me or Kylie he could have. He didn't seem the threatening type, especially handing me massive amounts of credits. For all I know, these bills could be fake. I don't know who this guy is or where he gets his money from. With the last few credits Kylie scrounged up, I set my sights on what I can afford for breakfast. Most places charge and arm and a leg for the smallest of things. Twelve credits for a burger, nine for meatball sandwich.

A boy runs up to me holding a small pipe. "Hey, you're Scrap, right?" I look down and see him. He looks like me when I was young, long brown hair, brown eyes, dirty white tank top, and ripped up jeans.

"Yeah?" I say and I take a small step back and ready myself for any sneak attacks. "How are you?" I say defensively.

"I'm good," he answers harmlessly. "Can you sign my pipe?" he holds a dirt covered rusty pipe out for me and a marker. It looks like he just found it in a garbage can. Ironic, because that's where I found mine.

My eyes light up in excitement, but I try and stay modest. "Of course." I write out "SCRAP" in my best script writing, but I always forgot how to write S's. and hand it back to him.

"Thank you so much, Scrap. You were so awesome in your fight," the boy says. He runs back to the group of little boys and they praise the young boy in a jealous fit.

The festivities are in full swing as the quarter finals begin with its first battle. The announcer comes on the loudspeaker. "Let us get this thing underway with our first quarter finals battle. Please come to the stage, Vector, and King Chris! The combatants make their way to the stage. I clap as Vector walks on. I'm rooting for him. But King Chris looks monstrous. His suit looks like an ancient spartan warrior you see in history books. He's well equipped with dense bronze armor. The man's enormous, exposed arms pulse up and veins shoot out like lightning as he roars and smashing the stage with his fists as the battle begins.

As the quarter finals begin, I remain vigilant going from food stand to food stand trying to find something I can afford.

"You hungry, kiddo?"

I cringe to the sound of that word. Kiddo, my parent's favorite name to call me. It haunts me now, hearing it makes me think of them. My dad said it to me the night they died. *"We'll play tomorrow, kiddo. I promise."* It makes me angry, enraged even. Another broken promise to add to the book of hundreds he had made over the years. I always resented him for it, but every time he promised me something, I believed it, like a good son should. I find that man Jinx behind me holding up two styrofoam boxes, but no helmet in sight, yet another broken promise, I'm sure.

"Yo, stop calling me that," I snap at him, but my nose betrays me as I smell the savory aroma of freshly cooked bacon. My mouth begins to salivate. "What do you want?"

He gestures the food to me, basically pushing the boxes into my hands. "Eat up, kid—, Carson. Sorry, I call my son that all the time, it's quite the habit."

"Well, I ain't your kid, mister. Why are you doing this?"

"I just thought I'd help you out. You two seemed alone over there and Kylie looked homeless picking change out of people pockets so I wanted to help."

Ugh, Kylie. I roll my eyes to it, thankfully he's not threatening to get us kicked out. "We're fine. Thanks." I open the boxes and my mouth starts to drool. Freshly scrambled eggs and six pieces of bacon. Holy saints it's been so long since I had bacon. I reward him my attention. "How do you know my dad is still alive?"

"Who told you your parents were dead?"

"Fox Legion. In particularly, a soldier named Omega Robbins. Him and another delta raided my house and told me it wasn't my house anymore. They took me to an orphanage and—" I realize I am getting way too personal with a stranger.

Jinx's eyes flashed at the sound of the name. "So, you *are* living at the orphanage?"

"How do you know my parents?" I quickly change topics.

He hesitates. "Win this tournament and I will tell you everything you need to know. Let's just say I know a thing or two about the Proving too."

"What are you, a scout or something?"

"Something like that. Go give some food to your sister. I dropped off your new helmet too. Damn girl nearly took my head off with that pipe of yours. I hope it works out for you. I'll be rooting for you," he says and walks away.

Just as I turn and walk back to Kylie, a flash of armor rumbles in front of me and crashes into the wooden fence surrounding the festival. I jump back, nearly dropping my food and find Vector unconscious in the wreckage. The crowd erupts in a frenzy. I turn and see the judge hold up King Chris's hand with Vectors glove device in his hand. Holy saints, what did I miss?

"Wow, what a stunning finish! King Chris is moving on to the semifinals!" the announcer shouts.

20

Scrap up one more

"*Ladies and gentlemen, is there any contestant out here that can match that kind of intensity?!*" the announcer demands. "*Let us find out right now! Amphibicus and the junk yard warrior himself, Scrap! Your time is now!*"

I take one more look at Kylie before I walk up the steps. Going over everything, making sure everything is tight and in place. This new helmet is amazing. Comfortable cushions inside squeeze my head like earmuffs. A shaded visor covers my entire face, giving me a full range of vison. There's also a target scanning system inside I've been toying with. If a marked target runs or flies off my visor, a beeping noise goes off in my ears, and a light point in the direction depending on where the target is. The capabilities of this thing feel endless. I walk on stage feeling like a real fighter now. My confidence is through the roof, but I can't be too confident. I haven't won anything yet.

"Hex you, Scrap!" I hear from the crowd. "Go home! No one wants you here!" Boos erupt from the crowd. A chant begins slowly but becomes a crowd sized chant in seconds. "No one likes you!" *Clap, clap, clap-clap-clap.* "No one likes you!" *Clap, clap, clap-clap-clap* "No one likes you!"

I drown out the noises as well as I can. I find their chants comical. I didn't come here to be liked, I came here to win. I accept the villain role after beating the former champion in the first round. The momentum has changed, I do not fear anymore, I have the upper hand. Although, that numbing serum is wearing off, so I got to end this quick, no toying around.

My opponent, Amphibicus, wears a sleek padded helmet completely covering his face. He wears camouflaged padding and reinforced hydraulic leg casings wrap his legs. I have to be conscious of that. In his first fight he did a fair amount of jumping and kicking so if I hurt even one of his legs, his game plan will crumble.

The judge brings us to the center. "Welcome back, gentlemen." He goes over the rules and asks if we have any questions.

Amphibicus instantly points out the new helmet. "Yeah. Where in the saint's holy underworld did you get that?" his voice is deep, really deep, like he has a voice dampener in his mask. "You didn't have that in your last fight."

"I bought it," I lie.

"Right. So, you can magically buy a military grade A1X5 carbon nanotube Titan helmet. Yet, you still have a stop sign on your chest?" he argues. "Judge, this is cheating. He obviously stole it. He should be investigated for—"

"I bought it," a voice interrupts my opponent from behind me. I turn around and see Jinx next to my sister with his arms folded. "He's my student. There's no rules implying the use of outside help, or the retaining of new equipment." He turns around and opens his arms. "What are all these overpriced armor stalls for?!"

"He is right, Amphibicus. It's fair play," the judge states.

I smirk and give him my hand to shake. "Good luck. Love your suit by the way," I tell him. Both Amphibicus and the judge look at me in complete confusion. I guess it is not every day that someone comes to one of these things and is a good sport about it.

Amphibicus smirks and smacks my hand like a high five. "You smell like sewage," he says and turns around to walk back to his side. I back step to my side where my new apparent coach, Jinx, and my sister await me.

"Did you really just try and shake his hand?" Jinx asks surprising me with his presence.

"Yeah, why not?" I ask him.

He snorts to himself and shakes his head. "You are something else."

"Gentlemen, are you ready?" the judge announces, he looks at me, then Amphibicus. "Begin!"

Amphibicus launches in the air by the power of his hydraulic legs. I snap my head up in amazement, but instantly petrified by the sheer power he excels. With the help of my new helmet, the scanner in it locks on to my opponent and beeps when he jumps out of my field of vision. I find him easily and evade his downward strike. His spiked knuckles impale the stage. I get behind him and cup my hands over his face and pull his head backwards. He hits the stage and I swing my pipe into him with an overhead strike. I nearly connect before he was able to roll out of the way and propel himself back to his side.

The crowd chants for more from Amphibicus as he readies himself, with the crowd on his side. He jumps again, just like before, in the sun. He must have rocket boosters or some kind of shock system in his light armor being able to jump so high. My helmet targets him easily shading the sun rays out of my sight. I read his trajectory perfectly, completely throwing him off of his strategy. I glide backwards leaving plenty of room for him to land. He lands and instantly takes off again, soaring horizontally towards me. My helmet beeps louder and rapidly as he quickly approaches me. He headbutts me violently, knocking me off my feet.

"What are you doing, Scrap!?" I hear faintly through the ringing in my ears.

Amphibicus jumps on top of me. Quick, and unavoidable combinations collide into me. I can't catch any of his strikes, my timing is off, none of my attempts to block him stick. Finally, I push him off me but get kicked in my face as I roll out of his reach. The crowd cheers and roars as Amphibicus jumps in the air once more. I quickly find my wits and a small, jagged crack runs down in front of my left eye. My helmet quickly targets him coming towards me. I stick my pipe up in the air and block his strike coming down at me. I get pushed back but I stay grounded. Amphibicus continues his onslaught, swinging hard and fast, coming from all directions.

"That fancy helmet won't save you, Scrap," he says.

"Who said I need saving?" I weave around a haymaker and drive my foot into his side, activating my boot and forcing him backwards. He topples over and nearly falls out of bounds.

"What are those things?" Amphibicus asks in his deep altered voice.

"Turbo Boots," I answer catching my breath.

He smirks. "Oh, did daddy buy them for you too?"

"He's not my father."

"Whatever. All I know is I know what I'm getting when this is over."

The fight continues longer than anticipated. His agility is astounding, and he's in much better shape than Mean Machine. We exchange punches, dodging and weaving through blows like a full-blown kick boxing match. I finally hit him after he ducks under a left hook. I pivot my body around his counterattack and hit him in the shoulder with the back of my fist, a perfect hit on a lightly armored body part from my new gauntlets. He wobbles to the side holding a dislocated shoulder. A powerful force collides in my stomach. His reinforced knee slams into my temple and another solid mass crashes into my face one more time and I fall. He rushes me to get on top of me again so I quickly try and kick his knee backwards as I did Mean Machine but he's too fast and strikes my jaw before I'm able to sneak into his chest and blast him back with the Turbo Boot.

I got to think fast. My broken rib is screaming for me to stop. It cries wondering why I still fight. I ignore the aching sensation and try to control my breathing as I find my feet once more. What is something he won't expect? I can't beat him with speed, I can't wear him down, so I need to do something he won't expect and hit hard when he exposes himself.

"You look tired, Scrap. It's a shame that your daddy spent all that money on that helmet only to lose it to me," he laughs.

"He's not my dad you—" Ugh... can't yell. Control yourself. Breathing hurts, the soreness becoming uncomfortable is an understatement. This is truly the worst pain I've ever experienced. I cough up blood and my leg uncontrollably gives out, and my knee hits the stage.

"Scrap, no! Get up!" I hear Kylie. Cheers for my demise begin once again.

The judge rushes to me, but I force myself up. "Don't you even try and call this fight," I say straight to his face.

He backs off. "That's one. If you can't keep yourself up, I'm calling the fight."

"Oh, just call it, judge. He's obviously had enough," Amphibicus says.

"If he can stand, he can fight," the judge argues.

"Then let's make sure he won't get back up this time." He pops his shoulder back into place. Panic dives deep into my gut. I can hardly breath, the pain in my chest is excruciating. just keeping myself up is a chore. "This is the end, Scrap." He rushes me, I can hardly move. My helmet starts beeping louder and faster as he approaches. "Tell Mean Machine I said thanks for giving me such an easy win." He winds up and swings but misses. I duck and pivot around him. I pull out my pipe and swing wildly, a new wave of energy immerses me. I clash into his exposed back then once more in the temple before he can turn around. He spirals and falls to a knee. I wind up and shatter his kneecap before he can get his balance. The sound of tyketanium to bone rattles the tournament as everyone in the crowd voices the unfathomable carnage. He screams and tumbles holding his knee in absolute agony.

The judge pushes me away. "Stop! STOP!" he yells, waving off the fight. The judge throws my hand in the air, declaring me the winner. I wake up from the blinding rage that came over me. I stare out into the crowd, there are hundreds of people staring back at me. All of them wanting me to lose but bad news for them, it's going to take a lot more to take me out.

I can't help but make eye contact with my unlikely opponent as he comes to. The medical team runs into the stage and rips his helmet off him to check his head. It's a boy, not a man, but a boy, not a hair on his face to be seen. His mangled leg looks horrifyingly painful. There's no way he's going to be able to walk for months because of me. Dread and sorrow fill my stomach to imagine if I suffered his fate. In my circumstances, Kylie and I would struggle for months to recover the time we would lose. I'd have to relearn how to walk, or worse. I rip out of the judges grasp and grab on to Amphibicus' wrist. I pull him up and over my shoulder and help the medical team escort him over to the medical tent.

He squirms and tries to get me to let go. "What are you doing? Get off me." He struggles out of my grasp and tries to walk on his own, but it is no use. He falls again and growls in pain.

"Let me help you. It's the least I can do," I plead to him. I get him back up over my shoulder and bring him down the stairs. I set him down in the medical tent just off the side of the stage where they can examine him thoroughly.

"You didn't have to do that," he mumbles.

I stare at the crooked mess I made of his leg. Three welts puff up on his head, his dirty blonde hair covers them, but they are noticeable.

Sweat drips down the young boy's face. I'm unable to take my eyes off him, he can't be older than me. I picture his future in a wheelchair, surgery after surgery, physical therapy, and the time this boy will need to recover.

"Scrap!" a voice says. I'm nudged and realize the judge was talking to me. "Pick a prize, what do you want?"

A dozen eyes watch me. I look back and forth from the judge and the boy and don't have the heart to take anything more from him. "I'm good," I tell the judge.

Amphibicus looks up at me with his astonished eyes. "No. That is not how this goes." He fixes his posture for the medical team. "What do you want?" he says in a much higher pitch voice than his helmet portrayed.

I wave him off. "I'm good. I don't want anything from you."

129

Kylie and Jinx join us in the tent. Curious about why I did what I did, I'm sure. "Carson! You were amazing!" Kylie cheers and looks at my opponent. Her face turns instantaneously seeing what I did. "Oh saints," she says terrified.

"Scrap? Are you sure? You can pick anything," the judge asks again.

"Nothing. I'm good, sir," I answer.

"What are you, a mad man?" Jinx questions. "You have to, it's the rules. You need to pick something that can help you in your next fight."

Amphibicus throws me a pair of metal stubbed knuckles. "Those are tyketanium. Stronger than those steel gauntlets you got. They're made to pierce through most armors. They're yours. Please, I don't like owing people anything."

"Is that what you want, Scrap?" the judge asks.

I feel guilty taking more from this kid than I have to. "I really don't think—"

"They're perfect," Jinx butts in. He turns my shoulders and walks me out of the tent.

I watch from behind me as the medic takes hold of the broken knee and snaps it back into place, the noise of bones popping makes me cringe. He screams in agony, but the deed is done. My conscience will forever be tarnished knowing I destroyed that young boy's future.

The judge grabs my attention as I walk out of the tent. "Scrap, I just have to say, I've never seen anyone like you before. In all my years, I haven't seen such sportsmanship. Harmony has been known for well," he hesitates. "well, scum. They don't care for anyone but themselves. But you, you're something different, kid. I can tell you're special. Are you even from Harmony?"

"Redding, yeah."

"Far from home, huh? So am I. I'm from Willowsburg." I nod, not really knowing how to relate to him. "I'm rooting for you, kid," he adds. "You would make a fine titan one day if Alannah actually accepted us."

I smile at my new fan. "That's the idea, sir."

130

21
Pablo

Hundreds of people have flocked to Levi to witness the Tournament of Titans, all to watch Levi's best fighters go at it to see who deserves a chance of a lifetime. Although, from the looks of it, I could be our only hope, yet another reason why I can't lose this tournament.

One fight remains until the final four contestants are announced. One that stands out from the last two fights is a man named Leaf. Cursed by his short stature but has rigorous discipline in his fighting skills. He wears a basic set of armor but has what is called a Forcefield, a shield of some kind that surrounds the wearer and deflects objects from hitting them. Leaf has shown insanely successful tactics in his fights, knocking a wildly overpowered opponent off the stage without even swinging his spear, just from the shear recoil of the Forcefield.

While we wait through the intermission, Jinx hasn't left our side. I decide to trust the man for the time being. He has done nothing but good since he has shown up. He's fed Kylie and me, and he was right about the helmet. I would not have been able to track Amphibicus as well as I did with a spare helmet. We seclude ourselves to the corner where we made camp and I relieve myself of my suit for the little time that I have.

With some fresh air to clear my mind for a moment, I find myself pondering an obvious question. "So, why are you helping me so much, Jinx? What are you possibly getting out of this?"

Jinx looks at me curiously sipping on a soft drink. "I told you, I just want to help. I want you to win," he continues to say his only excuse for hanging out with two kids.

131

"I understand that, but why me? Why me out of every contestant here?"

He huffs and drops his head. "Because I owe it to your father." He looks at me with concern in his eyes. "As I told you, win and I will tell you everything."

"And if I lose?"

"Then you die," he says without hesitation.

I take an eerie step back. I can't tell if he is kidding since his facial expressions hasn't changed. "Not if I kill you first," I say gripping my pipe on my back.

He starts to laugh but the awkward mood remains the same. This guy is so weird and mysterious but seems to be loaded on credits. This helmet alone must be worth hundreds.

"You either win or you die, it's a simple hypothetical metaphor," Jinx explains.

I look at Kylie, hopefully seeing her reaction in her eyes. She doesn't look scared. "He means there's no turning back."

"Precisely," Jinx says.

I let go of my pipe and put his words in the back of my head. "So, you said you know our dad? You owe him something? What did he do for you?"

"I know Christian Paul, yes."

"Is he alive?"

"He's," Jinx hesitates. "I know he's alive. Has to be."

I stand up in disbelief, an actual punch of hope strikes my heart. Finally, some hope in this entire mess. "What's that supposed to mean? Where is he?"

"He's, well... um, he's safe... kind of."

"Kind of?!" I snap.

Kylie intervenes seconds before I lose myself. "Do you know what happened to him? What about our mother? Is she with him? Is she ok?"

He hesitates again. "Unfortunately, this conversation must end, children." Jinx stands up. "I'm going to go scope out the competition. Get a look at this King Chris fellow and the rest of the competition."

He leaves us in a rush and puts our questions to rest. Jinx disappears in the crowd of people walking around the festival, leaving us in an awkward state of panic, and relief.

"Do you trust him?" I ask Kylie.

"I'm not sure, he doesn't seem like us," she says. "Why would he help us and spend money on you if he didn't have other intentions for you."

"I don't know, such a strange individual," I answer. I get up and try to push my thoughts aside. "You want dinner? I have enough money for that shishkabob thing you wanted."

Her eyes light up and agrees. I leave her to do some minor repairs to the suit, tighten some bolts and some other thing, I can't remember she wanted to do. It feels weird walking without the massive power of the exoskeleton around me, lugging around over four hundred pounds of car parts, iron, steel, and tyketanium. Feeling the air blow through my sweaty white t-shirt, drying my sweat drenched long hair that I tied up in a man bun, I stand in line watching the same man from before taking orders and laugh in his Daltonese accent. What's a Daltonese guy doing here anyway? The stench of the grill engulfs my nostrils, and my mouth slowly salivates from the familiar aroma given off from the food truck.

As the man in front of me finishes his order, I walk up to the window and I'm greeted by the Dalton native. "Ello youngling, how you doing? Looking for more free samples?" he laughs. "Where's the little lady you were with before?" The owner of the stand recognizes me from earlier in the day.

"She's tending to the suit. She's actually the one who made it," I say. "But no, no more samples. I'd like three orders of the shishkabob."

"Wonderful. That'll be thirty-six credits," he says delighted as I pull out the stolen credits Kylie swiped from a few drunkards by the bar. "You're Scrap, aren't you? You know, youngling, I wouldn't have guessed you had that kind of fighting spirit in you. You put on quite a show beating Mean Machine and the other guy with the weird name. You're the new talk of the town, you know that?"

"Yeah, I see he's a big deal around these parts," I say kindly but trying to rush my order. I'm salivating just from smelling his food while waiting in line.

"I'll get them to you right away, Sir Scrap." He turns and stops then he turns back to the window. "Say, let me make you a deal," he says in a quieter voice leaning over to me. "You think I can get an autograph? My son has been watching you from the food truck and he says you're his favorite. I'll give you a fourth one for free, how's that sound?"

I smile at the persuasive gesture. "Yeah, of course."

"Great, let me get your food. My son will be right out." I see him walk back to the grill and start cooking. "Pablo!" he screams. He mutters something else, but I can't quite understand what he says. Something about him not being scared.

While I wait on the side, I see a young boy peak his head out the side of the window. I'm guessing it is his son. "What's up, little man?" I say hoping the little boy saw me. He pulls his head back in hiding so I can't see him. Must be shy. About a few minutes later, the man returns with my food. "Did your son come out?" I ask. "I think I saw him stick his head out, but he never came out."

He looks at me with a bit of confusion and chuckles. "He didn't come out?" I shake my head with a slanted confused look. The man turns to his side. "Pablo! Get outside. Scrap is waiting for you."

"Tell him I want to meet him," I say loudly enough for the little boy to hear me.

The man laughs. "You hear that, champ?" He looks down and to his side. "Scrap wants to meet you. Go out there and give him something to sign. C'mon, go, get outta here. I gave him a free shishkabob so you can meet the guy. Go on, get!"

I hear quick little footsteps walking out of the back and a door closing. I walk to the side of the stand with my four trays and find the boy with his toy helmet and a marker. "Hi, Scrap," the little boy finally says. I put my food down on a picnic table and kneel to get eye leveled with him. He hands over his helmet and marker looking down. He must be shy.

I find a good spot on the top to sign my name. "Your name is Pablo, right?"

His head sprouts up and he nods.

I smile and look down at the helmet. I write. "Always be strong, Pablo. From Scrap." I hand it back to him. But when he grabs it, I don't let go. He looks up at me with confusion. "I want your autograph too," I tell the boy. "Can you give me your autograph?"

The boy's eyes light up and he puts on the biggest smile he can give. "Ok! I'll be right back," he says in his accent. Daltonese for sure. Most Daltonese people have relatively darker complexions like Anderson does. Poor Anderson, I wonder how he's doing. Hopefully, next time I see him, he isn't high on stims. Such a horrible habit for a young kid. The little boy runs back into the shop and comes back within seconds with a piece of a receipt. "Here you go." He hands me a receipt paper with a scribble of his name. "Thanks for being so cool, Scrap. From Pablo."

134

I can't help but smile at this childish handwriting. "Nice to meet you, Pablo. Do you want to be at titan too?"

He shakes his head. "No, that looks scary. I like cooking with my dad on his truck. I want to have my own food truck one day. Make all the food and money I want so I can buy all the toys I want."

"Very cool. Tell your dad I said I love his cooking too." I rub the top of his head. "Well, thank you for this, Pablo. You truly made my day, whether I win or lose."

His joy must have overwhelmed him as he runs up into me and hugs me. "Thank you, Scrap." He lets go and looks up at me. "I have to get back the work now. Hope you enjoy your shishkabob. I made them myself." He turns around and runs off back to the food shop.

The crowd behind me erupts in a wild frenzy. I peak over and see a slender man holding up two crossbows in his hands on stage. The announcer comes on the loudspeaker. *"Let's give it up for Needle! What an amazing victory over The Marathon Man. Sorry, pal, your race is officially terminated!"* The crowd echoes through the whole place, laughing and throwing food and soda cans at the losing fighter. *"What an amazing finish to the quarterfinals, ladies and gentlemen. You're devilishly handsome announcer will be right back. Please walk around and see all the fun games and unique food we have to offer. Semifinals will begin in exactly one hour."*

22
Semifinals

Jinx eventually finds us in our corner after lollygagging around the festival. He walks up to us intensively, looking worried or has something on his mind.

"Hey, so, I did some snooping around on your next fight. It is either going to be King Chris, that guy who knocked out Vector and won that Sonicfist. Beware of him, Carson, he doesn't seem like the rest of the competition. Let's hope one of the others can knock him out before you have to. Next we have Needle, a smaller adversary, but lightning quick with two crossbows and a rapier sword, so if you're caught up with him, watch out for flying arrows. Lastly, there's Leaf, he's a great spearman, but what's going to give you trouble is his Forcefield. He'll get you with his reach and stop you if you get close. All completely different opponents, so you need to game plan accordingly," Jinx explains.

I jot down these notes in my head. "Ok, so explain the Forcefield. Is it like what you see in cartoons?"

"Kind of. You see, movies exaggerate it. This is simply an electromagnetic aura that takes kinetic energy and deflects it in another direction. The way movies portray it is ridiculous, in my opinion. How it can catch a nuke and ~~can~~ throw it back to the attacker a thousand miles away is far from realistic. No, no, the odds of it coming back at you are slim, unless you hit it yourself. Like, if you swing your pipe at the guy and he turns it on, your pipe will bounce off it. So, if you go up against him, try to make him use it first before you go for any kind of frontal attack.

"How long?"

"Depends. Some models are better than others."

"Should I be worried? I ask.

"Worried? No, but conscious of them, yes. King Chris is your biggest threat though. Let's just hope Leaf or Needle can beat him in the semis, and you may just have a smooth road through the finals. If you end up facing him, well—" he pauses.

"Well, what, Jinx?"

"You've seen him, Carson. He's powerful, more powerful than your dinky pipe. He looks like he eats pipes for fun."

My eyes open wide in dismay. "Dinky? This is tyketanium, it's stronger than steel, iron."

"Compared to him, yes. He's got a lightweight compression suit with bulletproof Kevlar padding, tyketanium won't even dent it. I don't know who he is, or where he is getting his equipment but it's definitely not from here, and neither is he. There's no way, and now he has a Sonicfist… He's turning into a real threat, a Titan threat if you can understand that, so you'll have to wear him down, maybe even play a little dirty. I'm sure a cheap shot to the old family jewels won't bat an eye to the judge." I peer over to Kylie and see her reaction. Definitely sounds like something I told her before. "Let's just see where the semis end up. But if you have to face him, I'd be prepared with some kind of strategy."

He's right, we all saw what he did to Vector, and he was a skilled fighter himself, sloppy, but he had weapons. I was worried I would have to face him in the semis, but now I might have to face someone who is double his size and just as talented. I start to doubt myself. My ribs are numb from the serum, but I am out after this last dose. I won't have enough for the finals unless I go back to the paramedics and I know they're going to try to push stims back on me. Pshhh… if I even survive long enough to make it to the finals. Is this all even worth it? Will any of this actually matter if I do win? This Proving doesn't sound like a walk in the park either… Ugh…

"Ey! Focus! Your fight is coming up any minute now. This is your fight. Remember, if you lose, you die," Jinx says with a smile. "I'm going to go try to win one of those stuffed toys over there. I'll be back." He turns and walks away.

After more than an hour, the announcer finally comes on the loudspeaker. *"Sorry for the extended break, ladies and gentlemen. You know the ladies love them some Chippie."* He chuckles to himself then clears his throat. *"May I have your undivided attention!? We have our final four competitors. Leaf, Needle, King Chris, and by some miraculous feat, the newcomer, Scrap!"*

137

"Miraculous feat, huh?" I mumble to Kylie. I put my arm around her shoulders. She looks up and smiles at me. "This is all because of you, little sister." I point at her. "I wouldn't be here without you." She wraps her arms around me in a hug.

"Oh, I guess I'm chopped liver," Jinx jokes holding a giant stuffed blue dragon.

"Let's get this going, shall we?!" the announcer shouts. *"Scrap! Bring you and that rusty pipe of yours to the stage."*

"That was provocative," Jinx mutters.

"Good luck, Scrap!" Kylie screams.

I smile at her one more time. May the saints watch over her if I don't live through this fight. My nerves rattle as I climb the three stairs up to the stage. The crowd roars in a mix of cheers and boos. Camera drones pan back and forth trying to find the best shot of me. My ribs feel numb as they did the last time. I pinned myself with the last of the numbing serum so it should last the majority of the fight as long as it doesn't take long. I take a deep breath and feel minimum pain. A pound of anxiety leaves my body as I exhale.

"And for his opponent, coming from the back alleys of South Harmony, give it up for the cunning, the fearless, the reigning champion of Harmony's Marksmen Mania competition, give it up for Needle!" Chip shouts. The crowd cheers as my next opponent makes their way onto the stage.

Marksman champion? Those crossbows are no joke. Finally, I can see him up close, he wears a dirty white suit with a white biker helmet. A black visor covers his whole face. He has a quiver around his back with crossbow bolts, two crossbows clipped to his belt, and a rapier sword sheathed across his back, used mostly for stabbing and poking into pockets in armor. I've got to be careful with that. The judge comes to the middle and commands us to him. He goes over the rules, as usual, and asks if we have any questions. I shake my head and stick out my arm for a friendly handshake.

"If you really think that is going to make me pity you, you are sadly mistaken," a woman's voice comes from Needle and she grips my hand.

I'm taken back. "Are you a girl?" I ask without hesitation.

She rips her hand out of my grasp. "Of course I'm a saintdamn girl, you hex," she snaps. "What? You scared to fight a girl? You think I can't take it? Good, this will be done faster than I expected."

I backpedal back to my corner. It's a girl. Needle is a girl! Oh saints, I have to fight a girl. I never did that before. I walk back to my corner in deep thought. Jinx is in my corner. "You never told me Needle is a girl."

"He's a she? I didn't know," he shrugs nonchalantly, looking ridiculous with a drink in one hand and a stuff animal in the other.

I frantically look back at Needle. Oh saints, what am I going to do? Am I really going to have to fight a girl? I'm sure being a titan means you could either be a guy or girl. This makes no difference. I take a deep breath… Ok, let's get this over with.

The judge points to both sides. "Are you ready?" he asks both of us. "Begin!"

I pull out my pipe and tap it in my hand nervously. Let's make this quick. Beeps begin to chime as I see multiple arrows come flying at me. I drop to the ground and miss nearly getting skewered. Loud screams of panic come from the crowd. I look up and a thin blade shines in my eye as a piercing pain scores flesh in my thigh. A sharp pain courses through my body as her blade punctures through a pocket in my scrap yard armor. I anticipate a second move and tilt my head to the left and catch the blade against my pipe. The blade comes inches from my neck with blood dripping from it's tip. Before she can strike again, I come around and punch her side then I grab her wrist, spin around, and flip her over my shoulder.

Hoping to end this quickly, I swing my pipe down, but she squirms away. Again and again I chase her across the stage driving my pipe and clanking against the stage like a whack-a-nowa game. She retreats to a corner of the stage and has nowhere left to run. I let out a scream and heave my pipe down at her but she pulls a crossbow and shoots it six inches from my face. I jerk backwards at the last possible second and the arrow ricochets off my visor and flies up in the crowd. Screams from the citizens engulf my ears as the arrow plummets to the ground. This tournament is insane. There's no precaution for this madness, everyone is at risk with her here. I retreat and ready myself with my weapon. She goes into some foreign stance with her blade above her head pointing at me.

"Yo, Needle, watch where you're shooting that thing, there are innocent people here. You could kill someone with that," I say.

"You think I care about these lowlifes?!" she screams. "I wouldn't care if anyone here gets hit by a train. All I care is winning this tournament and getting out of this horrid territory."

Boos and threats surround us as the crowd becomes a roaring frenzy of angry Harmonians.

"Shut up!" she yells back at them. "All of you are worthless putrid animals. Every last one of you."

"Hex her up, Scrap!" a man screams from the crowd. More angry fans join in on the ranting. The crowd suddenly deviates from hating me to hating her. The crowd starts chanting. "Scrap. Scrap. Scrap."

She lets loose a loud cackle. "You don't have what it takes, Scrap. You're no soldier, you're just a loser. A puny little runt of the litter." She charges at me, sword high in the air, screaming in her high-pitched voice. I block her strikes back pedaling but get clipped in the same leg right above the knee, giving up the little room I have left. She tries sweeping my legs and I jump in the air.

"Gotcha!" she shouts manically.

I panic and anticipate arrows. I clinch up and prepare to deflect them, but none come. I land awkwardly and my knee buckles. *Beep, beep, beep-beep-beep.* An arrow finds my shoulder and another one ricochets off my chest plate. A searing pain scorches through my body. I scream in agony as my eyes meet the end of the bolt halfway through my body. I never felt something so devastating before. I grab the shaft of the arrow and pain sizzles down my torso as I pull it out of me. Luckily, it doesn't seem to have penetrated through my body as much as I thought. A small amount of blood covers the head of the arrow. I stand up on my good leg, using my pipe to get up, taking the weight off that bad knee. Breathing hard hurts. I'm winded already, and the numbing serum is wearing off. I hold my side, my arm hurts to hold up, and my leg stings. I can barely stand up straight.

"Wow, I'm surprised you can stand. Stay right there, darling, I won't miss this time," Needle says as she reloads another arrow in her crossbow and locks it in her holster. She pulls out her sword, laughs hysterically and charges me swinging hard, trying to catch me while I'm hurt but she comes up empty. I lean back and forth dodging each of her mighty swings.

"Stop dancing around like a little fairy and fight me like a man!" she yells.

"Fine!" I answer rabidly and fight back with the last bit of my energy. I strike her in the chest with my bad leg. My Turbo Boot pulses and shoves Needle across the stage. My thigh screams in pain but I fight through it, got to finish it now. I don't have much left in me to go on.

She quickly recoils and gains her feet. She pulls out both crossbow and sends two bolts hurling at me. I roll to dodge them but come face to face with her once more. Her blade slices another scratch in my visor before I pivot my body, and duck from her blade coming back around for my neck. I sweep to the side, pull out my pipe, and strike upwards at the crossbow, knocking it out of her right hand. I swing again and break her collarbone. A bone cracking sound erupts throughout the stage and I continue with another strong swing. Needle blocks it with her elbow, and she cries in pain as her arm shatters on impact, then I thrust the blunt tip of the pipe into her visor and finally, she falls.

She's slow to get up, only able to use one arm, she looks up at me in obvious pain. Her arm is mangled. A lone bloodshot eye is exposed out of a cracked hole in her visor. The judge goes to her side and asks if she can continue.

"I'm sorry! I really didn't want to hurt you," I call out to her.

She shoos the judge away and gets to her knee. "Why?! Because I'm a girl? I'm a saintdamn warrior, you hex," she screams and pulls out her last remaining crossbow and fires at me. No arrows fire. I push myself between her hands just in time and drive my knee into her chest.

She recoils back. I swing my pipe and break her last remaining crossbow. Then I blast her backwards with a forceful push of my boot. Using the force of the push, she's launches backwards to the edge of the stage. She saves herself inches away from falling off the stage and ending this ruthless fight. "Please, I don't want to do this," I beg. "Just quit. Please." She still refuses to give up. "Stay down, Needle!" I yell. "Fall off the stage and save yourself."

"Make me! No man will ever tell me what to do. Not now, not EVER!"

Ignoring my emotions to pity her, I wind up and, with a three step follow through, unleash havoc. Connecting on a tremendous swing, her body flails backwards and crashes outside of the stage. The crowd goes wild in celebration. I hear my name chanting in the crowd. New fans are finding a likeness to me. An underdog everyone wants to get behind. I feel bad for doing what I did to you, Needle, but there can only be one winner today.

The judge grabs hold on my wrist and throws it in the air. "The winna!"

23

Only Two Remains

Needle is carried out of the festival and into an ambulance. They had to cut her helmet off with a torch because the contusion in her head has swelled to the point where it could cause more damage if they tried to pull it off. I'm beside myself, I rush myself in the bathroom contemplating everything I've done to get to this part.

I'm in the finals, but only by sending a woman and two other men to the hospital. Does she have a family that I just ruined? Even though it was either me or her, I always have to choose myself. Does that make me selfish? She would have killed me if I let her. She wouldn't care to do it, she was crazy. What was I supposed to do? Who would protect Kylie if I had died? Jinx? I really don't trust him just yet. I have no idea who he really is or where he comes from. What is his past? Or better yet, what is his motive? Why is he helping us? What is he getting out of all of this? So many unanswered questions, it is driving me mad.

"Everything come out ok?" Jinx asks as I walk out of the bathroom.

"What? Yeah," I say waking up from my nightmare daydream.

"Great, because while you were playing with yourself in the bathroom, King Chris beat Leaf in less than thirty seconds."

"Yeah, twenty-two seconds actually," Kylie chimes in.

"That is impossible, how did he do that?" I stagger ~~up~~ off the examination table.

Just then, I see Leaf being delivered to the medical tent. He lays motionless with a caved in face and missing several teeth. My jaw drops in shock at the sight. My stomach lurches, it takes all I have to swallow it.

"He shattered Leaf's Forcefield with the Sonicfist. A perfect strategist he seems to be," Jinx proclaims.

"What do I do, Jinx? How do you beat someone like him?"

"Honestly, I'm at a loss, but take tonight into consideration, because tomorrow at the finals, it's going to become reality. You need to come up with some kind of technique or a way to weaken him enough to get him off his feet. Once you do that, give him hell. Don't let him up and get an advantage."

"Right," I say feeling defeated even though I haven't lost. My body aches, and breathing is indescribably difficult. "Well, do you mind giving us a ride home?"

"Of course, let me take a leak and I'll be right out. Go get checked out, you'll need that leg wrapped up and a refill on your medicine."

When I finally get my turn in the medical tent, I get it bandaged up by the medical professionals and they ask me again if I want stims. I regretfully have to refuse. As tempting as it sounds, I don't want to subject myself to Anderson's level. I won't risk it.

"Look, kid, you're not going to be able to walk. Just take a small dose, it'll help tremendously," the paramedic says.

"No, it made my friend into an addict. I will not subject myself to it."

"Pshhh," the man makes a noise of frustration. "If you abuse this, you'll be addicted. The numbing serum will help your ribs but now you got a hole in your shoulder and a gash through your leg. Buddy, you will not be able to fight tomorrow. I'll be surprised if you can get out of bed tomorrow."

"What's the commotion over here?" Jinx makes his appearance along with Kylie.

"I don't want stims. Just give me more of the numbing stuff, I'll be fine."

"Wait, you haven't been taking stims? Carson, are you insane? Aren't you in pain?" Jinx asks.

"What? Yeah. Everything hurts," I reply.

"Then take the stims, boy. They're not going to hurt you. You afraid of needles or something?"

"No, I—" I pause, knowing Jinx knows nothing about me.

Kylie butts in. "He had a friend who was addicted to them. Believe me, it was bad. The poor kid couldn't function correctly without it."

"Then your friend must have been taking high doses several times a day," the medic says. He shows me the a stim dispenser. "This is a 5mg dispenser, with ten doses in it."

"Ten? My friend would be out of it in like three shots."

"You see, now that is abusive." He hands it to me. "Use it if you want, I'm not trying to hurt you, kid. I've been a medic for years. I know it's bad for you, but unless you want to go to the hospital and quit, then this is your best bet for the finals." I take the dispenser. The temptation of feeling relief pressures me. The pain hurts, my shoulder throbs, and my ribs screech with every breath. I can't live like this. I'm not going to be like Anderson, I'm using it to help the pain, not numb reality.

I make up my mind. I uncap the top and point it to my neck like Anderson did. "Am I doing it right?"

The medic looks, and his eyes open wide. "Woah, hah, sorry kid." He twists something on the dispenser. "It was on twenty milligrams, now it's on five."

Unbelievable. I slowly pin myself and press down on the plunger. A slight pinch shocks me but a head rush of flowing ecstasy soon follows, it soothes my pain in a matter of moments. I stand up and feel like normal. I feel lighter, as if I am walking on clouds.

"Woah…" my voice even sounds slightly different.

"Take it easy, Carson," I hear Jinx's voice.

Kylie grabs my arm and looks at me with a slight smile. "Ready to go home?"

"Sure, you ready?" I look at Kylie, I told her to pick what she believes would be the best thing we could gain from Needle. "What did you pick?"

"Her crossbow," she giggles to herself. "It's not like she will be using them anytime soon," she jokes.

24
Fire

Jinx tells me to get in my suit one last time so I can get the suit in his truck. We find our
way out to the parking lot where Jinx parked. He has a huge silver F-350 hover truck.
It is the nicest car in the parking lot by far.

"Woah, is this your truck?" I ask astounded.

He nods and tells me to strap the suit down in the bed of the truck. I find reinforced straps
already connected to multiple steel bars on the outside of the truck. Never in my life have I seen a
truck like this. It has leather seats and a sweet looking stereo system, too. Nothing like dad's old
beater car, nothing like any car I've seen in Harmony in fact. I feel insecure stepping into this
pristine hovertruck. I don't want to be the guy who ruins the interior.

"Ey," Jinx snaps and grabs my attention. "You know you made it to the finals, right? Why
do you look so gloomy?"

I take a few breaths to test out my rib. The pain is numbed but I still feel the bone is broken.
"I just feel like all this is going to be for nothing. That King Chris guy looks unstoppable." I flail
my arms out. "How do you beat someone in less than thirty seconds?"

"I told you. Go for the knees and—"

"And why did I have to fight a girl?!" I interrupt abruptly. I see Kylie look up at me through
the side window. I avoid her eye contact and look at Jinx. "You knew she was a girl. You said you
went and scouted them out. Why didn't you tell me?"

"Why does that matter?" he snaps. "I wasn't trying to find you a date to the prom. I was seeing what kind of fighters they were. And what if I did? Would you have forfeited? What exactly would you have done with that information?"

I'm taken back by his louder tone. "I, well, I—"

"You know the military has no discrimination to gender, right? You know Atlantis University doesn't either? Hell, I know plenty of men who had to fight women, lost their lives to female bandits or cannibals out in the west. I had to watch them breathe their last breath. Can you do that, Carson? Can you protect your friends, your family, if a woman wants to hurt them?"

"I, I don't know."

"Needle would have messed you up, she could have killed you if you underestimated her. Just look at your leg, you second guessed yourself for one second." He holds up a finger. "*One hexing second, Carson,* and she crippled you. Honestly, I'm surprised you won. I saw so much doubt in you, it was laughable. How do you expect to win tomorrow when you pity every opponent you face? Do you know what happens to people who pity their opponents? They die, they're captured, tortured, do you want that? Is that the kind of titan you're going to be?"

I drop my head and find Kylie staring at me in the side mirror. Jinx is right, I was one shot away from being crippled. Ugh, what was I thinking?

"Hey, that's not fair," Kylie says from the back seat.

"No, he's right," I tell her through the side mirror. "I underestimated her. I just—"

"Let me tell you this, Carson," Jinx says more calmly. "I have been *destroyed* by women in my days." I look up at him and see his stern face. His eyes looking deep into mine, it's intimidating. "Black eyes, broken wrists, broken ribs, I've had to follow orders from plenty of female titans and—" Jinx hesitates and I catch him. I finally catch him.

"Ahha! You're a—"

"No!" Jinx exhales and looks back out his window. He curses under his breath. "Never mind that," he dismisses. "Don't get me wrong, bud, men should never hit women out of rage or what not, be a gentleman in any situation in public. But this was a threat, an enemy nonetheless, regardless of gender. She would have had no remorse ending your life." He leans into my face more intensely. "*Your life,* Carson." Jinx takes a deep breath, and exhales. "Sorry for yelling. But you need to get your head on straight, quickly." He shakes his head and turns the truck on. It sounds like a large vacuum at first, then shoots off the ground. We start driving out of the complex and down the main road.

"What kind of engine does this truck run on?" Kylie asks.

"Hydrogen, why? You never seen one before?" Jinx answers.

"No? I didn't know Harmony manufactured hydrogen cars."

Jinx dismisses the topic quickly again. I choose not to let it bother me and ponder in silence for a moment. I look in the mirror and see Kylie looking out the window doing the same as what I'm doing. I finally get the courage to express myself. "Ok, who are you, Jinx? What are you?" I ask. "You're obviously in the military, or some millionaire that doesn't live here, so stop hiding things from us. You said you wanted to help, yet you're holding back information that could help me. My dad was working on some kind of project. Do you think that has to do with anything?"

He hesitates again and takes a deep breath. "Yes. Project SPINE, he calls it."

"So, you do know about it? What is it?" I ask.

He refuses to answer. "Where are you staying?"

"Where am I…? Why are you hiding so much from me, Jinx? You say my dad is alive. He's my dad, not yours. I want to see him, I want to know he's ok. Is he hurt? Is he in danger? What about our mother?"

"I don't know where he is, or what he is doing, or how to find out. He was arrested along with your mother for treason. Treason, Carson. So whether or not they are guilty of that, they are most likely in prison. If you were to know where or plot to get them out, you would be arrested on sight."

I calm myself down. "So what is it that you're telling me if I win?"

"Listen, Carson, you're running into a pitch black cave if you did this alone. I just want to make sure you have the right guidance along the way. Now, where are you staying?"

"9th street. Just drop us off in front of the Weekends Inn. It's the hotel right across the street from the scrap yard."

"Ok, you obviously can tell I'm not from around here, but win tomorrow and I will help you with everything involving the Proving, ok?"

"So that's it? You just want me to win. You just go to these tournaments and pick someone to coach or something? Or are you some kind of stalker looking to befriend young kids? I don't understand you, Jinx. Who are you?!"

"No! What? Are you insane? Carson, look, I need you to just focus on—" His eyes open up wide and his jaw drops in disbelief. "Carson, look."

In the distance, a giant smoke cloud looming over where the scrap yard would be. We're about two blocks away but it seems to be in the general vicinity. Sirens blare louder as we approach the scrap yard. The smell of fire is in the air when I roll down the window.

"Kylie, you see that?" I ask her.

She peers around my seat and sees the giant black cloud emulating. "Is there a fire somewhere?"

We turn down the street to where the scrapyard would be and our nightmares have come true. The scrapyard is completely engulfed in flames surrounded by fire trucks parked all around the road. I'm speechless as I watch the flames dance with each other over my home. I get Jinx to pull over and I hop out the truck and run over to the main entrance. I get stopped by a fireman.

"Stay back! It is too dangerous. Go home, kid. There's nothing to see here," he says through his fireproof helmet.

"I have to go in there!" I shout. "You don't understand, I need to—"

"Are you saintdamn mad? What could you possibly need in there?" Jinx replies catching up to me.

"Oh my saints, our home!" Kylie wails as she reaches me. Her cries echo through me like a lightning bolt. She weeps for our home, all the effort we've put into it, the countless hours of work, the planning and time it took to compile the supplies all burn in a fury of flames right before my eyes.

"This is my home! All my stuff is in there!" I snap at the fireman and run back to the truck to hook up the jumper cables to my suit and rev the generator. I jump in my suit and squeeze myself inside as quick as I can. "Kylie, zip the back."

She sniffles and wipes her nose as she rushes towards me. "Carson, what are you doing? I don't think this is a—"

"DO IT!" I snap. "We're wasting time. Hurry!" At this point, nothing can stop me. My father's gun is in there and that is all I have left of my parents. No pictures, no watches, bracelets, nothing from my parents that I was able to bring with me. I have to, no, I need to get it. Kylie hops up on the truck's bed and zips me in. I jump off and blitz the wooden fence surrounding the scrap yard. I hear screams from multiple voices to hold on and wait but I ignore them all and pummel through the front gates.

Flames dance all around me, spreading quickly throughout the piles of trash, catching anything and everything it can to grow larger and more uncontrollable. I have to be fast and get out of here. I activate my Turbo Boots and dash as quickly as I can through the mountains of miscellaneous things piled up in this yard over the years. Countless piles I've never rummaged through are all surrounded by a blaze. Finally, I reach the transporter and it's up in flames. Oh no! I am too late!

The fire eats away at our home, digesting it slowly as it melts before my eyes. There's nothing I can do to extinguish the flames, it's too late. I have no fire resistance shielding, no coolant to cover me. Nothing but hopelessness as I watch everything my sister and I have created turn to ash. The distinct smell of gasoline in the air, did we forget to cap the gas can?

I hear Kylie calling for me. I catch her slipping through the entrance we made. Tears slowly form in her eyes as she enters the same state of disbelief I'm in. She quivers at the sight and drops to her knees.

"Kylie, you have to get out of here!" I scream. "Get out!"

"No! Not without you!"

I find myself ironically frozen to the ground. My body feels lifeless as I watch our home burn. I try to get myself to move but what do I do? The flames slowly spreading their way outward, catching anything it can to expand its mighty blaze. The heat makes me sweat; the uncomfortable feeling of dread consumes me. The universe seems to be laughing at me with every decision I make. Karma is taking her turn with me for all the violence I've caused today. I deserve this, I deserve all of this.

"Carson!" I hear Jinx's voice and it wakes me up. "Get out of here! What are you doing? Don't be a hero!"

A hero, what I've always dreamed of being. My holoposters in my old room showed me what a hero was every day. AlphaTitans who've stood the test of time fighting crime, and saving people from harm. Memories of my dad rummage through my mind, his long shaggy hair and his cleft chin. A smile on his face but a tired look from days of no sleep, my dad was a fighter, maybe not with his hands but with his mind. He may not have been the best dad in the world, but he supported us and kept a roof over our heads. If there is any hope that he is alive, I have to get that gun. It's his and I will get it back to him. I hear the voices of my sister and Jinx beg me not to go. I take one more glance at Kylie. My world in one ball of love and jean shorts watches on as our home melts in a fury of flames, destroying a year of stressful and grueling work. I have to do it. For him.

"I'M COMING, DAD!" I rip the doors off the transporter and lunge myself inside. It's a blazing frenzy inside. The walls melt away in a smoky black ash, that blinds me from seeing no more than two feet in front of me. A piece of metal ceiling falls through and crashes inches away from me along with a dozen flaming rods of PVC pipes. I hear Kylie's frantic screams from outside the house. I quickly find the box where the gun is supposed to be. The gun lays on top for easy retrieval if we ever need it. It sizzles in my hand; I can feel it scorching through my metal gauntlet. I turn around and dash towards the entrance, but a large mass of fiery metal drops on me and pins me to the ground. Several more cracking noises follow, and heavy weights collapse on top of my awkward laying body. The threshold of the door collapsed on me. I try to pry it off of me but something is caught in a pocket of my suit. I scream for help and watch the flames dance in front of me. Rotten wood and rusted metal surround me like a wild hoard of canahounds. I try and toss the gun out of my hand and feel the stinging burn of the heated metal searching for my palm as I try desperately to squeeze my way out. Nothing budges. Sweat drips down my forehead and into my eye. The heat starts to seep in through the pockets of my suit, it becomes unbearably painful. Fire sizzles my back, pinching little spots through my shirt and skin. As the burning sensations start to wreck my body, a sense of panic erupts in me. I hyperventilate and start to cough uncontrollably. Oxygen becomes harder for my lungs to find as the smoke blinds me from the light outside and clogs the air filters in the helmet.

"Carson!" I hear Kylie's voice.

"Kylie?! I'm stuck! Call for—" I cough. "Call..." I can't find words. "Help..."

"Oh my saints! Someone help! He's over here!" her voice fades.

I ignore the stings of the blaze and try one more time to wedge myself out. As I try to push, I feel the makeshift roof on top of me feel weightless. I shove it off me and a giant claw looking thing appears above me with half the roof on its hands. A man in a fireman's outfit is homed in the cockpit of this machine, controlling massive mechanical arms. He makes eye contact with me and he pulls me out of the wreckage. "I got him!" I hear. Light fills my eyes, and the sun shines down on me. "Put him out, put him out!" another voice says, and I'm then drenched in a heavy stream of freezing cold water. I try to breathe but from the smoke and now water around, I cough again. I beg for the water to stop and try to squirm away, but my body doesn't listen. I feel paralyzed on all fours as the several streams of water penetrate through my suit and smack my sore and tiresome body. "Carson, you're on fire!" Kylie screams. "Stop moving."

Water drips into my helmet and down my face. The water finally stops, and I am able to gather oxygen again. Defeated and worn out from today, it's hard to get up. "You are one crazy kid," a fireman says. "I hope that was worth it." I look up and watch as a team of fully suited firemen extinguish my home, or what was my home. The man pulled me out with one of his mechanical arms. Hoses were attached to the bottom of its forearms. Gallons of water are projected onto the pile of burning wood, plastic, and metals. Finally, the water stops and I can relieve myself of my blinding soot filled helmet and breathe. My suit is charred black like an overcooked piece of bacon. I plop myself on the ground and breathe in the flame smelling air, steam sizzles off me into the air as the rest of the fire squad extinguishes the pandemonium around me.

"It's all gone, everything is all gone," Kylie says walking up towards me. She sniffles her tears away, trying to be strong. "Are you ok?" I nod trying not to say anything. "Did you get the…" She looks around. "you know."

I cough to clear my throat. "I threw it over there." I point to the front of the transporter where Jinx is now walking up to us.

"What the hex was that? You could have gotten yourself killed!" he yells in a whisper so no one can hear besides us.

"I needed to get something in there. This was our home."

"You're home? You lived in a scrap yard?"

"Yeah, about a year now," Kylie adds.

"So that's where you went…" he trails off. "What were you looking for?"

"My dad's gun. He forgot to bring it the day he was arrested. So, if what you're saying is right, if he is al—" I can't catch my breath and start to cough. My ribs remind me they're broken with every uncontrollable cough I let out. "If he's alive, then I want to give it to him," I say hoarsely.

Jinx pulls out my father's 96 plasma pistol. "You mean this?"

"Yeah. That's it," I say emotionless. I feel ecstatic he found it, but I have no energy to be excited.

"Holy saints, Carson, you're absolutely insane," Jinx says and tosses it to me. The firemen are right in front of us trying to control the flames. Delta patrolmen start arriving to the scene and I hide the gun in one of the pockets in between my armor. "C'mon," Jinx says. "Let's sneak through the back and around to the truck."

As Kylie rubs the ointment on my back on the bed of the truck, I'm reminded of all the hexed up things I have done today.

"Let's go get something to eat," Jinx suggests. He feels for us and knows food is one of the best medicines for depression, or sorrow. I wonder if he's ever felt this kind of way, if he has ever lost someone dear and priceless to him. "My treat," he adds.

"I'm not hungry," I mutter. I just lost everything. With the finals bearing down on my back, this was the last thing that should have happened. Finally, the universe gives me hope for something good in my life, and the saints in the afterlife laugh as this mysterious fire destroys my home. I'm not thinking of food. I'm not thinking of the tournament. I'm thinking where am I going to sleep tonight?

"I'm kind of hungry, Carson," Kylie mumbles to me.

"Since when are you always hungry?" I ask her. She looks at me with a face itching for free food. "Fine. I guess we need to get out of here anyways."

25
Tito's Burgers

We make our way to a local diner named, Tito's Burgers. I try to walk the best I can, but my leg is getting the best of me. Every step feels like pins and needles being jabbed into my thigh. I plop myself in the booth closest to the door next to a large window. This long day has finally turned to night, Magnaluna and Parvaluna light up the sky along with the billions of stars mankind has yet to discover. The restaurant is empty except for a small family across the diner and an older man typing away on his tabletop computer with a cup of coffee. Some sticky substance sticks to my sweaty arm and makes me second guess Jinx's pick for food.

As I uninterestingly stare at the menu tablet, swiping through fake pictures of how the food would look if it was walking down a runway, Jinx talks to Kylie about something I don't understand, something about the magnetic pressure sensors in the Turbo boots and how they were made. I'm not really paying attention anyway. I have so much on my mind. I have the biggest lopsided fight of my life tomorrow, and I'm on the wrong side. Even when I got jumped in middle school by four kids, I still feel my chances were better than this.

That isn't even the end of my worries. For the first time in my life, I have no home. No bed, no roof over my head, nothing. At least at the orphanage, we had that. I have my sister and this random man who is *still* a complete mystery to me. He tells me my dad is alive and yet, keeps certain things a secret. Only if I win tomorrow will he tell me what he can do for me, but I don't even see that happening. I can barely walk…. to think, I have to fight a monstrous man who didn't seem to get hurt at all today.

The waitress approaches the table. Her blond hair is wrapped in a ponytail with bags under her hazel eyes. Maybe a little older than me by the looks of it. Her apron is dirty, she must be having a long day. "Good evening, y'all, I'm Sandy. Can I get you some water or coffee to start or do you know what you want?"

I turn back to the menu, I can't decide on what I want, my mind keeps wondering. All I can think about is the fire. The heat, the fear, it consumed me. I felt my body melting in its clutches. How stupid I was to risk my life over such nonsense. I look down at my hand and gaze at the bandage wrapped around it, a burn that will stay on my hand for the rest of my life, a constant reminder of a stupid and selfless act for a man who may not even be alive. All he ever did was work on this so called, Project SPINE? What could that possibly be? Was that the scar in my dad's neck? I always thought it was a birthmark that him and Kylie share.

"Carson," I hear Kylie's voice. I jump out of my thoughts and realize the waitress was waiting for me. A smile stretches over her face and I realize she's actually kind of cute. My face reddening, I have no idea what I want. I start to stutter, "I'll, uh… I'll just have whatever he's having." I gesture to Jinx not even knowing what he got. "Oh, and a coffee, please, milk and six sugars, please."

She jots it down. "I'll put this in right now, your food will be out in a bit. Thanks, y'all." She turns around and walks away.

Jinx waits till the waitress is a good distance away. "Six sugars? You ok, Carson?" he asks.

I snap and punch the table. "Does it look like I'm hexing ok?" I yell in a whisper.

Jinx leans back in his seat and folds his arms with a slight grin. "Nah, you look like you already lost the tournament."

I exhale my frustration and grab a couple of napkins to wipe the sweat dripping from my head. "I don't know what to do. What are we doing? Any bright ideas?"

"What do you mean?" Jinx asks.

"After this." I point to the table. "You're going home, right? Or you must have some fancy motel you're staying at. With all this money you've been flaunting around, you must own one, right?"

Jinx smirks. "Well, actually I—"

"We have nowhere to go, Jinx. That fire you saw me jump into, that was my home, *our* home. We built that place with our blood, sweat, and tears. We don't even have clothes." I pinch

154

my sweat filled ripped up shirt. "This and that saint forsaking hunk of hexing junk in your truck is all I have."

"Carson…" Kylie says looking insulted.

Jinx nods blankly. "Right… Well, for tonight, I'll rent you a room at the motel I am staying at and I'll drive you to the tournament. After you win tomorrow, I'll send…" he hesitates. "I mean, Atlantis University should be able to house you and Kylie until the time of The Proving. After that, we will go from there.

I ignore his suspicious hesitation. I have no energy to argue anymore but something in me still questions everything that comes out of his mouth. "How do you know I'm going to win? What if I lose? I need to figure out a backup plan."

"Then you die, Carson," he said plainly.

"Probably." I say with no energy to fight back.

"Carson," Kylie snaps. "Don't think like that."

"But he must," Jinx says. He points at me. "If you lose, you die. You'll leave your sister to fend for herself and then she will die, because you couldn't pull yourself together. Do you really want to die knowing that?"

"What is your deal, Jinx? You got a bet on me or something? Am I just a game to you?"

Jinx rolls his eyes. "No, you stubborn, *stubborn* child. It's a figure a speech you close minded buffoon." His words anger me. I felt my eye twitch in the sudden urge to reach over this table and punch him. "It means there's no going back. There's no, if I lose then… Then nothing, you fail. You go to war, you either win or you die. You lose the war, you come home a failure.

"And what exactly do you know about war, hmm?"

"That is none of your concern right now. You need to focus on how you're going to win tomorrow. This isn't my fight, this is yours."

"I just feel hopeless, Jinx. This was my only chance to get into Atlantis University and I can barely walk. How am I supposed to compete against a man like King Chris?"

"I don't know about you, but you were running pretty fast into that fire." He smiles and glances at Kylie and points at her. "For her sake, you have to win. You're fighting for more than yourself in this tournament. You're fighting to find your father, right?" Jinx says. "If you channel your anger, embrace your opportunities and drown out the doubts, the pain will go away. You—"

"I don't want my father back!" I stand up out of my seat and shout back with every last bit of energy I have. Emotions finally getting the best of me from all the stress and violence I've endured today. I fall back in my seat as tears start to form in my eyes. "I want… my mom back." Kylie hugs my arm and nestles into my shoulder. "But apparently my father was arrested for treason? The man did one thing my entire life and that was work. My mother is a stay at home mom, she didn't do anything treasonous. It's all a lie. Why would the military lie to us about something like this?"

Jinx goes quiet. Speechless even.

"We'll be ok, Carson," Kylie says. I look at her, her heart shattering along with mine at the thought of our parents. This is the only way I can get any closer to finding them, and it just seems so out of reach now. I grab her hand and squeeze as I fight back the tears that fill my eyes.

"My… *our* dad, was full of empty promises. Every promise he ever made to me was just to get me off his back. All he *ever* wanted to do was work on this project of his. He wanted to change the world and help humanity but couldn't give me an hour to teach me how to throw a starball."

"Carson, you know that's not fair," Kylie argues.

"Well, it is the truth," I snap back. "His last words to me were, 'I promise.' He promised he would make time to play catch with me, that's all I ever wanted from him." Tears begin to flow. I wipe them away but with everything going on, I don't care anymore. "Why would he resort to kill himself if he promised he'd come back? Why would he shoot my mother if *he* was the one getting arrested?" I smack the table. "Why, Jinx? Do you know that answer? What's your big inspirational answer to that?"

"He didn't try to kill himself or your mother," he answers softly.

"How do you know?" I demand. "How do you know anything at all?"

"Because… I just know."

Our waitress comes over with our drinks and three dishes. She places our dishes down on the table and I look and see this monstrosity of a burger that is placed in front of me and I lose all train of thought. "What did you order?" I ask.

He hesitates again, looking confused of the changed topic. "Tito's deluxe double bacon chilly burger." he answers.

"Hope you're hungry," the waitress says.

I am. The look of this burger enlightens me. I put the stress of the day behind me for now and I engulf myself in this massive chunk of delicious meat. The savory flavors dazzle my taste buds. Happiness fills me in a delightful sensation of salty bacon and tender ground beef stuffed in a sandwich melting in my mouth. A sweet dripping chilly with beans and spices fall off onto my plate as I pick up the sandwich for a second time. I clean my plate in minutes. My nerves are soothed, my belly fills to the brim, and, for now, I just need to focus on what is ahead of me.

26

The Hotel

After paying for dinner and dessert, Jinx took us to his motel and bought us a room. It was nice of Jinx to pay for us and help me in so many ways today but it's been hard to trust him with all his secrets. It's weird to say he's growing on me, like he's a distant uncle I never knew.

The room wasn't anything spectacular but is far more exceptional than our old rust bucket of a home. Yellow wallpaper covers the room with two small beds with a TV with cable to occupy us, and a small bathroom in the back with a shower. After walking in, I instantly turn on the TV and find the cartoon channel. For the first time in forever, I can watch cartoons and snuggle in a bed like I did in Redding. Jinx told us his room is just down the hall and leaves us for the night.

First thing I do once he's gone is rush into the bathroom and I test the shower. When hot water starts to come out, I feel as if a saint just touched my hand. Oh, what a glorious shower it was. The sensation of hot water drenching my body felt absolutely invigorating. I haven't had a real shower since we left the farm. In the scrap yard, we made up some kind of rig with a dirty curtain to shower. We got an extended hose and hooked it up to one of the local businesses next to us. Our showers have been mostly cold freezing waters, but it was what it was. Or, if we wanted a hot shower, then we had to wait for a hot day for our rainwater buckets to heat up, or we settled with sponge baths in the slop sink at Here 'N' There. For the first time in a long time, I have an endless stream of hot water rinsing the day away. Kylie had to yell at me to get out, I was in the shower for nearly an hour.

Jinx comes back during Kylie's time in the shower with fresh new clothes. He didn't know our sizes, but he said he went to an outlet downtown and got us each a new pair of clothes for tomorrow. It's getting harder not to love this man for his generosity. I invite him in but he politely declines and says that we had enough of him today. He told me to enjoy the night and he will wake us up in the morning.

Later in the night, after forcing myself to take the stim to relieve the pain, we watched a few episodes of some random new cartoon we both never heard of. It was weird feeling like a normal kid again. A thought pops in my head and I feel the need to get Kylie's opinion. "Hey, Ky, what do you think of Jinx?" I ask. She is on the bed on the opposite side of the small table we have in between us.

"I think you're too hard on him," she says rolling to her side to give me her full attention.

"He's keeping secrets from us, Ky. He says our dad is alive."

"Yeah, and now all of a sudden you don't care?"

"I do, Kylie, I'm just…"

"Tired, stressed, nervous?"

"More than you know," I chuckle. "I'm scared, Kylie."

"Of King Chris?"

"Yeah," Jinx's ultimatum echoes in my thoughts. "*You either win, or you die.*"

She chuckles. "So can you tell me what happened to the Carson who told me to face my fears?"

I look at her confused. "What do you mean?"

"Remember that kid on the bus I was doing homework for? He was scary, Carson. Maybe not to you, but to me, he was intimidating. I didn't want to be teased so I did what he told me to do." I nod and close my eyes. I don't have much more to say to her, so I just listen. "He's like dad, you know?" I hear her say.

"Kenny?!"

"No, you dope. Jinx."

"Don't say that." I snare at her. "He is *not* like dad," I shake my head. "Why? Because he says kiddo?"

My sharpen voice caught her off guard. "Ok, ok. No one is like dad, but you can tell he cares. It's kind of weird, he came into our lives when we needed him most. I wonder if he has a family back wherever he lives. It's odd that he spends his time here if he doesn't live around here."

"Did you catch him when he misspoke and said he took orders from titans. My guess is that he has some kind of connection to the military. Maybe he's undercover. You think he knows Robbins?"

"Maybe. Who knows anymore? All I know is that wherever he lives, I want to go there. You think he will adopt us?"

I take a deep breath and roll over, feeling as if my eyes have weights on them. "Don't be ridiculous, I'm sure he has a bet on me or something. Harmonians don't give a crap about anyone else but themselves and their family. We are nobodies to him and the only reason he is helping us is for his own gain. However, I don't mind him helping us for his gain, because it is still helping us get closer to finding mom and dad. Anyways, I'm going to bed, don't stay up too late, ok?"

"Carson?"

"Yeah?"

"Do you have a plan if you do lose?"

"I guess we'll find another scrap yard," I said sarcastically.

She chuckles. "Seriously?"

I roll over to face her again. "Whatever happens, I will never, ever, desert you. We will figure something out and make it together. I promise."

She rolls over and, in a matter of minutes, I hear her find the sweet relief of slumber. After sleeping next to her for a year, I know exactly when she's asleep. She makes small snoring noises through her mouth. I peer over and see the time on a small clock we have in the room, it's midnight. As tired as I am, I can't find sleep as fast as Kylie. I find the need for fresh air, something about this room irks me. It's just not what I'm used to, although the bed is so much more comfortable than the makeshift transporter seat cushions I screwed together.

I find my feet and creep my way over to the door and slowly open it so Kylie doesn't wake up. A shock slides down my back as a woman appears on the other side with her hand up like she was about to knock. Her makeup circles around her blue eyes. Blonde hair mixes in with the pink strands falling behind her back. I jump back, but realize, it was Courtney.

"What are you doing here?" I whisper. Her mouth opens but no words come out. She stares with frightened eyes back at me with, but I know her heart is filled with anger or betrayal.

"I, uh, how did you know I was here?" she says stumbling over her words.

"I didn't," I whisper trying to keep my voice down. "How'd you know I was here?"

"I have my resources," she says nonchalantly and clicks her tongue. "Can't a girl—"

"Shhh," I shush her and wave her back. "Kylie's sleeping. Keep your voice down."

"Oh, Kylie's with you? Sorry. I mean uh, whatever, that's cool."

I look at her baffled as I softly close the door, but I leave it cracked enough to open without the room card. I limp past her towards the balcony and lean over it to stare into the night sky. I try and do one of those breathing exercises and take a slow deep breath but with my ribs broken and the smoke from the fire, it's been difficult even with the stims. My leg aches, my shoulder is stiff, and my back feels like it's been sunburned. I can already feel the blisters. Everything hurts. With streetlights taking the beauty of the star filled sky away from light pollution, it's not how it usually is in the scrap yard. There were no lights in there. We depended on the natural light of the stars, stolen flashlights, and candles to see. I take in another deep breath, reliving the fearful day I've experienced. On top of nearly dying in every fight, my home was turned to ash by a fire unbeknownst to me how it even started.

"Rough day?" Courtney sets herself next to me on the balcony.

"Yeah"

"Oh, I'm good, thanks for asking," she says sarcastically. I stay quiet, not knowing what to say, how to say, even if I should say anything. "Must be nice living in this hotel. Much better than the orphanage."

I look at her with only regretful words in my mouth, but I swallow them. "What do you want, Courtney? Don't you have new friends to hang out with?"

"I can do whatever I want. Brett Breaker doesn't control me and after today, he doesn't control anyone. You broke the Bone Breakers, you know that, right? There's a huge bounty on your head if you lose the tournament tomorrow."

I snap towards her. "What did I do? You talking about Mean Machine? Hah, that bozo got what's coming to him."

"No he didn't, you insensitive bastard. He's a good guy and a visionary. He had plans to make Harmony great again and you nearly killed him. Now all the other gangs in Harmony are going to think they can walk all over us."

"Oh, how selfish of me, I should have just let him literally decapitate me with that saintdamn hammer? He's lucky I didn't take that hammer for myself and bash his hexing skull in. He made me look like a fool, you expect me to pity him?"

She's silent and she clenches her teeth, this conversation has a much more deep-rooted problem to it. "Don't you dare think you can talk to me like that, Carson Paul. You're lucky I don't kill you right now for what you did and collect the bounty myself."

"Oh, and miss out on this awkward conversation? Please, you'd be doing me a favor."

She clicks her tongue. "You have no idea what I've gone through since you left," she says getting louder, but she slows her tone. "You abandoned me," she says plainly crossing her arms. "What happened?" she says softly. "I thought you died."

"I—" I start but hesitate. "I can explain."

"No. I don't want your excuses. I want the truth," she demands. "What happened? I thought you were dead." Her voice softens. "Why did you run away?"

I try to justify telling her about Kylie, but it's none of her business and blaming her would belittle me even more than how I feel. I see the beauty in her face that I remember gazing into. Admiring her body that's now seemed to morph a bit, she holds a bit more weight than she did at the orphanage, but what I remember most of all about her is the wall she keeps up when she's uncomfortable. She puts on this hard face to mask her fear, but I see through it now. I may be the only one who can. "I just had to go."

Without a second to react she wails me in my bad shoulder. Ugh, didn't even see it coming. "Stop hexing lying to me, Carson," she snaps. As much as I can read her, she can read me just as well, maybe even better. I've never been a good liar. Especially to someone who's been lied to her entire life. I've abandoned someone who's been abandoned before. I sense her pain now. I feel what I've selfishly done to her by leaving that day with Kylie.

I shush her again. "Alright, alright." I rub my shoulder. "Have you been working out?" I sidetrack noticing the definition in her arms in her sleeveless black denim jacket.

"The truth, Carson," she demands again, getting more tense. Her eyebrows slant, I can feel the anger pulsing.

"Listen, you need to calm down," I whisper. She punches me again. "Stop it," I snap keeping my same tone. She punches me again, harder in the same shoulder.

"Tell me the truth or I'm gonna keep going," she threatens.

"Courtney, it's difficult."

"Oh! It's difficult, huh?" She punches me. I don't react, I let her swings connect full throttle. It's nowhere near as hard as what I've felt before, but it still hurts. "It was *difficult* to watch my dad drive off without me and leave me at some gas station." She punches me again. "It was *difficult* holding my mother in my arms as she overdoses on stims." She swings with the other arm. "It was difficult living in that orphanage, watching little twerp kids get adopted instead of me." She hits me once more. It hurts but I know I deserve the punishment, regardless of the circumstances. "It was *difficult* to think I actually liked you." She hits the same spot. "It was *difficult* to open up to you." My shoulder starts to throb, and a pins and needles feeling collects in my arm and spirals down to my hand. "It was *difficult* to get over the fact that one day you were there, and the next day you were gone." The punches start getting harder as she believes she can swing wildly and openly at my shoulder. "It was *difficult* to grieve over the fact that I thought someone I cared about disappeared out of nowhere, never to be heard from again." She swings one more time but this time I see tears start forming in her eyes. "So please explain to me, Carson Paul, how in the *hexing underworld* is it *difficult* to explain to me why you abandoned me!" She swings one more time, but I've had about enough of the punishment. I slide around her swing to her side, kick my foot behind her calf and push her body backwards. Normally doing so will make someone fall, but I cradle her head and stop before she hits the ground. The sheer shock in her face makes me feel even worse for what I did as a small tear escapes her eyes and rolls down her cheek.

"I'm sorry," I whisper sincerely. "But, please, let me explain. I'll tell you everything." I pull her back up right. "And stop hitting me. You're not gonna get anywhere besides a door being slammed in your face if you keep doing that."

She wraps her arms and waits with a sneering look on her face. "It's worked before," she mumbles.

I tell her everything, how Kylie was pushed off the cliff and what Rocky did to her. I told her flat out that I'm sorry for abandoning her, but there was no way I would leave Kylie to herself. As much as Courtney felt betrayed with my actions, I hope she can find it in her heart to forgive me. I'm a brother before a boyfriend.

"So, all this time, you've been alive, living in a scrap yard because Kylie didn't want to go back to the farm knowing she'd be labeled as a hussy?"

"That's not exactly it, she felt hopeless and scared living at that place."

"I can respect that. It's basically a place for Harmony rejects."

I click my tongue and roll my eyes. "So what happened to you? I thought you didn't want to be in Bonez's gang?"

"Yeah, well, things change when your boyfriend abandons you and you get kicked out because you're preg—" she stops and blushes.

"You're, what?"

"Per… Practically eighteen."

"Wait, they kicked you out before you were eighteen?" I ask baffled.

"No. No, but they were hinting about it long before. But um—"

"So, is this Mean Machine guy your boyfriend? I know for sure you wouldn't dare date that sleaze ball Bonez."

"No," she says in a laughing huff. "We had a thing but, um… it's difficult."

I snicker. "Why? Couldn't *handle* you?" I shake my hands mocking her.

"Pshhh, you know it."

"Oh yeah, because you're *sooo* wild," I jest.

"Hush," she stops me from talking about our intimacy. "We had a thing a little way back but nothing serious."

"Nothing like what we had, right?" I say bringing our relationship back.

She laughs nervously. "We did *not* have anything serious."

"Right, of course. That's what I thought until I heard what you told Nala."

A small, intrigued smile wraps around her face. "What'd you hear?"

"Oh, nothing. Something about you being *crazy* about me, and that I'm *all* yours."

"Because I, uh, I just wanted to… shut up." she scrunches her face but smiles, knowing I still feel the same about her. Her walls are finally falling. "You know, it doesn't happen often, but since you beat Brett, you could technically be Head Skull. Or at least head of a faction of the Bone Breakers like I am."

"Court, no offence, but I do not want to be in a street gang full of people who want me dead. What about that bounty you were talking about?"

"Oh, I'll void it, and you will just have to be inaugurated into the gang as a peon."

I chuckle at the gesture. "No disrespect, Courtney, but no thanks. I need to figure out how to win tomorrow and after that, I'll be on my way to Alannah to compete in the Proving."

"And if you lose?"

"I told Kylie we'll find another scrap yard."

"You know that just sounds ridiculous. Come check out the hangout. It's really not that bad."

"Oh yeah, I'll just walk on in and you can give me a tour, right? Do you have a gift shop?"

We share a light laugh. Her make up really takes away from her naturally beautiful face. "The offer is there if you want to… I'd like you to come, you and your sister," she says. I see what these months must have done to her. I feel guilty for how I must have changed her by abandoning her.

I notice her hands out gripping the guard rail. I rest my hand on hers. "You really don't need all that make up."

She pulls back sharply. "Don't," she snaps.

"I'm sorry. You have to understand, I've thought about you every day since I left. But I couldn't go back knowing Kylie couldn't."

She looks at me with concern in her eyes. To imagine what went through her mind when I left. Her face cringes. "It's whatever… Rocco got abducted."

"Rocky got abducted?" I ask hoping I misheard.

"No, adopted," she corrects me. "Yeah, around the same time you and your sister left. It was weird, some military guy walked in and asked for someone older and he ended up picking Rocky."

"A military guy? Do you know his name?"

"No, definitely not from Harmony though. Which is even weirder considering someone wanted a Harmonian seventeen-year-old and doesn't even live in Harmony."

Hexing Rocco got adopted. That utter failure of life got a second chance after what he did to Kylie. How does that work? Why do I feel as though the universe punishes me but gives a guy like him a second chance? I hope he was adopted to be put into slavery, that monster. Another dampener on what was supposed to be a momentous day turns into an absolutely miserable day. "Hey, Court, I got to get some sleep. Maybe after the fight we can talk some—"

Courtney attacks me and wraps her arms around my head and pulls me into her. Our faces collide, her lips meet mine. My hands slide around the small of her back and pull her into my hips. Just as her hips are pressed into mine, she shoves herself off me. "Don't make me regret that. I have someone you'd like to meet. Maybe after, you'll reconsider staying around." She winks at me, turns around and walks away.

In a shocking turn of events, I feel forgiven but strangely not at all. Who could I possibly have to meet that she knows? Brett? I don't feel comfortable associating myself in her gang. Nor if I even survive after tomorrow. Does she think I'd join them? Would it be rational? The number of connections I could get from the people involved, plus where am I going to go afterwards? I have no home. This may be my only choice. "What about the bounty?" I call out for her.

"There is no bounty if you win." she says, confusing me even more. I taste her lip gloss on my lips. I guess my day wasn't all that bad.

27
The Finals

The rest of the night was cruel and unsettling. Courtney's mysterious person spun my mind in circles. Even after the day I had, I was restless. I wonder if King Chris is as worried as I am, if he's been doubting himself like I have all night. Who am I kidding, he's destroyed his competition in every round. That Sonicfist is terrifyingly efficient, and now he has a Forcefield to go along with his vast arsenal, size, and versatility. On paper, he looks invincible.

The time has come, the day I will either find glory or despair. We park outside the gates of the park where hundreds of people are tailgating. The parking lot is packed with Harmonians partying, the air is thick with scented burners, the ground is littered with empty hopsguzzler cans. I climb out of the truck and unlatch my suit out of the bed. It's still charred black from yesterday. That fire still burns brightly in my mind, the carnage that ruined my home and everything I've made, yet I still wonder how it even started. Was it the Bone Breakers? Was it that Blitzkrieg guy who said I will regret beating Mean Machine? How would he even know where I live?

"You ready, champ?" Jinx calls out for me from the front of the truck with Kylie and all her tools and equipment.

"Yeah, I'm ready," I lie. "Do I have any time to try out the crossbow?"

"Let's see when we get inside. I'm sure we can find an ammo shop," Jinx replies.

I look over to Kylie walking in next to me. She looks as ready as can be. She's such a trooper. She helps me in the suit, maybe for the very last time. Only the saints know my destiny after today.

"Scrap is here!" I hear. "Hey everyone, Scrap is here!"

"You should have stayed home, kid! King Chris is gonna clobber you, boy!" another voice goes.

I ignore the drunk tailgaters and march myself through a crowd of people shouting other positive and negative things at me.

A pack of black jacketed men walk up to me, each with a cracked skull logo on their jackets. "Scrap, follow us, we will take you inside." The group of men cut a path for us to walk through, making sure no one lays a hand on me. They push the surrounding crowd to the side as we follow them through. The civilians know not to push their limits with the Bone Breakers. Everyone steps back and gives us ample room to walk cleanly inside.

"What is happening?" Jinx asks.

"I don't know," I say just as confused.

All this tension in my body has been driving me crazy. My stomach is in knots, this is so nerve wracking. Profanities are spitting out of people's mouths, hopsguzzler cans are getting thrown, and screams for my demise are from all angles. Chants for my opponent start coming from behind me. The feathers on his helmet is all I see from the heart of the crowd. My stomach drops, the reality of this whole event is finally coming full circle. The group of brutish gentlemen escort us to a big tent with a giant skull on it. Courtney and Bonez stand in front, along with about a dozen more Bone Breakers behind them.

"Hey, um, what is happening? What was that?" I ask Courtney.

Bonez is about to lash out at me but hesitates as Courtney glares at him. "I figure you needed an escort, sir," she smiles. "Our champion needs to be escorted properly into the festival." She takes a skull sticker out of her pocket and stamps it on my chest. "Like it or not, you are an honorary Bone Breaker today."

I look at her even more confused. "Oh, you didn't have to do all that. Really I—"

She leans into me. "It was either this or the bounty would have stayed, shut up and accept it," she whispers. "You look good in black, I like the paint job," she says in a flirty voice.

I laugh nervously and look at the slanted faces both Jinx and Kylie give me. "Oh it's not a paint job, it's from—"

Bonez throws his hands up and rants. "This is ridiculous! We're really going to drop Brett just like that, after all he's done for us? You think I'm gonna follow this *child* in a gun fight, you've got another thing coming, Pinky.

"Then don't," she snaps. "As a matter of fact, if you think you'll be a better Head Skull then fight me for it right now." She clashes her fists together, knowing Bonez is a coward. "Take out that switch blade of yours, too." She readies herself with her fists up. "C'mon, Barry, you think you're so tough? You think you're better suited for the job? You think that I got to be Brett's second because I slept with him? You think I don't know what's best for this gang? Screw you. Fight me! C'mon!"

Bonez's eyes spread open in shock. "Woah, woah, Pinky." He lifts his hands up defensively. "I wasn't saying I wanted to fi—"

Courtney cocks back and rocks his face, completely unprotected. He falls flat on his back, knocked out cold.

"Oh my saints," Kylie says with a huge smile on her face. "That was awesome!"

"Excuse me, um, Pinky. I got to talk to Scrap." Jinx pulls me aside. "Kylie, you too."

"I'm good right here, Jinx. You go on ahead."

Before Jinx starts demanding my sister, I stop him. "She's fine. I know Pinky, it's ok."

Jinx pulls me aside. I look back and see Courtney show Kylie a pair of plated knuckles on her fingerless gloves.

"What is going on here? You're in a gang now? Who is that woman?" Jinx asks.

I laugh off the seriousness of the question. "No. Long story short, Courtney, that girl, found me at the hotel. I know her from, uh, school," I lie. "But since I beat Mean Machine, there's a bounty on my head so Courtney made me a Bone Breaker to… not have a bounty on my head. So—"

"Carson, listen to me," Jinx interrupts. "You do not want anything to do with these people. Trust me. Now, you know how to use the crossbow, right?" Jinx asks.

"Not really." I never held a crossbow a day in my life. This would be great to use against King Chris if I had even a little experience in this, but I would need days, weeks, maybe years of practice to use it efficiently in battle like Needle did. "Is it useable?" I ask.

"Yeah, it wasn't broken in your fight. Let's go find an ammo shop," he answers.

It is very tempting. I would love to use something like this against him. Chris' size and weight trumps mine by nearly two-fold. Being able to attack at a distance would give me an advantage. But on the other side, I have no knowledge, time, or money to spend training myself. Using it could ultimately be my downfall. I don't even know how to reload the thing, and Chris has a Forcefield so even if I do shoot him, he could deflect it. There has to be some kind of disadvantage I can find on this guy. I'm running out of time.

"Do you know how to use it, Jinx? Can you give me some kind of rundown?" I ask him as he looks around for an ammo shop.

"Yeah, sure. Let me see it." He examines it for a few moments, pulling levers, and bringing it close to his eye, aiming the sights down at the ground.

This could be crucial for me. Using this at the right time could be the deciding factor in this fight. I peek over and see Kylie talking to Courtney. She has her arms folded but they don't seem to be at each other throats so that's always a good thing. Kylie got excited when she saw her punch Bonez. Maybe Courtney isn't all that bad for Kylie, she could be the sister she's always wanted.

"Carson," Jinx says to get my attention back. He aims down at the ground once more, looking like he would shoot it. "Ok, this is a M.M.S.C. 100. A mini multi-shot crossbow. You fill your ammo up here." He points at a small tube. "You can use regular darts, or long darts. I prefer the small ones, you can fit about three or four at a time. It would be more effective."

Again, I am so amazed at how knowledgeable Jinx is with things. Could he be a titan? He doesn't look like one. Although, he does have a sort of physique to him, along with the sure signs of a dad bod. I figured he would give me some mumbo-jumbo he pulled out of a hat, but he goes into such unambiguous detail about it. I can't help but stare at Courtney. Her flowing pink hair is growing on me. Her outfit is tight around her magnetizing figure. I switch back to Jinx and realize he is still talking, I really should be listening. My eyes wander again, Courtney catches me staring at her and winks, my head instantly fills with vivid scenarios. That kiss yesterday, all the good times we've had…

"—here. Uh… so, you pull this back." He points the crossbow down and pulls a lever back until it clicks. "This is how you load it. Carson, are you watching?" he snaps.

I swing my head back to Jinx. "Yeah."

"Focus! Your darts go in here." He shows the small indent where you load the darts he was talking about. "Let's have it loaded for you to use. Got it?" Jinx insists.

I wasn't really listening at all. "Yeah, I got it," I say stubbornly not wanting to admit it.

He hands me the crossbow and I look at it with complete confusion. He walks over to an ammo stand to see what prices we can get for some darts.

"**Scrap!**" A deep and heavy voice catches me off guard.

I snap my head to the voice and am taken back to see King Chris walking up to me. He's bald with blue eyes. Helmet in hand, his black armor shines like a freshly polished car with shoulder muscles the size of my head. I step back. "Chris," I say trying to stay calm.

"**Just wanted to wish you luck today. You're a great fighter, very inspirational. The crowd really got on your side in that last fight.**"

"I, uh, ok. Thanks."

"**You a Bone Breaker or something?**" He nods to Kylie and Courtney.

"Does it matter?"

"**Just curious about the color change in your suit. All you need is a skull, and you'll look like one of them.**" he says. "**Interesting engineering, unorthodox, but effective. I've been watching your fights. I'm quite surprised you pulled off that fight with Mean Machine. That guy is such a grandiose idiot promising the world to these people. However, it seems like his whole gang has turned to you now,**" he says astonished. "**Crazy how things happen. How power changes hands so frequently here.**"

"Yeah?" An awkward moment of silence passes over us. I find myself gazing at the man. He stands at least four inches taller than me. His nonchalant bantering makes him so much more intimidating, as if he doesn't have a care in the world. "Where did you get your suit?"

He ponders for a moment. "**Can't say, or they may kill me,**" he squawks. "**You know what I'm saying?**"

We share a laugh. His is more real than mine. Now I wonder how far he's willing to take this fight. "What? You get it from the mafia or something?"

"**The mafia?!**" He bellows out another large laugh. "**No! No, that's funny, Scrap. You're funny. You're a funny man.**" He exaggerates an exhale. "**Alright, enough small talk.**" He looks over to my group, then back to me. His demeanor instantly changes. "**You should forfeit, or I may have to end your life,**" he says nonchalantly.

"Excuse me?"

"**Look, I need this invitation way more than you do. Or, well, *they* need me to. So, forfeit or well... you know.**" He laughs awkwardly but stops abruptly when he sees that I'm not following. "**This is getting awkward, you don't really think you can win now, do you? C'mon! I mean look at you, you're a laughingstock, Scrap. You made a good run and all, an *impressive* run but... look at you. You're a hot mess. I saw what Needle did to your leg, you can't even walk right. I know Mean Machine broke your rib so you're not breathing correctly. You're a life insurance nightmare. I'm sure you're hopping on pain stims too. It's kind of sad, don't you think? So, do you, and that whole gang of yours a favor, and don't show up when your name is called. Better yet, just go home. There's no reason to be here. Go to the hospital, go get better, enjoy the weather.**"

I am flabbergasted, he's trying to help me by threatening me. "I... I can't do that. I need that invite. I gave up everything to be here, I have nothing to go back to, my home caught fire yesterday."

"**Um, it appears you have *a lot* to go back to.**" Chris nods behind me. He is right. With Mean Machine incapacitated for the foreseeable future, I do have a home. Not what I expected, but a place with Courtney in it as well. I take a deep breath and realize I don't have to die today. I can live if I quit, but if I quit, then the Bone Breakers will see me as weak and the bounty will be back on. Either way, I'm going to lose unless I fight him. I can't forfeit. Holy saints, what is happening? "**I like your passion, Scrap. I see why you have it, but that doesn't change anything. I need that invite because my life is on the line, yours isn't. You have a home, a family to go back to that'll accept you. I don't, I have nothing if I lose. But I respect you, so I'm giving you the chance to quit now before I have to do something I don't want to do. You seem different than most people here, you have a heart, and that's odd to see with these, uh, sort of people. But like I said, go home, get better, and stay off that stage, or I will show no mercy, Scrap.**"

He turns around and walks away but stops when he sees Jinx. I can't help but notice a noticeable scar or birthmark on the back of his neck similar to what Kylie and dad has. I stare at it for a moment and realize Jinx and Chris shake hands. He comes back with three small darts.

"Hey, these are armor piercing darts. So if you can get a good shot on him, hit a pressure point or a bone, you may have a shot. Get it?"

"Get what?" I take the darts out of his hand. "Oh!" I fake chuckle at his dad joke. "Thanks."
Again, Jinx does something nice and worldly for me. "You didn't have to do that." I tell Jinx.
"How much were they?"

"Don't worry about that, just make sure you win today. Ok, kiddo? I mean, uh—"

"Thank you," I said gently. "Thanks for everything."

"It was nothing. Now, let me show you how to load them," Jinx says enthusiastically.

I hand over the crossbow, and he fits them in smoothly with a click after every dart. "It's
ready, all you have to do is release the safety, aim, and fire."

"Easy enough." I say, still remembering what Chris just said. "Why did Chris shake your
hand?"

Before he answers, the announcer comes on the loudspeaker. *"Welcome back ladies and
manly ladies. This is your humble, charming, and single announcer! Back with you to find out,
who will be our new champion?!"*

28

The wrath of King Chris

" *First off, we have a man with one of the biggest underdog stories of the year. Actually, scratch that, or should I say, scrap that, the biggest underdog story of the existence of Tyke! Give it up for the one, the only, Scrap!"*

Jinx pats me on the back and I give one more look at Kylie and Courtney. The whole gang behind me cheers for me. Confidence, Carson, confidence. The crowd has doubled in size from yesterday. Hundreds upon hundreds of people have traveled and collected in this festival to watch me go up against a man who should already be a titan. Walking up the three steps to the stage seem harder today. Anxiety races, my heart bounces in my chest. I look out into the crowd and see all the people cheering for me who wanted me dead yesterday. Chris was right, it is weird to see such a mood swing when power changes hands.

"And his challenger, standing a whopping six feet eight inches tall, he's conquered the mighty Vector for a Sonicfist, the cunning Leaf for a Forcefield, and crushed the young hopeful Winterbrand in the first round. All in an arousing two minutes, and forty five seconds combined! Can anyone stop this maniac? It's time to find out. Give it up for King Chris!"

King Chris, in all of his glory stomps up on stage shaking his head. A massive man from afar, but up close, he's downright horrifying. **"You're going to regret this so much more than I will!"** Chris roars. **"That head of yours is nothing but trouble. Hope you don't mind that I nail it on my wall."**

I say nothing as I try to keep my composure and my bodily fluids at bay. He stands strong with a sleeveless armor on his chest like an ancient spartan warrior with a feathered helmet like a knight in my school history books. His arms are solid muscle, his legs are covered in the same kind of metal his upper body has, and he has steel plated boots. He wears the Sonicfist in his right hand, and a glowing white diamond on his chest plate, that must be his Forcefield. If I can get inside his grasp and get a good hit on it, I may be able to break it. With his size, I can't allow myself to be in so close.

The judge walks to the center and gestures us to the middle. I'm eye level with his chest, a monster among men stands before me. "Gentlemen, let's give this crowd a good show. Scrap, how's your leg?"

"Fine, sir."

The judge nods. "Any questions from either of you?"

I shake my head no.

Chris puts out his hand. "**No handshake?**" he asks with an eerie smile and puts out an open hand. His hand is nearly twice the size of mine. Without a second thought, trying not to seem scared, I grab on to his hand and squeeze. He squeezes back and nearly crushes my gauntlet. I don't let up. I can't show weakness. I stare at him with a blank look, trying to hold in the agony of my bones being crushed. I heard a couple cracks too, but I think that was just the metal giving way on my padding. He scoffs as he releases his grip and walks back to his corner.

"Good luck, Scrap." The judge whispers to me as I walk back to my corner. A small crowd is in my corner. Not only do I have the backing of Kylie, but I have an unlikely friendship now with Jinx whose been nothing but helpful, and I have Courtney, the woman who's kept me sane throughout the orphanage and now is back in my life once again. With them, and the rest of the Bone Breakers behind me, I can't lose. This is it. This is the fight I've been anticipating. It is all or nothing; winner takes all; mono' e' mono; for all the marbles.

"Are the fighters ready?" the ref shouts pointing at both of us.

Oh saints above, watch over me. Mom, dad, if you are watching, look away.

"Begin!"

Chris lets loose a berserker like war cry and steamrolled across the stage. I quickly activate my boots and boost to the side to avoid him and dash over to the other side of the stage. "**Why did**

you even come on this stage if you were going to run?! You're a joke, Scrap! A saintdamn joke!" he shouts.

He flexes his hand and activates his Sonicfist. The metal hand illuminates, and he charges toward me. I shoot myself up in the air again. He then leaps up at me, jumping at least twenty feet in the air to reach me. He swings and clips one of my Turbo Boots. A wave of force blasts out of the glove and I'm shoved to the side by a crazy burst of energy. I flip and spin in the air and crash hard into the stage. I look at my boot and see it's completely inoperable. All the scrap metal on my right leg has been blown off as well, only the exoskeleton remains intact. Holy saints, that glove is destructive.

"Stay right there! Don't move!" Chris roars again. He activates his Sonicfist again and jumps in the air, his fist high above his head.

Got to think, got to think fast. I pull out the pipe and dive forward, a loud explosion erupts from the impact behind me and blows me to the corner of the stage like a leaf blower. I spiral trying desperately to hold on to my pipe and crash into the stage again. Saintdamn it!

"It needs to recharge Scrap! This is your chance!" Jinx shouts from the side of the stage.

He's right, it's time to go on the attack. I get to my feet and dash towards him with my only Turbo Boot left. I launch off it and slide around him just enough to clip his ankle, spin around him and get a clean kidney shot. I try for another but he's already caught up with my scheme. My eyes stay keen on his vigorous swings to cleave my head off my shoulders. Each of us grunting and growling as each strike clips our armor in close quarter combat, but neither of us are allowing any clean hits. He's yet to use his Forcefield, what is he waiting for? My tyketanium studded knuckles are doing work to his armor. What could he be planning? I dash around him on one foot just trying to trick him out and get behind him. His frustration grows, I can hear it in his swings. I duck under a rage filled swing, dash around him and unleash a solid kick in his manhood.

He grunts and coughs. His knee finds the stage. **"You dirty little piece of—".**

I unload a full powered right to the back of his head, denting his helmet. The crowd screams in a frenzy of astonishment and excitement. I scream at the top of my lungs as I finish my combination with a heavy swing of my pipe and break off the feather piece of his helmet. I cock back one more time and let loose, but he catches my pipe in his hand, inches away from his face. Everything freezes. Our eyes meet, his are more manic than I've ever seen a human can have, like something inside of him has been activated.

"You're going to pay for that." He pulls my pipe into him, and follows up with a strike to my midsection, I feel a rib crack. I'm flipped over and stripped of my weapon and then hit with it in my chest, cracking another rib. A fist the size of my head collided in my chest again and I'm picked up and flung across the stage. The car battery in my chest sparks and whines. A dent the size of a watermelon breaks through a solid plate of slate metal. I watch in horror as Chris bends my pipe in half and tosses it aside off the stage and into the crowd. Several hands reach up and grab it out of the air. A tussle begins in the crowd as another fight for my famous pipe brews in a mosh pit.

"Whoops. Did I do that?" Chris jokes and rips off his helmet. He then pulls it apart until it snaps clean in half and chucks the two pieces behind him.

I squeeze my sides as the pulsing pain fills my body. I squirm to find my feet. The car battery still operates but how much longer can I hold out until it dies. That's what he's doing, he's trying to break my battery, which will leave me completely defenseless. He roars and charges me once more, sending a barrage of strikes coming from all directions. His strikes are fluid and fast, I desperately try to evade them keeping my hands close to my chest, but a heavy foot clips my side and I'm hit with an elbow I didn't see coming. Then, before I can react, he twirls in the air and with the force of a wollybear, collides into my temple and I'm throttled to the floor. The pain continues, another cataclysmic force rocks my back and cracks another rib. Pain sears through me as I retreat away from him and cough out blood in my helmet. Chris is relentless, he storms towards me and stomps my face back into the stage before I can escape. The back of my head smacks the stage and my visor cracks. Never in my life have I felt something so devastating. He lifts his foot again and drives it down on my face again, but I catch it moments before it finds purchase.

"Give up, Scrap! Just give up!" Chris yells struggling to end me. **"I told you to go, I told you to stay off this stage. Now look, look what I have to do to you. Look what you've forced me to do!"**

My suit whines from the pressure. The car battery in my chest is dying, I can feel the weight slowly building. This can't be it. Am I really going to lose like this? In the mercy of this behemoth, getting my face clobbered into the ground until I either die or... no... This is not how I lose. I can't lose. I will not lose. Kylie... you have always been there for me, you've always had my back when I was down. I can't lose, not after I just got Courtney back, I can't lose her again. I will not, I cannot let her down! I have too much riding on this!

I snap back to reality. A fire lights in my eyes like the fire that burned my scrap yard home to the ground. I swing my leg up and blast his knee inward with the force of my Turbo Boot. He grunts and wobbles backwards, hopefully tearing a ligament. I swing myself up, adrenaline pumping faster than ever. I charge him and sneak a few quick strikes. One to the head and a swift kick to his injured knee. I dodge his next punch and catch the next one in my arm pit. I scream with all I have and heave him over my shoulder, pile driving him into the stage. The crowd erupts in a frenzy. Shouts and cheers of absolute astonishment sound off around me in the crowd. I hear Kylie and Courtney cheering together from my corner.

I get on top of him and make use of my tyketanium knuckles with all the energy and adrenaline I have left in me. I swing wildly and aggressively, flailing back and forth into his exposed face. His left eye blackens, a tooth dislodges from his mouth. I clasp my hands together and heave them down. He smacks them out of the way, and I lose my balance. An elbow collides into my temple and another swift punch find my side, cracking yet another rib and knocks me off him with a right hook to my face and cracks my visor again. He shoves me off him and collects himself. I slide myself back and distance myself before I find my feet.

"You're good, Scrap… quite impressive." King Chris said panting. A sweltering bruise slams his left eye shut. **"But,"** he spits out a bloody tooth. **"there may only be one winner, for there is only one invitation, and that invitation is MINE!"**

"Not if I have anything to say about it!" I yell back holding my side. Ugh, I can barely hold myself up anymore. That was supposed to end it. I can barely see out of my visor from all the abuse it's been taking.

Chris is definitely tired, he has to be. All of his fights would have been over twice, maybe three times by now. I'll use this to my advantage. I sprint towards him, trying to be quick before he gets his breath back. I spring at him with my Turbo Boot, dashing across the stage and swing my leg for his knee. He deflects my kick, stumbles to the side unable to hold much weight on his one side. I sneak around him and sweep my leg in the back of his knee and his leg buckles. I pull back and swing for his head, but he ducks just in time and rocks my kidneys, knocking the fight right out of me for a second time, then lands an open strike to my face, shattering my visor into pieces with shards penetrating my face. He grips me by my chest plate, spins me around, and throws me across the stage. I crash into the stage and skid to the edge of the stage and push myself back from the edge.

"Get up, Scrap! What are you doing?! Get up!" a voice echoes. People screaming for me to move, to show them I can be their champion. I'm winded, my head is spinning, at least five more ribs are broken, my jaw aches, my back stings, my shoulder's numb, I can barely get myself up off the ground. The car battery whines weaker after landing on it for a second time. My adrenaline fades, I can't catch my breath. So many people are counting on me, and I feel as if I have failed them all. My body won't respond, my suit is dying. Nearly four hundred pounds of pressure slowly weighs me down. The weight of my suit is becoming unbearable to hold up. I struggle with all my might to get back up on my feet. I'm not strong enough, my knees buckle and smack the stage. I muscle up enough fight in me to unclip my crossbow.

Chris looks tired and in pain from across the stage. Any minute now his Sonicfist is going to be functional again. I aim my crossbow at him, these piercing darts better work perfectly. I can barely hold it straight, my body screams for me to stop, to lay down and give up, but I can't. *I can't!*

King Chris limps towards me. He looks at his Sonicfist and smiles menacingly. "**It's over, Scrap! It is all over!**" He flexes and squeezes his hand and the Sonicfist comes to life. Emulating a bright red aura around it, it looks fully charged. He was just waiting for it. He growls like a demon possesses him, roars like a wild animal, and takes off like a rocket towards me. I take aim, trying to stay calm as the scariest man I have ever met stampedes towards me. I pull the trigger in quick precession. Miss, miss, and a green aura deflects the only one that makes contact. His armor deflected it, but how?

Oh, saints in the afterlife, his Forcefield…

Jinx screams for me. "Carson, fall off the stage! Fall off the hexing stage!" But it was no use. I loose grip of the crossbow and I can't hold up my weight anymore. I hear the battery give its last whining bit. Hundreds of pounds collapse on me and I'm paralyzed inside the suit, I gave it my best shot. Sorry, Kylie, it was either win or die. I just wasn't strong enough.

Chris laughs manically. **"Goodbye, Scrap!"**

King Chris hits me straight in the chest with a fully powered Sonicfist. My ears ring at the impact of a Sonicfist, and the electromagnetic forcefield surrounding it unleashes an enormous shock wave, detonating on impact. My armor implodes on itself and shatters like my dreams. I'm lifted off the stage like being shot out a cannon in the circus. I can't control myself, there was nothing else I could have done. *You either win, or you die.* I'm so sorry, Kylie. I accept my fate and close my eyes, accepting death and await the conclusion of my fate. Abruptly, I stop, and smash into something solid. I groan out in pain, open my eyes and see the grass. Then, with nothing left to stop my momentum, I'm pried off whatever I hit, and my dead suit pulls me into to the ground, pummeling my limp and exposed body into a dirt pile. My body slaps the ground with nothing to catch myself. I can't move a muscle, I can't move anything. My vison blurs.

Darkness.

29

On one condition

My eyes flutter open. I'm in a room. A bed holds me under an avalanche of fluffy blankets. The pillows are soft against my skin like a cloud. I make the slightest movement and my body screams at me. Pain wakes me up with a fury of burns and broken bones. Oh my saints, what happened? I look around and I'm in some kind of bedroom. I unravel the blankets off me, and I'm shocked with the brisk feeling of air condition. A weird looking vest is strapped around me.

Where am I? In the darkness of the room, a family picture is the only thing I can make out. I slowly maneuver myself to the side to get out of bed but it's hard to move. Breathing hurts. My ribs throb, my chest is tight, and I feel bruises all over my body and my face. Ugh, my jaw, it cracks when I open it. My leg is bandaged where Needle slashed me, and my back is wrapped up from where I was burned. I feel like a giant bandage. Two stim dispensers sit on a nightstand next to my bed with a small lamp on it.

I make my way over to the picture on the wall. My eyes adjust to the darkness, it looks like a young couple with a baby boy. Is that Jinx? If it is, he looks younger, sporting a thick mustache with a green button up shirt. The woman in the picture has long flowing amber hair. She holds a baby with a little suit on.

Footsteps creek the floor from outside the door. The door cracks open and a small figure peaks their head in.

"Hello?" I call out.

"Holy saints, you're up!" A shadow with a woman's voice says, sounding remarkably familiar to Kylie's. She looks back out in the hallway. "Jinx, he's up." I hear a heavy set of footsteps coming and see his body appears. She turns on a light switch and their bodies enlighten. It was Kylie. Jinx walks into the room behind her.

"Sit down, Carson, let me look at you," Jinx orders.

I slowly make my way to the bed and sit back down like he instructed me to do. "Where am I? Is this your house?"

"Yes. Please, Carson, sit down," he demands in a soft voice.

I sit back down on this paradise of a mattress. He's right, why did I even get off? I feel like I could live on this thing.

"What happened? Did I lose?" I ask.

"Oh yeah, big time," he says sarcastically. "I told you to watch out for that Sonicfist. You flew out of the festival and into an apartment complex probably close to three hundred yards away."

"It's a miracle you're alive," Kylie adds. "Every rib is broken. You're lucky you had the helmet on, or you probably would be brain dead."

I sulk in my sadness. I really did lose. "How long have I been out?" I ask.

"A few days. It's seven in the morning on Thursday," Jinx says, making sense why he is in pajamas. He unzips the vest and a pain shoots out of me like an animal being released from it's cage. I grunt at the sharp pain and he straps the vest back on. The vest constricts to my body and instantaneously the pain in my ribs subsided. "My bad." I see you still feel a good amount of pain, you want a stim?"

"Um, I don't know. I feel like I got hit by a train." I look up at the ceiling and try to breathe correctly, but my body just won't let me. "Sure, just do it." I bend my neck to the side and allow Jinx to pin me. As the medicine does its job, I feel the sweet relieving sensation slowly wrap my body in a warm hug. "So, what happens now?"

"What do you mean?" he asks.

I slowly adjust myself, fighting through the soreness. "I lost. I'm never going to get in the Proving now. My suit was destroyed, my home was destroyed, my life is over. You even said it, if I lose, I die." I fall back and let my head hit the pillow. I look over and see Kylie smirking at me. "What?"

"Jinx asked me something, but I wanted to wait for him to ask you first," she says.

I look over at him, slowly and painfully I sit back up again. He takes a seat in a nearby chair and gives me his full attention.

"How would you feel about me adopting you two?"

My mind spins, I'm taken back. This whole time living with Kylie for the past year has made me believe that this was it for us. We had our home, we weren't looking for new parents, we had each other. "I, uh, why?" I ask still in shock. A smirk inches its way onto my face. "You would really do that?"

"While you were out, I introduced Kylie to my," he hesitates. "our family, I talked it over with my wife, your soon to be mother, and well… she is open to the possibility of adopting two Harmonian teenagers who I've grown to, well, become accustomed to."

"Why did you say it like that? Where are we?"

Jinx chuckles. "We are in Greycott. Greycott, Alannah."

"We're in Alannah?" I spring forward. Kylie smiles at me. Our dreams of living in Alannah could actually come true. "I… How?" I'm speechless. After all this time, even though I lost everything, Jinx still finds a way to help us. "Jinx, who are you?"

"I guess this is a better time than ever." He takes a breath. "Carson, I am, what's known as a proctor at Atlantis University. My partner/superior, Proctor Quay sent me out to the tournament to get a fresh look at who wins. As much as Alannah… doesn't accept the norms of Harmony and its inhabitants, this tournament was suggested by the one known as Robert Fox. He alone authorized a sponsorship to the winner of this tournament to subject Harmony to a chance, a privilege to represent Harmony in the Proving. When I heard a *Carson Paul* entered the competition dressing up in a suit made from junk that he found in a garbage can, I had to check it out hoping you were your father's son. I knew I needed to meet you and help you win."

Still star struck and flabbergasted, my mouth can't make words from the happiness I feel in this moment. This bed, this room, air conditioning, oh sweet, sweet air conditioning, a bed that could be mine, and a TV bigger than any I've seen in Harmony stares back at me from the other side of the room. This blanket is soft like a cloud. No smell of mildew, or decaying garbage anywhere in sight. This is a real room. This is real life… "Ok Jinx, what's the catch? How can you be ok with adopting us? We're Harmonian. It's a felony for Harmonians to even step foot in

Alannah without proper passage, and even that is a stretch. You're putting your life in danger, *our* lives are in danger. What were you thinking? We have to get out of here."

"You're lives are perfectly safe here, Carson. Both you and your sister will be properly acclimated to the system and you can restart your lives here. I promise, everything will be ok."

"I've heard enough empty promises in my life to know that is complete canahound crap."

Jinx leans back and snickers. "Canahound crap, that's a good one." He leans forward. "Carson, in the truck you were slowly figuring me out. I am a titan. Suez Legion, Hopscotch Company, eleventh platoon. I've been a titan for nearly two years," Jinx explains. "I have the... authority to...forge documents if need be. Suppose I log into a friend's account in an Alannican orphanage and add, let's say two distinct names that so happen to be yours. Let's also say, I choose to adopt these two Alannican children and house them under my surname. "

"You're insane, Jinx," I mutter.

"Carson..." Kylie stops me. "He's trying to help. He's giving us a chance at a new life."

"I have everything under control, buddy. You will get new birth certificates with your new names, social security cards, everything. If anyone investigates you, you'll both be covered," Jinx explains. "Graycott is one of the gated towns here in Alannah. Carson, you and your sister are safe here. Anyone coming through the front gates needs approval."

Safe. Such a strange and openly used word. What is safe? How can someone know an outsider can be safe? "So, if we do accept being adopted, what now? I lost the tournament. How am I supposed to get into the Proving now?"

"Well, the traditional way. You're supposed to be a high school senior, correct?" I nod. "Perfect, I will enroll you and Kylie in Greycott Mountain High School. It's a fine establishment for Alannah standards. You can go back to school, get your diploma, and register to participate. In Alannah, all you have to do is sign up, it's really not that hard."

High school was the only word that caught me. I can go back to school. *Kylie* can go back to school. I look over at her. Her eyes tell me to listen, her heart begs me to try. I ponder the idea of going back to school; friends, homework, gym class... in Alannah. "Does this school have a starball team?"

Jinx smiles. "Why, yes. A good one in fact. Do you play?" I nod, getting myself excited. "I'll contact the coach and see if they can squeeze in another hopeful prospect in their workouts."

My smile grows. Kylie's smile copies me. She sees me being reeled in like a fish.

"So, you will go to school, get your diploma at Graycott Mountain High School, come home and train. Of course, I won't stop you from making friends while you're here but you should be focused on training. My wife, Julianna, your new mother, will make sure you're comfortable. My son, Raymundo, will look after Kylie while you're at school. I'll have her in his classes. If Kylie is as smart as she says, he'll need her to help him more than he can help her. I have everything you can need to train too, weights, treadmills, gravity condensers, a virtual simulator, whatever you need. Alannah is always coming out with new training equipment so I'll get whatever will help you prepare. This is your chance to do this, Carson, the right way."

I'm speechless, still nervous to say yes, but how can I say no? Where will I go if I say no? Will Kylie even follow me if I do? I can't do that to her, to us, not after all we've been through. Kylie grabs my hands. "Ray's nice, Carson, you'll like him. You'll love it here, I promise. We are finally safe," Kylie even says it. Does she really believe we're safe here? In this foreign land full of people who hate us for being who we are? What about this Raymundo? Who is he? Can I trust him?

My mind races with more questions that all need to be answered. "So my name isn't Carson Paul anymore?"

"Yes, of course your name is still Carson Paul but for now, to keep your real identity safe, you must take my surname, Marano," Jinx says.

Carson Marano... Kylie Marano... "So, I'll be Carson Marano?" Jinx nods. "I... don't know how I feel about that. It's weird. Like you're going to be my dad? I barely know you and it's like your trapping me with your name."

Kylie huffs. "C'mon, Carson, it's not that big of a deal what our names are."

"It's just to keep you safe," Jinx adds. "Here in Alannah, people take pride in their family name. They respect names like Fox, Brix, Marano, Caldwell, Leonidas... Once people see you are my son, your time in Alannah will be smooth. You just need to abide by our norms and customs so you aren't targeted as suspicious. If you act out of sorts, people will notice, and when people notice, questions arise and when questions arise, investigations begin."

"I thought you said we were safe?"

"We are as long as you don't goof off and say some kind of Harmonian slang like... what were those idiots saying, you heard?"

Kylie and I giggle. "Don't stress about it too much, Carson," Kylie says. "The people are so nice here, they're sophisticated and well mannered. I even met their neighbor, Mr. Matthews, he is such a sweet old man."

Kylie's already met the neighbors. "What did you say?" I say frantically.

"Settle down, Carson." Jinx lays a hand on my shoulder.

I smack it away. "Don't touch me," I snap. "What made you think bringing two Harmonians to Alannah was a good idea? I have a target on my back now. If anyone finds out I'm not from here, I'm as good as dead."

"Because if I didn't, you'd be dead in the mud I found you in," Jinx snaps back. "Take a look at yourself." Jinx grabs my blankets and tosses them off me. Bandages wrap over my leg, bruises stain my body. He grabs the strap on my vest and yanks it off. A shooting pain stabs my side like he flipped a switch. "This decompression vest is helping you breathe." I grab the strap and fiddle with it to tighten it back to my body. He takes it out of my hand and straps it back down. A suction noise compresses the vest to my sides and the pain goes away, such amazing technology.

I take a few deep breaths and realize Jinx was right. "Ok, you win, you're right, thank you. But before I say yes, you promised to tell me about my parents? I want to know everything."

Jinx looks at me and takes a deep breath. "Let me tell you the story."

30

Jinx's mission

(The day Carson and Kylie became orphans)

Before transferring to Suez Legion I was an alphaOmega in Fox Legion. The mission was simple, find Christian Paul and extract him back to base for interrogation. My commanding betaTitan Milo DeAngelo was placed in control of the operation. With a background of seventy-five successful missions, he chose my squad to do, what he called was, a light mission as a reward for our laborious work. We were told this was a rescue mission, but it wasn't, it this was a kidnapping operation.

"Ugh, this Harmony air smells like piss and depression," LowDelta Brennan says. Low man on the totem pole in his sophomore year of Atlantis University, full of ambition and sarcasm. We picked him up recently because my highDelta enjoyed a card trick this kid showed him.

"Right? I bet it's full of prostitutes," my second in command, highDelta Robbins adds. Five years away from retirement, this old man refused to promote his entire career. Said he wanted nothing to do with the titan spotlight, but still kicks just as hard as anyone here.

"So Brennan's ex-wife is here?" LowDelta Evans jokes to his classmate. Both are new to the squad but Evans is a senior in school. Lucky for me, my squad has thick skin and can take an edgy joke.

Laughter fills the truck. My squad is a good bunch, full of personality, and loyal to me from day one. I ride shot gun in an armored hovertruck with my team of four leading straight into

Harmony City. Robbins drives us to a restaurant named Brooklyn's. Seems shady at first, but we have our orders and we're prepared for anything.

"Hey, Omega, who is this Christian Paul fellow?" Robbins asks. I was omega at the time, which means I oversee the operation while my titan sits on his lazy hindquarters in the stealthshot helicopter and/or does recon. Normally, titans lead the operation on foot, but Daniels has his own way of doing things.

"Some scientist stole some world changing tech from Fox. Says he will be docile and understanding."

"Interesting. Why are we intercepting him at a restaurant? Doesn't that sound strange?"

"You're saintdamn right it does, but I don't question Daniels, and neither should you."

"What if this hex wants to fight back?" Evans asks.

"We do what we have to, Evans. Keep the hexer alive, we do not want blood on our hands," I snap. "Whoever this guy is, he is important to Fox."

"Copy, sir."

The drive from Alannah to Harmony was long and tedious. Once we grabbed Paul, he was supposed to hand over this Project SPINE. Robert Fox demanded we get it to him at all costs. If we failed to do so, we would be shamed and blacklisted, meaning we would be fired, and our pensions will be terminated. So, for the last four hours, Robbins drove my burner and bourbon smelling squad through the boarder and into the heart of Harmony. We park just outside the restaurant in the parking lot across from a dark blue quadmobile.

Robbins points out the subject's car. "You'd think the guy would have a nice car for being a scientist. The thing isn't even a hovercar. I haven't seen one of those things in ages."

"That's Harmony for you," Brennan says.

Reports also say he may be with an unknown woman of power, maybe another investor for the tech. It was our job to make sure the deal falls through and extract Mr. Paul before things get ugly.

So, we wait. An hour goes by and we see the couple walk out. They walk holding hands back to their car. The man walks smoothly while his partner looks drunk with a stain on her red dress. She's basically being held up by the man.

"What the hex?" I say. Our suspect opens the door for the woman and gets her in the passenger seat. He then walks over to the driver side and starts the car.

"Sir? Orders?" Robbins asks about to open the door.

"No, hold on for a second." I press my radio to talk to my titan. "Charlie squad to Patriot, threat seems docile, looks to be intoxicated. Do we have confirmation on the target?"

"Affirmative, omega, Brooklyn's. White shirt, black tie. Woman in a red dress should be with him."

"Sir, there must be a mistake here. Are you sure the information is correct?"

"Saintdamn it, Marano, get the scientist and get to the extraction point! Over and out."

"Start the engine. Follow them onto the skyline, we'll pull them over once they're out of town," I tell Robbins.

"Sir, he's right there. We can arrest them right now for driving drunk. Just look at her, they've obviously been drinking."

"No, there's cameras everywhere. We are way out of our jurisdiction to be arresting some random in a restaurant parking lot. Now, follow him."

"Copy, sir."

We watch as the car pulls away and we follow them. Twenty minutes of driving goes by, and they seem to be going in circles. Either they are on to us, or this man is lost.

Just as I am about to give the order to turn the lights on, the car makes a sharp right turn down an alley way. Robbins misses the turn.

"Turn around! Saintdamn it, he's on to us," I yell.

"I knew we should have got him at the restaurant!" Robbins is a skilled driver. He swings the truck around and floors it back the other way. He tries to cut the car off, but we end up empty as the car doesn't show up at the next turn.

"Ohhh, he's a smart one!" Brennan adds in the back.

"Charlie to Patriot, we lost eyes on the target, I need a bird's eye of the target," I say into the radio.

Static starts buzzing in the radio. *"Affirmative omega, target is half a mile north heading to Hope's Highway."*

"Copy. Move it, Robbins! Don't lose him."

Robbins floors it and drives like a mad man, nearly crashing into several cars making wide turns. We make it to Hope's Highway and still have no eyes on the target. We take an illegal elevation and floor the accelerator. Lights on, sirens blaring.

189

I click my radio. "Patriot, where is he? We need a visual," I ask my titan again over the radio.

"Target's—" Static.

"Hex! C'mon."

"He must be jamming us. How does he know we're on to him?" Evans questions.

"—passed him Charlie—" Static. *"—woods east north east side of the woods. You'll find a small dirt trail. Follow it, do not lose him omega."*

Robbins hears the radio and throws the truck in another sharp turn around onto the grass. He drives along the grass and turns it into a fire trail. We slowly follow the trail until we find the target's car smashed into a tree. I exit the truck, weapon drawn. I order Delta Brennan to approach the car and pokes his head in. He says there's no sign of them.

I stick my face into my communicator. "Omega to Patriot, target's on foot. Proceeding to target."

"Copy, Charlie. He could not have gotten far. Be careful, we need him alive."

We march, scanning the surrounding woods. There's about thirty miles of woods here. They couldn't have gone far but they could create a hell of a man hunt if they wanted to.

"Yo, omega, I'm not getting a good feeling about this. I've heard Fox wants this chip to give people super strength. What if this scientist attacks us?" Delta Brennan asks.

I click my safety off. "Subject is supposed to be docile. However, reports indicate this chip was meant to make people superhuman. I'm not sure what that means but stay frosty."

"Weapons hot deltas." Robbins orders.

"Copy sir. Drinks on me tonight, alright?" Brennan says.

"Hold you to that, delta. Tranquilizer rounds loaded, omega," Robbins confirms.

The storm brews. Raindrops by the billions fall from the sky, covering our path. The loud smacks from the rain hitting the ground disrupt my hearing. Lightning cracks followed by an enormous boom of thunder.

I switch over to my intercom setting on my communicator. "Christian Paul, by order of Fox Legion, you are under arrest." I call out. "Do not resist, we will use force, if need be. You are in possession of property that belongs to Robert Fox. Surrender yourself now, and no harm will come to you or your business partner." Lightning cracks again, the storm rumbles right over us. A wild wind gusts through the trees, nearly pushing us off balance.

"Christian Paul, you are now resisting arrest and will be charged with the highest extent of the law. You are committing treason, do you understand? Surrender yourself now before we have to take extreme measures." The pouring rain smears the foot prints we were following. Water seeps into my boots and my visor fogs. Saints, I hate the rain.

"Christian Paul! By order of Fox Legion, I—"

"Stop!" a woman's voice shouts. "Don't shoot." A woman in a soaking wet, dark red dress creeps out behind a patch of trees. "What do you want with my husband? He has done nothing wrong to you! He is an honest man."

Husband? I walk closer to the woman, I extend my hand outwards. "Ma'am," I push her to the side, and motion Evans to take point. "Christian is your husband?"

"Yes. Please, he means no harm."

"If he means no harm then why are you driving into the woods? Why are you evading us? Where is he? Tell us now!"

"Contact!" Several shots go off, Delta Brennan shoots into the darkness.

"Holy hexing shit, Brennan! Are you insane?" I whisper in rage pushing his gun down.

"Stop! You'll kill him," the woman yells.

"Stop!" a man's voice calls out. A man appears from the darkness. Soaking wet, Christian Paul emerges with his hands up. "Please, don't shoot. Isabella has nothing to do with this." His dark hair covers his eyes, his beard covers the bottom half of his face. All that is visible is his nose. "If you're not here to kill me, I surrender. Please, I have a family."

"Dr. Paul?"

"Yes. Please, that's my wife. She has nothing to do with this."

Delta Evans steps forward. "You are under arrest for treason, and theft of government property by order of Viceroy Alpha Titan Robert Fox."

"Robert Fox? Robert Fox?!!" His hands go down. "That bastard has been trying to steal my work for years and now he sends a goon squad after me? This is an outrage. This is *my* property, not his. I haven't committed treason. *He* is the one who—"

"Shut up!" Evans snaps, and points his gun at him. "Turn around, hands on your head. You can explain yourself on the moon." He points to the woman. "You too, ma'am, hands on your head. Do not resist."

"Sir, I have children, please, we can't just abandon them," his wife pleas.

191

"You should have thought of that before stealing government technology from the most powerful titan on Tyke," Evans snaps and manhandles the woman, bending her wrist to make her fall to her knees.

"Hey!" Christian yells. "Get off her! She's innocent!"

"Shut up!" Brennan shouts and points his gun at Christian.

"Hex you! You stay away from my children! I know what you will do to them. You monsters are going to use them for your experiments."

The woman twists and pries out of Evan's grip. Brennan turns his back to us and Christian immediately jumps on Brennan's back, and wrestles him for his gun. Several gun shots go off, and the woman screams and falls. Christian's fingers lodge into Brennan's eyes. Blood squirts out of his face as he screams for help. I freeze. Evans and Robbins rush over to them. Christian falls with Brennan on top of him and throws Brennan's limp body off him. Christian reaches for Brennan's gun and points it up.

"Stop, Christian!" I point the gun at him. Fully intending to fire.

Evans lights him up, unloading his entire clip into Christian.

"Hold your fire! Hold your hexing fire, Delta, are you mad?!" I shout.

"Omega! What is happening?!" the radio sounds off, I ignore him.

Evans looks baffled and steps to me. "He just killed Brennan! Hex this guy, omega!"

"He needs to be alive, you hexing moron!" I shout back. "When will you learn that—"

Christian still moves, he pushes himself up to his knees. "Stay away from my wife, you monsters," he wearily moans. "She's innocent, my children are innocent, he'll use them!" Electricity dances inside Christian. The tranquilizer rounds sizzles through his body, yet he fights the urge to give up. "You think Fox cares about any of you? He'll kill all of you to get what he wants. He's a menace! A SAINTDAMN—"

Robbins decks him in the head with the butt of his weapon. Christian finally hits the ground unconscious and Robbins handcuffs his hands behind his back.

"Saintdamn it, omega, what is happening?!" the radio goes off, I ignore it again. The woman is bleeding out of her side, a puddle of red under her. I quickly nurse her wound with a coagulated injection. The bleeding stops in seconds. Her pulse is slow, but she's stable. I radio my titan. "Charlie to Patriot, target acquired, one K.I.A., one wounded. I'll brief on the Patriot. Proceeding to extraction. Over and out."

My mission was simple, grab Christian Paul and escort him to the extraction point. Once I dropped him and his wife off to Titan Daniels, the mission was over. My deltas and I drowned ourselves in hard liquor for the rest of the night in honor of our fallen delta. For the success of a highly classified mission, Robert Fox promoted me to betaTitan and awarded me my own company. HighDelta Robbins accepted a promotion to omega where he now commands Charlie Squad. From reports of the operation, the scientist had Project SPINE implanted on his brain stem at the time of extraction and was unable to remove it without killing him. Dr. Christian Paul remains alive as a war prisoner to Fox Legion until he complies to the mass production of Project SPINE.

That was the story I told Carson and Kylie. The truth was too much to tell my new son and daughter so soon. The truth is that I went rogue and shot their father, not Evans. I disobeyed my orders and blamed it on my dead delta in our reports to save our reputation.

My grief and depression only grew from that day forward knowing what I had to do to right my wrongs. As my first mission as titan, I was ordered to go back to the orphanage three months after Robbins left them there. Robert Fox wanted them as peons to negotiate with Christian, just as Christian said he would. When they weren't at the orphanage, I was ordered to take the oldest boy there as an alternate, a seventeen year old pale red head with amber eyes. He was packed and sent up to the moon to meet his new father, Robert Fox.

Disgusted by Robert Fox and realizing Christian was right, I abandoned Fox Legion and transferred to Suez Legion, where the only spot open for a betaTitan was an assistant proctor spot at Atlantis University. From there, I put my old life behind me and housed my family in Greycott. My head proctor, a Daltonese native named Arthur Quay, got the idea to scope out a Harmonian fighting tournament in Levi, Harmony, exactly where the two children were sent. I jumped at the opportunity to go back and find the two children but to also scout out the winner of the tournament. When I realized the son of Christian Paul was actually a competitor in the tournament, I knew what I had to do. I ignored the rightful winner and focused all my efforts on finding out more about Christian Paul's children. I couldn't think of any positive outcome telling them the truth in my story, that I was the reason why he and Kylie were orphaned, that I was the sole reason his parents didn't come home. So, I did what anyone would, I lied, but I fed them, housed them, and now, with my back against the wall, I am the adopted father of a boy who wants nothing more than to find out the truth. For now, the truth must remain hidden. For now, I can shape the boy into a man who could dethrone Robert Fox before his plan goes into motion.

31

Do you trust him?

My mind explodes like an atomic bomb. Not only is Jinx a titan, but he was the commander of the squad who lead the operation after my mother and father. Anger builds, frustration piles on this wave of emotions building up my throat. "So, you know Omega Robbins?" I try to ask calmly. Rage igniting my small fuse with a flamethrower.

"Yes, he was a trusted soldier of mine for nearly—"

"Robbins was in my home," I snap. "Robbins pointed a gun to my face. He…" My body twitches in anger. I want to yell but I won't. I want to cry but tears aren't what fills my eyes, it's betrayal. I look over at Kylie and see her worried face. As the multitude of questions compiles, in my head, one already has its answer. "So, my father actually did shoot my mother. Robbins really wasn't lying about that."

Jinx's eyes flash. "He… He did and didn't. He scuffled with my delta and the trigger was pulled." He exhales and shakes his head.

I clench my fists. "He destroyed my family, Jinx! You and your squad are the reason why we became orphans! I lived in a scrap yard for a year, I was ripped away from the safety of my home. Now you come to me with your big fancy house and money and say you'll adopt me? You ruined my life. Why would I ever stay here? Why would I ever trust you?"

"Because I'm the best you got," Jinx snaps back. "I'm trying to help you."

"I'd rather take my chances in Harmony," I snap back. "At least there I won't have to change my name or live a fake life. I had the Bone Breakers in the palm of my hands. I had

Courtney. She wanted me to be Head Skull. They wanted me to lead, they wanted me to rule. I could have gotten whatever I wanted there, and you took me from that."

"Now just hold on a second there, Carson." Jinx stands up with his hands out. "Don't you think for a second you would have been adequate in a gang. That Pinky girl looked like nothing but trouble. You wouldn't have survived a day without my help in your current condition. I stitched your wounds, I bought you expensive recovery Vitastims, I even got that vest you have on. These things are exclusive only to Alannah, I'm the reason why you can breathe correctly right now. I brought you into my home and offered you a life of freedom. I didn't mean to hurt you or your family. I was only following orders. I saved your mother's life for saint's sake."

I clap my hands. "Oh, bravo, hero. Let's give it up for the participation winners. What am I, a charity to you? A redemption for your lack of better judgement?"

"You ungrateful piece of—"

"Either way, you would have taken my mother and father away from us. We would be orphaned either way."

"That's not true. He killed my men. He stole government technology."

"That's a hexing lie, Jinx. My father has been working on Project SPINE ever since I was a baby. He didn't steal anything! You have been lied to... Pshhh, if I were my dad, I would have done the exact same hexing thing if—"

"Carson, be reasonable," Kylie snaps. "You're acting like a psychopath. Just listen to him."

I look at Kylie in an unfathomable gaze. "Reasonable? Kylie, our mother didn't deserve to get shot. She was harmless. She was an angel and this man is the reason why—"

"You're alive?" Kylie stands up, defending Jinx. "Jinx saved our mother, Jinx saved *you*. You were being crushed under the suit. He ripped you out of it and bought everything you have on, have you looked at yourself? You think Courtney could do all this? You think the Bone Breakers would have done any of this?" I stop my thoughts of rage and violence and realize Kylie is thinking more logically than I am. I'm bandaged everywhere from my arms to my ankles. "He didn't leave your side yesterday. He cares about you. He cares about us. He's giving us a second chance for a better life. Now, apologize."

"Me? What do I have to apologize for?"

"Carson, stop being ridiculous," Kylie snaps. "You even told me that we can't change the past. We have a good opportunity here. It's not like Jinx was the one who shot them."

196

I stop myself from cursing at him and take an unsettling breath. "You're... you say you want to help but you're the reason we're in this mess in the first place. How can anyone trust someone like that?"

Jinx snickers and collects himself with a deep breath. "I... I'm sorry. I'm sorry about your parents but I only did what I was ordered to do. You have to believe me when I say, I never meant any harm to you or your family. We were told Dr. Paul had Project SPINE on his person, not already implanted. It was supposed to be a simple one, two, three thing. No shots were supposed to be taken but your father went rogue and put your mother in danger. He was only supposed to hand it over. We even were told to pay him an absurd amount of credits if it came down to it."

"Yeah, I've heard he's denied a considerable amount of credits before. It was one of the biggest arguments our parents had," Kylie says.

"If it makes anything better, I'm just a low level assistant for the freshman class. I basically grade homework for a living now," Jinx says. "I don't even go out in the field anymore."

I roll my eyes. "Just because you did what you had to do to save your own skin doesn't make it any easier to trust you. How do I know that anything you say isn't a lie to cover up another lie?"

Jinx clicks his tongue. "I don't expect to earn your trust overnight. However, there will be no more secrets between us, no more mind games."

"Ok, but how about—"

"Oh my saints, Carson, *shut up*." Kylie snaps.

I look at her with a crooked look. "I'm trying to get information out of him. Jinx has been so secretive, so closed, so cryptic. I want more. I want his real intentions."

"It's fine, Kylie." He puts his hand up. "These are appropriate questions."

He's playing with me. Making me feel entitled to ask but I'm nervous to know the answers to them. Kylie is nervous for them too. One slip up and she knows I'll turn around and walk right out the door. Doing so could jeopardize everything. How do I look my parent's captor in the face and call him dad? Does he feel guilty for what he did? Did he do all this to fill a void in his heart to make him feel whole again? Am I simply just a good deed to him?

"So... where are they?" I finally ask.

"Who?"

"My parents. Are they ok?"

"My best guess is your father is on one of the moons. That's where Fox Legion is stationed. Your mother was transported with your father. As much as I want to say she's with him, I have no knowledge of it."

I nod. I can understand where he is coming from. Although I never took a life before, I do understand how it feels to injure someone and feel remorse for them and their family. Am I just as bad as Jinx, all the fighting and the stealing? My past is extremely decorated in a multitude of petty crimes. "You a believer in karma, Jinx?"

"I am. Karma is the only disease that can never be cured, but the only medicine for karma is forgiveness, right?"

"There is no forgiveness for murder, Jinx."

Jinx makes a worried face. He sees the fire in my eyes. He knows what I'm capable of, what I'll do to accomplish what I want. "I'm the one who has to live with my deeds. It's not easy, it's hard to look at myself sometimes, but I walk out my bedroom and I see why I stay sane. I see my wife and my son, they are the only people who know me for me. When I saw you, I knew I had to help any way I can. Please let me right my wrongs and help you through the Proving. You're safe here, Kylie is safe here. Isn't that all that matters, big brother?"

I roll my eyes again. Not because he's annoying me but because he knows exactly how to persuade my reasons. Kylie's eyes meet mine, her eyes say please, her eyes say give this a chance. I look back at Jinx with one exception and smile. "You ain't calling me kiddo."

32
A New Beginning
Six months later

L ife has changed dramatically in these last six months. Instead of living on the streets with my sister, we now live with Jinx and his family in a gated community, two miles above sea level, in Alannah. My adopted mother Julianna's a professional stay at home mom, as she likes to put it, and a renowned chef. She's posts videos on her Novestream's page of herself showing off her complimenting outfits along with creating unique, and dazzling food dishes that leave her fans drooling and paying top dollar for her cookbooks.

I'll be completing my senior year of high school this year, two months from my eighteenth birthday, I slipped under the adoption age law, so Jinx adopting me and Kylie was perfectly legal. Kylie's the youngest in her junior class and she has never been more excited to be back in school. I was a bit worried about how I would be able to handle an unfamiliar culture. To be in an Alannican school is something neither of us know what to expect. Society is extremely different here compared to Harmony. People are friendly, but there's an eerie over-competitive nature with Alannicans. Everything is a race or a contest. Everyone has to be better than one another. Students constantly try to outdo their peers whether it's the best grades, the strongest lifts in the gym, or the fastest around the track.

Jinx's wife and son were, however, soothingly calm about our homeland, Julianna more so than Ray. He was quiet and stern on his feelings for the first few weeks, but he lightened up when he found a trust between us. Harmonians are not the plague or a disease as we are portrayed. We are the same as everyone else. We made sure to follow house rules and pitch in when needed. Sometimes, I even pitched in and did Ray's chores for him to get on his good side. Eventually our secret was secured and, for the time being, I finally felt at home here in Alannah. Jinx even got me a chance to play starball at school. I didn't make the team because I was absolutely saintdamn horrible compared to the unbelievable athleticism and size of some of the kids I had to go up against, but it wasn't a big deal. Jinx promised me something and he kept his promise.

Besides starball, I stayed focused and learned what I could in the classroom, but being from Harmony, it is difficult to fit in. Hiding my surname wasn't the hard part, keeping up academically with everyone was. My grades are above average for a Harmonian but for Alannah, I am below average. Half the students in my school score a perfect GPA. I had to up my game and try harder than I ever had to in school to even keep up with the average kids. That's where I met Norman.

Norman Vanhoozer, a sub average student, but one of the most levelheaded Alannicans I've met. He is constantly ridiculed at home by his strict parents and harassed by his teachers to act accordingly. He tries to keep up with the other students, but he talks about some kind of learning disability. Alannah doesn't believe in disabilities of any nature, they just see it as weakness, and weakness isn't coddled here. We found each other at the back of a classroom on the first day of school and we've been friends ever since. From there, I met his best friend, Phineas Deacon, an All-Alannah track star by day and a bachelor by night. He accepted me with open arms and forced me to be a normal Alannican kid and go out drinking with them every weekend. Norman's parents were usually out on business, so he would throw the *wildest* of parties. I tried to stay sober but, being the new kid, Norman and Phineas made sure people threw drinks at me everywhere I walked. Alcohol is in abundance, not a delicacy like it is in Harmony. You had to rob or pay top credit for any kind of alcohol in Harmony.

There was definitely a culture shock in the first few months. Alannicans are sophisticated, and live wealthy lives. I couldn't keep up with all the things they had. I was still getting used to having a Palmphone again. Now I have the most updated version, the Apex X9. Jinx has a three-story house, with a basement and a backyard with a massive in ground pool. It blew my mind how much stuff he had, how many rooms, and entertainment he could afford on a titan's salary. Even after living here for six months, I still hadn't explored the entire house. My bedroom was downstairs, so I stayed more towards the bottom floor.

Another new thing I have grown accustomed to is driving. No more hoverbikes, I now have a driver's license and drive one of Jinx's twelve cars. One for each month he jokes, but with steady grades and good behavior, he allowed me to *finance* one of his cars. He says once I get through the Proving I'll be making a little lower than a lowDelta's salary through my freshman year. So, if I can fill the tank, it's mine to use. It's been hard making money without stealing it but with the car I was able to pick up a digital news installer gig. It's simple, just annoying to wake up early three days a week to drive around town and install the latest articles of Alannah to people's mailbox tablets.

Jinx also told me if I want the car, I have to drive my siblings to school and back home as well. It's not a problem, the school shuttle always bothered me, but here in Alannah, they are much different. Instead of a rust bucket transporter driving around an overstuffed meat wagon of children, barely able to ascend off the ground, we have these sleek hydrogen powered shuttles that fly nearly twice as fast. They're all equipped with air condition, heat, soft cushioned seats, and a breakfast waiter that'll make you a fresh breakfast sandwich.

After school, I wait in my car exploring through my palmphone. It still feels like a dream to sit here in my own car, in Alannah. To think, two years ago, this reality felt like a fantasy. Kylie and Ray mosey on out of the front door of our castle sized school. Two twenty-foot-long doors stand at the front, with a huge lounge area around with a long fifty-foot awning going down the strip that leads to the parking lot. 'Welcome Back Roucars!' stands in front on a banner next to a brass plated sculpture of a fierce feline predator with fangs protruding out of its mouth. Our mascot stands proudly on a rock with one of his claws out in the air to swipe. It was made to high five for good luck.

"Let's go!" I yell, hurrying my siblings.

"Hold on!" Kylie yells back, still not making haste to my car.

"Fine." I start the car and activate the hover pad. The wheels invert up to ninety degrees and a push of magnetic force forces my car airborne. "Find your own way home."

As I inch away from the curb, I watch Ray panic a little. His curly brown hair bounces as he starts to run. "Woah, guy, slow your role," he calls out to me. He runs around the side and hops in the front seat. I turn back around and see Kylie still walking with her book bag stuffed. She still walks at the same pace, not falling for my bluff at all. She hops in the back with a huff and tosses her bag to the side.

"What's wrong?" I ask.

"Nothing. Just a lot of homework," she replies.

I look at Ray for confirmation, he's in most of her classes yet he doesn't carry nearly as many books as she does. He shrugs his shoulders and flips his wrist to unlock his phone. A 3D hologram of a pro starball player appears in his hand. He swipes around with his other hand to his social media page. I ignore my twenty questions I have for Kylie and pull out into the main road. I have a different agenda for today anyway, something that's been bothering me ever since I've arrived here in Alannah, something dear to me, something I should have done but couldn't because of my injuries. When I drop my siblings off home, I'm taking a drive back to Levi to find Courtney. She took me back in one easy swoop. She wanted to introduce me to someone, and it's been aching me for months. Who can it be? Brett? I wonder how he's doing, if he recovered, if he's the same, or even if he is still Head Skull. I can't tell Jinx nor Kylie. They'll tell me it's too dangerous and trap me with guilt and logic to stay. With Kylie safe, I don't need to baby her anymore. She's opened up enough doors for her to consume herself in her education. She's started exercising and going for runs on her own. Finally, I can confidently say she feels normal again. A new, special kind of normal, a bliss only we can describe.

I remember seeing the town for the first time. Never in my life have I seen clean, window filled buildings, people of elegance strolling down the road, not a vacant building in sight, no boarded-up shops, shady drug dealers on corners, or stoned bums passed out on the sidewalk with a stim in their hands. I look in the rear-view mirror and see Kylie smile looking down at her hand. She's texting someone. "Who are you texting?"

"None of your business," Kylie says nonchalantly.

"Oh, it's a boy," I say cheerfully. Not caring, but it's fun to get under her skin.

"No!" she snaps.

"Oh yeah, it's totally a boy," Ray adds his own comment. "Who is it? Alvin? Todd? No, its Demetri."

"Ew, no. No! Bleh," she says makes a puking sound. "It's none of your concern." She flicks her wrist and the projection dissolves. I keep my eyes on her through the mirror, we lock eyes, and she smiles and blushes, obviously getting embarrassed. "What?" she laughs.

"You got a boyfriend now?"

"No! Kind of... I don't know. No, not yet-ish"

"Not yet-ish? Kylie, since when do you talk to boys?"

"Since I can finally have a real intellectual conversation with one," she argues and a good point to make. "It's so weird, I actually have to try to have the best grade in my class."

"Yeah, I totally know the feeling," Ray says sarcastically.

Kylie rolls her eyes and clicks her tongue. "Maybe if you put your phone away and listen to the teacher, you wouldn't struggle all the time."

I stay quiet and listen to them babble on and on about something that happened today. When I land in our massive six vehicle long driveway of Jinx's mansion sized estate, I watch Kylie and Ray hop out. Kylie looks back at me confused since I didn't turn off the car. "You not coming inside?"

"Not right now." I tighten my grip on the steering wheel, knowing now I have to lie to my innocent little sister again. "I'll be right back. I, uh, gotta get something at the store."

"Oh, what is it?"

Damn it, Kylie, just leave it alone. "It's nothing. Just something I've been wanting to look at. A new game."

Kylie gives me a crooked look, probably seeing right through me. "What's it called? I'm sure you can look it up on your phone. I'm sure some Novastreamers already made videos to watch."

"I, uh, I know. I know. It's just better to see it in the store you know?"

She hesitates, thinking about my lie as if it was really the truth. "No, it's not… What's going on?"

"Nothing," I quickly say. I start to levitate the car. "I'll be back before dinner. Tell Julie I went out for a bit. Love you," I roll up the windows and back up away from her. The air from the bottom of my car pushes off the ground and blows Kylie's hair back. I see her eyes squint with a million more questions why I'm acting so weird. I pull down on the gear shifter and drive away. Leaving our glorious new home for an old one, a memory filled place of poverty and deception. I am bound for Harmony with a head full of excuses and redemption speeches for when I see Courtney. I don't know why I care as much as I do, but something inside of me knows what I'm doing is right. I just hope it doesn't get me in trouble.

33

Scrap Returns

I soar through the skies on the Skyline Expressway. Not another hover car in sight. My palmphone GPS guilds me through the air space and out the boundary line of Alannah. I drop into the urban altitude and make my way through some dirt trails and smuggle myself into Harmony.

My life has changed so much in these last few months. My hair's slicked back with gel. I wear a blue pullover jacket with my school starball team logo on it. I don't look like a Harmonian anymore. I decide to take a detour and pass by the orphanage again. I don't stop but the old house brings back thousands of memories. The food that was hardly edible, the constant screaming and yelling I had to blank out to sleep, and nights filled with laughter and splendor with Courtney. I pass through the span of woods Kylie and I traveled through to get to Levi. It took near seconds to pass but for us back then it took all day to cross. I cut into traffic on the main highway and make my way into Levi.

Once I'm in town, I pass by the scrapyard, or what was the scrap yard. I didn't recognize it at first but it's now under construction. The entire lot is gone, bulldozed flat with a big sign advertising low income housing. Wow. The lot is gargantuan compared to the space we had.

A thought rings in my head, I have no idea where to look to find Courtney. She never gave me an address or anything. What do I do now? I find myself aimlessly driving around town, ten, twenty minutes goes by and I have no idea where she could be. I can't stop and ask someone. "Hey where's the Bone Breakers hideout?" I'd be laughed at or robbed at gun point. I stop at a nearby recharging station and flip the man my card to plug in.

"Nice car, youngling. Where'd you get it?" the grungy attendant asks.

I'm caught off guard at his voice. I look at him with confused eyes, not only because he's talking to me, but because I don't know how to answer. "It, uh, it was a gift." I notice the stench of puffer smoke on the guy. His dusty brown jacket reeks of it.

"A gift, you say? Is that the newest palmphone too? Where you coming from, boy? You don't look like no Harmonian."

"I grew up in Redding."

The man nods his head and swipes my card. He hands it back to me. "Won't work."

My eyes bulge out my head. "Won't work?" I snap back to him.

"Yep. Won't work."

"That's impossible. I know I got credit on there." I stick my hand out for my card.

The man keeps it and flips it over. "Yep, must not work for you hexing Alannicans." He chucks the card behind him. "What do you think you're doing here, boy? Joy riding? You don't belong here and, quite frankly, I don't like liars here at my establishment."

My mouth opens but won't work. "I, I'm from Redding."

"Liar!" he snaps. "Listen here, boy, let me hold that fancy phone of yours and I'll let you leave. C'mon, fork it over."

I don't know what to do. He eyes me with a cruel smirk. I may be in a car but if I leave without my card someone will expose me. I'll have to explain to Jinx why purchases were made in Harmony. If I fight back and rush to grab the card, my car could be jacked. If I give him my phone, I'll lose my phone, all my personal bank accounts, social media profiles, everything could be revealed.

"No," I answer firmly.

"No?"

"Yeah, no. I came here for a charge, if you won't serve me, give me my saintdamn card back, and I will leave. Who are you to rob me when I'm simply here for a charge? I'm visiting family. *Family* whose been forgotten by relatives and all I'm trying to do is see if they're ok."

He laughs hoarsely, sounds like he spends most of his days sucking down burners. "I ain't ever heard of an Alannican with Harmonian family."

"Oh, well, nice to meetcha," I say trying to blend my words as most Harmonians do. "I was in the titan tournament last year."

"Oh yeah? Another lie, huh? Boy you're just adding them up now."

"I haven't lied yet," I lie. "I… I'm the one who sent Mean Machine to the hospital."

The man's eyes blink and his whole attitude changes. "You're… no way." His body tenses. "How *dare* you come to my shop with some preposterous—"

"If I was from Alannah, sir, how would I even know that? I'm Scrap."

The man takes a step back, he eyes the floor and picks up my card, he looks it over and swipes the dirt off it. "Carson Marano, huh? That's really the name of the boy who sent Brett Breaker to the hospital?" He hands back my card and eyes me up, he looks at his jacket and wipes a pile of dust off it, a name tag appears, 'Voltz'. A stained, but visible skull with a crack through it becomes visible. "You're supposed to be dead."

"You're telling me." A silence lingers. "So, you're a Bone Breaker?"

"The oldest," he says plugging a line into the charging port of my car.

"Then maybe you can help me. I need to talk to Cour… Pinky."

The man blurts out a loud obnoxious laugh. "Don't we all, Scrap, don't we all. You obviously haven't been around much. She goes by Pink now. What happened to you?"

Gotta play the part and get myself into my inner Harmonian. "Long story. I have friends in high places and had to take an extended stay in Alannah after the tournament. Got knocked pretty hard, yah heard? Broke my ribs and stuff, I could barely even walk. But my guy patched me up and I'm back. So, I need to see her, she needs to know I'm alive."

He peers over to me, then looks the other way into his little shop. I turn my attention to two bald men playing cards. Each wearing a much cleaner black denim jacket. He whistles a sharp chime, and their heads pop up. One hops out of his chair quicker than the other and walks towards my car. "What's up, boss? This guy giving you problems." He gets bigger and louder as he approaches. "I don't like people who give my boss problems! You want problems, boy?! You want—"

"Yo!" The man stops this raging animal. "Hop in and bring him to Pink," he orders.

"Boss, who is this guy?" the other bald man says.

"This is Scrap. Rose from the dead. Now stop arguing and hop in. Now," the grungy old man snaps. He looks over to me. "They'll take you to Pink and when you're done, leave. You've caused a mess here and you don't belong here anymore. Do your business and don't come back, yah heard?"

I nod and choose to trust the man. It's risky, but if he's telling the truth then I have no other way to find out. Then again, I can't show fear here. Harmonians aren't cunning, or evasive plotters. If they want you gone, they'll make sure you disappear. The doors open and the two men pile in. A reeking stench of burner smoke smacks my nostrils. "You mind if I smoke?" The one asks.

Jinx is gonna kill me. "Nah."

34
Pink

After both of them burn through two burners, my car finishes its charge. A cloud of toxic tobacco fills my car. I feel lightheaded, more than when I was induced on stims. "Alright, where are we going?" I ask the man in the front seat. He has a noticeable scar down his cheek.

He hacks up a lung in his hand and wipes it on his pants. "Just go round back here." He blows the last of his puffer out the window and flicks the butt of it out the window.

"Seriously?" I look at him baffled. "Why did…" I groan in frustration and start the car to hover around the back of the shop. Hexing Harmonians, I've forgotten how ridiculous some of them can be. I go slowly around a mixed pile of trashed cars and several car parts laying in the dirt. A wooden fence surrounds us with the sound of canines barking behind it.

"Drop down right over there." He points to the side where several other cars and a row of Varleyson chargerbikes are parked. All of the cars have blacked out windows, one in particular appears like it just got into an accident. I park and tuck my keys in my pocket. I get out and pray that the car is still here when I get back.

I follow my two companions to a door where they knock in an offbeat rhythm. A set of eyes appear in a small tab at the top of the door. "Who is it?!" The man recognizes them instantly. "Oh, what's up?" He then eyes me up and glares. His eyes pivot back to the bald man. "Who's that?"

"Pink's ol' boy, Scrap. Remember the tournament last year? This guy made Bonez look like a fool."

"Scrap, huh?" the man behind the door retorts. He glares at me again. "You're the one who broke Bonez's nose?"

I nod with a hum and push back my hair. "Sup, man? Is Pink here? I gotta talk to her, yah heard?" I say trying to act as Harmonian as I can. It comes naturally.

He completely ignores me. "I thought Scrap died?" the pair of eyes says to the man.

"Apparently he's back from the dead," the bald one with the scar says.

I lift my hands and smirk. "Alive and well. Listen," I inhale with no other answer besides a vague and simple one. "I got to talk to her, it's personal."

"Ay yo, I ain't talking to you. I don't care who you are, shut your mouth," the eyes snap then dash back to the bald guys. "Voltz ok with this?"

"Yeah, he told us to."

"I heard." The tab closes and I hear a loud clanking noise. The door opens with an eerie squeaking noise. Darkness follows behind the door and a bearded man appears. He wears a black bandana with a ripped sleeve jacket, a well amount of extra weight rounds his belly. His muscles exceed the size of his head with a large vein pulsing on his bicep. "She's downstairs."

I follow the two men through the door and down a flight of stairs. A familiar smell of burners contaminates my nostrils. Old grey walls with peeling paint and scuff marks line down the stairs with a flickering light that needs replacing.

Chatter fills the room as we walk into a bar. Dozens of grimy looking men and women sit on circled tables with drinks in their hands and burners in their mouths. Smoke fills the room and heavy metal music engulfs my ears. Guys are playing cards and billiards around the room. There are two small windows in the corners and a few fans on the ceiling. I search around the place. I don't recognize Courtney from any of them.

A heavy hand drops on my shoulder. "Ey, Scrap, go sit at the bar and order us a couple shots. We'll be right back," the bald guy says. I feel uncomfortable here. I look like a fish in a tank of carnivorous sharptooths. The man's hand leaves a burner stain on my sweatshirt. I'm an eye sore to the rest of the people inside. I look around and see several sets of eyes glaring at me. People who don't know who I am or why I am here. I don't belong here, I'm not safe. I scurry to the bar where a man with an afro sits on the other side. Two dark skinned girls surround him with smaller black jackets that wrap around their revealing breasts over a tank top. Knee-high hard toe boots and black stockings cover their legs up to a teasingly revealing short skirt. The woman behind the bar cleans a glass as she sees me. I sit down a few stools away from them. They glare at me like I don't belong here. I nod to them, to greet them.

"You lost?" the deeply voiced man asks across the bar.

It takes me a second to recognize he was talking to me. All eyes are on me. "Nah, just waiting for someone."

The bar tender on the other side of the bar looks the same as all the girls but she wears a red bandana around her tied up hair. A towel over her shoulder covering her name plate. She leans on her counter and looks me dead in the eyes. "You sure you're not lost? You look very, very lost." Her voice is seductive, but her slanted eyes make me caution her.

I try to remain calm. "I'm, uh," nervous is what I want to say. "I'm Scrap. Or at least I was. I'm waiting to see Pinky."

Her eyes glare at me like I called Courtney a rude name. "It's Pink. Don't insult her name again... Scrap, huh?" she asks unconvinced. She stands back up.

"Yeah, thee Scrap. Why'd she change her name?" I ask leaning forward, peeking over the man across the bar, knowing all of them are eavesdropping.

"Head Skull does what Head Skull wants, yah heard?" She pulls out a shot glass from under the bar and pours me a shot. "You're supposed to be dead by the way." She slides me the shot glass.

"I've been told." I raise the glass to her, and down the shot as manly as I can. The liquor tastes bitter and foul, nothing like the liquor I'm used to having in Alannah. I try not to make a face. I reach in my pocket for my wallet and drop a few credits on the bar. "Pour yourself one."

She slowly reaches for the credits and smirks. "Daddy always told me to respect the dead."

She pulls out another shot glass and pours us each one. We cling glasses and each down the liquor. My high school parties are returning to me. I should remain sober though, I came here for Courtney. I shouldn't be drunk when I see her. The bartender looks above me and waves her hand over. I peak over my shoulder and see my two bald companions walk up to the bar.

"You buying shots for everyone right, Scrap?" the man asks, sounding more like a demand. I look over my shoulder again and figure the number of shots. Looking more towards three to four dozen shots. Saintdamn it.

I click my tongue and look at the man to see if he's joking. He looks stern with a small, convincing grin on his face. I look back at the bartender, and hope she intervenes. Her eyebrow lifts in curiosity. I can't say no, I got the credits. I groan, feeling the regret of my logic. "Sure. Why not?"

The bald man turns and shouts. "You hear that everyone? Shots on Scrap!" The crowd lifts their drinks and cheers. The man slams the counter. "Pour em out, Asia!" The glasses fill the bar and the red bandana bartender walks down the bar filling each glass with precision. As each man and woman walk up to the bar and receive their free drink, I cling glasses with the two bald men and we down our liquor.

My head starts to spin, and I realize I am getting ahead of myself. My inner filter that blocks nonsensical words dissolves as the burning alcohol rushes through it, breaking its walls and letting my loosely lipped words find my vocal cords. I find her heavenly more attractive than I did five minutes ago. "What is this stuff?" I ask the bartender feeling the buzz of social freedom.

She whips the towel off her shoulder and uncovers her name, 'Asia.' "It's the gang special called Neverclear. It's a mix of pretty much everything we can get our hands on. Supposed to knock you on your ass."

The alcohol is going straight through me. My belly warms, my head lightens. "Oh," I giggle. "well, I'm already on my ass." Asia snorts out a laugh and shakes her head. I look over to the scarred face bald guy and see him chuckle as well. "Do you drink this stuff all the time?"

"Nah, only when we can get it. We smuggle this stuff in from Dalton. They got the best distillers on Tyke."

I nod. "Hey, where's Pink?"

"Head Skull is busy with her boy," the other bald man next to me says. "Take a load off, Scrap. Buy us another shot."

Busy with her boy? I should have known she would have gotten over me by now. It was pointless to come all the way out here thinking I can make amends with her. "Her boy? She has a—"

"Yeah?" the bar tender interrupts. "You... don't know?" her eyes brows slant, the bald men look over to the bartender, they eye each other with suspicion.

"She has a boyfriend?!" I blurt out, trying to stay cool in my tipsy state. "It's fine. I figured. Hex it! Fill me up, Asia." I smack the shot glass on the bar.

"What? No, you idiot. She has a baby."

My mouth has a different user. The alcohol takes the reins of my mind and tells me what to say. "A baby?! When did she have a baby?!" I blab out loud.

I instantly feel the entire room stare at me, like I betrayed each and every one of them. Chatter awkwardly silences the room. Not a sound, besides the rolling guitar rift of the music playing.

A door slams open. "Where is he?!" A loud raging woman's voice enters the room. I whip around and see the woman I've been waiting for. A thin, blonde woman with knee high black boots. Faded pink strands of hair are tangled in a mesh of blonde all tied up in a tight ponytail. Pink is the name on her dirty black jacket. A crowned skull with a crack going down through the eye planted on her jacket sleeve. Her head swivels around and finds me at the bar. She marches over to me.

"There you are!" I stand up to give her a hug.

"Come with me." She grabs the collar of my sweatshirt and pulls me off the stool. "No one comes through this door without my say!" she shouts into the bar.

Nearing tripping over my own two feet, I'm dragged out of the bar and down a hallway into another hangout room. A raggedy brown couch is in the middle of the room pointing at a TV with some kid's show on.

"Sit," she orders pointing at the couch. Her voice is nothing like the girl from the orphanage. I sit down trying desperately to gain my sobriety back. She pulls a chair from the table behind me and sits backwards on it. Her blue eyes remind me of who I came here for but the person who's eyes they belong to tells me she's not. She squints at me. "Are you hexing drunk?"

"Uh, a little. I can explain," I chuckle.

"Famous last words…" she huffs. "How do you keep coming back from the dead, Carson?"

"I… I can explain that too."

She clicks her tongue and rolls her eyes. "I'm sure you will and what the hex are you wearing? Since when do you like starball?"

"I've always liked starball," I say confused. "And again," I lift my hands up hoping to calm her down so I can sober up, which is not working as well as I would have hoped for. "I can explain."

She folds her arms. "I'm getting really sick of hearing that come out of your mouth. Next time you say it, I'ma smack you." She looks at my hair, and her eyes drop down to my clean pants and unreasonably priced designer shoes. "Well," she says sounding impatient.

"I... I don't know what to say. I just wanted to find you."

She clicks her tongue and looks away from me. She stands up with a huff and walks to turn off the TV. "Well, you see me, don't you? Listen, I'm busy. I have a lot going on, and you are the least of my worries."

"I can imagine, I hear you have a kid now."

Her head snaps to me as she clicks the off button on the TV. "Yeah, well, so what?"

"Is he Brett's?"

"How did you know I had a baby?" she deflects.

Thinking quickly, my Harmonian past has trained me to conceal rumors. Never snitch, even if it was little. The smallest of snitches could lead to a world of consequences. "You told me you had someone you'd like me to meet. Is it him? When did you and Brett have a kid?" I ask.

"Me and Brett didn't'..." Her face scrunches like she's about to explode. "The father of *my* child is none of your concern."

"Fair," I dismiss it. I realize the pain in Courtney's eyes from a mile away, there's no sugar coating what I need to tell her, so I'll just say it plain and simple. "I live in Alannah now."

"You what?!" she sneers. "Is that why you look like a hexing cheerleader?"

"Pshhh, c'mon, Court."

Her eyes bulge. "No, no, no, you did *not* just call me that. You do not have the *privilege* to call me that anymore, do you understand?" I nod and understand. "How did you get into Alannah? Harmonians aren't allowed anywhere past the border without a written consent from the Viceroy."

"I, um... Remember that guy I was with at the tournament. He uh... he saved me when I lost the fight. He brought us back to his home and well, he kind of adopted us. I've been going to school there too. My plan is to graduate and go to the Proving."

Courtney looks insulted, betrayed, and baffled all in one facial expression. "Well isn't that just hexing fantastic. So happy for you, Carson. So hexing happy for you." She throws her hands in the air and shakes her head. "How is that even possible? How is any of this possible? You were hit by a Sonicfist encased around a Forcefield! You should be dead, Carson Paul, *dead*!"

"So I've been told."

She grunts and walks in a line back and forth in front of me. "How did you survive?" She stops in front of me. "How are you able to walk? I... I looked for you, for days."

"Wasn't easy. I went through months of physical therapy. Jinx, he, um, he helped me get back on my feet. Alannah's medical equipment and vitastims helped me dramatically. His family has been a great help. I honestly don't know how it works but the last thing I remember is smashing into some building a quarter mile away from the festival, and the next thing I know, I was in Alannah."

Courtney clicks her tongue and shakes her head again, feeling the unbelievable events that unfolded in my life. Nothing that spectacular has ever happened to her. From what she told me, Courtney has had zero luck in life besides having a certain way of persuasion to get what she wants. "I don't believe this," she says sounding frustrated.

I feel nervous to ask. She feels more intimidating than she ever has. That crown on her jacket intrigues me. She's actually Head Skull now. "I, um, I wanted to uh…"

"What? Beg for me back? You're lucky I haven't put a bullet through your head for coming here."

"I mean, I bought everyone shots. So—"

"Shut the hex up! Like you're such a saint. Hex you, Carson. How dare you think you can walk in here and expect anything other than a bullet in your skull."

My loose mouth starts flooding with composure. As much as I believe I deserve everything she's been throwing at me, it wasn't my fault. I had no control over what happened after the tournament. "Look, give me some slack here, I didn't mean to leave, Courtney."

She folds her arms. "Well, you did. For a second time now, you abandoned me when I've never done a single thing wrong to you.

"Lies," I snap. "You stopped talking to me for two months at the orphanage, like I did something wrong." I watch her face tense, I fling my arms up, starting to feel annoyed for always looking like the bad guy. "When I woke up in Alannah, the first thought I had was crap, I left Courtney." Her face loosens. "I'm sorry, but I could barely get out of bed. Every rib was broken," I pull my collar down to show her the arrow scar in my shoulder. "You know that arrow I was shot with against Needle? I could barely lift my arm. I had to go through six months of physical therapy to get back full range of motion." I unbutton my pants to show her that scarred gash down my thigh.

"Um, what are you doing?" Courtney asks confused.

I ignore her and pull down my pant leg to show her the foot-long scar from a sword I also got when I fought Needle. "You see this?" I watch her stare at my scars, full of words but none to say. I pull my sweatshirt off and show her the burn scars from the fire in the scrap yard. "This is what happened when I ran back into that fire in the scarp yard." I can't see her face, but I know it isn't a pleasant sight. "I had my own problems to deal with, Courtney. So, please, let me be the first to apologize," I say sarcastically, but full of meaning. I step closer to her. "I'm sorry I left you again," I say sincerely. Trying to change the mood of the conversation. "I didn't come here to rub my new life in your face. I came here to see if you're doing ok, if you need help, if... if I can make it up to you. I think about you all the time. I just... I couldn't come see you when I barely could walk out the front door."

Her eyes soften, her arms untangle. "How do you expect to make it up to me?"

"I don't know but what I can do is—"

I hear the door creak open and it stops me. Thinking it is one of her goons checking in on her. We haven't been quiet, so it's to be expected.

"Mommy?" I hear a toddler's voice. A little boy no more than a couple years old peeks through the door with a dirty blonde mohawk, freshly cut, with a white t-shirt on and a diaper.

"Riley!" Courtney panics. "Go back to your room, mommy's busy."

"Are you ok, mommy?" the baby says holding his hands. His brown eyes look up at us with worry.

"Yes, mommy's fine," she says motherly. Courtney pushes me out of the way and picks up the baby. "C'mon, let's go back to bed." He hugs her and lays his head on her shoulder. I watch her motherly instincts kick in as she rocks the baby. Her world turns to him as our conversation becomes voided and meaningless. I don't think twice before I follow her out the door and down the hall into a room that looks designed for a child. Big race car stickers fly around the walls with checkered flags and green flags crossed together. On the other wall is a cracked skull with the name 'Rampage Riley Breaker' on it. She lays him back down in the crib in the corner of the room.

I walk over to her side. "He's got your nose."

"Shut up," she says cheeringly disguising her words to sooth her baby. She doesn't give me her attention, her eyes are glued to her child. I watch as the young boy snuggled with his small blanket and fades back into slumber. He looks older than one, maybe two. I gaze at Courtney's

215

tired eyes looking down at him with a small smile on her face, petting his hair. In that moment, I realize something that shakes my very being.

"He's mine, isn't he?" I finally ask.

"Yes," she says keeping her sincere voice she used to talk to her son. My mind spins, my stomach drops, and my world instantly evolves in a way where life has a new meaning.

"He's... how? His name? It's—"

"How else do you think babies are made, you idiot?" she says softly, still keeping her eyes on him. She finally looks over at me and I see the woman I've grown to care for, now in a way that I've never felt before. She's not just some girl I fell for at the orphanage, she's the mother of my child. I'm a father. "C'mon," she leans her head out the door and I follow her out.

"How is he mine?" I whisper while we're in the hallway walking back to the room.

"Because I was pregnant at the orphanage," she huffs. "I didn't know how to tell you, so I just stopped trying to see you. I didn't want you to be worried. After you left, I... I was with Brett for a while and when I was..." She clicks her tongue, obviously pushing through the embarrassment. "When I was, *showing*, he assumed and well, I said it was his. He was ecstatic and when he found out it was a boy, he cried, Carson. Riley is his son, but you're the father. When you put him in the hospital, I took over as Head Skull and Riley hasn't seen him since."

"Wow. How is Brett now?"

"He's recovering, I guess. I don't know. Haven't really talked to him. I don't really care anymore," She looks deep into my eyes. "He hasn't been the same, Carson. You really messed up his head. He doesn't know what to do with himself. He's suicidal, he's always angry, he doesn't want to see Riley anymore...."

"I didn't mean to I—"

"It's fine," she stops me. "We've managed without him and quite honestly, he's kind of a dope. He's not... he's not educated. I can't talk to him like we used to talk, he doesn't challenge me like you did, I don't know. It's just now we're in the middle of a gang war with the Sky Kings and the Onyx Ghosts and, well, things have been rough. The gang isn't the same without him and his inspirational leadership, and that's what he was, an inspiration. I can only do so much. I'm a mother now, I don't have time to do raids and stick guns in people's faces while teaching Riley how to read and go to the bathroom on his own."

216

I'm feeling guilty for doing so much damage. I can't regret what I did, but the repercussions I have made to someone I care about is what bothers me the most. I feel lost for words but all I want to do is make amends with her. "Can I help?"

"You gonna stick around?" she asks optimistically. "Because Scrap would be a huge help to me right now. You bested Brett, you're good with words and fight with passion. I could... I would appreciate it if you stayed around."

A million thoughts race through my head. I become speechless as the immense weight of the situation bares itself on my back. "I, I don't know."

She folds her arms, disappointment rolls over her face, then a huff of disgust. "You don't know?" she snaps. "You don't know if you want to raise your son?"

"How do I know it's really mine?"

"It's hexing yours, Carson!" she roars in my face.

"Ok... But, what about when Brett comes back?" The awkwardness is making my stomach turn. "I'm going through the Proving in a few months. I can't miss that."

"Right." She walks away from me. "Real mature, Carson." She walks to the door and opens it. "Go then. Go to your *Proving* and go be a corrupt slave to the people like you've always wanted to. I'll be here being your son's mother, and I'll run this gang while you go play hero. I'll devise a way for peace from two vicious and blood thirsty gangs while you can run and fly in your little battlesuits and arrest people like me, right? Because that's what you've always wanted to do, right? Be some peacekeeper, right? You want to save the world from villainous monsters who roam the streets of your town, make your city safe again, like in the movies, right?"

"That's not fair, Courtney. You hid this from me for *how long?* You expect me to just drop everything?" I walk up to her. "Courtney, this is the only way I can truly find out what happened to my parents."

"My name, is Pink," she sneers. Jealousy and betrayal in her heart, I can feel it, she never knew her parents. She feels betrayed by them and knows that they are meaningless to her. Now she's a mother and all she's ever wanted is to have a complete family again. "You know what happened to your parents, Carson, they're gone. They don't exist anymore."

I hesitate by the sheer idea of it. I know they're alive. I know it. Jinx wouldn't lie to me. "Hex you."

"No. Hex you, Carson. You want to know what does exist?" Her eyes start to get puffy. She chokes up but sucks it back inside. "I exist." She points to herself, then to me and back to her. "Our son, exists," she says with a lower voice. A sincere plea, a beg for me to reconsider. My dream ever since I was a child was to be a titan. To somehow, and some way, make my way to Alannah to accomplish what I thought was impossible. With that on my shoulders, it is up to me to find out where my dad is, to find out for certain if my mother is alive. If my dad is as important as Jinx makes him out to be, with this Project SPINE thing, I need to go. I can't stay. The fate of humanity rolls its magical dice with me in it. Now, more than ever, I believe I was put on Tyke to be something, to be a titan, but how? How can I walk away from the mother of my child? Do I even believe her? Can this boy be mine? Those brown eyes, he looks nothing like Brett. I have a son...

What kind of father would I be to abandon my child for my own personal reasons? Saints, I am my dad's son. I stand in front of Courtney speechless. She eyes me down, her mental wall building thicker than it's ever been. She doesn't trust me. She knows my answer, but she hopes it can be altered. Unfortunately, it cannot. "I can't."

"You can't?"

"If there is any way I can do both I—"

"Both?" she laughs. "No, there is no *both*. You don't deserve *both*. You abandoned me and him when you left that orphanage and now, *now* I give you a chance to stay and you say, 'You can't.'"

I throw my arms out. "You can't expect me to be able to make this kind of decision right now Cour—" I stop myself. "Pink. I've been wanting to do this my entire life." I try to think of an alternate situation, it is hard, but my drunken mind still won't cooperate. "Look, Brett wanted to expand to Alannah, right? I can do that. I can—"

Courtney raises her hand to me and shuts her eyes. Her face tenses, she shudders in another betrayal. A lone makeup filled tear rolls down her cheek. "Let me be crystal, saintdamn clear with you. Brett is *not* Head Skull anymore, I am." She points to herself. "I control what happens and where we expand. We are staying in Harmony because we are at war because *you* put us in it... I will give you, one, last, chance, Carson... Stay here, join the Bone Breakers and help me fight off these hexing nobodies who think they can walk all over us, be the father that Riley needs, and stick by my side while I bring the respect of the Bone Breakers back to Levi. You can do whatever you want, screw who ever you want, all I ask is you're there for the boy. Or..." she sighs. "You can go back to your pretty and luxurious home in Alannah, and for saint's sake, do, not, *ever*, come back," she demands firmly. Her heart's about to crack, she trying to hold back her emotions from the amount of stress I've put her through the last few years. I left her with a baby, I left her to join a gang she didn't want to join in the first place. Now she runs it during the brink of a territory wide gang war. "Choose," she demands. "Choose right now, Carson."

With a deep breath and a heart full of regret, my mind is made up. "You're not going to keep me away from my son, Courtney. I'm going through the Proving and when I am done, I'm coming back for you. I'll bring you to Alannah and I'll give you and Riley a home. Jinx can make it happen. I will make it happen."

A second tear rolls down the face of my first love. My heart breaks to see her so distraught, but my mind is made up. The idea of justice and revenge runs deeper than this.

"I don't want your hexing charity. This is my home, and this is *my* gang, my family. This is all I have, this is all my life has given me. Alannah's really changed you, Carson, so gunho with glory and all that. You forgot what it feels like to be left behind... Get the hex out of my face." Forcing back more tears, she whips around out the door. "Knuckles! Fury!" she calls out, I hear several skids of chairs. "Take out this trash for me! Make sure he can't get back in."

Two gruesome men encase the doorframe and pass Courtney. They eye me up with demons in their souls and metal knuckles on their fists. They instantly pounce on me. I'm able to evade a few swings and land a couple more but it is no use. There's no room to move around in this small room. Regret flourishes as the metal knuckles rock my shoulder, and wrists. My body is slammed against the wall, I'm kicked, and my sides are thrashed. I flop to the floor and cover myself hoping these two monsters don't kill me.

After what felt like an eternity on the floor, she calls them off. She pushes through them and pulls on my collar. My bloodied face inches from hers. "You ever step foot in Harmony again, I won't show mercy." She pushes me back and kicks my face. I feel a tooth go through my lip. I'm yanked up off the ground and dragged through the bar. My eyes flutter as several dozen eyes watch me being dragged away. Every one of them despise me. I have betrayed everyone here.

The sun blinds me. I close my eyes and feel myself being thrown. My body smacks a sleek metal surface. My eyes adjust to the sun and I feel a dent the size of a boulder on my passenger side door. A slimy ball of phlegm smacks my cheek and a loud creaking door slams shut. I pull myself up and feel the temptation coursing through me to look at myself. A black eye and a busted lip make their appearance on my face. Blood stains my teeth and drips down my lip. Dread fills my heart, I feel ashamed of my selfishness. I feel worse than I ever have. I made eye contact with my son. My baby… and I said no to him, and to *her*. I deserve this. I don't deserve him, and I don't deserve her. How am I ever going to explain myself out of this to Jinx?

35

Time to move on

It's been a month since I've seen Courtney and my son. His face is embedded in my head. Courtney's pleading eyes makes me regret ever leaving her in the first place. What could I have done differently? Any other decision could have led to dire consequences. What would have happened if I stayed and joined the Bone Breakers, if I didn't go to Alannah? Kylie would never survive in a gang. What would she even do as a new member? What kind of initiation do they have? Probably nothing good for the women. I'm sure I'd have to get beat up or something ridiculous like that, maybe even rob somewhere, or kidnap someone. I haven't slept well all month. Some days I would drain myself to exhaustion just to get myself to sleep. Only downside of that is I have to train harder and harder every time because my body's adjusting and getting stronger every time I do it.

Kylie gave me one look after I came home the night I saw Courtney. She just shook her head and ignored me the rest of the night. Ray was wildly curious and so was Julianna. I ended up telling them my story, leaving the baby part out of course. That is something I'll choose to keep to myself. Saint forbid if Kylie ever found out…

Jinx laughed and called me names. Then he saw the car. Hah, he had another few choice words to call me. He said the damages will be added on to my debt to him. I couldn't argue with that, so I sucked it up and suffered through the consequences.

With that thought lingering, it's time to train. I have four months left before the Proving so I need to get my head on straight. Jinx tells me the Proving changes every year so the secret behind it is to keep your mind open to any possibilities. All I've gotten out of him is I better be ready to think outside the box, and the surprise production of Chris Turner in Fox House. He was bigger, stronger, faster, and an absolute genius through his freshmen year of Fox House. Senior deltas are jealous of him, and underclassmen are terrified of him. Apparently, he's going into sophomore year a betaOmega. Robert Fox himself has already opened a spot for him on his personal team of subordinates on the moons.

After breakfast, we go downstairs to the basement. I walk into a massive open room where he has his own collection of battlesuits of all different classes lining the walls in showcases. He has Warmongers, Demons, Ghosts, even a collapsible Mecsuit that the firemen had when they saved me from the fire. Down in the next room is his armory. Guns upon guns line the walls along with swords, war hammers, crossbows, spears, and even a few different styled Sonicfists. He is quite the collector.

Today, Jinx wants me to use his virtual reality gravity compressor machine. I'm not sure what it's named but he calls it his Box of Doom. I suit up in a sensor filled onesie and step into a massive metal cube that Jinx said had cost him a small fortune. It allows me to train virtually while he can control the gravity and the difficulty of what is coming after me whether it is bandits, soldiers, animals, or even laser beams being shot from different directions. I feel a pinch and a shock on my suit depending on what is able to hit me. Alannah's technology is astoundingly more advanced than Harmony by lifetimes.

"You ready, kiddo?" Jinx asks.

"You bet," I confirm. He's been calling me that lately. It's still slightly awkward but I'm not uncomfortable with it anymore. I think it's because I've slipped and called him dad a few times. I've learned to trust him and doing so helped me learn to be an Alannican. This is my new life and, for now, I must wear a last name I wasn't born with. I must be Carson Marano of the Marano family.

When a simulation starts, the cube dissolves into a realistic looking environment, whether it's the forest, the beach, or even space. My body is encased into this machine and my onesie morphs into a battlesuit. I consume my conscious to my new surroundings and train as if this was real life. I feel as if I am living in the moment, it's the only way to truly train your instincts. A few simulations go by and my heart is already pumping. The degree of difficulty Jinx puts me through has honed my senses twice over. I have gone from a punk kid with a heavy fist into a natural fighter. My combinations are fluid, technique is strict. I'm balanced in mind and body with perfect precision, movements are quick and lethal, breathing properly, and stellar weapon accuracy. I can complete any difficulty Jinx has thrown at me. Until today, where he ups the gravity by two times normal gravity, causing my legs to tremble just from holding myself up. Wave after wave of vicious carnivorous animals and a platoon of level ten soldiers, my body feels like it is holding a thousand pounds of sand. I call it quits and scream for Jinx to stop as my legs buckle and I'm shot eight times across my body. Every virtual laser burns and stings as I'm pushed to the floor. As a faceless soldier rushes up to me and lifts its sword up to impale me, it dissolves, the forest environment dissolves, and I open my eyes to the familiar surroundings of the metal slates that close me into the cube.

Jinx groans. "That was embarrassing. Are you seriously going to give up that easily in the Proving?"

"I can't even stand up!" I yell still unable to get my chest off the ground. "I'd like to see you do this any better."

"This isn't for me, kiddo. It is for you and you alone. I don't need this training."

The gravity releases me. I try one more time after getting a drink of water. I can't figure out a system. I try to remember where the soldiers come from, but they don't respawn in the same spots as last time. As one comes in front of me, two come from behind; completely unlikely, but then again, anything could happen. The shocks and pinches continue until I give up once more and shout for the simulation to stop.

"Horrible, absolutely horrible," I hear Jinx. "You know you're not going to be able to say stop in the Proving."

"Hex you!" I scream out the window where Jinx can watch me. "How am I supposed to prepare for something when I don't even know what it is?"

Jinx slams his hand on the control pad. "What'd you say, boy?!"

A pack of canahounds virtualize in a circle around me. Vicious hounds that run on four legs and sharp teeth like razors that can tear into flesh with ease. They're small, but as a pack can take down any prey they can find, including me. They growl angrily and dash towards me.

I am able to dive out of the way but can't find my feet in this dense gravity. They pounce on top of me and bite at my shoulder trying to find my neck. I rip one off and shoot a blind shot but another one grabs hold of my arm and brings me to my knees. I punch it three times and hurl it into another one. My arm burns from the pain receptors in the suit. I gain some space between the pack and unload my weapon into them. As the animals are hit, they dissolve into the abyss of the simulation. I hear a tiny snarl behind me and I snap around but it's too late. Two of them pounce on me and I shriek as the animals maul me. They dig their noses into my neck and I can't get a grip of them in time before the sensors sting me, stimulating an uncomfortable pain that tells me I lost.

"Stop!" I call out and the canahounds disappear. Holy saints, that was intense. Sweat drips off my face as I try to catch my breath but my ribs still haven't fully recovered. Every time I overexert myself, I feel an uncomfortable reminder of my past. The gravity still doesn't budge. "I need a break!" I say panting. "Turn it off!"

"A break?! Sure, let's wait for little Carson to get a drink of water while a saintdamn war is going on. Ok! I'll wait."

I try to fight through the gravity but I can barely get to my knees. "Can you turn down the gravity? Please."

"Turn it up you say?" Panic smacks my heart. I watch him out of a small window where he looks down at the gravity control and I feel the pressure push me down with a force I have never felt before. My knees give out and my body smacks the floor. "I'll tell you what, you get up, and we are finished for today," Jinx wagers.

I try and scream to push myself up. I yell and grunt my heart out, desperately forcing my muscles not to give up, to exceed its limitations and push beyond my breaking point. A titan can do that. A titan never gives up, a titan always finds the will to finish the mission. I push myself up and force my knee up using all the might of my arms and legs to get myself upright. My back pinched, a sharp pain shoots down my lower back and I drop to my knees again. "Jinx, I can't. Turn it off!" I yell.

"Get up, Carson! Don't give up!"

"I can't!"

"You can! Get up! Kylie is in danger! Get up!" He uses my sister as motivation. If I can believe Kylie is in harm's way, I always find the strength to push through. I use it to my advantage. My heart fills with adrenaline as I imagine my baby sister being strangled by a man, something to get me angry, something that will drive me off the floor.

I take a last long breath, and strain. I power through the gravity and force my leg up and find the ground. I can do this! For Kylie, I have to do this! I let loose one last scream, and I push through the gravity like a rocket ship through the sky and extend both legs up. My body erects straight. "Turn it off!"

The gravity returns to normal, and the weight on my body returns. I no longer feel the strain in my muscles, or the density of the gravity I once felt. The relief of normal gravity makes me feel like I'm floating on the moon.

"Nice job, kiddo. You were at three times normal gravity. That is an awesome achievement." Jinx opens the door leading outside. "C'mon, go shower before dinner is ready."

36

Are you serious?

The night sky is different here than it is in Harmony. The star constellations I once gazed at are unseen and a whole new array of stars fill the darkness of the late hours. It's been one year since I woke up in a bed with every rib broken and was barely able to walk. That family picture I saw of a younger Jinx now shows two more smiling faces in it and a much older Jinx. He's really sacrificed a lot for my sister and me. He cares about us and really sees a future for me, and especially my sister. After she finished her junior year at the top of her class, she has really been shining here. I'm happy that she finally feels normal. She deserves the world and I plan to give that to her. She even has a "friend." Apparently, this friend doesn't go to our school, she's very secretive. Whether or not I accept this friend of hers, we are truly fortunate to have Jinx in our lives and I hope I can make him proud of me when I go through the Proving.

I lay in my bed reading the acceptance letter I got on my phone. Smiling from ear to ear as I read the words "Congratulations, you have been cordially invited to Atlantis University's 239th annual Proving." I read on towards the bottom. "You must be through the gate by 0500 hours, so plan accordingly. Formal attire is mandatory. No running shoes or any athletic wear is acceptable. Anything other than formal attire will be turned away and your invitation will be null and void." They are serious about this. Why the stress for formal attire? The last thing I would want to happen is showing up wrong, or unprepared for this. Anxiety bubbles up in my throat. I set out one of my tailored suits and get ready for bed. Everything is laid out perfectly, ironed and pressed to impress.

My shoes are polished enough to blind someone and my hair is neatly cut short. I waved goodbye to my long locks of brown and hello to the skin on the back of my head.

I get a knock on my door and Jinx comes in my room, his eyes looked worried.

"What's up?" I ask.

He doesn't answer. A stern look singes on his face. He moseys on into my room with his hands behind his back, looking... looking for something. I stare at him in the awkward tense moment I was dumped into. Jinx walks over to my suit, and he picks up my shirt to examine the crease in the sleeve. A hum escapes his mouth, he nods and places it back down. He checks his watch and finally speaks, "Are you leaving soon?"

"Excuse me?" I ask confused.

"Are, you, leaving, soon?" he says obnoxiously slow.

"Uh," I look at the time on my wrist, it's not even ten yet. "no?"

"Wrong."

"Wrong?" I open my phone and scroll to the e-mail. "The e-mail says I don't have to be at the University until five. It takes forty minutes to get there."

He lets out a disappointing breath and sneers at me like I just insulted him. "Do you know how many people go to phase one? On average about a thousand people show up every class."

"A thousand?"

"A thousand. I want you out this door in no less than an hour. That is an order."

"An hour?! I—"

"Shut up," he snaps. "Math question for you, it takes our gateman an average of thirty seconds to log one person into the system to accept their invitation. What is point three, times a thousand."

"Three hundred."

"Correct. Three hundred minutes is five hours. If you arrive at Atlantis University anywhere past twelve midnight, at the back of a line of one thousand cars, you may just make inside the gates by five. It doesn't matter if you wait in line all night, if you are not past that gate by five you will be turned around."

"Are you serious?" I hop out of bed and start to panic. Anxiety heightens, I look at the time again and it's the same time as it was but now five o'clock seems so much closer.

"Don't ask me. How serious is this to you?"

By 2258 hours, I am out the door, fully dressed and on the Skyline Expressway heading to Atlantis University. By 2340 hours I descend off the Skyline into Alannah City, the home of Atlantis University. My ride was full of hard rock music blasted to keep my doubts in the back of my head. I stuck to bobbing my head to the beat and trying to enjoy myself before I have to sit in a line of mayhem for hours to get through the front gates.

The line ends two miles from the University. It's barely midnight and hundreds of cars are already lined up to enter. Jinx was right, if I left at three like I was thinking, I would never have made it inside. Better get comfy, I unwrap an energy bar and endure this slow ride.

By 0206, I am one block away from the golden gates. In the distance, twelve feet high, these legendary arches are the symbol of Alannah; powerful, luxurious, and sturdy. They are there so no intruders can invade its luxurious land, until I showed up, the one and only Harmonian to ever approach these gates. One step forward, a thousand more to go. What if a movie was made after me? It should be called, the Harmonian Avenger? The Harmonian Revenger? Nah... The Harmonian Smuggler? No... Oh! The Harmonian—"

"Name!"

37

Invitation accepted

I snap out of my daydream and realize I pulled up to the gateman. "Uh… Carson, Carson Marano, sir."

He looks down at his hologram data pad on his forearm. A list of names reflects backwards to me. He swipes on it scrolling down the names that are supposed to be here. He clicks a name, and it highlights. "Ok, Marano. Invitation accepted…You're Proctor Marano's boy?" He looks down at me from his booth with a less stern look and a more pleasant looking face but still just as intimidating.

"Yes, yes, sir."

"No kidding." He clicks his communicator on his ear. "Denning to Marano, your boy's here."

"Good, copy," Jinx responds.

"Follow the cones to the parking lot and do as the proctors command. Don't hex up," the man tells me.

"Thank you, sir," I say quickly and follow the road to a massive parking lot where cars are being coordinated into spots by a group of proctors. The ginormous parking lot is split off into quadrants, north, south, east, and west. I follow the line of cars up to a few gentlemen and a woman all in formal military attire who point and yell at the simpletons to park or go to another parking lot. Some take forever to park. A proctor with a hard chin is in the window screaming at this poor guy as he inches backwards into his spot. The woman looks at me and my stomach nearly drops, she points at the next open spot and I nod and follow her direction effortlessly. Filling into the spots one by one, I slowly rotate myself into a spot next to an outrageously expensive sports car. I unbuckle myself and message Kylie that I'm at the school.

From there, I sit patiently waiting for 0500 hours and relax with a power bar and scroll through my social media.

Time passes by and as the clock hits 0500, the gateman walks out of his booth and closes the golden gates in front a huge line of cars. Then he starts screaming that everyone is late and has to turn around.

"EVERYONE OUT OF YOUR CARS!" the sharp chinned proctor screams. "FACE FORWARD, MOUTHS ARE SHUT!" I rush out of my car and stand as straight as a line in front of my car. Sweat building on my head, I feel my damp armpits already making its way through my shirt. "ANYONE WHO SPEAKS OUT OF TURN WILL BE DEALT WITH ACCORDINGLY. YOU WILL ANSWER ONLY IN YES PROCTOR OR NO PROCTOR. IS THAT UNDERSTOOD?"

"Yes, proctor!" I yell along with everyone else. Our combined voices echo through the parking lot but still somehow doesn't match the lungs on this proctor.

"Brilli—" He turns to someone sharply with fire in his eyes like someone just slapped his wife. He sprints over to a man and stops inches from him. I watch in horror what he is about to do. "WHAT DID YOU SAY?!" I can't hear the response. I just continue standing firmly thanking the saints it wasn't me. "YOU THINK YOU'RE FUNNY?! YOU THINK THIS A GAME?! I'LL SHOW YOU A GAME!" The proctor drags the man out of the line by his suit jacket and brings him into the center of the parking lot. He makes the man stand straight up with his hands by his side.

"EVERYONE LISTEN!" the proctor orders. "WHAT IS YOUR NAME?" the proctor shouts at this poor guy.

He swallows quickly and gains some composure. "Rex Cambridge, sir."

The proctor smiles and turns back to the line. "IF ANYONE ELSE WANTS TO TALK WHILE I AM TALKING, YOU WILL END UP LIKE REX," he snaps back at Rex. "FRONT LEANING REST POSITION, NOW!"

The boy doesn't understand what that means, and honestly, neither do I. The boy is frozen in place looking at the loudmouth proctor in pure fright. "Wha... what does that mean, sir?"

The proctor growls. "PUSH UP POSITION!" He turns to us. "SAINTDAMN IT! EVERYONE GET IN THE HEXING PUSH UP POSITION! DO IT NOW!" I drop to the pavement and get in a pushup position. Nearly one thousand people from all over the world are placed on their hands. Sweat already drips from my face. The humidity is torture in this suit. The pavement is hot and needs to be repaved. Small rocks dig into my hands. I squint and endure the suffering as I hear this proctor, who should be an opera singer, yell at Rex. Along with him, the other proctors are giving him the works too, each going on about how big of a loser he is, and that he won't last a day in the Proving.

"Get off your knees, this isn't gym class anymore!" a female proctor screams. Her voice isn't as intimidating as the others, and her short and stocky body doesn't pose much of a threat to me. "You all came here to be titans, but all I see are a bunch of sorry, pathetic weaklings. If you can't follow simple directions, you will be expelled! Does everyone understand?!"

"Yes, proctor!" I answer along with the rest. Ugh did I really wait hours in my car for this?

Another proctor takes command and starts shouting orders, "Now, when I say down, you drop down when I say up, *push up*. Welcome to the first day of the Proving, ladies and gentlemen. This is called front leaning rest position. You will be in this position a lot in your time here, if you can survive today. If any of you can't handle this, get out while you still can, but don't you dare ever come back!"

A few moments pass and my hands are starting to hurt against the pavement. A sharp rock feels glued to my palm, digging deeper every time I try to reposition my hands. Another drip of sweat releases its hold on me and splashes into the pavement.

"Down!" I drop my body. "Up!" I push up. "You will be doing this until little Rexxy here can't feel his arms anymore!"

Oh saints in the afterlife, I hope he is weak.

We continue this pattern forty-five times. Rex finally can't get his body up and his arms fail him. Thank the saints, I'm nearly finished myself. My hands burn from the heat and the rocks. I tried pivoting my hands to other positions but there is no way to get comfortable. Every time I moved it just got worse and worse.

The proctor laughs at him. "Is that really all you got, Rexxy?" He whistles in disbelief. "We are going to have fun with you. Keep going!"

Rex is struggling. He is basically flopping on the road and pushing his body off the road. The proctor picks him up with one of his massive hands. In one motion he yanks Rex to his feet. "Get to the back in line, Rex Cambridge! I don't want to hear another peep out of anyone, is that clear?"

"Yes, proctor!" I shout along with the whole group of about two hundred people.

I watch his scan of the line and find his next target. "I didn't tell any of you to get up! Get back on your face!" Some people were stupid enough to think we were done. I hear some groans and grunts around me, some whispers filled with profanities.

A few more moments go by. "On your feet!" the proctor orders. I spring up as fast as I can. "Too slow! Front leaning rest positions!"

I drop to the pavement again, hate and anger dig into me for this clean cut proctor. He's not as loud as the other one but he knows how to make us hurt ourselves. Sweat droplets race down my face. I can already feel the puddles in my armpits. Is this how it is going to be every day? He finally walks up to the front of the gates and orders us off the ground. He then instructs the first man to follow the pathway. The group isn't slow to get up this time. I get on my feet and follow the first man through the gate and down the dirt path into the University grounds.

Relief fills my head. I'm winded and dripping in sweat but I try to keep calm and still. These proctors are looking to weed out the weak. I will not show them weakness. I will not be weak. I stare at the back of a blonde boy's head as another proctor stares me down when I pass.

I exhale as I pass through the gates. The bright blue grass is swaying with a soothingly cool breeze. Fresh flower bushels are planted down the path. A massive flag of Alannah flaps in the distance behind a library with a huge clock planted on top. Students walking to various other buildings stare at the long line of potential recruits. A small group of girls point towards us and stare as we pass. We march across the entire campus to the entrance of the Four Houses, and the entrance into the military grounds. Inside the grounds, it's completely different, the landscape isn't maintained, even the smell in the air is different. Passing that gate was like crossing into another realm.

"Stop right there," I hear from the front. The line stops. I look around the blonde boy and see another man in his formal military wear. A few medals on his chest shine as the sun glistens on them.

A decorated proctor waits for the other proctors to join him and they have a quiet few words with each other. The man nods, then breaks character and snorts a small laugh. He quickly recovers and composes himself. He salutes the proctors and walks towards the middle of our line. "Welcome, ladies and gentlemen. You will all do exactly as I say, when I say it, and you will do it properly. Does everyone understand?"

"Yes, proctor!" the vast group yells in unison.

"Alright, ladies and gentlemen, follow me. You all look like you've been working out. I hope Proctor Albanese hasn't been working any of you too hard," he jokes. No one dares to make a comment in fear of the consequences. He has a dominatingly deep voice, speaks in a gentler tone, a less threatening tone, but I'm not fooled. Every proctor here is paid to be rough, strict, and by the book. We're escorted into a gymnasium. Large tables are set up in rows with chairs, with a stack of papers laid out with a black pen.

"Fall in and sit down." We do as the proctor says. I file into a seat next to the long curly haired, blonde boy. "Fill out the papers and wait for further instructions."

I look at the first page, it is all personal information. I write out my Alannican name, my address, and some more personal information. Next page is the waiver. Blah, blah, blah… school can't be sued for any death caused during my stay… Wait, what? I could die? I guess if guys like Chris Turner walk in here I have no doubt that behemoth could take someone's life. I finish the paperwork and set my pen down. One proctor I haven't seen before calls the papers to his side. I slide my paper over along with the others given to me by the other side of the table, and the man looks through them.

"Carson Marano?"

"Yes, proctor!" I spring to my feet and stand straight up.

"Proctor Marano is your father?" he asks.

"Yes, proctor," I answer him.

"Come over here," he orders.

Oh saints what now? What did I do now? I make my way out to the aisle and stand in front of him.

"So, you're his adopted son he's been talking about," he says amused. "He tells me you're quite the fast learner."

"Yes, proctor," I answer shortly.

He eyes me up, creating more attention from the other proctors as they all surround me. They all eye me up like I am some fresh piece of meat they all want to jump on and devour.

"You think you have what it takes to be a titan?!" the proctor yells in my face.

"Yes, proctor!" I yell back.

"Just because you're a proctor's son doesn't mean we're going easy on you, kid. You have to earn it like everyone else. Do you understand?"

"Yes, proctor!" I reply. I know that, they're just trying to get in my head. I keep a blank mind and listen closely to him, so I don't misspeak.

Another proctor sneak attacks me from my side. "I doubt you have what it takes!"

Another voice yells in my other ear, "Look at these scrawny arms, what are you going to do with those?!"

Back and forth three, four, I don't even know how many proctors scream and yell in my face, calling me names and shouting things that would make a normal kid crack, but not me. I know better than to believe any of this abuse.

"What are you still doing here?! Get out of my face!" the proctor yells in front of me.

"Yes, sir."

The proctors back off of me and I go back to my seat. I make my way down the row, my arm pits sweating profusely from that verbal beat down, but I pushed through it, I didn't crack and talk back.

A deep voiced proctor makes his way back up to the front. "You will all be given a permit to return after today, unless for some reason, you don't make it through phase one. If that is the case, you were never supposed to be here anyway. We do not accept weak. Titans are strong, capable, we are the answer to all questions. We are the saviors of this world, the best of the best!

"AHHHOOO!" the proctors chant. It jolts me and awakens me. Yes! This is what I wanted to hear.

"Be ready to prove yourself, ladies and gentlemen. We are not done here yet. The Proving will be something unlike anything your privileged lives have ever been through. Your lives are at risk. You must be strong, quick, and you must never give up. You have to—" the proctor stops and stares towards the back of the class. I flip around and see a boy with glasses on waving his hand in the air. "What?!" the proctor shouts.

Someone in the back stands up. "Sir, what exactly is the Proving?"

The proctor stares at the boy with anger and frustration in his face. Then points to the side of the room. "Go over there and do pushups. How dare you interrupt me like that! Go! Now!"

The boy is startled at first but slides out of his seat to the side and starts doing pushups.

The proctor clears his throat. "As I was saying, the Proving is a test of might. As of now, not all of you are destined for it, for there is a test within a test today. Only half of you will be eligible for the Proving. The other half, well, I hope you all said your goodbyes to your family. Everyone up!"

I stand up as fast as I can. Said your goodbyes? What in the saints could that mean?

"File out the doors behind you and follow your proctors. You will be seated in classrooms until it is your turn. Good luck and may the saints bless you with strength and wisdom." the proctor says as we walk out.

As I stand up and face the exit of the gymnasium, I realize I may be in over my head. A small handful of people walk the other way and towards the parking lot, quitting this thing all together. Should I have listened to Kylie, is this really all going to be worth it if our parents are dead? The line starts moving and the man behind me pushes me forward. No, this is what I want to do, there's no going back now. I'm here, the Harmonian Wanderer... No, still stupid, got to work on that.

38

Maximus Brix

We get placed in a long classroom filled with rows and rows of seats all facing a massive holoprojector board where a professor would write. Each seat has a computer with a virtual screen up asking for login information, much more modern than the pen and paper we were just given. I file in and take a seat at the end of one of the rows in the middle. As the last person files in and takes their seat, an unknown proctor walks down the stairs and to the podium. I still haven't seen Phineas or Norman. I hope they got in the gate in time.

"Welcome everyone," a new proctor greets calmly. "Everyone needs to remain quiet. You may talk with your peers but do it in a low volume. I will be outside, there will be no further questions. You will remain here until the next phase of your invitational is ready. When I get the call, the last row will come with me. Until then, keep it down. If, for any reason, you feel you do not want to continue, you may leave, no one is forcing you to be here," he says professionally. He leaves and a varied collage of chatter engulfs the room.

"What's happening?" I ask the curly blonde haired boy.

"I'm not sure. My dad never told me about this part."

"Your dad went through the Proving before?"

He looks at me crooked. "Yeah, do you... do you not know who I am?"

I mimic his crooked look and shrug my shoulders. Is he a celebrity? Why would I *have* to know this guy? "Um, yeah, sorry I'm not good with faces. I'm more of a name by name kind of guy."

"Pshhh, do you live under a rock, my good man?"

"It's a nice rock. We've done renovations, but yes, it's still a rock," I jest.

"You card," he chuckles. "Well said my good man. I am Maximus Brix, son of Titan Mason Brix. I am the heir to Brix Company. I am a household name. Are you not from Alannah? You don't look like those savages from Dalton, nor oddly proportioned like Lunens."

I laugh to give me time to think of a rebuttal. "I am from Greycott. It's a large, gated town. I meet new people every day, so I apologize if your name slipped my memory. But of course, the Brix family is well respected in my family. My name is Carson, my father is Jinx Marano, he's a proctor here."

"Yes, yes we all saw that verbal beatdown those gentlemen were giving you, I thought one of them was going to bite your ear off. May I say you took it quite well. But do inquire my good man, we Brix are more than well-known. My father is next in line to be alphaTitan, supposably, alphaTitan Malcom Suez is ready to retire."

"Is that so? Well, it's… um… it's a privilege to meet you, Maximus." I hold out my hand. He grips it harder than I'd imagine. I try to keep a straight face, but it hurts. Yet another small competition for an Alannican, I squeeze harder trying to match his strength.

"Ah, a fine grip you have, Carson. A man among boys you seem to be. Reputable, respectable, composure under pressure… You'd be a fine wing man for me at the bars." He releases his grip. "After this we should get a drink. I know a place not too far from here. They serve stiff drinks and the girls, ho ho ho, the girls will make you stiff as well, my friend."

My mouth opens but nothing comes out. His charisma is astounding. I feel as if we've been friends forever, yet I'm somewhat threatened by his overwhelming confidence. "Um, sure?" I answer halfheartedly confused.

"Marvelous!" Maximus celebrates. "I've been meaning to bring my younger brother there some day. He is a fine man. Not as sharp as I, or quick witted, or charming, or well anything… But he means well, and his heart is where it needs to be."

"Is he of age?"

"Of age?"

"Yeah? Is he eighteen? Can he even get in?"

Max bellows out a laugh. "Oh my friend, you really don't know my family well, do you? This is haunting for me, I have never met anyone who was so oblivious to my blood line before.

Yes my twin brother is of age, of course. I call him younger because I beat him out of the womb by fifteen seconds."

I click my tongue and shake my head. "Really? You're the card, Maximus."

"Please, call me Max. Maximus is such a mouth full."

39

A Test within a Test

The doors slam open and the proctor orders my row to stand up. We're escorted down the long dark hallway and into a set of three elevators. The proctor stops us and counts us off, sending the first ten into the left and so on. I'm the tenth person into the third elevator, just missing Max. I make eye contact with my new pompous friend just as the doors close. The proctor presses a button on the side panel and the number six lights up. He talks on his communicator saying that we are coming up and walks out of the elevator. Silence surrounds our clogged bodies. Stuffed in like aquatix in a can, I can barely move in this tight square, and the man next to me reeks of body odor. The elevator pulls us up and the doors open to a room with twenty doors laid out in front of us. Two proctors stand at the entrance of the elevator.

"Fall in, stand in front of a door, it doesn't matter what one," one proctor says. I walk slowly towards one of the doors in the middle. A female and an older man stand beside me facing their own doors. "Face your door. No talking unless spoken to," the other proctor says.

Suspicion and utter terror trickles in my head. What could this be?

"Now, everyone listen to me closely. Start undressing yourself," the proctor orders.

What? My eyebrows curl as I stare deeply at the mysterious door in front of me. I peek to the side and the same goes for the man next to me.

"Did no one hear me?!" The proctor gets louder. "Everyone take your clothes off, down to your undergarments. That is an order, do it now."

I slowly do as I'm told, trying not to stare at the woman next to me. This is so awkward. The man next to me has no shame and strips butt naked in seconds.

"Socks and shoes too. Fold everything up and place it to your side. Saintdamn it, sir, put your drawers back on!" the proctor snaps. The man next to me quickly realizes his mistake. "Bras, and briefs people, bras and briefs... Saint Peter, give me strength," he exhales as the other proctor next to him lets out a quiet chuckle.

"Uh, question sir?" a girl down the hall speaks.

"No more questions! Face your future head on, no matter what is in front of you," the proctor dismisses.

"Sir, I don't feel comfortable doing this," the woman says. "There has to be some kind of mist—"

"This is your preliminary test for the Proving, miss!" the proctor shouts on top of her pleading voice. "This will prove to everyone that you belong here, that you deserve to move on to our real Proving. This will determine if you are capable of fighting for your life, if you can deal with adversity and follow orders when they are given to you. Does everyone see the red light in front of you?"

"Yes proctor," I answer along with the group.

A big, bulgy light protrudes out of the wall above the black door.

"When it turns green, go through the door. Are we clear?

"Yes, proctor," I shout, as do some others but it was a lot less enthusiastic. Not everyone knows what is about to happen. They only know stories of the past. They could have changed it up somehow, no one knows. I feel exposed to the world, uncomfortable standing here with my manhood nearly poking out of my boxers. Why couldn't Jinx tell me about this? This is so weird, so embarrassing, so confusing, so... exactly how they want us to feel. They want us to doubt, to be scared, and second guess ourselves. I try and numb my emotions, do as your told and you will prevail. You've trained for this, for months, dreamed of this chance for years. Whatever is past this door, you will face, and you will succeed.

"This is to show us that even though you came here today to be welcomed into our fold of brothers and sisters of Tyke, you will be placed in situations where you are most uncomfortable. You are always to be mentally and physically sound. At any time during your travels, whether it be business or casual, you can be faced with danger. Titans do not back down, and neither will any of you. Behind that door will be someone who may or may not want this opportunity more than you. Today, you will be fighting another recruit. Fight hard, fight well, and survive. There will be a two minute timer inside each room. In those two minutes, you will be judged. Winners move on to the Proving, losers go home or sent to the morgue.

Instantly, a blaring buzzing noise fills the room. I look up thinking my light turned and I grab the doorknob. My light is red. I look left and right and see some green lights down the hallway, but not mine just yet. I release the doorknob. My hand is shaking, the anxiety of all this is turning my insides. Another blaring noise goes off and the green light flashes to the man next to me. He hypes himself up with a few growls and fast breaths and storms into his room.

My heart starts racing. Jinx never told me about any of this. Why would he keep this from me? Goosebumps ride up my naked legs. Anxiety startles me, my heart races with anticipation. Holy saints, calm down Carson, it's just another fight. Nearly a minute goes by and I hear screams of anguish from beyond the walls. Oh saints, what happened? A roar followed by a bone snapping noise echoes my ears, then an eerie thump into absolute silence.

"I can't do this," someone whispers a few doors down.

"Quiet!" the proctor orders from his chair in the corner of the room. "Wait your turn in silence."

Just like that, the man's light turns green. I see him hesitate as he slowly turns the doorknob and enters the room. I turn the opposite way and see only a few more people waiting their turn like me. Clear your mind, Carson. No matter what they throw at you, you will win. No matter what comes at you through this door, you will succeed, you will dominate, you either win or die. Win or die. Win, or…What if Norman or Phineas is on the other side of the door?

"You ready, Scrap?" I hear the proctor's voice behind me.

I straighten up sharply. "Yes, proctor." My stomach drops. Oh my saints what did I just do?!

He chuckles menacingly to himself. "Gotcha."

I turn my head and see an unknown face looking at me. He's tan with bright blue eyes that remind me of someone I can't think of. I look at him with fear for myself and my family. I just saintdamn blew it! "I, uh—" I stutter not knowing what to do or say.

"I know all about you, Scrap. But don't worry, your secret is safe with me."

I start to sweat. All this training and preparations just got thrown out the window. "Sir, I uh, don't know what you're talking about."

"Carson Marano, a.k.a, Carson Paul, right? Born in Redding, runner up at the Tournament of Titans last year?"

I start to hyperventilate. "I have no idea what you're talking about, sir."

He chuckles. "Smooth, Scrap, real smooth. Good luck in there. Head Skull sends her regards."

What did he just say? I obviously misheard him. There's no way.

A loud buzzing noise jolts me out of my head and I look up, my light has turned green. I stay frozen to the floor. How could I be so stupid?! What do I do? Do I run? Do I stay? Did I really just blow it? Who was that guy? I search the long hallway for him and the other proctor yells at me to go inside. I burst through the door and jump in a fighting pose. Another man is on the other side of the room. I look around at our peculiarly small room, maybe the size of two wide hallways with a high ceiling. A large window is in the top left corner of the room. Two people sit inside looking down upon us. Under the window is a large timer with two minutes on it. The door closes on its own behind me and the timer below the window begins to count down.

"Welcome, gentlemen. Today you will be involved in hand to hand combat. I'm sure you have been told the rules by now so, begin," a voice over a loudspeaker says and the timer starts ticking down.

I look across the room to my opponent, a smaller man, maybe my age, firm body type with long blonde curly hair. Oh no, is that Max? Am I really going to have to face the heir to the Brix Company? I could use that long hair to my advantage. Jinx told me to buzz my hair for a reason. Holy hexing saints I'm so screwed.

I swallow my fear and inch closer. Making my approach up to him in a ready position. Fists are clenched, up by my face to block. Don't be scared, be brave. Fear is only excitement leaving the body. You've trained for this, Carson. Be ready for him to do anything like a sprint at me, or a quick combination of jabs after a war cry. However, none of that happens. His feet look glued to the floor. His heels are down too, he isn't in any ready stance, he looks scared... This can't be for real.

"Hey! Hey! We don't have to fight," the boy shouts at me. He sounds nothing like my curly haired friend from before. Much more... squeamish. I'm about twenty feet from him, still in a

242

ready stance. It's not Max, just some scrawny blonde kid. Don't believe him for a second, Carson. This is just the kind of deception I would fall for.

"Yeah, we do, kid. You heard the proctor," I entertain him.

He drops his shoulders and takes a deep breath. He looks up at me and readies himself, still trembling. His face looks like he is about to cry, and his hands are shaking.

"I never fought anyone before. Please go easy on me. I'm just doing this because my father made me."

This kid can't be for real. I can hear the fear in his voice... No... this is a trick? It must be. Hex this kid, I won't fall for it.

I slowly inch closer to him. "Listen kid, a wise man once told me, you either win or die."

"I don't want to die!" the boy shouts and shoots his hands out at me with his fingers extended. I back step and tighten up thinking he is going to attack. "Please don't kill me," he pleads.

Oh my saints. This kid is pathetic. No! This must be another trick. I inch myself closer to him to where I would be able to strike if needed.

"Ok, here is what we are going to do," I tell the boy conjuring up my own plan of attack. "Put your hands up like this." I show him my hands, he mimics me. Perfect. I take one last quick short step and launch my foot between his legs. Making full contact with the boy's manhood.

He shrieks in pain, and he grabs hold of his family jewels. He falls to his knees, exposing the top of his head. I take a step back and wait for the right moment.

He looks up at me. "I thought you said—"

I strike him, full force with a wild roundhouse kick aiming for the side of his head. I miss slightly and break his nose. He wails and flops to the ground, blood spews out of his nostrils. He screams again in agony and rolls around holding his nose and himself.

I look up at the judges in the window. All I see is two shadows watching over us. I put my arms out gesturing if this is over. The shadow makes a small circle with his finger, insinuating to keep going. I look down at my poor foe. He holds himself squirming in pain, wheezing in agony.

It is either win or die, never forget that. No mercy, no pity. I take one last look at him. Blood covers the bottom of his face, he looks terrified when our eyes meet. I push him back down on his back with a shove of my foot and mount him to continue my onslaught. Punch after punch

I lay into him. He tries to block and squirm out of it but I won't let him, I've come too far. I am not giving my deplorable opponent any means of figuring me out. Not today, and not ever again.

After a minute of constant abuse, I grow tired. I give up on trying to hurt this kid. I pull his wrist out from covering his face and pin his hand down with my knee. I grab hold of his other wrist and raise my left hand high in the air.

"Please stop! Please stop!" he begs. "I don't want to die, I don't want to die! Please, I give up!" I stop and gaze at his cowardness. He starts to whimper, then turns to full blown crying.

The unthinkable has happened, I made an Alannican cry. I get off him and watch him pant on the ground. I turn my back to him and look at the judges with my hands out. The timer still rolls. Forty-five seconds remain. "He said he gives up!" I shout into the window.

"There is no giving up unless he is not breathing! Now continue to fight or you will both be disqualified!" the shadow in the window says.

Then out of nowhere, I feel cold, wet arms wrap themselves around my neck. It was him. How did this happen? He locks his arms and wraps his legs around my waist. Pressure continues to squeeze and blood rushes my head. My vision blurs, he's choking me!

No, no! This can't happen, I had him. I HAD HIM! With all my might I grab his hair and pull. He shouts in my ear, making my ear drum pound like a heavy metal drummer. I punch and swing around trying to break free. Pure animalistic fear comes over me and I start attempting to gauge his eyes out. I hook an eye socket and he screams in my ear again and tightens his grip. Adrenaline kicks in. Rage engulfs my body. I flex my neck and try to pin my chin in between his locked arms to allow air to flow. Once I can inhale the tiniest bit of oxygen, I charge the wall. I dive full force into the metal padding wall and turn my body, so this bastard feels the full extent of solid metal to his body. We bounce off the wall with a thud and I hear several cracks echo from the impact. We fall and our bodies separate. He tries to squirm back on top of me, but I am able to lift my legs into his stomach and force him backwards. He stumbles and checks his back against the wall again. He can't breathe right; He sounds like I did during the tournament when I broke my ribs. Perfect. I'm furious, anger from today builds in my heart and pumps through my veins and into my fists. I told myself I wasn't going to pity him and then I do, and he tried some little stunt like that? This is why you don't pity anyone, never again.

He gets to his feet and sticks a handout in fear. "I'm sorry..." he struggles to breath. "I didn't... I didn't mean..."

"You didn't mean it?!" I question manically. I cough hoarsely trying to catch my breath again. "Are you kidding me?!"

"You don't understand, my name is Leonardo Brix, my father is the legendary titan, Mason Brix. I must win. He'd disown me if he knew I lost." He attempts to put his hands back up. "He'll hunt you down if he finds out you killed me."

Holy saints I am fighting a Brix. The runt of the litter but a Brix, nonetheless. Fifteen seconds left on the clock. I smack his hand out of the way and immediately come back around with a full left swing. "I don't care who your father is, kid." I swing and collide into his jaw. "I don't care who you are." I swing once more in the other side of his face. "All I know is that I am done pitying you!"

I put all my might into my next punch. Without any protection, or skill in fighting, he doesn't attempt to dodge, or change up his blocking. His face is wide open. I stomp on his foot to hold him and unleash a haymaker that ignites in his cheek bone. Blood sprays out of his face, and a tooth falls out. His head bounces off the back wall and his body flops to the floor. I mount him again and this time, I'm not giving him anything. I pin his hands down under my knees and annihilate his face. Punch after punch I throw, four, five, six clean open shots. I put my hands together and swing down like a sledgehammer. His nose crunches from the impact. His eye is closed shut while the other one looks gauged out, and his mouth is missing three or four teeth from his shattered jaw. He is out cold.

The timer rings. I turn and see four large zeros and two men clapping in the booth above it.

"Well done, Mr. Marano. Go to your door and accept the ticket out of the dispenser. That is your ticket back to the university for the Proving. Best of luck."

I stand straight up, hands by my side in attention, and salute the two people. I take one last look at my squeamish foe. He isn't moving. He's not twitching, and I can't quite even see him breathing. Humanity collapses back into me and I become the man I once was. A scared little boy. Did I just kill him? His father is… Mason Brix, Max… his brother? Thoughts fly through my head like a merry-go-round. What did I just do? How could I explain myself for this? I stare at the motionless boy, he didn't deserve that, did he? He didn't even want to be here. He—

"Was I unclear recruit?" the voice says over the loudspeaker.

It catches my attention, and I turn back to the window. "No, sir. Sorry, sir."

40

ROCCO

I walk out of the door and feel a gentle breeze against my wet, bloodied chest. I try to wipe it off on my boxers but that just makes this sight look worse. Saintdamn, this looks ugly. I grab my shirt and put it on. The wet blood seeps through my white button up shirt instantly. I awkwardly slide my socks and shoes back on as well and take my time tying them up. I am in no rush. My mind is going crazy, but I try to remain professional.

Did I just kill that boy? No, I saw him breathing, did I see him breathing? Almighty saints in the afterlife, am I a murderer? Could I get in trouble for this? No… No! I signed the waiver, which means he did too, so I am safe. Can a piece of paper justify killing a Brix? Oh saints, what have I done?

It is scary to think just one piece of paper could determine if your family will have retribution for their child's death if it so happens. Saints, I feel horrible, I never wanted to do that. He just attacked me and I don't know what came over me. Even after I tried to stop the fight, for him nonetheless, for his benefit and his wellbeing. Those people in that booth saw it coming too. I bet they just laughed their heads off at it.

I get my shoes tied way faster than I wanted to and I finish getting dressed. That shady proctor is reading his tablet in the corner, the one who told me Head Skull sends her regards. Does he know Courtney? Is he a Bone Breaker? I thought they didn't expand to Alannah? I walk up to him, a splitting pain in my head makes me want to ignore him and go home, but I can't. I need answers.

"Ugh, what happen to you?" he asks disgusted.

"I, I did what I had to do, sir."

He cackles, then stretches his body in the seat, sits up and points towards the door. "Walk out these doors and take your third left. You'll find the far end elevator. Take that down to the ground floor and follow the path back to the parking lot. Dismissed."

"That's it?" I ask softy.

"That's it."

"How is that it? Who are you?"

The proctor's eyes snap to me above his news tablet. "You did what you had to do, right?" I nod. He eyes the winner's receipt in my hand and smiles. "Then you'll receive an e-mail from us in a few weeks that entails what is required for the Proving. Now get out of my face."

"Are you serious? You tell me Head Skull sends her regards, and you don't reiterate?"

The proctor stays prominently still, keeping his eyes on the tablet. "Say another word to me and I will end your life right here. Do you understand me?" His eyes flash to me. "Not another word. Everything will be explained when and if, and only if, you survive the Proving."

I do as he says without another word. I walk past him and out the door.

"Hey, Scrap," he calls me back.

I snap back and scan the room quickly to see if anyone else heard. It's just me and him, thankfully.

"Wipe your face, you got something nasty on your lip," he says.

I wipe my face, and in doing so, I smear the blood on my hands onto my face, blood that isn't mine.

The proctor cackles and leans back in his seat.

I ignore his humor and storm out the double doors to find the elevator down the hall. It guides down silently without a sound. Before leaving the building, I find a men's bathroom. Inside, two others had the same idea I had. They look just like me, blood smeared all over their shirts and face. I go to the paper towel dispenser and unravel a handful of towels. I wet them in the sink and wipe my face. I choose not to look at myself in the mirror. I don't want to be reminded of what I did. I hear whimpering in one of the stalls, these trials are putting us through something that mentally, some cannot comprehend, me included. Pink agrees to my deal, what does that even mean? Does she really expect me to push the Bone Break influence into Alannah? How am I supposed to do that? Holy saints, what do I do now?

The wet paper towel turns red as I lift it off my face. I rinse it out and continue wiping my face one more time. I feel someone behind me, I twitch and throw my hands up at him. He leans backwards and does the same thing.

"Bro, relax," he says defensively. His sweaty hair drips past his eyes. He's just as tense as I am.

"Sorry, I—"

He puts a hand out at me to stop me from talking. "Same," he says softly with a nod. "Good fight?"

Flashbacks rev through my mind. The sounds of bone cracking, his eerily cringing voice, his pleas of surrender. "Yeah," is all I can muster.

"Right on," he says and walks out of the bathroom.

I turn back to the sink and look at myself in the mirror. It kills me inside to see someone else's blood smeared all over my face and body. My once long brown hair I could tie in the back of my head is now shorter than it has ever been. Jinx told me to keep it like this, it looks more professional this way. I remember being back at that scrap yard when professionalism wasn't a thing. It was live another day, whatever it takes.

A bead of water drips down my face and falls into the sink. I take a long, deep breath. "You animal," I whisper to myself. I look at the multiple stains of red streaks down my shirt. I take my shirt off and clean my body as well with wet paper towels. After collecting a nice pile and satisfied with how I am going to present myself, I throw the wad out in the garbage. It hits the pile of other red and damp paper towels in the garbage bin. Ugh, what a mess.

I walk out the door and bump into a broad-shouldered man covered in blood from head to toe. A shockwave bubbles over my entire body when I recognize the giant man. "Rocky?"

He looks at me confused when we make eye contact. "Who are you?"

"Who... How did you get here? What happen to you?" I feel absolutely baffled when I see the man who pushed my sister off a cliff. The long-haired ginger boy with piercing amber eyes I once knew has transformed into a behemoth of a man. He stands near a half a foot taller than me and looks like he can pick up a car over his head.

"Um, do I know you?" he asks. "Sorry I'm a bit of a mess, if you don't mind me scooting by I—"

"Rocky McKenzie, right?"

That name stops him in his tracks. He looks around with wide eyes and he picks me up by my collar and pins me against the wall with both of his brawly hands. "How do you know that name? Who are you? Speak now!" he growls. His strength is remarkable. I have to be close to two hundred pounds and he just lifted me like I was a grocery bag. His amber eyes dilate, his face tenses, he looks like he is about to kill me for saying his name.

"Woah, woah, woah. It's me, Carson... From the orphanage."

He swivels his head back and forth. "Carson? Carson Paul?" he whispers. His face loosens with his grip and I find the floor again as he lets me go. He looks shocked and delighted, like a light bulb that turned on in his head. "I thought you were dead."

"You're not the only one. But um, it's actually Carson Marano now, I got adopted."

"Oh, nice. Me too."

"I've heard. You were turning eighteen, who in their right mind would adopt—" I stop my insult short. He could rip me in half for saying something off putting.

"No go on, say it. Who in their right mind would adopt a seventeen-year-old? Funny story actually, Robert Fox. I'm a Fox now."

My eyes open wide, and my jaw drops. *Thee* Robert Fox adopted some seventeen-year-old kid? For what? How? Why? I completely forgot Courtney told me that at the hotel. I stutter to get words out but can't find anything to say. "Wow, uh, congratulations." I search his eyes and can't find the rage or confidence to demand answers about why he did what he did to Kylie. He's terrifying, and massive, like he's been on muscle enhancing stims for years. He reminds me of what Chris Turner looked like during the tournament. "When did you get adopted?"

He ponders for a moment. "Around the same time you disappeared. What happened to you?"

The day flows back into my head. A spurt of something inside me rushes through my chest and out of my mouth like a water geyser. "Well after you took my sister into the woods and pushed her off a cliff for not sleeping with you, she didn't want to see your ugly hexing face again. So, we left."

His eyes open in fright, a secret he must have held on to all this time comes shooting at him like a bullet. "Woah." He puts his hands out, they're twice the size of mine. "I don't know what you're talking about."

An easy excuse, a lie he's probably been telling himself for years. It's believable, but not something I can believe. "You don't know what I'm talking about? I saw what you tried to do. She had bite marks on her neck."

"Well, hex what you heard," he laughs.

Blood boils. "I can expose you, Rocco. Kylie would sing if she knew you were here."

He laughs confidently. "Maybe you don't understand, I'm a Fox now. My father is the most powerful man in the territories, he has more influence than that drunk bum we call a Sovereign. You think a tall tale with no evidence can get me? Hah! How about a boy from Harmony in the most prestigious academy in all of the world? You won't survive a month with the truth out."

"Chris Turner did. He's from Harmony."

"How do you know Chris?"

"Don't worry about it."

"Don't worry about it huh? Well, here is one for you, Chris is actually from Parvaluna. Got papers to prove it and everything, all signed by Robert Fox himself and Chris's family. So, I don't know where you're getting this information, but it seems like you just blatantly admitted you're from Harmony to the son of Robert Fox."

My stomach drops. I'm speechless, scared, and baffled all at the same time. I check the bathroom for any eavesdropper. Luckily, we are alone. "You... you're from Harmony."

"Wrong again, I live on Parvaluna too. Proud citizen and alumni for a few years now. What else you got?" He gets in my face, I can feel his breath against my face, the drying blood sweating down his cheek. He sticks a bloody finger in my face. "If you think you're going to try to jeopardize my time here, I'll ruin you, Carson, I'll ruin everything." He walks to the sink and splashes some water in my face, grabs some paper towels and walks out.

"Rocco," I call for him as he walks away. He turns back at me with a blank stare. His back muscles are protruding out of his suit jacket. He's turned into an absolute monster. "You keep my secret, I keep yours," I say before he walks out the bathroom.

Rocky turns back to me and clears his throat. "Listen," he gets uncomfortably close to me again. "the difference between our secrets, is one is false, and the other one is a felony. I can *easily* get away with whatever story you tell the authorities because if you do, all I need to say is you're from Harmony and everything would be swept under the rug. Plus, I'm a Fox, no one will believe you. What they will do though, is they'll look you up, see who you really are, question whoever the hex thought it was a good idea to bring you here, arrest them, and throw them in a cell after they see that you're just some orphaned loser from Harmony. They'll banish you, or possibly kill you since you got this far, just like your treasonous parents, right? That got swept under a rug really quick, didn't it? No one even knows about them anymore. No one even looked for them because they were simply just some Harmonian scum with stolen technology. No one cared. So, if you know what's good for you, stay out of my hexing business, and stay out of my way during the Proving. Or I will expose *you*. You heard?" He laughs manically. "See you around, Carson. Good luck in the Proving. You're going to need it."

I hold my tongue. I want to yell but I can't. His voice is utterly intimidating. He can say whatever he wants because I had to threaten him and expose him for what he did. Now he's got me by the balls, and I have no room to stand on, yet again by a member of Fox. He turns around with a smirk and walks off down the hall.

"Oh, and one more thing. That Rocky kid you're talking about, is dead. My name is Rocco now, Rocco Fox."

41

Pinky Promise

Nightmares have terrorized my dreams ever since I watched the fainting eyes of that boy in that box. Blood drenched my chest, blood stained under my nails, the eerie feeling of watching the boy's last breath escape his body unnervingly haunts me. Was it worth it? His name rings through my head, *Leonardo Brix.* On top of that, I completely ditched Max for drinks afterwards. There's no way I could sit at a bar with the twin brother of the kid I hurt and think nothing of it.

I lay in bed scrolling through meaningless pictures of my old classmates and other people on my social media. I found his online profile, a happy go lucky kid in high school who played starball with his All Alannah starback twin brother. He has a picture of the seven accepted university letters from all over the world and the moons, benching impressive weights in the weight room, girls upon girls commenting on his posts. Saintdamn it, this guy is legit, yet no pictures of his dad, just him his mom, and his four brothers, all just as tall and big as him besides Leonardo who stands shorter than all of them.

I've received the e-mail that details the entire Proving from where we start to where we finish. A sixty-mile hike starting from the Alannah shoreline and end at the border of the campus property. There's also something about stations and talismans that I haven't been able to figure out. I haven't been myself lately. Ever since phase one, I haven't trained or even eaten well. That kid's face haunts my head, I stalked all four of his brothers and still haven't found any evidence that he is alive or not.

Regardless, I am in the Proving, and tomorrow I step out of this house with Jinx's old rucksack and the sleeping bag he used for his Proving. I hope his good luck rubs off on me. I've already said my goodbyes to Julianna, Ray, and Kylie. Jinx refused to let me say goodbye to him. He told me some spiritual line he must have seen, 'There is no goodbyes, only see you soons.' So, with that, he hugged me tightly and said he would see me soon.

I lay in bed contemplating if this is even all worth it. I don't understand why they made us do that. A fight is fine, but they wanted blood, they wanted death. Why? What kind of cruel territory is this?

A knock comes from my door and makes me jump out of my daydream. "Yeah?" I look at the clock and it's about nine, almost time to go to sleep to wake up at two in the morning to get there by four. Then everyone has to get their rucks searched, and an 0600 hour departure into the wilderness.

Kylie creeps in the room with her face leaning against the door. "You got a minute?"

"Sure, Ky, what's up?"

She grabs my desk chair and sits by my bedside. "You know what you're getting yourself into, right?" I nod. "You've researched the Proving, right?"

"Um, yeah, kind of?" I lie. "What do you mean?"

"Do you?" she asks harshly. She throws her tablet on the bed and a blog titled 'The truth behind the Proving' is on the screen. I read the first couple lines, explaining a fight to the death in a closet sized room.

"Ok? Yeah? What am I looking at?" I ask.

"Did you even read it, you bonehead?" She scrolls down, and a disfigured and mangled face appears. The man's eye is swollen shut and a hole in his mouth where his front teeth used to be. A piece of hair is missing, and his nose looks bitten off. "Is this what happened to you? Is this why you haven't talked to me all week? Did you kill someone, Carson?" she questions me.

I'm caught off guard. "No, I, um, I'm not sure."

Her jaw drops, she scrolls back up to the top of the page where the blog explains they were forced into a room, butt naked, and was forced upon an ogre looking man who beat him senseless. "How could you keep this from me?"

"Kylie, I had no idea. I went there in a suit and tie. I thought I was just going to fill out paperwork. Plus, it's fine, I'm fine." I scoot myself up in a more comfortable position to talk. "I've fought people before, it honestly wasn't anything new to me."

"Yes, but you were naked?"

"Not naked. I had boxers on," I think back. "If anything, it was better than the Levi tournament."

"No, it's not!" she cries. "I talked to Julie and she told me all about Jinx's time in the Proving. The man nearly died, he got a severe concussion. He still gets pounding migraines to this day, did you know that?"

"No."

"Of course not. You know there's more to it, right? You have to go on some hike or something through some trap filled woods," she explains scrolling through her E-tab. "This guy says he almost died eight times. People become savages for these talismans. There's the Rampart River you have to cross, the Great Mountain of Alannah you have to climb filled with traps, there's wolleybears, poisonous flora, flesh-eating fish, the saints only know what else." She keeps scrolling and reading off the page. "What in saint's name are you doing this for, Carson? Go be a doctor or a lawyer or something, you like to argue about everything."

"Kylie, Kylie, slow down. Why would you show me this, to scare me? This is the only way I can get in the military. This is how I'm supposed to find our parents. I need to do this, you told me I had to do this."

"I know, but does it really matter anymore?" she argues back insensitively. I'm taken back. "I'm sorry, it's just at first, I was worried for you, but now, I'm petrified." She starts choking up. Over the months we've been here she's hardened up, sucking up her childhood fears and replacing them with a stern and braver attitude like most Alannicans. Her face starts getting puffy and tears start to form. "You could die. I don't want to lose you too. I—" She starts to tremble. I sit up in my bed and grab hold of her. She locks her arms around me. "I lost everything when we lost them, Carson. For that, I'll never forgive them. I just don't want to lose you too," she says. "I don't want to hate you if you die, not after everything we've been through."

Can anything I do go smoothly? I've been in such a rut these past two weeks and the day before I leave, she comes at me with this curveball? I've come so far. The whole reason why I'm here, the reason why Jinx adopted me was so I could do this.

Kylie sniffles and wipes her nose. "I just can't bear to lose the last piece of my family. Not like this."

"And you won't, I promise."

"How can you promise something so complex? This isn't something you can control."

"I have a titan as a mentor who's trained me all year. I have you to always inspire me to be better too. Kylie, this is my dream. I finally have a chance to be something I thought was impossible. I can't give this up. I promise I will come home."

She sniffles one more time and takes a deep breath. "What if they're really dead? You'd be doing this all for nothing. You could die tomorrow for no reason. We have a family again, Carson. You have a dad who gives you attention and plays starball with you. We even have a little brother. Remember how mad you were when you found out I was a girl?" We share a small laugh. "We have everything we could ever want here. Why do you need more? When is enough, enough?"

"So, you just want me to say, enough? Quit while we are ahead? Who are you? Why are you doing this?" I start to feel aggravated with her, distant even. She's the one who cried for days when they didn't come home. I had to be strong, I had to plan out a way to find them. Now that I have a chance, she wants me to... quit?

She clicks her tongue. "I gave up on them, Carson. It's been two years with no signs of them that they are alive besides the words of Jinx. Who, for all we know, has no idea if they are still alive. Also, what if they are? What's your plan? They were arrested for treason. Whether or not it's true, they are probably in prison. You expect to break them out and give them a normal life? They'll be fugitives, *you* will be a fugitive. You'd put this entire family at risk. It's not like you can break them out and send them back to Harmony. Robert Fox will find them, he'll find you."

As I listen to my pleading sister, I realize Kylie has become more Alannican then I could have ever imagined. Her logic is there but her emotions have dulled. To think, one year ago she miraculously made me a junkyard battlesuit to give me a chance to find our parents. Now that we are here, now that our plan has finally reached its climax, it seems pointless. "Robert Fox took dad because of this Project SPINE. Whatever it is, it makes people into... monsters. King Chris had the same scar that you and dad have on the back of your neck."

She feels her neck. "Ok? What's that supposed to mean?" Kylie snaps back. "I thought that was a birth mark. But either way, dad nor I are anything like Chris Turner. If you haven't noticed, I am quite the opposite."

"I know. But if Robert Fox arrested our dad for this brain chip, he must be using it the way he wants to." I want to tell her about Rocco, but not now, not before the Proving. If she knows how big he is, how powerful he has become, she would never let me leave this house. "I need you to trust me."

"I do, but that's a long shot, Carson. You and I both know that—"

"I need to see this through. It's some coincidence that our father gets arrested and we're sent to an orphanage to be forgotten. Robert Fox is trying to cover his tracks. I know he's up to something. I can feel it and I'm the only one that can stop him."

She exhales, letting out the last of her efforts to keep me home. "Swear to me that you'll be careful." She holds out her pinky. Childish, yet effective, I lock my pinky around hers, giving an extra incentive to fulfill a promise. A pinky promise.

"I swear."

She attacks me in the biggest hug she has ever given me. "Good luck tomorrow."

42

The Proving

At five o'clock sharp, five hundred fifty-two people gathered in the Silva Auditorium at Atlantis University for inspection. With only a rucksack I acquired from Jinx, a sleeping bag, and a pair of clothes, I am escorted into one of four wide transporter shuttles to be taken to the Proving grounds. An unnerving feeling twists my stomach. I sit next to my two high school friends Norman Vanhoozer and Phineas Deacon. We made sure to arrive together this time so we don't get separated.

We are seated on metal benches that line the sides two stories high with at least a hundred people on each level. Traveling deep through the Brimstone Forest, gliding through the air at nearly six hundred miles an hour towards the Great Mountain of Alannah, soft chatter fills my ears from the other passengers. My rucksack sits in between my legs with a sewed-on patch made from a pair of pants stitched on the bottom from a wolleybear attack Jinx experienced during his Proving. I stare at the empty pockets of my BDUs and the boot laces loosely hanging off of my boots. Phineas' foot bounces rapidly up and down while Norman appears more relaxed than both of us. I hear him whistling a tune to himself.

A loud beep echoes the transporter. "*Attention passengers, we will be landing shortly. Make sure you have everything you brought; you will not be allowed back on this transport unless you are forfeiting your admission. Good luck to everyone who is aboard. May the saints rest their wings upon you today and guide you down the path of success.*"

Anxiety rushes, my body tenses, the time has come.

"Do you know what these talismans are for?" I whisper to Norman.

"They are supposed to be like points," he says. "I'm not sure though."

I turn to Phineas and ask him the same question. With his longer blonde hair tied back in a man bun, he has a different vibe coming from him. "What? Uh, no," he says leaning over, still rapidly bouncing his foot. He's anxious, but that's how he always is before a big event.

"Alright, listen up!" a loud roaring voice catches my attention, a proctor with the University's logo on his shirt stands in front of the cockpit door. "When we land, everyone is to walk out in an orderly fashion. If I have to yell at any of you, I'll have you doing pushups before you even start. Does everyone understand?"

"Yes, proctor!" I answer back along with every contestant on this transporter.

As instructed, the transport lands near by a beach along the coast. As we reach ground, I watch out the window of the other transporters landing as well. Wind gusts around, grass is blowing from the breeze, the sounds of the transporter's hydraulics lock into place, and the front doors clank open. The proctors immediately start shouting at us to get off like a bomb is about to go off.

"This is it gentleman," I hear Norman's voice behind me. He slaps my shoulder and squeezes it.

As my foot hits the blue grass, I realize I am absolutely in over my head. A proctor lunges into my face screaming for me to get in formation. I'm instantly flustered. Another proctor shoves a folded-up piece of paper in my chest as other proctors line us up in lines all facing a large podium. The yelling finally settles, and nature becomes the only sounds I hear. Ocean birds caw in the distance with the sound of ocean waves brushing up on the sand. I am placed diagonally facing a podium, my friends beside me, as I hope they stay. I scan the field and find Rocco. He towers over everyone in his group. His flush skin reflects off the sun, shaved bald, and fearsome amber eyes that still haunt me to this day. Nearly three times the size he was two years ago, he is a completely different person. Even against the massive physique of the proctors, he outmatches them. He wears a tight black, long sleeved compression shirt, probably four sizes bigger than mine but fills it out to the point of ripping the fibers of the shirt with one measly flex of his muscles. His ruck even looks like a child's toy compared to him. Knots fill my stomach with anticipation. My throat feels tight as well as my chest. Nerves shake my bones. Just him standing in place is more intimidating than when I faced Chris in all his armor.

"EYES STRAIGHT!" a terrifyingly familiar voice explodes in my ear. I snap forward. The familiar proctor from phase one walks up on the podium and stands fiercely at attention. "Good morning," he speaks.

"Good morning, proctor!" the near six hundred people echo.

"My name is Proctor Albanese, and it is my privilege to see a fine group of future titans here. I am also displeased to say that I see a *whoooole* bunch of corpses here today as well." Murmurs start around me. Proctor Albanese looks at his watch. "I sincerely hope some of you said your goodbyes because, during your time here, you will be tested, you will be brought to the point of exhaustion, you will be judged, betrayed, relied on, depended on, threatened, and most of all, you will be watched. Not only by me, or the other proctors here, but by the spirits of the Brimstone Forest as well. You will be tested by the raging rapids of Rampart River, the steep hilltops of the Great Mountain of Alannah, the animals in the wild, and the animals you stand next to today. Sixty miles will be your hike today. At every seven and a half miles, there will be a station where you can rest. Small huts will be located around the camps and fire pits will be there as well to cook your food. Each station holds a hundred fifty water canteens, a hundred fifty pieces of food, a hundred and fifty med kits, and a hundred fifty Proving Talismans." He takes one out of his pocket. They look like a man in a battle suit standing at attention. "These talismans are what you are hunting for. The object is to finish with a grand total of eight." He pauses and scans the group. His bald head shines from the beaming sun. "Now, there's a catch. At each station you may only take one," he raises a finger up. "yes, *one* item," He points to four elevated boxes filled with the items he was talking about. "If any of our camera drones catch you taking more than one, you will be disqualified. Show some discipline, and you will prevail. Show weakness, and you will die." Proctor Albanese pockets the small statue. I watch as a few hands shoot in the air. "THERE WILL BE NO QUESTIONS!" he roars. "YOU ARE GIVEN A MISSION, AND YOU WILL DO IT OR DIE TRYING. THAT IS THE TITAN TRIBUTE. YOU WIN OR YOU DIE."

Wow it all makes sense now.

He points to a path to the left of him. "That is the path you will all take to the first station. In your hands, you've been given a map of the area, that is my gift to you. The rules are simple, survive. Do what you have to do to survive. If you are quick, you can get yourself a talisman here or a first aid kit to bandage your boo-boos. You may work together, you may hunt together, you may even hunt each other and take another's equipment, you may steal, you may barter, you will do what you have to do to finish with eight talismans. If you finish with *less* than eight talismans, that is ok. Most of you will not finish with eight. More than half of you will finish with an average of three. That is ok, just don't expect to be drafted high, or at all. There are only two hundred spots in this year's draft. So, if you survive and you're not chosen, better luck next year. Maybe next time you'll try harder... With that, I send you on your way. May the saints guide you down the path of success." He smiles and looks around. No one moves in fear of doing anything we weren't supposed to. His face changes, his eyebrows curl, his teeth show. "GO!" he barks.

His roar jumpstarts everyone and I take off bolting to the opening. Pushing and shoving from all around me as everyone steamrolls over to the boxes. Cursing and shouting, pandemonium ensues as six hundred men and women attack the four boxes in a mosh pit of bodies. Fists are swinging, blood spatters as a head is rammed against a tree next to me.

"Get out of my way!" someone shouts behind me. I'm lifted from behind and heaved over the boxes into a pile of fallen branches. I fall awkwardly and look back to see a hoard of people clawing over each other over the scattered items on the ground. It looks like a zombie apocalypse movie. I feel frozen to the ground at the sight of six hundred people fighting in a mass pile of simple survival items and wooden figurines. A boy's head is concaved from being thrown into a tree. That could have been me... What did I get myself into?

I'm picked up and I rip out of the grip of... Norman. "You ok?" he asks.

"Yeah." I look over myself. "Yeah, I'm good."

"C'mon, guys. Let's go!" Phineas shouts.

Norman pushes me forward and I start to run. Phineas waves us in and breaks a hole in the group. Bodies scatter the ground, both bloodied and broken already. This is ridiculous, this was not what I signed up for.

We go at a steady pace. Already down one talisman because of my fall, we travel more towards the back of the pack. Some contestants run out of steam within the first couple miles, but with Phineas holding our pace, being a top runner in high school, I can keep pace with him. My training regime was excruciatingly strict. Twelve-mile runs, heavy power lifting inside the gravity cube and also some hand to hand combat simulations with Jinx. I had to be in the fittest shape I could be to compete with these people who have trained their entire life for this one chance.

Norman begins to pant as we approach the first station. It was a straight path down to the beach where two small square huts are homed. Camera drones glide around the enclosure. A fire pit in the middle with dozens of people there guzzling down their water canteens and tending to their wounds. One man has a gash going down his entire leg. In the middle there are these wooden boxes, one is completely empty, the other one has about a dozen med kits, the food is completely empty, and six water canteens remain. Norman and I grab a water canteen, while Phineas takes a med kit with a huff.

"Saintdamn it, I wanted that talisman. Hex! We're already down two." He peers over to me and I look at him with confused eyes as I take my first sip of warm water.

"What? It's not my fault." I snap.

"You're damn right it is. If you didn't trip, we would have gotten two talismans already."

"Are you serious? I was thrown!"

"Whatever, man," he snaps. "I'll leave you if you keep slowing me down." He slips a small hand sized med kit filled with a stim, some medical ointment, gauzes, bandages, and a small ace wrap. "You ready to keep going?"

"Yeah, let's pick up the pace then," I say. We look to Norman chugging his water canteen. "Norm, slow down. Savor it, we got a long road ahead." I look beyond the camp where some people already look a mile or so down the coastline. "We got a lot of sand to track through."

He breaths heavily. "Ok... one second." He takes one last sip and clips the canteen to his backpack. Norman doesn't look good, his shirt is soaked with sweat. His demeanor is alarming as well, like he's stalling.

With nearly eight miles down, we're ankle deep in a four mile stretch of beach. Sand seeps into my boots, running is awkward against the soft terrain. Phineas wanted a faster pace, but Norman simply can't keep up. Wearing hiking boots was not the smartest thing to wear, my feet are burning. I already feel a blister forming on the sole of my foot.

About three miles of sand left in front of us, Phineas peels off the beach and found a detour down a dirt path that brings us through another chunk of the Brimstone Forest. As time rolls by, the sun beats down harder on us. I sacrifice a few more sips of water as the sweat builds down my shirt. Phineas holds strong without water. I'm feeling a bit winded by mile ten, but Norman was not ready for this kind of hike. He's brought our steady jog to a measly walk. Phineas voices his frustrations, but at least we're not passed by anyone. From what Phineas guesses, people are already at the second station. He urges Norman to push through with insults and mild threats to leave him behind, but Norman just isn't built like us. His water canteen is dry by mile eleven. He complains of cramps in his sides and begs to stop, but Phineas refuses and threatens to leave him behind. He picks up his pace while I slow down to stay by Norman's side.

"Phin, you serious? You're gonna just leave him?"

He stops with a huff. "Normmy knew he had to train," he snaps pointing at him. "You knew and what'd you do? You drank, ate junk, and played video games all summer."

"No!" Norman pants. "So did you."

"Yes, but I trained! You are ruining my Proving! Maybe you don't want this as badly as I do, but this is everything to me! Both of you are jeopardizing my chances!"

"Woah, Phin, relax," I butt in. "Let's walk the next mile. People have to be wearing down by now. This thing wasn't meant to be a run, it's a hike."

"No! I want to be first! Like the proctor said, you either win or you die!"

"Do you see anyone dying right now?" I snap.

An ear piercing scream catches me off guard. It's not from any of us, it sounds in front of us. Agonizing screams continue as we rush down the path through a multitude of several different trees. Cries for help with whimpering sobs come next. What happened? Are we running into a herd of canahounds or a trap of some kind? I pull Phineas back and tell him to be careful, we inch our way upwards as the scream get louder. "Help! Help!"

The tree trunks darken as we walk further in. Danger signs with crossbones are nailed to the blackened trees. They don't appear dead, but they are black like death, grim trees, the best kind of wood to start fires. I watch my step as we inch ourselves closer and closer to the raging bellows of this poor person begging for assistance. I pick up the sturdiest stick I can find just incase it's an ambush.

A haunting reality hits me in the face as I see a severed leg cut from the knee in a snap-trap made to catch woolybears. A few yards up is a one legged bloody teenager no older than me. Life rushes out of him in a spraying red stream. He looks at us with a helpless pale face, his eyes flutter, and his screams are silenced as his head falls back and hits the truck of a tree.

"Holy hexing saints," I panic to myself.

Phineas walks up to him and rips off his bag. "Looks Lunen, no way this snap trap could sever an Alannican leg. Not with our bone density."

"What are you doing?" I ask.

"Uh, seeing what he has. We can use his stuff." Phineas opens up the kid's bag and pulls out a talisman. "Nice!" he celebrates with a smile. Norman huffs a disappointing show of jealousy.

"Guys, this kid just died?! This can't be part of the rules. We have to tell someone."

"Bro, did you hear Proctor Loudmouth? There are no rules, this was supposed to happen."

"Are you kidding me?"

Phineas walks up to me and shushes me. "Keep your voice down. They're probably listening to you panic right now. Don't let them know your scared. It'll hurt your draft stock."

"My draft stock?" I stare at the lifeless child. He probably had a family, friends, pets. All gone, wasted for nothing.

Norman looks at me with confusion. "Why are you acting so weird? You knew this would happen. You're acting like you knew him. The kid's dead, so what?" I ponder the thought; what kind of childhood do Alannicans have? Jinx did tell me Alannicans think differently than Harmonians. Once their worthless, it's like they don't exist. The only thing worth something is the bag off his back and the talisman inside. Poor kid.

"C'mon." Phin swings his arm down the path and insinuates us to go. Norman rips off the kid's shirt and tucks it into his pack, says it'll be good for a tourniquet. I shake my head in disgust. I have never seen this side of them before, so unamused to death, so nonchalant to it.

The dark forest creates a massive tension. My head spins with the idea that traps and obstacles are aligned in our path to kill us and decapitate limbs off our bodies. Norman and Phineas march ahead of me while I stare at the ground begging the saints to leave here with all my limbs together. Jinx never told me anything about traps.

Phineas now holds the only talisman. In his head, he is the leader of our group. He's confident, and physically and mentally in the right state of mind for this but what he lacks is actual leadership skills. He hasn't faltered once or shown any signs of panic as we pass nearly twenty more people who've stopped to catch their breath. Phineas wants to ambush several smaller people but I talk him out of it. We just need to get out of these woods and to the next station.

Another hour goes by, we find the clearing where the smell of fire and smoke creep into our noses. Laughter and chatter consume our ears as we enter station two. Talismans stare us down as we approach them. I grab my first talisman and push it deep in the hidden pockets of my bag, under the bottom flap of my pack, the pocket where Jinx urged me to take advantage of. Phineas races to grab yet another talisman while Norman decides on a second water canteen. Norman sits next to me on a bench and gulps down his water. Phineas takes out his map and plans our path towards Station Three. Only time will tell what's next in our long journey ahead.

43
Clay

I urge Norman to keep his drinking to sips as we extend our hike up slope to the third station. Reading the small map we were given, it shows that the trail splits after the second station. This gives us nearly three different paths up towards the Great Mountain of Alannah. My feet ache, blisters are burning my raw flesh on the soles of my feet. A sign nailed to a tree says we have reached the sixteenth mile of our sixty mile hike, not even halfway done. Combined, we have no food, three empty water canteens, and three talismans in the first four hours.

Doubt follows Phineas, he had the idea of running the entire distance of the Proving. I don't disagree with him, but even that is something I've never thought about doing. He urges us to pick up the pace but Norman just can't keep up. He trails behind us about a step off pace of Phineas. If we can't make it to the next station at this pace, we're for sure going to be spending the night in the woods, where only the saints and the proctors are aware of what's around us.

Is Jinx watching me? Are these camera drones really all that protect us? Is that proctor who knows Courtney keeping an eye on me? What protection can they really provide? I've seen more dead corpses in these woods than I have in my entire life.

"We have to pick up the pace, guys," Phineas says. "If we can't get to the next station by sundown, we're dead for sure. We're not hiking these woods in the dark. The last thing we need is stepping on a trap we can't even see."

"Do we even want to camp at the station?" Norman considers.

"What do you mean?" I query.

"Well, if everyone wants to make it to the station, and everyone camps out in the huts by a big fire, wouldn't you think someone could try and steal everyone's stuff while they're sleeping? It's like that level in Ghost Raiders, remember, Carson?"

"Yeah, sounds like a plan. What do you think, Phin?"

"So, you're saying we shouldn't be trying to get to the station? That we should camp out here for the night?" Phineas asks.

"Why not? We have no idea who's in there. We should wait till night, then quietly go in and sift through everyone's stuff, taking anything we can hold on to, and booking it."

The smell of smoke clogs my nostrils. A steaming grey stream lifts in the air in the distance at the top of a hill side. Half a mile in the distance, we find Station Three with a line of staggering bodies sitting outside the walls.

"There it is, boys," Phineas says. "If you guys want to set up camp and get a fire started, I'll go up there and do some recon. Maybe see if they want to trade for food or something."

"By yourself?" Norman asks.

"Yeah, I'll go in there and scope out the place. No sense for all of us to go. I'll be quick."

"Phin, no, I don't think that's a—"

As I try to get my friend to stop, he bursts ahead of us, leaving us. We watch him run at a ridiculously fast pace, but for him it's nearly a jog in the park.

"He's so impulsive," Norman says.

"What do you mean?" I ask.

"He wasn't even listening to us." Norman flings his hands up and walks off the path towards a bush. "He never listens to me, ever. I don't understand. All he's ever done is… Oh, look, there's berries over here." He walks over to a bush plucks a few and pockets them. "These will be great to trade for real food."

I walk over to the bush and examine the berries. Bunches of blue berries with little pink hairs. I can't remember what kind they are. Norman throws one in his mouth. "Norman, spit that out, they're no good."

He looks at me wide eyed and spits it out. "What's wrong with them?"

"I can't remember, but I know they're not for eating. They're for dyes and stuff, I think. Good for trading though, so hold on to them."

Norman gathers the majority of the berries and bags them in the shirt he took off of the dead boy in the woods. We stretch out off the beaten path and gather some wood for a fire.

The sun finally dips under the horizon, light becomes sparse and still no sign of Phineas.

"You think he's in trouble?" Norman asks.

"Probably. You think we should go and find him up there? How much trouble you think he's in?" I ask.

"What's the plan? We're just going to walk on in and ask for our friend?"

"He's probably in there sucking face with some random girl. I'm sure he's fine."

Norman can't argue with that logic and packs up for the walk up the steep rocky path to the campsite. Muscles are tightening as we climb up the massive hillside towards the woodsy smell of a fire burning. Spiked logs stack together vertically surrounding a small camp site. A banner atop reads, 'Station Three.'

Laughter and chatter mix in with the smell of fire and burning meat. I'm tired, my feet swell from hiking. We pass the front gates and come upon a group of nearly twenty various people. The first I see plays with a stick in the sand, he sports a black eye swelling with puss. The smell of a meat aroma is in the air. A crispy rodent is rotating over the fire pit. I scan the place but find no signs of our blonde curly haired friend. As we approach the fire, the eyes of the group bend to us, the chatter dims, an awkward aura makes my stomach drop. There's no sign of Phineas anywhere. There are no more talismans in the boxes, so I grab a bag of assorted fruits and power bars.

"Stop," a rugged man with disheveled hair shouts. We stop quickly. He holds what I can only guess is a tree trunk chiseled down to look like a sledgehammer.

"Woah!" I marvel at the complexity of his weapon. "Where did you get that?"

"Silence!" he demands. "Leave, now!" He points towards the exit.

"Hey now, what's with the hostility man. We're cool," I say with my hands up trying to deescalate.

The man growls and threatens us by slamming his hammer into the ground. "I did not give you permission to speak!" The group stands as one, each holding their own makeshift weapons. Eyes from all directions stare us down. A nervous rumble in my stomach makes me feel uneasy.

"Woah, brother, my friend, we don't want any trouble," Norman chimes in.

"There are no friends of yours here, Alannicans. If you wish to be allies, pledge your obedience to me and drop your bags."

Chatter from all around cheering for their supposed leader. They threaten us to do as we are told with long pointed sticks in their hands.

"Drop my bag?" I question. "No, that can't happen. Listen, like we said, we are just looking for our friend. Tall, blonde hair, probably making out with some girl right now."

The shaggy man tightens his grip and whistles a sharp tune. The group points their weapons at us and creeps forward. Sharp points of knives, spears, and other makeshift weapons creep towards us.

I step into my fighting stance and swivel my head around. Three, four, six, ten, and four more come out of the huts. We're surrounded.

"Woah, woah, buddy. We mean you no harm. Can we talk this out like civilized human beings?" Norman argues. "I am a full blooded Alannican citizen, and I will not be subjected to the likes of barbarianism. Please, lower your weapons and let's talk this out."

"You do not give me orders, Alannican. I am Clay Douglas, master blacksmith of Parvaluna and we Lunens do not negotiate with your kind. Drop your bags or it will be your heads that will. You have three seconds to decide."

My stomach drops. We are completely surrounded. No weapons, nothing to barter, and no ground to escape. "What do we do?" I whisper.

"Three," Clay starts.

"We can't fight all of them," Norman whispers back. "Can you?"

"Two."

"I can try," I say.

"One."

"Don't be foolish," he says slowly detaching his rucksack. "I don't see any other choice, buddy. Stay alive, do as he says. Fight another day." He walks forward, detaches his rucksack and chucks it in front of him. "There, happy? Let's talk like men." The group laughs and slowly surrounds us, two or three already in my blind spot. Norman never steered me wrong before, but I wouldn't have given myself up so easily. He knows more than I do, right?

As disgruntled as it feels to give up so easily, he's not wrong. I unclip my ruck and throw it in front of me. The spear wielding man nods to his guards beside him and they rush to grab our bags. "Now bow. Bow to the future alphaTitan, Clay Douglas." I hesitate to do so, Norman drops to his knees instantly. Baffled and confused, I know this was never part of any video game Norman played. I think to rush him and rip that hammer out of his hands, but before I take a step my knees are kicked in and I fall to my knees in a bowing position, and something digs into my back.

Clay snickers, then it turns into a full on bellowing laugh. His group of followers join in on his rampaging racket. He stops mid laugh. "Tie these worthless bags of bones up and throw them with the other one."

A blunt force hits me in the back of the head. Three knees pin my arms down and then two more on my hamstrings. Pain shoots up my body like a cannon as my arms are forced back and tied. Two fists clobber my face with a few kicks in my side for good measure. I'm left with my friend in the same predicament, his forehead digging into the sandy floor. He's panting with a gash over his eye.

I'm picked up from my hands and feel my shoulder nearly dislocate.

Clay's huge dark green eyes meet mine. "No ally of mine would ever bow down to the enemy. Rule four of the Brotherhood of Titans, never submit." The group cheers and celebrates their new captives like a horde of barbarians.

44
Trapped

Clay personally picks me up over his shoulder and drops me into a dark hole. My hogtied body plummets into a hard floor of dirt, landing on my tied-up hands. I lay there angry, confused, and atrociously embarrassed, utterly humiliated. This is the second time I have been thrown today, and I am tired of it rather quickly. I would have never bowed to that man if I wasn't forced to. If Norman had even the slightest bit of backbone, we may have stood a chance. Hexing Lunens, hexing recycled air breathing psychos. As I squirm to the side another body is dropped on my ankle. The weight shocks me and I shriek at the bone crushing pain. I shake my foot free and curse a mouthful at him. "You hexed us, Norman, you really hexed us. What are we supposed to do now?"

"Norman? Carson?" a voice calls out in the darkness.

"Phineas?" I say in a lethargic gasp. In the darkness, the natural light adjusts to my eyes and I find the eyes of my lost friend.

"Holy saints in afterlife," Phineas says. "It is you."

"I see you met Clay," Norman says. "I guess you bowed to him too?"

"Saints no. I pounded a guy to a pulp before they ganged up on me and ripped my ruck off. Said something about a brotherhood always looks out for each other blah, blah, blah. Lunens, man, you can't trust them."

I give Norman a stink eye. He sees it but Phineas doesn't. A weird aroma is in the air. "Did you pee in here?"

"No!" Phineas snaps. "I am a saintdamn Alannican. I do not soil myself! Are you mad?!" I look at Norman, he gives me a crooked look. "I didn't ask if you soiled yourself?"

"I know what you said! Don't be ridiculous, they threw us in their saintdamn latrine." Phineas snaps.

This is degrading. Alannicans are not slaves. They are established businessmen, CEO's, lawyers, and doctors. Alannah consist of sixty percent of the military. Hours seem to pass, the moons glisten down the hole, and I finally get a good look at Phineas. Both of his eyes are bruised, blood dried up around his fat lip, his hair is messy and filled with dust and dirt. At several times during our imprisonment, we are targeted with urine. We're laughed at and ridiculed as the Lunens take aim on us.

Phineas snaps on them, "Just you wait! I will destroy you. I'll rip your saintdamn arms off you inbred, test-tube abominations."

The last of them leave and the moons sit at its peak in the night. The hole reeks of urine. It's hard to hold my breath so I don't have to inhale this foul odor. I put my shirt over my nose and sit with my knees up in my chest.

"We got to get out of here," Phineas says finally calmed down. "Those insignificant creatures will pay for this."

"Do you have a plan?" I ask.

"More like an idea. I have a knife in my sock. I took it when I was fighting, slid it in before they tied me up. If you can get it we can get untied."

"Why haven't you said something?" Norman snaps.

"Well I was, but there's the other matter of getting out of here." We all look up at the holes entrance. We're about eight feet deep. "Now, with you guys here I can—"

"You can what, go scout out the area again?" Norman chides. "Your little stunt is the reason why we're in this mess. I lost my berries because of you. If you would have listened to me, instead of your stomach, we wouldn't be in this mess. We could have taken them on together."

"Do you have a plan then, pretty boy? No? I didn't think so." He shimmies over to him and lifts his legs at Norman's face. Norman recoils with a disgusted face and rolls his eyes as he maneuvers himself around to grab the knife. It's quite comical to see two grown men basically spooning each other as Norman uncomfortably reaches behind him to grab a small pocketknife dug into Phineas' sock. "Great, now untie me." Phineas and Norman go back to back. They do this

271

humping motion that makes me giggle like a preteen boy hearing private parts in health class. Phineas' hands break through the rope and he lets out a relieving sigh.

"Wow, get a room you two," I jest.

"Shut up," Norman sneers embarrassingly but laughs it off.

Phineas cuts both of us free and now it's time to get out of here.

"Great work, Normmy," Phineas says. "Now, lift me up. I'll go find us a ladder or something."

"What? By yourself? No." He waves his hands. "I'll lift you up and you can pull us up. Then we will find a way out. We work together, as a team," Norman interjects.

"Yeah," I agree. "C'mon let's get out of here. Hopefully, everyone's asleep."

"Great, fine, whatever. I'm going to go find our bags. Did you guys get your item out of the boxes? Did you see any more talismans?"

Norman shakes his head.

I nod. "I grabbed a bag of food before we were stopped."

Phineas groans. "Ok, whatever, no big deal." He points up. "There's a hut filled with people next to the exit, go see if you can sneak in and grab anything you can hold. Weapons, rucksacks, food, whatever." He points to Norman. "Normmy, you're with me. You go get something out of the boxes. I'm going after Clay, that lunatic is getting what he deserves for dishonoring me like he did."

"*No!*" Norman snaps in a whisper. "You want to wake the entire camp? We're as good as dead if you do."

Phineas growls angrily. He thinks it over and argues his point, but Norman is stern and refuses to help. "Fine."

We hoist Phineas up out of the hole, and he leans back in to pull us both out. Phineas and Norman sneak around to the other huts and leave me to myself. I creep over to the side of a hut full of people snoring. I peak in the window and see six bodies sleeping in hammocks. Rucksacks cover the ground and spears are leaning against the walls. I lean to the side of the building to check if the coast is clear. A shorter woman with a makeshift spear is casually walking around the fire. I hop into the window and cautiously grab the rucks and carefully drop them out the window. An inconsistent snore shocks me as I snap to a sleeping man rolling over in his hammock. I stay still as a frightened ovat who dares not to move in hopes of evading its predator. Quickly, I hop through the window and land back outside. Norman is back looking over the side towards the fire with a rucksack on his back.

"Behind you," I whisper and squeeze his shoulder.

He looks over his shoulder. "I think she fell asleep," he whispers.

"Where's Phineas?"

"I don't know. That idiot was right behind me a second ago."

Six bags lay next to us as we ponder our next move. Wherever Phineas is isn't our main concern. He can handle himself, hopefully.

Before we plan our next move, a shadow creeps up to the woman and wraps her up in a choke hold. The shadows constrict the girl as she wakes and starts flailing her legs trying to escape but it is no use. We think it's Phineas before a voice scares us from behind. "I told you guys to get out, what are you doing?" I snap around and find Phineas looking at us with a crooked look insinuating we move. He carries his own bag with four other rucks in his hands. "I got your ruck." He tosses it to me. I spot Jinx's stitched patch, so I know it's mine. "C'mon, let's go. Is the coast clear?"

"Wait, that wasn't—" I look back and the shadow that knocked out the lookout is gone. "Ok, coast is clear, let's move."

We clear the camp and race down the hill nearly running another half mile before stopping in a small patch of trees, a perfect place to camp for the night. We scurry ourselves inside the pocket in between the trees and unload our stolen goods.

Finally back together, we can relax and regain our strength for tomorrow. For tomorrow, we take on The Rampart River. As legend has it, the raging rapids rush through this at all hours of the day, but one. After counting our findings, we got twelve talismans, five med kits, five bags of fruit and power bars, a bunch of pointed spears with some kind of sharp pointed rock on top, and a good amount of rope. I feel like a neanderthal holding something so primitive, but that is all we can get here. We survive off the fallen and learn how to live without the means of technology. Jinx really meant it when he told me to think outside the box.

Splitting our loot amongst ourselves evenly, I now hold four talismans, a spear, a few water containers, and a good amount of food to last me the rest of the Proving. For the first time this entire hike, a calm sensation tips me over as we tuck ourselves away off the path and chomp down on the first piece of food I've had all day. After a day like this, I would be knocked out cold in my bed. As I roll out my sleeping bag, I realize we may be in for more than we can chew. Clay and his mob of Lunens aren't going to be happy when he realizes we robbed them blind and escaped. We need to keep our heads on a swivel.

45

Through the Rampart River

I wake to something nibbling at my nose. I open my eyes to a furry scrunched up face of an ovat. I shriek and smack it out of my face. It freaks out and makes a whining noise as it scurries away. As my heart pounds, my watch shows five o'clock. I got three hours of sleep.

"What was that?" Norman groggily says waking up.

"Nothing, I don't know," I lie. Embarrassed to admit a harmless ovat startled me.

"Ugh, what time is it?" Phineas groans.

I check my watch as if I didn't just look at it. "It's about five. We should get a head start on the day. Clay could find us any minute."

I swing my ruck over my shoulder and make my way towards our first challenge of the day, the Rampart River. Twenty miles in length, the rapids roar downstream to a waterfall that falls into a lake at the bottom of the mountain. If we can't figure out a way upriver, we will die at the bottom of that waterfall.

"Any ideas, fellahs? I really don't want to get wet," Phineas says.

"Maybe we don't have to swim, maybe we can just walk up stream," Norman suggests.

"How do the proctors except us to cross the river with no battlesuits?"

"There's no way we can go through it, maybe up ahead there will be a narrower part we can jump across or a bridge even. There's no way a proctor would expect anyone to swim through this."

My feet are still raw from the near twenty-three miles we traveled yesterday. Still waking up from a rough night, I fear we overstepped stealing the Lunen's stuff. The best thing we can hope for is to keep moving and hope that Clay and his goons don't catch up to us. Hopefully, no one got a good look at our faces in the dark. Phineas on the other hand fought them. He gave himself a huge target on his back for doing what he did.

The sounds of the roaring waters crashing down stream is intimidating.

"Hey, Norman." He doesn't respond. "Norman?"

He blinks and finds me. "Hey, sorry. What'd you say?"

"You ok?"

"I'm fine."

Norman's holding his stomach. Did he have a bad piece of fruit? Did those Lunens poison our food? "You don't look fine. Did you eat any of those berries yesterday? I told you—"

"No. I'm *fine* though. Just have to uh… relieve myself."

"Ok, there's a tree right there." I nod.

"No, like… the other one."

"Hey!" Phineas shouts catching my attention. He stares over the other side of the river where a smaller boy is wondering around collecting wood. He stops in his tracks and looks around. "Hey! Over here! How did you get across?" Phineas calls out. He looks over to us and flips us the middle finger and walks off.

"Did you really expect anything different?" I ask.

"I guess not, but how did he even get over there?"

A loud whistle overpowers my ears. Behind me a hoard of wide eyed angry Lunens point at us. One screams for Clay, others jumps in animalistic joy. Spears dance in the air, a rabid look in all their eyes. The Lunens found us.

"Get them! Bring them to me now! They will pay for their crimes!" a voice thunders. The wild gang of Lunens charge us.

"Holy saints! Run, run!" I yell.

Phineas bolts ahead of us. Making distance between Norman and me. Norman is falling behind, he holds his stomach like there's a dumbbell in it slowing him down. I grab his wrist and pull him along.

"Go. Go on without me," Norman says.

"No! C'mon don't be ridiculous."

A spear nearly skewers me, another flies over my head and sticks the ground. Yelling and shouting come from behind us. A panic dips into my stomach as I look behind and see a wild gang of Lunens gaining on us. What do I do? What do I do?

"Look!" Phineas yells in front of us. In the distance, a path of rope and wood lines itself perfectly over top the rapids. A bridge. A saintdamn bridge. "C'mon! Follow me!" Phineas yells. Phineas grips the railing of the bridge and dashes across it in six wide leaps.

"Don't let them cross the bridge! Stop them now!" the thunderous voice yells behind us.

I pull Norman on to the bridge. We race across and nearly fall off when it wobbles. The wood is old, the rope holding it together is worn, and the creaks and cracks scare me as we get halfway across. At any second this bridge could—

A loud crack pulls me backwards and a yelp of my name scares me more than the Lunens. Norman falls in the river and I lose grip of his hand.

"No!" I scream. I can't hold him. "No! Norman! Phin, catch him!" I scream in shock.

Phineas doesn't attempt to save him. He pulls me on to the other side and cuts the bridge with his knife. A wild gang of Lunens shriek as the bridge gives way to the weight and collapses into the water. Nearly a dozen of them are pulled by the current.

I get to my feet as fast as I can and race down the river. "Norman! I'm coming!" I yell trying to find Norman. "Get out some rope, Phin. Hurry!"

Phineas follows. "Carson! The waterfall!" he shouts.

I spot Norman holding on to a large boulder dug into the ground. Before I'm able to get to him, two Lunens bump into him and he loses grip. His head falls under the water and I lose sight of him. My friend is in danger, I have to save him. Without a second thought, I leap into the roaring stream after him. The current's immense pressure overwhelms me.

"Carson, are you crazy?!" Phineas shouts at my insane gesture.

Norman's head bobs above water, his arms splashing around trying to grab onto anything.

Desperately thinking of what to do, I swim over to him and grab his shoulder strap. He clings on to me as we bounce off of another boulder the size of both of us. The air is knocked out of my lungs as we spiral out of control tumbling under the water. With a gasp of air I find the surface once again and realize we're seconds from the falls. The roaring waters are eager to consume another two weary souls. Norman holds on tight to me as I see the horizon at the end of the rapids.

"Throw me the rope! Phin! Throw the rope!" I yell. I spot Phineas sprinting at our pace with his hands out. "Throw me the rope! Hurry!"

Phineas launces the rope and a Lunen nearly grabs it for themselves but misses it. I eagerly have to stretch backwards and catch it with the tips of my fingers. I quickly twist it around my wrist and hold on to Norman as tight as I can. The last thing I see is the sunrise over the horizon, and the lake at the bottom of the waterfall.

Time slows. As we descend to our doom nearly nine hundred feet in the air, I realized this wasn't worth it. Norman cries and screams in my ears and my mouth can't make words. This feeling is nothing like a roller coaster. Gravity pulls us down and for the first time in my life, I felt as if I was flying. Then suddenly, the rope tightens around my wrist and we're flung into the cliff side. Air is shot out of my lungs on impact. An eerie batch of various screams echoes as a dozen bodies catch the corner of my eye. The unfortunate Lunens that were on the bridge the moment Phineas cut the rope falls to their deaths at terminal velocity into the lake below. I don't even hear them splash at the bottom.

As we hang off the side of the cliff being supported by my one hand, Norman's wrapped around my waist, clutching my rucksack. My hand burns and stings from the weight of me and Norman. Almost a quarter mile in the air, Norman looks down and shrieks when we're jerked downward suddenly. Then he hollers with absolute indecency.

"Shut up! Shut up. We're ok," I exhale. "We're ok," I say gently cupping his head trying to calm him down. I hold on to him, both of his arms are around me and his feet tangled around my waist like we're spooning lovers dangling nearly a thousand feet in the air over the largest waterfall on Tyke.

"I got you! I got you guys!" I hear, I look up and see Phineas looking down at us holding the rope. "Hold on!" he grunts and growls. Slowly, I feel myself being pulled up.

Every inch we're pulled is a devastating burn on my wrist. As much as my body wants to let go, I refuse. I choose to hold on but the rope itself is constricting around my wrist so hard, it's making my hand change color. I tighten my grip for as long as I can, trying hard not to look down. Norman's screams turn to measly whimpers as the realization of our near-death experience slowly comes to an end. I reach for the ledge and make sure Norman makes it to solid ground before I pull myself up. Phineas grabs my hand and pulls me up. Once I make it to solid ground and feel the sweet relief of grass in my face, my hand throbs, heartbeat slows, and reality comes back into focus. I'm going to be ok.

"Hey, Carson," Norman says.

"What?"

"I don't have to go to the bathroom anymore."

"Ugh, shut up." On top of a near death experience, this man has the nerve to joke with me.

"Thank you, for saving my life," Norman finally says.

Annoyed, wet, tired, and caffeine deprived, his voice instantly annoys me. "Don't thank me." I stare at my swollen hand and watch the water droplets fall off me and take a deep breath to calm myself down. "Thank Phineas, he just saved both of us."

Phineas is at the shore flipping off Clay and his remaining few followers on the other side. I can't quite hear what they are saying but I'm sure it's not pleasant things.

As my nerves settle and danger is averted, I realize my ruck is waterlogged. Everything inside is ruined besides the talismans hidden in the bottom compartment. All my food is ruined. None of it survived. I turn my ruck upside down and with a long, sad exhale I dump everything out.

"Sorry," Norman whimpers.

"Don't be sorry either. It's ok. We're ok. That's all that matters." I lay my hand on Norman's shoulder and we share a relieving smile.

46

The Daltonese group

My hand still hasn't changed back to its normal peach color as we find our way to Station Four. It's numb and irritating but at least I can say I have both my friends still with me. Without any food, my stomach growls for breakfast.

A chipped sign with the words 'Station Four' is placed on an arch made of tree branches. A fire brews in the middle with only five others. A basket load of talismans and all the other choices we have are still in abundance. We're hesitant to make our approach inside with deja vu in full effect. I announce myself with hands open begging for safe passage, pleading we mean no harm. In return, they laugh and welcome us into their fire circle. They insist I strip and dry off my clothes and sit by the fire. They say fungus will grow on my toes if my socks remain wet.

With their dark complexion, bushy hair, and tribal tattoos all over their bodies, I know they're Daltonese. Even our silent and cautious approach wasn't enough to be unheard. All five of them turn their heads to us.

"Welcome, gentlemen!" a deep voiced man yells.

"Did you guys go swimming or something?"

"We mean you no harm," Norman pants. "Please, we're just passing through. We've—"

"Is this the guy you flipped the bird to, Oober?" the broader shouldered man asks his shorter companion. He has a familiar sounding voice as the man next to him. They appear to be identical. Also accompanying them is a long legged woman who is roasting sliced vegetables on a stick over the fire. Another boy is off to the side sharpening sticks with a Dalton multi tool.

The familiar shorter boy looks at us with a devilish smile. "I don't know. I flip off a lot of people."

"Did you guys fall through the bridge or something?" one of the big men asks.

"Bridge?" Norman blurts out. "That was no bridge! That was nothing more than wood and rope. Whoever made that was a saintdamn moron."

The smaller boy hums to the woman. "I didn't think it was that bad."

The big one rolls their eyes. "Come, friends, sit down. Dry off and cook your food on our fire. We can share if you'd like, we have plenty to go around" He scooches over and allows us to sit. I take in the opportunity, but Phineas smacks his hand against my chest.

"It's fine. They're Daltonese, not Lunen, c'mon," I speak softly to Phineas and shake hands with them. I set my ruck down next to the fallen log and take my shirt off to lay it on their makeshift drying racks.

Phineas and Norman refuse to sit or undress. The woman smiles at me and compliments me on my confidence. I try to make small talk and ask what Dalton is like and they all look at me like I have two heads.

"What's it to you?" the stick sharpener snaps.

"Nothing, just curious. I had a Daltonese friend back in the day."

"You did? When?" Phineas asks with his arms folded.

I stutter realizing I slipped. "It's uh, long story. Foreign exchange student."

"In Greycott?" Norman asks.

"Ye… no. No. Don't worry about it."

The group looks at me crooked but I'm able to shrug the topic off. They explain how they're not used to people asking so kindly before. They're always sincere to out of territory citizens but were always treated differently when they are out of their home territory, like they are inferior to Alannicans.

Oh, how I can relate.

"Well, any friend of Dalton is a friend of mine. I'm Griffin Daltonson," the bulky man with a long braided ponytail says. His voice is deep and profound, sophisticated and strong. He lays his hand out to an identical man with a tribal tattoo going across his neck and face. "This here is my twin brother Ezekiel and our shadow over there—"

"Oober," the little one snaps in a raspy voice, standing half a foot shorter than me. "and I'm *not* your shadow!" he snaps at Griffin.

Griffin laughs. "He is. He never leaves our side. Whether we were hunting or gathering for the tribe, this little guy was always by our side."

Oober folds his hands and huffs.

Griffin continues, "This here is our other cousins Morganna and her little brother, Blitzen." He leads his hand to the thick legged, green eyed woman with deep purple hair. Only Daltonese usually hold that exotic hair color. I notice Norman eyeing her up. The boy nods to us as he continues sharpening his stick.

Their last names catch my attention. "You said Daltonson? Like—"

"Yes, *thee* Daltonsons. My father is Viceroy and the descendant of the founder of Dalton. We are—"

"Royalty," Phineas insinuates.

A confused look appears on Griffin, but he shakes it off with a laugh, "Hah, I guess you can put it that way. Grateful, is what I was going to say. But yes, our family bloodline runs deep in Dalton."

"I bet your pockets do too." Phineas gives me the vibe he wants nothing to do with this group. Most Alannicans don't do well with outsiders, especially when their masculinity feels threatened.

"That will be enough out of you, blondie," Morganna speaks.

"What did you just call me?"

"Blondey!" Oober chides in and nearly falls off his seat laughing.

Phineas' face reddens and I snap him back into the light with a grab of his shoulder. "Stop," I simply say and he cools down. I look back at the group. "Thank you for your hospitality. I will make sure to keep my friends in line."

"Very good! It seems Alannicans can be normal!" Griffin celebrates. "You owe me five credits, Zeke!" he laughs.

Over the next hour, I've gotten both dry and fed by the Daltonese. My friends eventually lightened up and take their seats next to me. I openly asked some questions of their homeland and the mysteries about their culture and ways of life. I hold off on my friendship with Anderson, as I would be dripping with red flags for Norman and Phineas. They share their roasted vegetables and although it wasn't filling, it was delightful to get food in my stomach. Without asking my friends, I insisted that we stick together. Alannicans and Daltonese never have lived well together, but for now, I know this is the best case scenario. Griffin accepts with open arms, but the rest seem to be closed to joining us, as do my friends behind me. It seems Griffin and I are the voices of reason. With no real argument against it, we leave the sanctity of safety of the station as a group. Each with a new talisman to add to our collection.

As we close in on Station Five, excitement grows in my belly. We clear mile marker thirty-five and pass the halfway point of the Proving. As conversations feel light and flowing, I find Norman including himself more in the conversations. Then, finally, Phineas expresses a mild gratitude of their generosity. He explains his trust issues with not only Daltonese, but everyone. He explains his father's views on Dalton, saying his family is prejudice against the other territories, but if his friend can befriend them, then he can live with it, for now. Oober eventually apologizes for not helping us, he too has the same experience as Phineas coming from a household of ignorance towards Alannicans.

Those two begin sharing stories and laughs as they reveal embarrassing stories of the past and clicking better than I could with the smaller man. I stick to the twins and find out more about their royal life. Norman finds himself closer to the female of the group. Her confidence is staggering along with her bright green eyes, and other worldly strong figure. Her voice is smooth but powerful like the twins. Her arms are lean, her shoulders are broad, but she sounds gentle and innocent. A difficult judge of character for me, she looks like she can choke me out but can make me a nice home cooked meal like Julianna can. I always wondered if Courtney could cook. Knowing her, my best guess would be that she would burn cereal. Griffin shares a banapear with me, a tough fruit you need to peel with a sweet but tangy aftertaste. He pulls out a Dalton multi tool like it's nothing and cuts the fruit in a few pieces with the pocket knife setting.

"Where'd you find those?" I ask.

What? This?" he lifts the tool. "Found it off a…" he chuckles. "a man who didn't need it anymore," he says eerily cheerful.

"So, you've seen some dead bodies too?" I ask.

"Plenty my friend, plenty," Griffin answers. "It's quite a shame. Some can't even be saved by the proctors in time. Some are attacked by the predators of the forest, some just don't want to be found. You Alannicans have a… a unique way of dealing with the dead."

I look over at my friends to enlighten me.

"People are stupid here," Ezekiel adds. "Stepping on pressure traps, getting caught in snatch traps, like don't you people have any survival instinct?" he says chomping down on his fruit.

A nerve catches my attention as his insults hit home. "Stupid? I'd say Alannicans are exceedingly more intelligent than any of the other territories. Atlantis University is the most prestigious University on Tyke, including the seven trade school on the moons."

"Here we go..." I hear Morganna whisper behind us.

Griffin gives his brother a look and Ezekiel's attitude changes instantly. "Oh... yes. My friend, my apologies, I didn't mean to offend. I just... I just find it quite, uh... unwise for some certain people who... you know what I'm saying right?"

"No. No we don't, friend," Phineas answers for me.

If I may," Morganna chimes in. "If it wasn't for Dalton, your scientist would have never found rune. Alannah would never have invented the battlesuits we use today without us and especially without Magnaluna's raw material exports. You Alannicans talk so much praise of your lands and wonders but it is your neighbors that made you as strong and smart as you think you are. If you cut us out, you're just as worthless as you made Harmony.

"Guys, guys, don't get your panties in a bunch," Blitzen says. "Let's let bygones be bygones. Right now, we are all in this together. Now I don't know about you but I'm in the mood for—"

An arrow pulverizes the young Blitzen through the back of his head. His body drops to the ground with a thud. He's dead before he hits the ground. Morganna screams for her little brother and Oober pushes her out of the way of another arrow. Roars and chants of battle shout from behind us.

"Ambush!" I yell.

"Get to cover! Find a tree!" Griffin yells.

I drop to the ground and roll to my left into a nearby bush and plant myself behind a tree. Phineas lays belly down near my crotch while Norman is behind a tree with Morganna and Oober in front of me. She sulks and cries for her brother, I can only imagine what she's going through. I peak over my shoulder and try to find a body, but I don't see anyone. Screams of war echo in the distance. Several more arrows soar by, our path fills with blood and brain matter of the Daltonese boy who just turned eighteen. I look to my left and see the twins rummaging through their bags. Oober gives Morganna a decent sized rock and chucks another into the bushes in the distance.

The bushes shake. "There they are!" Griffin shouts to me. I snap my head around to the right and catch the abnormal bloodshot eyes of a Lunen.

The man exposes himself with a long staff with a dozen arrows wrapped around it. As he extends back, I pull my spear up to block him, but a rock clobbers the side of his head and he drops motionless. Morganna dashes over to us and ends the man's life with a clean snap of his neck.

"*Torcaja!*" she screams at the top of her lungs.

"*Torcaja!*" the rest of the group roars. They stampede down the path. Phineas rolls off me looking embarrassed. He joins the fight and charges down the path. I try to hold him back but he's too fast. Roars from the Daltonese overpower the squeamish cries of dying bodies. Two arrows slip by them and puncture a distance tree. I run up to the next tree and catch the final moments of another boy getting clobbered by Griffin. Ezekiel scores a kill shot in another man's heart while Oober distracted him. Several crossbow shots sound off in the distance then horrifying screams of panic from voices unknown to me. There is so much mayhem, so much blood and death around me. I feel frozen to the ground.

"Retreat! Retreat! Everyone, full retreat!" I hear in the distance.

Phineas' head springs up and we both recognize the voice. I lunge forward and stop him before he sprints after the man, I know he wants him dead more than anyone. I have to fight him to the ground. "No! Stop! He's right there! Stop!" he growls and argues the entire way to the ground.

"We'll get him, Phineas. We'll get him, I promise."

He shoves me off him and brushes himself off with a glare of betrayal in his eyes.

The Daltonese regroup to their fallen family member. We circle and kneel around him. I rest my hand on Oober's shoulder. "I'm sorry for your loss."

"He's making his way up to the afterlife, he suffers no more, his aches are gone." He looks up into the sky. "Take care of him, *nomma*."

47

Norman

We bury Blitzen in the woods as best as the Daltonese wanted. It was hard without shovels so we found as many big rocks as we could and laid Blitzen to rest. It was a funeral more fit than what the proctors would have done with the body. My friends collect the Lunen's rucksacks and I get handed two talismans out of the pot of things we collect. A loud rumble of thunder booms in the distance. Ezekiel advises we make haste for shelter as soon as possible to avoid the storm. As we run towards the next station, Phineas refuses to talk to me. He blames it on running but I know he's feeling a certain way after I stopped him from pursuing Clay.

With a storm brewing in the west, we're forced to scale majority of the Great Mountain of Alannah. As dangerous as it is to climb higher before the storm hit, it was our safest option. The map was atrociously confusing when it comes to these trails but Oober found traces of a path off the trail that led into a cave. We rushed into the cave and found the trademark sign with 'Station Five' on it. Once we were all settled in the cave, we dropped our rucksacks, and set up camp. The fire brews hot from the collected grim wood the Daltonese have collected. They skewer their food packages and creates a nice meal for each of us.

"What does torcaja mean?" I ask out of the blue sitting by the fire.

The Daltonese look at each other like it's a big secret.

"Torcaja is like a code for us in our village. It means, 'To the last.' Torcaja doa brisses is 'To the last breath.' We say it to strike fear in our prey on hunts, and also to vow a pair together

286

during matrimony ceremonies," Morganna explains. "It's just what we do. I say it to announce the beginning of war, and my cousins say it after me to let me know they are beside me."

The rain didn't let up all night. Lighting seared down in the distance. Thunder boomed and woke me up several times throughout the night. Morganna couldn't hold her emotions and sobbed for her lost brother. I wanted to comfort her but I felt that I wasn't the right one to do so, or even worse, I'd go there and say something off putting and get kicked out of the cave.

I lay restless in my sleeping bag for the second night. My sleeping bag is still wet from the river and my clothes have yet to fully dry from my sweat filled day. I catch Phineas staring at me with eyes of confusion and discretion.

"I forgive you," he says. "But if you *ever* hold me back or slow me down again, I swear it'll be the last thing you do."

Norman overhears us and shakes his head. "Why did you tackle him? We could have hunted them down, took them on together. Do you understand we could have stopped them permanently? We could have stopped Clay but instead… instead he still breaths and hunts us. We're not safe now."

"We had him, Carson. My moment of glory to show the proctors that I can handle myself and do what is needed to be done is gone. You took that from me, you *stole* that from me," Phineas says.

"Do you even know how many people he has? Dozens. What if that was his plan? He wanted us to chase him out of rage after killing one of us. We could have run straight into a trap."

Phineas points a finger at me. "That wasn't your call to make, it was mine. I'm the leader here, not you. If you're too scared to face him head on, then you should have stayed back, or better yet, quit. Now we may never get that opportunity again. Now we have to sleep with our eyes open just in case they decide to ambush us again."

As the storm passes and the sun peeks itself over the horizon and shines its rays on the third morning of the Proving, I stretch out and sit by the edge of the cliff to gaze out into the forest. I watch the tops of the trees sway back and forth with the wind. I even see a few contestants walking through the woods. The trees are slowly changing colors as we get into the fall months.

Norman taps me to get up, the group is ready to descend down the mountain. As we pass by a fallen tree, we meet a group of soaking wet stragglers limping themselves up the path. They look on the verge of passing out. As easy as it may be to take everything they have, the two royal sons eye up Phineas, knowing he wants to ambush them. He shakes his head and huffs with disappointment. He sneers at me and I look the other way.

A steaming argument ensues as we descend the mountain. Cultures clashing back and forth about integrity and stability. Phineas argues that if he was alone, he'd be done with this Proving by now, he would have finished with a perfect score, but we are the ones that are holding him back. This relationship between Alannican and Daltonese only gets harder as the Daltonese tell Phineas to hex off and go if he wants. They look at Norman and me, but I have no problem with how we are moving. With a perfect set of seven talismans secured in my bag, I too, don't feel the need to steal anymore. Is that right to feel as an Alannican?

By mid-morning, my new Daltonese friends have guided us halfway down the mountain side. Griffin preaches how their ancestors were the hunters and gatherers of the original settlers and they're vast knowledge of feeling out the land and using what the almighty saints blessed us with was how they survived. As the path narrows, I find myself feeling nervous. One wrong move and I could slip off the entire mountain. I catch myself looking down at the pile of sharper edged rocks under us. Cracked and serrated boulders inch out looking like spikes for corpses. It makes me think how many people have actually died from the Proving.

"Be careful through here, Alannicans. Do not rush. Stay close to each other and do not look down," Griffin advises. I watch Oober shimmy himself along a slotted ledge over to the other side where the path widens. It seems something must have broken the pathway here. Morganna goes next, flawlessly making her way across. Then I go, followed by Phineas and the twins. Norman hesitates to go last. It's like the river all over again.

"What's wrong, buddy?" I call out.

Norman quivers, "Nothing. I'm… um." He starts shaking, hesitant to move closer to the ridge.

"You afraid, Alannican?" Oober laughs. "Check out this guy. Pshhh, C'mon I thought you were all fearless?"

"Shut up!" he snaps.

"Stop." I chop my hand out to stop Oober's insensitive mocking. I lock eyes with Norman. "Keep your eyes on me," I inch myself closer to the edge and extend my hand. "No one's leaving you behind."

Norman's petrified eyes doubt me. As he slowly maneuvers himself closer, he starts taking tiny steps along the ridge. His hands squeezing the sides of the mountain. He inches closer and closer, shivering like a blizzard is blowing. A cracking noise shocks him and he shrieks to a standstill. "I can't. I can't do it."

The group sighs but I haven't given up on him. "Yes you can. C'mon, man, you're halfway there." I take another step forward and stretch out my hand.

"Uh, Carson don't go too far," Morganna instructs. "Your weight could collapse the ridge, be careful."

"It's fine." I close out the doubts and keep my eyes on Norman. "C'mon, buddy, just a few more steps I inch closer and stretch my hand out further.

I see him start to hyperventilate. Fear drips from his eyes as he powers through another tiny step. "Carson, I can't move. I can't—"

"Yes you can," I insist. "C'mon, be the titan."

"You got it, Normmy," Phineas encourages behind me. Soon after him, the rest of them voice their encouragement.

I take another step closer to him and reach out for him. "Just one more step." He closes his eyes and takes a deep breath. He takes one more step and the rocks crack underneath him. It ripples down and crumbles the ledge under us. "Norm, jump! Jump now!"

He panics and freezes in place. Our eyes meet in a devastatingly silent goodbye.

"Norman!" I cry out. I reach for him, but I'm pulled back from the crumbling rock path. My shouts for him do nothing as his body plunges into the rock filled abyss. He tries to grab on to something, but his uncontrollable momentum flips him into the gravel graveyard down below like a pinball machine. I don't see him land.

A newfound energy consumes me. I race down the mountains path, clearing nearly another mile before I reach the bottom where I search desperately for my friend. Tears roll down my face, it was because of me that he fell. I had too much weight on the rocks, it's all my fault!

"Norm! Norman!" I shout at the top of my lungs. I'm all alone at the bottom. My friends weren't as fast as me, not even Phineas. I walk around the spot where I imagined he would have landed. At long last under a small pile of rocks I find his boot. I dig him out, panting at the horror and sorrow that fills me for not being fast enough. His body is torn, legs crooked in mortifying positions, bleeding from multiple places. I drop my ear on his chest, and feel his pulse, he's still breathing. I pull him out of the wreckage and into the grass. He's ruined, mutilated even. My friend lives, but how much longer does he have? I sit there next to him sobbing, begging his unconscious body for forgiveness. I do my best and use every bandage I have to seal the wounds. Tears fall endlessly on his chest from me as I work. How could he ever forgive me for this?

My group of friends eventually find us. Phineas is beside himself while the Daltonese pull out their med kits to help finish wrapping him up. Oober splashes him with a bit of water and Norman finally comes to. He's delirious and can't feel his legs. I ask him to flex his toes, but he can't... he's paralyzed; the boy who showed me how to play video games, who introduced me to his friends at parties as his best friend. He saw me and didn't hesitate to ask for my name or how I randomly enrolled in some school in Alannah out of nowhere with a lie to persuade anyone I was one of them. He didn't question anything. He saw me as another kid in the back of the class. My friend Norman may never walk again.

He tries to get up off the ground, but his legs simply just won't hold his weight as he crumbles to the ground every time, we pick him up. He punches the ground, cries an unfathomable plea to end his life.

It takes a moment to register. "What? No way." I sit him up. "Doctors can fix this. Modern prosthetics are great. We... we can save you, buddy."

"Stop." He smacks me away and mumbling something to himself. "Just kill me."

"No, absolutely not," I snap

"Carson, what are we supposed to do?" Phineas voices his concern.

"If he wants to die, we should honor his wish," Ezekiel says. "That is your way, isn't it?"

"No! Absolutely not, he has to finish! C'mon, buddy, I got you." I grab his arm to pull him up over my shoulder, but he squirms out and begs for me to stop. It pains me inside to see my friend like this, so eager to end his life. "We'll get you home, buddy, I promise. Everything will be ok."

"Everything will *not* be ok, Carson. Who are we kidding? He's only going to slow us down. What does he have to prove? The man can't walk. He's done. His family won't accept him like this. He's as good as dead," Phineas argues sincerely. "He's—"

"I will not leave *my friend* behind," I snap.

"Carson, there's really not much we can do, he needs surgery," Morganna adds.

"Saints, he needs more than that," Oober chimes in.

"Hex you!" I snap.

"Carson, they're right," Norman says softly. I look to my friend with betrayal as he looks at me with concern and heartbreak. He knows it was because of me, the whole group knows it was because of me. "My life is over. My mother forced me to do this. She said it would make my father proud to see me doing something other than drinking or playing video games, that I was wasting my life. Just…" he whimpers, hesitating to say his last words he may have left. "Just end it. Let me find peace." He flips open his switchblade and hands it to me. "Do it, please."

"C'mon, Normmy, don't talk like that. Put that away. You're stronger than that. We've been through so much together. You can't give up now, I won't let you." I pull Norman's arm up and hoist him over my shoulder.

"Woah, woah, woah," Phineas stops me. "What do you think you're doing?"

"Helping our friend get back home. No one gets left behind," I snap at Phineas.

Phineas stares at me dumbfounded, unable to make sense with what I'm doing. "Left behind? Carson, he's paralyzed. He's only going to slow us down. He's going to get us all killed."

"He's right, Carson. Please, just stop." Norman tries to squirm out of my graps, but his body isn't what it used to me. His miserable attempt to break free only tightens my grip on him. "My parents were right, I'm not cut out for this. I'm not cut out to be an Alannican. Just put me down. The proctors will find me."

"No! Hex your parents and hex the proctors. We're going to finish this together, buddy. Me and you, I promise, I got you." I walk on down the path. My group of friends follow me.

Phineas gets right in my ear. Confusion and concern wrap around his face like a blanket around a newborn. "What do you honestly expect to do here, Carson? We got sixteen miles left. You're going to carry him through the Darkwoods? There's canahounds everywhere. We need to get to the station as soon as possible. At least there's scent deflectors around so we're safe beyond the perimeter. We can leave him there, he'll be safe."

This ridiculous Proving has torn me apart from my friends more than I could ever imagine. I don't think I'll ever understand Alannicans; how they think, how they rival against one another, and shun the ones who need help. Norman continues to beg me to stop and let him down to die but I won't. I can't knowingly desert someone that accepted me on the first day of school. Phineas' confusion quickly turns to anger. He demands an explanation for my actions and tries to rip

Norman off my shoulders but luckily Ezekiel interjects "Let the boy go. If he can keep up, then there's no problem."

The path to Station Six feels like a marathon with the extra weight on my shoulders. My arms are weak and my legs shake after every step. I was able to keep up with the group till the next station. Phineas was able to get a talisman. I got a med kit for Norman and tended to more of his cuts and scrapes. I used the stim on him to help him with the pain.

Instead of waiting out the day, Phineas wanted to get to Station Seven before nightfall. He told me to stay with Norman and wait for the proctors to pick him up, but I refused. I want Norman to finish. He has to finish and show his family he can be accepted, paralyzed or not. I feel like I'd be abandoning him. Who knows if the proctors would even come to his aid? Who knows if the scent deflectors actually work, or if other competitors would come and do something even worse to him?

As we get deeper into the Darkwoods, the path is hard to see. Even with the lone flashlight we have left, the eerie howls of the night start to settle in my stomach. I march on but slowly I start falling behind from the group. Norman notices and insist I leave him, but I refuse. We are nearly ten miles from the finish line. About a mile and a half to Station Seven. I can do it, I can—

A sharp pain shoots up my leg. My ankle twists in a small puddle that was deeper than expected. I stumble and my knee crashes into the dirt. Norman topples over my head and indents my face into the mud.

My friends turn around and see the embarrassing sight of fresh mud covering my face. "What happened?" Griffin asks.

"I twisted my hexing ankle," I grunt.

"Can you walk?" Oober asks. Morganna runs up to me and grabs my leg. She checks it over and feels for swelling.

"Leave them," Phineas mutters. "He obviously can't keep up anymore and it's getting late. We need to hurry if we are going to make it to the station before nightfall."

"What is your problem?" Morganna snaps at Phineas. "Don't you care about your friends? Carson is doing everything he can to save him and all you're doing is complaining and shunning him."

"My problem? My problem?! Of course I care about them, that's why I told him to leave Norman at the station. The proctors will find him and give him the care that he needs. But it'd be better for Norman to die here with some dignity instead of go through all the surgery just to be rejected by his family. I don't understand you people. Norman is done, he's useless, he's not Alannican anymore. The only thing he is doing is slowing us down. He is delaying the inevitable. You Daltonese don't understand the purity of an Alannican, and you, Carson, I have no idea what has gotten into you."

He shakes his head and takes a breath. "Say you were a wild bird, a baby bird. You fall out of a tree and break your wing. Do you think your flock of adult birds and able baby birds are going to fly down to the ground where you are all exposed to the dangers of the world, to pick you up and help you fly? No, they'll leave you and let you die because if a bird can't fly, it's as good as dead. If they all fly to the ground and help it, a predator could sneak up on them and kill them all, simply because they were trying to help a helpless bird. Now instead of one dumb bird dying, the entire flock dies.

"The strong bloodline of birds that can fly, dies. They can't reproduce to make stronger, bigger, or faster birds. That is why Alannah is the best, that is why Alannicans have the strongest bone density in all the territories. That is why our immune systems are impeccable. Alannah has never seen a plague like Harmony. We don't believe in weakness, we believe in power. I believe in power, *I* believe in dominance. All we have now is a bird with a broken wing who's only going to get us all killed."

"Norman isn't some baby bird, he is a human being and our best friend. You'd abandon him just like that?" I question. Baffled by his logic. "If that's what an Alannican is, then I don't want to be one."

Phineas tenses by my comment but I don't care. I walk over to Norman whose set himself up against a tree.

He smacks my hand out of the way from picking him up. "He's right, Carson. We all know I'm worthless now and—"

"And he's only going to get us killed," Phineas insensitively finishes Norman's sentence.

"Stop saying that!" I yell and get in Phineas' face. "If you want to leave, fine. LEAVE! If this Proving is more important than our friendship, then go!" Emotions sweep over me, exhaustion weighs me down, but my heart is still whole. I don't want to be separated, I want to finish as a group, as friends, but Phineas just doesn't see it like that. He hesitates and glares at me, processing my threat. His tongue slides across his teeth, his face tightens like he's thinking of hitting me. I see it in his eyes. If that's what I have to do to knock some sense into him, then fine. As I wait to embrace a fist, I feel a presence behind me, all the Daltonese stand beside me, against Phineas.

"Go ahead, Blondie. Go finish by yourself, see if we care. We will take care of your friends while you seek glory and satisfaction with yourself, and only yourself." Griffin defends me.

Phineas looks like a volcano about to erupt. "FINE!" he shouts. Just one word breaks my heart. He turns around and starts to run, sprinting faster than I've ever seen him into the darkness of the forest.

48
Glowing yellow eyes

We decide to set up camp along the path in a clearing not too far from where we separated. The Daltonese gather some wood off of a fallen tree and make a fire. The fire is different here in the Darkwoods. The black wood gives off a deeper red flame, which kind of smells like cinnamon. I sit beside Norman while he lays in his sleeping bag. He's quiet, quieter than he's ever been. I try some exercises to see if he has any mobility in his legs, but nothing works. No feeling at all, no pain receptors, nothing. He really is paralyzed, and it finally hits me that my friend will never be the same again.

As the night goes on, my friends fall asleep around a fire. Snare traps are set around the camp. I asked Norman if Phineas was right about the bird thing. He nods and explains how his parents think the same way. It's just the way of Alannah, survival of the fittest.

Griffin's snoring blocks out the midnight noises of the forest. I stare at the back of Norman's head as he sleeps. Does he hate me? Does he resent my actions? I was only trying to help, to get him back to his family. Does he even want to go back? Would he really be disowned if he showed up home in his current state? I know if my mom saw that I was paralyzed, she'd do everything she could to make sure I was comfortable. My dad would design some kind of crutch to help me walk or move around. We'd find doctors and surgeons to correct my spine to get me walking again, but here... Here you're as good as dead if that happens. What if I was the one who paralyzed myself? Would Jinx throw me away? What if I finish and go undrafted, would my family resent me for failing? Are the proctors really watching us? Does that mean we're safe? I don't feel safe...

"Was I wrong to save you?" I say to the back of Norman's head. Not expecting an answer. The wind blows, the fire crackles, nature sings its song of insects and animals in Norman's silence. "No," he finally answers. "No, and yes." It takes him a bit, but he rolls over to me. "Can I tell you something?"

I snicker and nod.

"My parents told me if I don't go through the Proving, I'm not allowed home. She didn't kiss me goodbye when I went to phase one, my dad didn't shake my hand... They didn't sympathize when I told them I had to snap a girl's neck during the fight. My dad simply said, 'Lucky you.' My mom basically said the same thing... But you, you're different. You care... I never had someone care about me like you do."

"Is it a crime to be a good friend?"

"No, but it is to lie about your heritage." My eyebrows raise. I try to deflect it but he goes on. "You said you and your sister were adopted, so I figured it had to be from an Alannican orphanage." I watch his eyes wonder and look at the ground, embarrassed about something. "Can I ask you something? And, for saint's sake if you lie, I understand, but at this point in time, you may as well be honest with me. I really won't be able to do much."

I nod.

"Are you really from Alannah?"

The question I saw coming a mile away. I don't want to lie, especially to Norman in his current state, he's been through enough, but what would he think of me if I tell him. "Why would you think anything else? Where else could I come from?"

"I don't know, the moons, maybe you're one of the few light skinned Daltonese, I mean, you clicked with them so well. I know it's crazy but you're just, different. Even when we first met, you were nice. You didn't try and beat me in all my video games, you played to make it a close game. You invited me over to your house and helped me with my homework. You made me feel like I wasn't inferior like everyone else does."

I take a deep breath and let it out. "We're adopted, Normmy, yes, but it's hard to talk about. Kylie and I have been through a lot. We lost our real parents one day and from then on, it was just me and her. We had to look out for each other, so I understand how it feels to be alone." For the first time, I feel comfortable talking about myself. This entire year has been all about keeping secrets and watching what I say to people but here, in this moment in time, Norman looks at me differently. He's listening, not judging. "It's a long story." I scoot closer to him. "We um… We ran away from our orphanage and lived in a scrap yard for about a year before meeting Jinx."

"Where is a scrapyard in Greycott?"

"We didn't live in Greycott, we lived in Lev—"

My eyes bulge out of my head. Over Norman's shoulder, in the darkness beyond the campfire shines three sets of glowing yellow eyes. Three becomes twelve, twelve into twenty.

"Lev? Carson, what's wrong?" Norman tries to turn around. I slowly reach for my spear.

They were scary in Jinx's virtual training cube, now they find me again. This time, it's real.

"Shhhh," I shush him and whisper. "Canahounds. No sudden movements. You have your spear?"

"Yeah," he whispers back.

"Good." I stand up with my spear, tighten my grip and say a short prayer to myself as this may be the final moment I have with my friend. "Norman…"

"Yeah?"

I look down into his eyes, his worried eyes. No betrayal, no anger, just two of my best friend's eyes looking back at me for guidance. "I'm Harmonian."

"You're what?!"

"TORCAJA!" I shout the Daltonese battle cry of war at the top of my lungs. Not only to wake up my friends but hopefully my voice will scare off the canahounds. It does not, it only riles them up. They howl in unison and charge out of the bushes. Nearly three feet tall, these small hounds can run up to twenty-five miles an hour with two sets of teeth to dig into their prey and sharp claws to pin bigger prey and pounce on them as a group. Seeing a dozen of them charge me at the same time is one of the most terrifying moments of my life. Some tangle up in the snare traps but a dozen more charge out of the bushes. The Daltonese wake up behind me and scream their war cry back to me.

The first one lunges at me and I smack it away with my spear. Another lunges towards my ankle, and I jump back and swipe its head. Oober rushes to my side and digs his spear in its throat. Three more hounds zip by us and the twins get in the action by drilling the hounds and throwing one into the other. Morganna shoots off several small bolts from her crossbow, three more hounds fall. The rest of the pack emerges and surrounds us. One by one the hounds are dealt with. Spears swing and hounds are mutilated. One finds Griffin's forearm, but Ezekiel makes quick work of it. He grabs it by its jaw and rips its jaw right off. Morganna shoots away on her crossbow with deadly accuracy until the unfortunate noise of an empty magazine clicks, Morganna is out of ammo. I climb over the sleeping bags and fend off the remaining two trying to bite her.

"Carson!" Norman's voice scares me. I turn and see two more hounds circling him. One chomps on his dead leg and pulls him off his sleeping bag. The other goes for his neck but Norman is able to fend it off before I kick the one biting his leg and it jumps away with a sharp cry. I follow up with throwing my spear right through its skull, then grip the spear like a bat and swing the dead carcass around to hit another one. Both tumble to the side and I follow through with a strong finish and end their lives through the abdomen.

A calming silence fills the camp. Dead carcasses spread out all over the camp. "Is everyone ok?"

Griffin grunts in pain from his bite, as he wraps his wound with his shirt.

"We're not done yet," Morganna calls out.

She's not wrong. As the words come out of her mouth, the loud growling comes over the camp again. Except this time, there's more. Glowing yellow eyes surround us. Dozens upon dozens of eyes linger over to us in an unrelenting horror. I back up to my friends, blood dripping down Norman's dead leg.

"They're surrounding us!" Ezekiel screams.

"I'm out of bolts! Give me a spear!" Morganna shouts.

"Maybe your friend was right about that bird thing, Carson," Oober says.

"Shut up! Shut up, let me think," I snap. My mind is blank, nothing can help us. I've fallen into their trap. Phineas was right. Helping Norman not only slowed us down, but it's going to kill us all. He's the broken bird and we're the dumb flock that flew to the ground.

"Carson, we have to run!" Griffin yells.

"No, we can't run with Norman!" I stare at my friend. He looks at me terrified with a bloody spear in his hands. Telepathically, he speaks to me. Our minds talk to each other, horrible words are exchanged. His eyes look tired, he shakes his head. Knowing exactly what I want to say to him.

"Go!" Norman shouts. "If you don't, we're all dead. At least you stand a chance if you run." I shake my head, knowing exactly what he wants to do.

"No, not without you." I run to him and pull him up, but he smacks my hand and points his spear at me.

"Go! Run! You've saved me enough already… Now it is time for me to save you."

Without my approval, Norman throws me his ruck and pulls himself up on the fallen tree. He takes off his shirt and throws it at one of the hounds.

"Come and get me hounds! Over here!" He waves his hands and shouts a suicidal distraction. Tears form in my eyes. I'm yanked away by a thick hand and pulled into the depths of the forest. "C'mon, you stupid dogs! I'm over here!" Norman continues. I can't help but pull away and look back. He swings his spear around like a mad man and slashes a hound. He chants and screams and swings his spear pushing the hounds back until one finally creeps around him and finds his neck. Another pulls him off the tree and I lose sight of him in the mob of furry monsters that pounce on top of him. A wet gurgling scream is all I hear before I turn and run.

I run as fast as I can to keep up with the group. My ankle still throbs and tears blur my vision. Dodging through tree branches and jumping over puddles, the sound of the hounds dim. We run into a clearing and find Station Seven. We weren't even a mile away. If we didn't camp and kept walking, we could have made it. Norman may still be alive. Lanterns fill the huts surrounding the campfire and bins of our choices line around the fire. I drop to my knees and sob. Morganna wraps her long arms around me and lets me cry. What Norman did was the bravest thing anyone has ever done. Norman Vanhoozer, my best friend, I hope you finally found peace.

49

Bound and Beaten

I'm sick of death and I'm sick of losing people I care about. My stomach turns with nausea at the thought of seeing Norman being mangled apart by a pack of vicious canahounds. Those little monsters… I punch the ground and have to leave the campfire. Morganna tries to comfort me but I don't want to be comforted, I just want to be left alone.

I sit down in the sand by the lake. The waterfall I fell off of is in the distance. It's so majestic being down here, and not at the top of it holding on to a rope for dear life. It's crazy to think that was only a day ago and in that time, I lost both of my closest friends, but gained four more.

I unload Norman's ruck and found that Norman was actually hiding twelve talismans. Where he got them, I have no clue. He must have done some snooping behind our backs. A miracle of grace.

I don't fear death, I fear what it's like after death. There are many assumptions in the Harmonian Bible, but they are merely stories to promote religion. To meet your loved ones in the afterlife means you were accepted by two of the three saints to gain acceptance into their holy lands. Was Norman accepted by the saints?

I bury Norman's empty rucksack in the sand and say a prayer to the three saints, James, Peter, and Nicholas, to please accept Norman into their holy place of eternal bliss. It was the best I could do to sooth my sorrows before I join my remaining and unforeseen group of friends. After a small meal of a power bar and some fruit, the group decides to hike out the rest of the Proving during the night. As we reach nearly three miles left, the sun tips above the horizon and we're gifted with walking through the Darkwoods with a little bit of light. Oober snatched one of the lanterns from the station so at least our path is brightened up. It's difficult to read the map with barely any light. Lucky for us, Oober was a tracker in his village. If there are any kind of footprints leading to the sanctity of the finish line, he will find it. People must have finished by now. There's no way we're going to be anywhere near first place but, at this point, I just want to be done with this. With as many talismans as I have, I find my chances of getting drafted much higher than I have this entire hike. The thought of Phineas' wellbeing haunts me. For what it's worth, I hope he is ok.

We approach a swamp and have to cross to get to the path that'll lead us to the next station. Knee deep in mucky water, hundreds of bugs buzz around us. Some try and bite, but most mind themselves. Morganna's scared of them, she feels violated with all of them landing on her and flying close to her face. Ezekiel then catches one out of the air and shows her the dead insect to freak her out. I don't care for the bugs, what I worry about is if man eating footfangs are swimming around my ankles. Both carnivorous and protective of their territory, these swamp fish are the canahounds of the aquatic world.

Suddenly, Oober's head snaps to the left and he lifts his hand up. The group stops and I bump into Morganna.

"What's going on?" I whisper from the back.

"He heard something," Zeke shushes me.

In the distance, I hear a faint high pitch scream.

"You hear that?" Oober asks.

Griffin nods. "That's not a good scream either. Sounds like they are in trouble."

"So what? Let's get a move on," Morganna insist.

Griffin looks over his shoulder. "Would you like it if someone ignored you in agony? Do I have to bring up you know what, when you know who, needed you know who, and—"

"No! No, fine. Whatever. Let's just be quick about it. I want to get out of this swamp as fast as possible. These bugs are annoying the hex out of me." She smacks her thigh and ends the life of a bloodsnatcher.

"Lead the way, Oober," Griffin orders.

We cross the swamp and go off trail towards the frantic screams. As the screams get louder and louder as we pass through the thick of the woods, a light flickers in the distance.

"Camp," Oober says.

"Alright guys, stay low and don't do anything stupid. If there's nothing we can do, we leave, fair?" Griffin says from the front.

I nod along with everyone else. At a crawl, we move quieter towards the light. Oober spots people walking back and forth in front of a person bound between two trees. We lay down to conceal ourselves from the camp. A bulky man with shaggy hair walks up to the bound prisoner and says something to them. The prisoner cocks back and spits out a wad of saliva into the man's face. He instantly retaliates and punches the bound man, then motions his goons to take their shots as well. Two men then start taking turns swinging full force into the man; face shots, body shots, the man groans and screams, then tries to spit at them.

"Is that the best you got?! My grandmother can hit harder than you!" The man screams threats and profanities at them when he's kicked between his legs. His fingers are black, burnt to a crisp, his face is bloodied and bruised. He's been tortured for quite some time.

"I recognize that voice. That's Phineas, we have to help him," I say.

The bigger shaggy man pushes through his two companions and wails Phineas so hard in the face, he knocks him out, then spits in his face for revenge. "Hah! What do you have to say now?! Huh!" the man bellows and leaves my friend bound and limp.

"Holy saints…" Oober whispers.

"We got to do something. We got to get him," I say.

"What can we do?" Morganna questions.

"How many can you spot?" Ezekiel asks.

"I'm seeing twelve, possibly thirteen," Oober counts. "All Lunens. Look at their eyes, they're huge. Hexing freaks, all of them."

It's Clay, it has to be. They have been a pain in my side this entire time. Clay must be that bulky guy. That's probably how Phineas got in this mess. He went straight for Clay like a rabid animal.

"We need a distraction," I suggest. "No way we can take all these guys head on. Especially if Clay is here. He'll kill Phineas if he sees us."

"You sure you want to help this guy?" Morganna asks. "He was a real—"

"You still have ammo?" Griffin interrupts Morganna. She nods finding two blood stained bolts in her quiver.

"Ok, who is this Clay person you are speaking of, Carson?" Griffin asks.

"That big one near Phineas, long hair, looks like a wildling."

"Ok, Morganna, take out the big one first. If one doesn't take him out, two will. The rest will either cower or charge unorganized and we can easily pick them off in the shadows. We can take these guys no problem. Carson, you roll around and cut blondie loose. Try not to get spotted. If you attract them, you'll have all of them to deal with before we get to you."

I nod and arm myself with a knife. If I bring my spear, I'll stick out like a sore thumb. With that, we split up, I roll around to the west side and the twins and Oober to the east. At a signal, Griffin gives Morganna a whistle like a common small mouth bird. The arrow is launched. It hisses through the air, and smacks into Clay's back shoulder. He spirals and hits the ground, screaming in agony. He grabs hold of the arrow and grunts as he orders his followers in her direction.

He groans as his group approaches him. Some girl screams in shock and the others swing their heads around to look for an ambush. "Alpha down! Arm yourselves!"

The Lunens freeze in place. With their attention pointed away from me, I slowly inch myself to their flank. Another shot goes off and slices through the shorter woman. She flails on the ground in a chalkboard scratching screech, releasing pain throbbing shouts that gives me goosebumps. The group dives for the ground holding their heads, and yells to take cover, shouting for where the arrows are coming from. Their heads swivel in Morganna's direction, simply just waiting to be slaughtered, yet it's unfortunate she's out of ammo.

Silence envelops around us, like a calm before a storm. Fingers are pointing to Morganna's location. Bodies slowly reach their feet, anxiously waiting for a sign of movement. Sweat drips down my face, my palms getting sweaty holding my knife.

"*Torcaja!*" the Daltonese scream.

They emerge from the woods, barreling through the field at breakneck speeds. Griffin is the first to spill blood. He heaves his spear and punctures a man. Zeke pulls the spear out of the man's chest and swings it like a propeller, slicing two more. Blood splatters. Oober closes in and disarms an archer moments before she shoots an arrow. Morganna joins in shortly after, making sure she gets her fair share of the fight. Shouts of anguish and fear cover the campsite in the mayhem these Daltonese create.

Overrun by pure dominance, the surviving Lunens scatter, and the Daltonese chase after them, laughing and shouting at them to fight.

I inch myself closer. With my knife in my hand, I slowly creep over behind Phineas. His head dangles limp. Phineas groans as the rope loosens and looks over at me with two puffy black eyes. Our eyes meet.

"Carson?"

"Hey, buddy. Hold still. I'll cut you free and get you out of here."

"Ey! What are you doing?!" I hear violently behind me. I look over and Clay has spotted me. An arrowhead protruding at me through his clavicle and a swelling black eye covers his left eye. "I know you! You're that hex I threw in the pit. How in the saint's unholy underworld did you guys get out?" He breaks off the arrow in his shoulder in a manic grunt and holds it in his hand like a dagger. "Take your grimy hands off my prisoner!"

I lift my hands up in surrender. "Prisoner? Why are you taking prisoners? This is supposed to be a race to the finish. Why are you torturing my friend?"

"Don't tell me how to live my life!" Clay barks, he inches closer. "This little hex stole my rucksack. I had to eat bugs and berries for two days." His voice is ravenous, his eyes are oddly bloodshot red like the man Morganna killed yesterday. What happened to them?

"I don't have your rucksack," Phineas shouts. "You're so stupid! How would I have your ruck sack if the only one I have is my own you unintelligent, subhuman abomination."

"Shut up! You're a liar! All of you are liars! None of you can be trusted! None of you!" Clay screams.

"He's right," I say. "He doesn't have it, because I do. I have it." I take off Jinx's rucksack and show him. The morning fog clouds his vision. It'd be hard to tell mine from anyone else's at a quick glance.

"You have my rucksack?! Give me my rucksack, now!" Clay screams and steps to me.

"Now, hold on!" I stop him in his tracks. Let's trade," I suggest. There's no chance I'd actually give him my ruck but all I need to do is distract him like I did with Kylie's bully all those years ago. I just need to fill his hands before I make my move.

Clay ponders the idea, his face loosens. "Is that really my bag? Do you still have everything in it? My talismans? The pictures of my family?"

I'm surprised this is actually working. "Yup, even collected some more for you. You can have them all but *only* if I get my friend back."

"You idiot," Phineas mutters and drops his head. "He'll kill us all. You really think he's going to just—"

"Shut up, Phineas," I snap. "What do you say?" I ask Clay.

Clay must be on some kind of drug. Lechons cover his face and arms as well. What happened to him? What did he go through after the bridge?

"Friend? Yeah, sure, whatever. Just give me back my rucksack. Give it here, now."

"Not until you release my friend. No one needs to get hurt, let's do this and go our separate ways. Remember we could all be working together very soon. Me and you, we could be drafted in the same legion, we could be brothers in arms, fighting on the same team. So, whatever we've done to each other is forgiven, we need to be civil, ok? Lunens are very resourceful, and very intelligent, I know you are both, right? You said you were a master blacksmith, right?"

He nods, eerily so, but he's seemed to calm down from the gentle banter.

"Me, you, Phineas, we are the same. We, are, the same, right?"

"Yeah… Yeah, we are… I… I just want this all to end, so badly I… I miss my family, my friends… So many friends have died here, I… I don't know what to do. I just want to be liked, I… I wanted to make, *him*, proud," he says. Finally giving in to my hypnosis, he shimmies over to Phineas and starts cutting the rope with the arrowhead.

Without warning, Phineas lunges at him before the rope is fully cut. "Ahhrrrggg! You piece of vile garbage, I'll kill you for what you done to me!" he screams, and flails but is still attached. He kicks and jolts, but the rope keeps him in place.

Clay retaliates and clobbers Phineas' jaw. I take my chance and charge him. I pick him up by the waist and spike him into the ground as hard as I can. In one motion I mount him and grab his weapon hand to break his wrist. It's empty. He grabs my collar and pulls me off him. Before I even look up, my head is bashed into the tree. I'm manhandled and my ruck is stripped off my back. I try to get up, but a foot is shoved into my nose and the back of my head meets the tree once more.

Dazed, and on the verge of consciousness, I desperately try to find Clay. My hands are up to block, but nothing comes. "You liar!" my eardrums ring. "This isn't my ruck! Where is it?!

What did you do with my rucksack?! You promised me you had my rucksack and you lied! You lied!"

I'm hit again, more devastatingly than the last. My feet leave the ground and I'm shoved back into the tree.

"Where is my rucksack?!" Clay barks and punches my stomach. A blood filled cough projects out of my mouth and spatters into Clay's face.

Clay screams and releases me. I regain my vision and see Phineas swinging manically at Clay, crushing the back of his head with a rock the size of my head. Phineas mounts him and delivers a horrifyingly crunching blow into Clay. Two, three, four times. Blood sprays out. Five, six, seven sledgehammer like strikes. A wet crunching noise gives me goosebumps and Clay goes motionless. Eight, nine.

"I'll show you a sorry excuse for an Alannican!" Ten. "I'll show you honor." Eleven. "I'll show you dignity." Twelve. "I'll show you what it means to be worthy!" He lifts the bloody rock over the brain matter that used to be Clay.

"Phin, stop. This is enough!" I shout out. He ignores me, thirteen, fourteen. I grab the rock out of his hands before he hits him again.

He turns on me, his eyes bloodshot red just like Clay's. "You don't tell me when to stop! What did I tell you before?! Stop me again and you will regret it, Carson!" His voice is rabid as well with spit dripping out of his bloody mouth.

"What's going on?" Morganna calls out behind me.

"Business!" Phineas shouts, and dismounts Clay. He snaps around and lifts his hands like he's about to fight us.

"Oh my worlds on fire, what did you do?" Morganna shutters. "That is how you do business?"

"This is how Alannicans do business!" He turns to her and walks up to her, his bloody fist clenched, a fire still alive in his eyes. "You want some too?!"

"Who do you think you're talking to?" Griffin steps in front of Morganna. Zeke and Oober join them with weapons of their own.

Phineas finally shuts up and looks around. He turns to me. "Where's Norman?" he asks.

Guilt smacks my heart. "Um, I... We... We were attacked by canahounds... I... I did everything I could, but there were too many of them." I shudder at the remembrance of my brave friend. "He distracted the pack. There were too many of them," I repeat. I can't help but stutter over my words. "He... he sacrificed himself."

Phineas smiles and huffs. He walks up to me, his bloody hand rests on my shoulder and looks me in the eyes. "Say I was right." Phineas looks numb from the abuse he has been through. His bloodshot eyes worry me, what happened to him? He looks possessed. "Say it, say I was right."

"You were right," I admit. "You were right all along, buddy. I'm so sorry I ever doubted you."

"A baby bird with a broken wing will only slow down its family," he says blankly.

"Yeah. Yeah, Phineas, you were absolutely—"

"*Every* Alannican knows that," Phineas cuts me off. His face changes. Eyebrows slant, teeth show. "Why don't you?"

My stomach drops. "I—"

A massive pressure enters my stomach and twists inside me and yanked out. Phineas stabs me with the arrowhead. Shock builds with panic, horror, and betrayal. The pressure releases in the worst stinging pain I've ever felt. Phineas swings for my face, the arrow in between his fingers twinkles as it swipes across my face. I lean out of the way, but it slices the side of my cheek before I stumble and fall. Griffin steps over me and punches Phineas. Ezekiel joins in and stomps him but Phineas rolls out and runs away.

Red gushes from my abdomen. I try and press against it but it's no use.

"Stay back!" Phineas roars pointing the arrow at the Daltonese, then at me. "I don't know who you are anymore, but what you are, is a liar! If you ever talk to me again, you better hope there are witnesses! Because I will kill you!" He backs away from us and eventually runs away.

Morganna drops to my side and screams for a med kit. It hits me like a hydrogen train, I know we don't have any. We used the rest of them on Norman to cater to his wounds. Morganna screams again and orders her cousins to find something to help. She looks me dead in the eyes and pushes her hands on my bloody stomach. "It's all good, Carson. I got you, I got you. No one is leaving you. You're going to be ok."

I can't make words. My mind races with regret. This would never have happened if I didn't stop for Norman on the beach, if I didn't jump in the river for him, if I didn't pity his inability to train with me to be ready for this. I hate myself, and I deserve this. I let my friend die and I betrayed my other one all in one worthwhile action that I thought was for the best. Something hits my head and I look over to it, it's a med kit.

"Morganna," I point. She looks and spots it immediately.

"Where did that come from?" she says, opens it up and mends my stomach with a full dose of coagulation stim and pins me in the neck with a pain reliever stim. The bleeding stops in seconds. She continues her work and bandages me up with the gauze and wraps inside the med kit.

As the pain subsides and my head starts feeling lighter, I focus on her eyes. I never noticed how pretty she is. "You're really cute."

She laughs and blushes. "Looks like the stims are working."

50

An unexpected generosity

My rucksack is missing. Everything inside it is gone, my talismans, my food, my water canteens, everything... Jinx is going to kill me.

I can't fathom the way Phineas looked at me, how he behaved even after I rescued him, like he wasn't grateful at all, like there was something deeply wrong with him. Finding out Norman died must have triggered something in him that he's been holding for a long time. Does he know I'm not Alannican? Was it that obvious?

We search through the thirteen bags of the escaped or dead followers of Clay's little gang. We find a measly three talismans, no food, no med kits, but plenty of empty water canteens. With disappointment in my heart, I sling over a random rucksack and follow my friends to the finish line. All I know is I'm ready to go home, regardless of how many of these ridiculous talismans I have.

The sun nearly peaks as we finish out the last few miles of the Proving. Going all downhill, we hiked the last six and a half miles with songs and stories. With no signs of Phineas, my group of Daltonese friends and I cross the finish line together. Proctors stand by in air-conditioned tents with TVs watching a starball game. Very anticlimactic. Griffin bellows out a greeting and shocks the distracted proctor out of his seat.

He walks over to us with a stopwatch in his hand. "Time! Three days, twenty three hours," he says.

Another proctor taps it in on a palm sized tablet. He asks for our names and orders us to empty everything out of our rucksacks and count the talismans. Knowing I have nothing to show for, I feel like a complete loser and stall to even take my stolen one off.

A heavy hand on my shoulder, nearly dislocating it from my tired and worn out body, I nearly fall over. "I need to talk to you." I turn to see Jinx, fully suited in his battlesuit.

"There you are," I say masking my emotions but happy to finally see him again.

"Here I am." He looks down at me, and I drop my head in embarrassment and refuse to empty out my bag that isn't my bag. "You lost my rucksack?" he notices.

"I... I didn't mean to. I—"

"Phineas threw it in a ravine. I got it, don't worry about that. That punk finished not too long ago, had thirty-four talismans and severe lucaberry poisoning. It was so bad, medics had to hold him down to stick him with a stim to knock him out to send him out for detox."

Lucaberry poisoning? That's what those berries Norman was picking were! Lucaberries have psychedelic properties that heighten the amygdala. Clay must have taken those berries off of Norman. How did Phineas get a hold of them? That has to be why he was acting so irrational. My eyes sparkle with joy and a fulfilling excitement. Then it hits me. "You... you threw me the med kit."

"I don't know what you're talking about." He smirks and winks at me.

"You cheat."

"You can't cheat if you're the one making the rules, kiddo."

Morganna, and Oober empty out their bags, talismans are filled to the brim. Griffin and Ezekiel watch on as they empty their bags full of food and water canteens.

"Where are all your talismans?" I ask Griffin and Ezekiel.

They look at me strange. "Morganna and Oober were holding them. We got so many that we couldn't fit them with all of our other stuff, so we stuffed all of them in their bags and we took the food and supplies," Griffin explains.

"I don't understand, I thought we all needed to hold eight separately?" I ask.

"That wasn't the rules I heard." Ezekiel says.

"You see, Carson, we Daltonese aren't like Alannicans with all that glory and selfish honor and stuff. We work together, as a tribe," Griffin explains. "Back home, our community flourishes by our citizens working with one another to make us stronger as a whole."

"So those are all yours?"

"Ours you mean, we are sharing with you, you idiot. There's no rule that we have to finish separately. That's an Alannican thing."

"Yeah, you Alannicans are so weird, no offence," Zeke chimes in. "But seriously, why fight each other when you can help each other grow stronger? This way we all share an equal success in our mission."

Griffin walks up to me and pats me on the shoulder. "Yeah, so fork over those three talismans and add them to the pile," he jests.

My heart fills with joy. "So, you're letting me be part of your group? I almost got you all killed. I—"

"You did nothing of the sort. What you did for Norman, any of us would have done. So, c'mon, the proctors are waiting."

I unload my measly three talismans and add them to the rest. Several proctors mumble to each other looking at me like I have three heads. They eye Jinx as well, wondering what he thinks but he lets it go. He knows this is only helping me.

"Fifty talismans, Griffin," Morganna finishes counting.

"Fifty?! Holy saints on a Sunday, that's ten each," Griffin says.

"You heard them, Jeffrey, ten each. Jot that down," Jinx orders.

The proctor taps his tablet. "Copy that, sir. Carson Marano, ten talismans, three days, twenty three hours, sixteen minutes, two seconds."

"Congratulations, Carson," Jinx says squeezing my shoulder. I look up at my adopted father and realize he was watching me the entire time, knowing he always had my back. As dependable as he has been during my journey through the tournament in Levi, through high school, and everything else, he has earned the name, dad.

I accept the gift from the Daltonese. Ten talismans are marked to my name, and the Proving is finally over. Relief and success embellish me, but a wild suspicion engulfs me about Phineas and my future here. My body aches, my stomach in knots, and my head is light from the blood loss. I'm given a water bottle and I don't even know what to do with it. My friends celebrate their victories clashing their bottles together. Morganna walks up to me and gives me a hug. There's a certain look in her eyes when we detach. I smile, finding peace in my little gang of unexpected friends. But something is wrong, my stomach gurgles violently.

"Carson, are you ok?" My eyes flutter, I hiccup, and turn just in time before I hurl something foul out on the ground. I stumble backwards. *Darkness*.

51
Welcome Back

One moment I was talking to Morganna, the next I open my eyes to the back of a van, or an ambulance. I pick my head up and see a woman with a face mask on.

She touches my head and lays my head back down. "Slow, Carson, slow." I look around and see tubes coming out of my arms, and an empty IV. A device touches my head. "101.8" the device reads.

"Where am I?" I mumble.

"You're being transported to Southern Alannah Shore Hospital. Just relax, everything will be ok." the paramedic says.

"What... what happen?" I look over my shirtless body and see my entire stomach covered and wrapped.

"You passed out. Heat exhaustion, dehydration, fatigue, blood loss, you name it."

The last thing I remember is throwing up, then... nothing. Ugh, I threw up in front of Morganna, in front of everyone. I lay my head down and stare up at the lights shining down at me.

"Where's my dad?"

"Right here, kiddo." I hear the familiar voice behind me. A few clattering noises rings my sensitive ears as he grunts and complains about the million things in his way from the cock pit. Eventually he makes his way to the bench next to me.

"Hey," I murmur. "Did I really throw up?"

"Oh yeah. All over the place, in fact. What did you eat that was purple?" he chuckles.

Thinking back, was it Phineas, or Norman? Someone said showing weakness would drop my stock. Throwing up and passing out in a puddle of my own excretion probably wasn't the greatest way to show my worth. Ugh, in front of all the proctors too. "Did that ruin my draft stock?" He laughs. "No, no, I don't think so. At least I wouldn't imagine... maybe? I don't know. I'm sure you'll be fine, kiddo. You did good, great actually. You scored ten talismans, that's more than what I finished with."

I lean my head back towards him and examine his facial expressions. Jinx wouldn't say this lackadaisically. His face is stern with a pinch of worry but all together, I think he means it whole heartedly. "You're not sugar coating this, right? I really don't want to do this again."

I hear the paramedic chuckle, Jinx looks at her, smiles and shakes his head. "You're fine. Trust me." He looks down at my side and pokes my wound. It's completely numbed. "Although *that*, was foolish. You should have seen that coming, buddy."

I groan and roll my eyes. "I know," I grunt out frustration.

"Yeah, now that may knock you down a few draft picks. However, you exceeded most of the proctor's expectations. Jumping in the river, fighting Clay and those cananhounds, that was insane, Carson, absolutely terrifying. *I* didn't even know what to do. You showed that you can handle yourself and think quickly in crucial situations. That's what we proctors like to see."

"I guess so."

"In fact, you're a hero," he adds. The word catches my attention and instantly gives me goosebumps. He smiles and leans into me. "Proctor Quay is extremely interested in you. Both you and all your Daltonese friends."

"What about Phineas?"

"Hex him. There's no chance Quay would draft him after what he did. I'll be surprised if anyone does, regardless of how you acted towards him or... I'm sorry about Norman."

Norman... Alannicans don't understand death as I do. Death hurts. Death is inevitable, but death has taken loved ones away from me, uncles, aunts, grandparents, and my biological parents. This world is ruthless and so are its people, but life goes on. The world keeps spinning and the trees still grow even if one falls. It'll die and get eaten by bugs or animals and the ones who survive will grow and strive. It's the circle of life. I think I finally understand how Phineas thinks, how an Alannican should think, why death isn't a bad thing. Death relieves pain. It ends suffering. It still hurts to know I'll never be able to share memories with my friend ever again. "It's fine," I lie, trying to be like them and numb my emotions. "So... how well did I do?"

"You did good, kiddo," he repeats himself. "Talisman wise, you are in the top fifty in count, time wise closer to the bottom of the top one hundred. So, you're averaging around the seventy fifth pick if you want to think of it like that."

Shock smacks my face, and I can't hold back the expression of his words, supposedly. Such carelessness in that word, like we are just bodies to these people. "So, that's good?"

"It's draft worthy. Now, it all depends on how the proctor's liked your attitude, leadership, companionship, personality, it's all got to be looked over in the coming month. Look, buddy," he looks at the nurse in the cockpit then turns back to me. "you may have gotten a perfect score talisman wise, which is good. But the way you got them is well... unorthodox, especially with the Alannican proctors. Quay is Daltonese, so working with them really drove you up his charts. On the other hand, Proctor Torvin from Fox House is Alannican, and he wouldn't find that so charming, but it's not a deal breaker. Proctor Zendaya, however, is from Parvaluna so all the fighting you did against her people, well... it's all about perspective."

"I just don't understand the division between every culture. A solider shouldn't be left behind, regardless of their race."

"In the field is different, when you're on a mission you put your heritage aside, this, however, was meant to be an individual experience. Plus," he looks back again. "what you did, saving Norman was totally uncalled for. Don't you know Alannicans must have a funeral service to ascend into the afterlife. What you did, what Norman did, his body isn't going to be found. Religiously, he may never get to the afterlife. Theoretically, he's going to live in purgatory for the rest of eternity."

"What?!" I snap and it gets everyone's attention.

Jinx settles me down. "Unless his body is found or at least something is, then his spirit may have a chance to ascend but...

"Oh my saints. I'm... Jinx I didn't know I—"

"It is what it is, and you can't take any of it back. You know better now and for what it's worth, you're still breathing and that's all that counts. Next time, listen to your friends. I would have got him before he passed, he could have survived."

What have I done? Norman will never ascend... He... he knew... and he sacrificed himself so I could live. I can't believe he would do something like that for me...

"Anyways," Jinx snaps me out of my trance. "you got to see this one kid, he finished the first day. He didn't stop running. Didn't eat, drink, nothing. Just ran for sixty straight miles."

"The first day?!" a shooting pain stabs my side, I grunt and hold it. The nurse touches me to relax me and asks if I want more stims. Before I refuse, Jinx answers for me and she deposits it into my neck without my consent. Feeling the smooth release of pain leaving my body, my nerves calm and my body soothes into the gurney I lay on.

"Yeah, he even jumped the Rampart River. He just saintdamn jumped," Jinx continues. "Boy must have been taking his vitastims because that boy sure is something."

I'm baffled at it, but my head is spinning. Not because of the stims, but because of Norman's actions. Phineas stabbing me, working with the Daltonese, and now someone is some superhuman man who jumps rivers? "That sounds... unrealistic, what's their name?"

"Um, Rocco, I think? It's Robert Fox's boy. I'm surprised I don't know of him. The boy did say he wanted to join the Olympics, but Fox wouldn't let him. He was crazy, Carson, like he was in a video game and he had unlimited stamina and all the cheat codes," Jinx jokes but is completely serious. "I've never seen anything like it."

Rocco Fox finished on the first day... That monster is only getting stronger and faster by the day... I have to say something. "Jinx, dad, there's something I got to tell you about Rocco, he's—"

"Sir," an unknown voice calls behind me in the cockpit. Jinx looks over to him. "We're here, sir."

"Great." Jinx stands up. "We're at the hospital, kiddo. We'll talk later. They're going to check you out and stitch you up, so take this time to recover. You have a lot of work ahead of you after the draft next month.

The ambulance doors open, and three bodies face me as I get wheeled out. The first face I recognize as I get out is a concerned look on a brown-haired girl with her mother's hazel eyes. She's had my heart since the first day I saw her come home in a carriage. "Hey, baby sister."

"Hey, big brother. Welcome back."

52
Draft Day

Buttoned up shirt, *check*. Jacket, *check*. Shoes shined so clean you can eat off of them, *check*. Pants creased tight enough to cut a piece of paper, *check*. Cameras flashing, heart racing, stomach turning, it's the day of the draft, the day I could be chosen to attend Atlantis University's Titan Program, where I will train with my new brothers and sisters to be fit for the world's military.

I arrive at the luxurious Silva Auditorium in Atlantis University with my family by my side. With a capacity of nearly ten thousand, this place is packed with families from all over the world, from here in Alannah to the southern depths of Dalton, to the domes on the moons. The four house flags line the auditorium as we enter. Armed soldiers in battlesuits stand along the sides of the auditorium. To think, one day I could be one of them, standing in a suit made of tyketanium, powered by rune, armed to the teeth and ready at a moment's notice.

As we take our seats, I notice everyone is dressed to impress, all outfitted in their territorial accustomed attires, each with their own personal style and class. I sit impatiently waiting for the draft to begin. Kylie sits to my right, she keeps my mind busy by talking to me about each House. She's fitted in her new golden dress, supposedly some Alannican designer made it for her. Her hair bound up with sparkling beads entangled in it, she looks as elegant as ever. Raymundo sits beside her in a blue suit jacket, looking like he just got out of bed with his unproportioned hair. He means no disrespect to me, he's just lazy and doesn't see the point in doing his hair. Julianna sits to my left. As supportive as she has been, I still feel a slight disconnection between us. My insecurities say it's because I'm an outsider and could jeopardize her entire family if I slip up, hopefully it'll never come to that. However, the shady proctor from my deathmatch is nowhere in sight. Jinx recognized him as Proctor Forrick, a man of few words, but strong, and sharp minded, also part of Suez Legion. If I do get through, I need to watch out for him. His words dangle in my mind, *"Head skull sends her regards."* What could that possibly mean?

The lights dim, chatter quiets, a spotlight shines down on the stage, and an eruption of applause fills the room as a hefty man with graying hair enters from the right of the stage. The Sovereign of Tyke, the man who controls everything, the man whose family bloodline has led the human race from the days on the Gateway Space Explorer. Donavan Silva waves to the crowd as every single person in the room gives this man a standing ovation. I stand and clap to join in, whistles sound off and screaming cheers blend into the applause. He sports a white tuxedo and a black vest underneath with a white top hat to go along with his outfit.

He speaks into a microphone that wraps around the back of his neck, "Welcome, everyone, to the draft of Class 239!" The room thunders with more applauds for our Sovereign. "Everyone, please take your seats." The spotlight follows him as he walks across the stage. "This Proving has been one of the greatest yet. Please, everyone, give yourself a round of applause." The room erupts yet again in claps and cheers. Whistles all around as ten thousand people from all over the world try to be louder than the rest. "It is an honor to be standing here today before all of you. Statistically speaking, ninety percent of the chosen will graduate as deltas. An arousing sixty five percent of that ninety percent will promote to omega. Now this is all statistically speaking folks, but fifteen percent of those omegas will be titans, now can you believe that?" The crowd roars in applause. Kylie shakes my shoulder in excitement. "But one, and only one of you, statistically speaking, could be a future alphaTitan. That, ladies and gentlemen, is something we can all be grateful and proud to think about. A true, honorable, brilliant, and perfect soldier is in this room, right now.

"Ladies and gentlemen, you are all in my debt. I would not be the man I am today if it wasn't for each and every one of you doing your part. I thank you." The crowd accepts his sincere compliments and cheers.

He continues, "Those who are called up here today will be given what many of you have dreamed about, a chance. A chance to learn from some of the greatest titans this world has to offer. So, without further ado, let's get this show on the road." Another frenzy of an applause shakes the ground of the auditorium. Music plays, the spotlights dance around, and a holographic projector illuminates into a massive square on stage behind the Sovereign. "Like we do every year, I will call out the names of the chosen participants and when you are chosen, please come up onto the stage, take your picture with me, and you will be escorted to the back to get fitted for your uniform."

The projection changes to a timer counting down with 'Round One' on it. Fox House, and Proctor Torvin are now on the clock. Before fifteen seconds elapse, the screen changes and Fox Legion's insignia of an Old Earth depiction of a fox shows with 'Pick is chosen' displayed on it.

"Wow, Torvin," the Sovereign says surprised. "that was fast." He gulps down his glass of wine and walks up to his podium to announce the first pick of the draft. "Proctor Torvin is elated for the first choice. This man has demonstrated nearly superhuman abilities during the Proving. A man I have certainly come to adore myself, and one who will certainly give Fox Legion a run for their credits. I would like to announce the first pick of Class 239's draft, the son of AlphaTitan Fox himself, Rocco Fox, of Parvaluna!"

An outburst of loud claps and cheers rocks the auditorium. Rocco stands up in the front row and hugs a pair of women seated next to him. The camera drones surround him as he bows to the Sovereign and turns back to the crowd and waves.

"Is that…?" Kylie can't even finish her sentence.

"Yeah. That's him," I answer hating to admit it.

"How? How did… You knew?"

"Courtney told me at the hotel. He was adopted by Robert Fox."

"How did he get so big?"

"I don't know, but I think it has to do with why Fox wanted dad's project. I think he's using it to make people into giants."

"That's impossible. Dad's project wasn't to make people like that, it was to make people smarter."

"I know, that's why I needed to do this, Kylie. Something bigger than anything we can imagine is happening. I need to find out what," I say.

The man formally known as Rocco McKenzie towers over seven feet tall, about twice the size of our hefty Sovereign. The top of his head barely peaks over Rocco's elbow as they embrace and stand for hundreds of flashes from cameras all around the auditorium. A highlight reel starts playing behind them on a projection screen. It shows Rocco barreling through the woods. A speedometer on the side of the screen shows he's running close to twenty-five miles per hour. He then sprints down a hill and launches himself up and over the Rampart River without even flinching or hesitating. Wow, incredible!

A long and stressful hour passes, and twelve rounds have elapsed out of the fifty. My name has yet to be called.

The Sovereign comes to his podium after downing yet another full glass of wine. "For House Calloway's thirteenth pick, Proctor Bernie chooses the young eighteen year old, Phineas Deacon, of Alannah."

Dread collapses over me as I spot my former friend from across the room. He swings his hands in the air and runs down the red carpet and up to the stage. He has a sleezy smile on his face as he turns to the cameras. I can't help but grip the chair in anger. My scarred side aches in a constant reminder of his unforgiveable betrayal. Even if he was poisoned by lucaberries, what he did was past the effects of the hallucinogenic fruit.

Doubt creeps in as another hour passes. An unnerving feeling in my gut tingles with regret and aggravation for the mistakes I have made. The Sovereign is now on his ninth glass of wine. Names are called to the stage, all of them are different than mine. All four of my Daltonese companions were chosen by Proctor Quay of Suez House in consecutive rounds. He even traded up one spot to select the twins back to back. I can't be discouraged that they all go before me, I couldn't have gotten this far without them. If it wasn't for them, I'd probably be on the wrong end of a pike by one of those Lunen psychos.

Round forty-one out of fifty begins and Jinx has to be in Proctor Quay's ear. He knows how much this means to me.

Fox House starts the round and chooses a woman from a wealthy family.

I slam my hands on the seat railings and Julianna grabs my hand and insinuates that I sit up straight.

"This is getting ridiculous, Julie," I snap.

She violently shushes me with an aggressive sneer and peaks around before speaking. "I don't want to hear it, Carson," she whispers. "Your father knows how important this is to you. Just give him some time, I'm sure he has everything under control."

Round forty-three out of fifty starts. Proctor Zendaya from Cannon House announces that she will trade her next pick for Proctor Quay's pick and a switch of picks for next year. What is this, the starball league?

Kylie holds my hand as Proctor Quay's clock begins to tick. Coming from a poverty ridden family in the southern tip of Dalton, Proctor Quay has fought for everything he has. Jinx told me he liked me, he liked my drive and passion for my friends. With that in mind, he seems like the only logical one to pick me, so every time he is on the clock my heart skips a beat.

The clock dissolves after twenty seconds and the screen announces that the pick is in.

I catch Julianna look at her wrist at a message, she peaks over to me and smiles as she shuts her screen off.

The Sovereign approaches the podium. "With the one hundred seventy second pick in the forty third round, Proctor Quay has chosen a man that he has great plans for. With countless recommendations from certain proctors, he has been deemed a true sleeper in this year's draft. A man who would jump on a grenade for his friends or in his case, dive in the Rampart River to save a friend from certain death." I sit up and my eyes spread open in anticipation. I squeeze Kylie's hand as we lock eyes. Her eyes sparkle with joy, my heart drops, and Julianna's smile grows at the sight of ours. The most powerful man in the world takes a deep breath. "Proctor Quay would like to welcome Carson Marano, of Alannah, to Suez House!"

"Yes!!!" I shout. "Yes! Yes! Yes!" I throw my hands in the air. I grab Kylie and twirl her around in a monster bearhug.

Julianna has to break us up and gives me a genuine hug and a kiss on the cheek. "Go," Julianna says. "Don't forget about us when you're famous."

I scoot down the row shaking hands with random people I don't know and make it to the red carpet. I follow it down to the stage and see my name boldly printed on the screen with Malcolm Suez's insignia planted next to it. The stage looks smaller from where I was sitting, it's massive when standing against it. I climb the stairs along the side and lock eyes with the most powerful man in the territories as he waits for the mightiest of handshakes I have in store for him. A smile spreads across my face, I can't contain myself as I reach for the Sovereign's hand and I grab it tightly.

He pulls me into him. "Congratulations, kid." Donavan's words slur a bit. Alcohol has gripped him in more than one way. His face blushes, like his wine.

"Thank you, sir. It's an honor to finally meet you," I say.

"Of course it is. Ho-ho, you have quite the handshake buckaroo. Lighten up a bit will ya?"

"Holy saints, sir, I apologize I—"

"I'm only messing with you, boy. Now turn and smile for the cameras."

I look out into the crowd and soak it all in. Thousands upon thousands of people clap and cheer for me as I soak it all in. Cameras flash and drones hover around me as the realization of it all comes true. I stand with my hand around the most beloved man in the world and let realty take hold. I will be attending Atlantis University's Titan Program as a member of Suez Legion along side of my adopted father and all my friends.

A highlight film plays behind me of my most daring events. It begins with me jumping in the river and hanging from the waterfall with Norman on my back. The crowd coos as a close up of Norman and me holding on to each other for dear life as Phineas pulls us up. Then it flashes to me carrying Norman over my shoulders, then to striking a canahound in the chest with the spear. The camera's shot was from deeper in the woods, it pans out to show a herd of snarling canahounds waiting to pounce. Holy saints, the cameras caught it all. The film ends just before I have to turn and run, leaving Norman to get mauled and eaten alive by those blood thirty beasts.

Norman... my friend, my savior. His sacrifice will not be in vain. He may not have known my true intentions, but it is because of him that I am here to finish them. I am now one step closer to finding my parents. Now it is time to train, for the real test has begun. I will give it my all, but will that be enough?

<u>*Epilogue*</u>

Robert Fox

A week after Jinx's mission

Tyke's moons have been my home for over twenty years. I have built, maintained, and funded fifty-two out of the two hundred four domes spanning between the two moons. While my legionnaires handle the terraforming aspect, I lead my Lunens as their Viceroy and alphaTitan.

Living in recycled air, growing our own food, and filtering the deposits of water deep under the moon's crust is part of everyday life. There is no discrimination with race or religion, we are one, and welcome any motherworlder to join our efforts. The buildings, the artificial air pumping into the domes, the food that is grown in hyper vegetation chambers and farms that have cloned cattle, chickens, pigs, goats, horses, anything we want, it goes through me.

I constructed the moons to sustain a new kind of life, the Lunen Life. My grandfather was the first to engineer the first dome on Magnaluna and started his global plan of terraforming the moons to live on. Over the last hundred years, these dead rocks have grown its first gardens, grass, and ecosystem with exported genetically modified animals from Tyke that we mate in mass and send out into the domes to adapt and feed my people.

Several housing domes line up through the window, all are connected by a series of tubes, filters to keep the people of the moons safe and healthy. My people respect me. They see me as a god, but I am not one, not now, but soon. Soon, I will be what my people believe I am, and I will not fail them.

I am escorted to a discreet room far off the populace domes where I reside with my wives and close Titan Commanders of my legion and through the prison domes. Armed guards salute me as I pass and allow me into a special, off the grid, shed where a special prisoner resides so I can talk to him privately.

The door is opened with a special code and I take a seat next to a cell. A lone body sits helplessly in a wheelchair inside. His beard extends down past his collarbone, his shaggy hair falls below his eyes, his arms pale, and frail. Project SPINE has done a number on him ever since he was shot. The nanites inside him feed on the stem cells to regenerate his body. After he was shot sixteen times, the nanites went into overdrive to save him. Doing so, has made the forty-two year old look like a withered old man.

"Good morning, Christian."

"What do you want, tyrant?!" my brother barks.

He is strapped down to his wheelchair but has nothing binding him aside from his purely physical inoperable body he was destined to live in. Ten of the sixteen tranquilizer rounds punctured deeper than expected and shattered his L3, L4, and L5 vertebrae causing him to lose function of his legs. The nanites, however, has healed his bones but in doing so, has made him ironically paralyzed.

I chuckle at his misfortunate state. "Now, now. You should be grateful, Christian. You're lucky you're not on life support."

He wheels himself closer to the iron bars of his home. "What do you want, Robert? Are you here to gloat, to torture me? We are brothers, remember? How could you do this to me? After all we've been through."

"I plan nothing of the sort, brother," I say picking moon dust from my fingernails. "What happened to you was simply just, bad luck. You shouldn't have resisted," I say nonchalantly. "Oh it sure has been a while, hasn't it? How long has it been, twenty years since we've been in the same room together? Although for you it looks more like a hundred and twenty."

"Bad luck?! You killed my wife!" he outrages. "They nearly killed me," He flails his arms. "you might as well have."

Aggravation grows, I lean over to him and stick up two fingers. "You killed two. *Two* of my finest soldiers, Christian. You committed treason, *murder*. You are *lucky* I am not holding you accountable and bringing you to court." I get in his face but still behind the bars. "How dare you think you don't deserve this cell. You are *lucky* I gave you that wheelchair. You are *lucky* I haven't had my scientist rip that blasted piece of tech out of your neck and let you bleed out on my floor. You are *lucky*, Christian, that I have plans for you."

Christian spits in my face and rolls back to the wall with a smirk on his face and folds his hands. Anger engulfs me and I pull out my pistol and aim it directly at him.

His eyes spread out wide. "Do it! End me! Do it! C'mon, put a saintdamn bullet in my brain and end this whole thing once and for all!"

The fact that my brother was shot was a matter of insubordination. I instructed the commanding titan several times that no shots will be fired during that mission. An alphaTitan does not usually acknowledge what is out of their control. Luck is unexplainable, and my career has been calculated to the finest detail. Luck is for fools. If luck truly did exist, it was certainly on the side of that omega. Against my better judgement, I agreed to transfer him as long as he never sets foot on these moons ever again.

I drop my pistol to my side. "That's not an option right now," I say wiping my face with my sleeve and holstering my weapon. "What your options are, is to mass produce Project SPINE the way I want." I take my seat next to the cell so we can talk eye level. "Or, as I said, we extract the device out of your head and copy it ourselves. You could die, you may even become a quadriplegic. With that, I will have it anyway, and produce it myself. It's a win-lose, or a lose-lose situation for you, Christian. It doesn't take a robotic engineer to see that. I will rule this world, Christian. All that matters is where you sit when it happens."

"You think I care about myself anymore? Even if I could work, I can barely lift up my arms." He tries to and his whole arm trembles as he struggles. "All I ever wanted to do was to make mankind better, and you took that from me. You've stripped me of everything. My work, Isabella, my children… Where are my children, Robert? Answer me that," he demands.

It took me a second to realize my worthless niece and nephew were still alive. "Hmm? Oh yes, I had them escorted to an orphanage, they won't be a bother anymore."

"A bother? No, I want them here. I want to see them. I won't do anything until I see them and know they are safe."

I squint my eyes, and find it entertaining to see my brother try to negotiate. I will play his game, for now. "Very well. I will have them adopted by me and have them delivered to Magnaluna. I will father them and give them the life they deserve."

"You'll what? No! I am their father, you think you can be a better father than me? Kylie is a saintdamn genius. She's smarter than anyone on this saint forsaken base. Don't you dare corrupt her!"

Oh, hit a soft spot. "What about the boy? Is he one of your experiments too? Did you do the *dirty* to him as well?"

"Carson? No, I... I didn't want to do it to him. He's... special. He was my first born so..."

I spurt out a laugh. "Hah, oh Christian, so not all your seeds have your prototype? Why not? Was he not compatible? What, is he in slow classes or something? That must be hard for you to live with. Your first born being a dud is always the hardest."

"No, you rotten hex! Like you would know anything about having children. Thank the saints they cursed you with infertility."

"Shut up! I am not infertile! You have a lot of nerve after everything I—" I step back and close my eyes. Deep breath in... deep exhale... That's better. "When they arrive, I hope they will be grateful to know their mother is alive."

"She's—" He's stunned. "You're lying, she's really ok?"

"Why yes, that pesky omega must had a soft spot in him. He sealed her up before we extracted her. Our technology and medicine are miracles up here on the moons, Christian. Gravity is also a miraculous thing when it comes to blood flow and surgery. My surgeons were able to patch up Ol' Isabella with a state-of-the-art prosthetic core in her heart that will keep it functional, for now."

"For now? You monster... How dare you treat my Isabella as an experiment. She is a human being! Why would you do that to her? Just let her die."

"If that's what you wish. I just thought being able to see your wife one last time before you wither away would be a courtesy."

Christian tenses. "What do you need me to do?"

"Simple, really," I lean in closer. "we take you to surgery, get that little chip out of you, safely. Study it, see how it works, replicate it with mine, then we will just, *pop*, it inside your wifey and if it works the way we think, your wife will heal and she will go on like nothing ever happened. If it works, and you agree to relieve yourself of all the rights of Project SPINE over to me, we can file a plea deal for you to work for me instead of jail time. Once you are my employee, I will personally make sure that my little brother is properly taken care of and restored to his former glory. Why do you think I look so young? Ahh, fifty-five and still have the physique of a twenty-five year old."

His eyes stare at me, his mouth gaping open. "That's... that's generous of you."

"Right? I thought so. So, we have a deal?" I hold out my hand.

He looks down at my hand, calluses cover it from years of physical work and training.

"Sir?" I turn around and see one of my soldiers at the door, he stands at attention and salutes me. "Alpha Fox, sir, you are needed at Dome Thirteen."

Dome Thirteen is the intake dome where shipments and trade ships land to exchange goods and trade. "At ease, Robbins. What is it? I am busy."

The soldier relaxes. "My apologies, sir," He looks at Christian then back to me. "Your visitors are here. They have come for negotiations."

"Ah! Wonderful." I get up and walk out the door "Chao, Christian, it was fun talking to you."

Christian's eyes bulge. "Visitors? What does he mean, Robert? Wait! Robert! Wait! I accept! I—" The door shuts on him. I knew he would agree. Something as worthwhile as that, I don't know if I would be able to resist. Ahhh, I can be too nice sometimes...

My soldier escorts me down a series of corridors and out of the solitary cell unit. "Did anyone speak to the Sovereign, betaOmega?"

"No, sir. No one has had contact with the mother world," he says sternly.

"Very good. Silva doesn't need to know about this." This is my project, and no one needs to worry. Pretty soon, we won't have to worry about him if all goes to plan.

"Do you have your translator, sir?"

I pull out a small microphone looking device I acquired at my last interaction with my special friends. "Right here, you dare doubt me, omega?"

"Never, sir." Robbins is a good man, and an even better soldier. He's everything I like, obedient, modest, and consistent.

The automatic doors unlock and slide to the side where we walk into Dome Thirteen. There they are, a small group of four amphibious looking creatures. Dark green scaly skin covers their bodies with eyes a third bigger than mine, a flat nose with a small mouth, they have brain colored bulbs coming out of their forearms and are dressed in robes. Aliens. No armor or weapons in sight as far as I know. The group looks at me in unison and bows to me simultaneously.

327

Gull, the tallest and rightful leader of his people takes out his translator and brings it to his mouth with his long three fingered hand. The translator works by the user speaking directly into the voice assimilator. The translator then projects a vibration into a surrounding being's ears that'll render the user's speech as the hearer's language. As Gull finishes, the vibrations find my ears.

"Greetings. Robert Fox, it is satisfactory to see you again." The translator was a gift on our first encounter, an amazing piece of technology they made on their stripped home world of Jingoty, Tyke's neighboring planet.

I put my translator to my mouth and speak. "Hello again, Gull, it is nice to see you and your Jingoty monks again." The translator rumbles off a series of noises completely foreign to me. Gull nods with a heavenly hum.

"Pleasure is ours, Alpha," Gull rasps into the translator, it comes out cheerful. "We have come as requested. Do you wish to trade yet again? Your, how do you say, *chocolates* were delicious in our last visit."

As the Jingoty monks bend to my whim, so will Tyke. I, Robert Fox, am the first human to interact with a celestial being. I bring the translator back to my lips and smirk. Time to put my plan for Sovereignty into effect.

"Follow me to my office if you don't mind. We will discuss terms more thoroughly."

Acknowledgements

Greetings fellow Bone Breakers, Titans, and little Tyke Titans,

Let me just start out and say that you are the meaning to my life. As a little tyke, I wrote *horribly* illustrated but comically inclined, and adventure filled comics called, "The Jingoty Warriors". They were a riled little bunch of teenagers who somehow got superpowers and beat a massive evil man robot in three pages. How? Pshhh, a super powerful beam of awesomeness, that's how. But that, my friends, was just the beginning.

One day after moving into my new home I found a small yellow bin with my name on it. Inside was the series of comics of those wacky named warriors. I read them all back to back and realized that I should give this book writing thing another go. Unfortunately, I still don't have the prowess to create people with pencils and colors so this time, I left it to you, my amazing audience, to create my world with your imagination.

My wife and amazing editor, Maria, pushed me from the start to make a world like none other, a place filled with animals, plants, people, and an environment that can flourish into someone much bigger than anything anyone could ever imagine. Harmony, the ironically named territory took the stage. She continued to push me to the elevation of full blown Italian screaming matches about the smallest of things like 'hex', or 'saintdamn it', or why does Courtney have to be blonde. She knew my potential before I did, and I cannot thank her enough for everything she has done for me and my work.

Then there's my sister in law, Gina Nagy. Out of the kindness of her heart, she grabbed hold of my book and took on the name of my second editor. Thanks, Gina, our table talks at our weekly taco nights are always heartwarming, and hospitable.

On to the next, my amazing cover designer, the Scotland native himself, Mark Reid found out about me from a mutual friend on Facebook. This humble, and patient man sprang into action and jumped at the opportunity to make me the eye catching cover I have today. Thank you, Mark.

Speaking of Mark's, I have yet another Mark from Europe that I would personally like to thank. My first beta reader, and newest friend from England, Mark Lane, another Facebook friend I made from a random author support group. It was a simple post about how my prologue looked, nothing more. He asked for a review on his work, "The Bretz", (Check it out!) in exchange to read mine. So, let it be known to the young authors who place my book in your hands that even you can find the humblest of friends from all over the world.

Enough about Mark's, and on to the enormous group of helpers I've had along the way. I couldn't begin to count the number of times we formed little brainstorming circles and I went over the entirety of my book, and each and every one of them had something to say. RC, GB, KP, KL, I'm talking about you guys. You took my unfinished work into your hands and I watched you turn page after page, completely enveloped in it, jotting down small notes along the sides and always asking for more. I want to thank each and every one of you for your generous time.

Now, I've talked about a boat load of people, but I never got to mention my support team I've had since the day I was born. Mom, dad, aunts, uncles, brothers and sister and especially my grandparents, you made me into the man I stand before you today and there is no possible way I can repay the amount of patience you had for me. You raised me up right, and you pushed me in the right direction every step of the way. I love you guys. You mean the world to me.

Finally, just one more shout out to my fellow Bone Breakers and Titans. Carson's journey does not end here, oh saints above no. The sequel is underway as we speak. Or it may possibly be out, depends on when you read this. April 3, 2021, 4/3/21, the greatest release date ever.

I have to tell you all, I am super excited to hear from each and every one of you. If any of you would like to contact me on the socials, please do not hesitate to do so. I would like to hear back from each and every one of you and thank you personally for taking a chance with me.

ABOUT THE AUTHOR

At the prime age of 27, living in a thriving town close to the Jersey Shore, being a writer has always been a dream of his. It is because of you that his dream has become a reality. He's a huge fan of science fiction, loves playing sports, and working out at the gym in his free time. If he's not at the gym, he's with his huge Italian family either having a heated conversation of who can be louder than whom or playing pool with the in-laws for bragging rights.

If you loved this book, or have a concern or some criticism, please consider leaving a review. Every review helps and every positive and/or negative review will press the author forward in the world of writing and will motivate him to make bigger and better novels for you. His fans are his biggest motivator, and he thanks you for giving him a chance.

May the saints guild you down the path of success.

Made in the USA
Middletown, DE
05 April 2021